SUMMER RAIN

Also by Bob Manion

The Treehouse

Springer's Heart

Sabrina's Promise

Summer Rain

Bob Manion

The Write Place
Spokane, Washington

Summer Rain 2nd Edition 2017

Published by
The Write Place
Spokane, Washington

ISBN-10: 0-9788507-5-1
ISBN-13: 978-0-9788507-5-3

Cover photo credit: Sami

Dedication

This book is dedicated to those men and women who keep our forests safe for us to enjoy; the smokejumpers and firefighters who risk their lives to protect the forest and wildlife, and the rangers and wardens who enforce the laws protecting the forest and animals from abuse and ensure we have the wildlife and wilderness to enjoy for ourselves and our children. I must also acknowledge and dedicate my stories to the men and women of the United States Marine Corps whether active, reserve or retired. All our lives are richer for knowing and honoring the men and women who serve in our Armed Forces. Semper Fi!

Acknowledgements

There are many who have influence over this writer. Among them is my father, Allen Honey, one of the original smokejumpers for the Forest Service. The men who first used parachutes to get to fires in the forest were responsible for the development of the Smokejumpers at Winthrop, Washington. I urge you to go to the small airport at Winthrop and see and meet the young men and women who protect our valuable forest and wildlife. I must also acknowledge those writers of my author's group for their valuable input to my stories.

Chapter One

Smokejumper

The whine of the engine starter and the ticks of the port propeller could be clearly heard through the aluminum skin of the old airplane. The starter turned the propeller and the pilot choked the engine until it coughed, the cylinders fired and the engine roared to life. The port engine ran a bit unsteadily and sent vibrations through the cabin. As the engine warmed, its sound and vibrations smoothed into the sound of a well-tuned motor. The pilot started the starboard motor. Soon the engines purred and propellers were ready to pull the aircraft into the sky. The pilot added power and the plane's propellers spun and again sent vibrations and noise through the cabin and the twenty smokejumpers seated along both bulkheads in the cabin.

The smokejumpers sat strapped into the red webbed bucket seats above the scared and worn aluminum deck. The only ventilation came from the open cargo door of the seventy-five-year-old Douglas DC3 transport plane. The plane, a veteran of World War II had seen action on D-Day, 6th of June 1944. The then, C47 Dakota delivered the paratroopers of the 101st Airborne Division to the continent of Europe to battle the German Army. Since that time, hundreds of paratroopers and Forest Service firefighters jumped from the plane into harm's way.

Today the plane's passengers were Forest Service smokejumpers scheduled to do a qualification jump into a small landing zone surrounded by trees. Warm sunlight streamed in through the small plastic windows. The heat in the plane's cargo space combined with the body heat of the smokejumpers in their padded protective suits caused minds to wander. The strong smell of aviation gas further dazed the passengers.

Cargo and jumpmaster Carl Brenner stood at the nose of the plane with a fire extinguisher during engine start. When both engines ran smoothly, Brenner walked around the tip of the port wing to the open cargo hatch. He climbed the aluminum ladder into the plane and pulled the ladder up after him. Brenner locked the fire extinguisher into its place on the rear wall and secured the ladder beneath the web seats. Carl counted the jumpers and attached the heavy safety strap across the open cargo hatch. He hooked the cargo master's personal safety strap to the figure-H harness he wore and inserted the plane's communications jack into his chest receiver.

Carl could hear the pilots talk to each other and the air traffic controller. He was in charge of all the passengers and cargo as long as they were in his airplane. He spoke to the pilots using his throat microphone and the plane began to move forward.

Sara Bennett sat relaxed in her seat with her eyes closed. She appeared asleep to the casual observer, but her mind was occupied with the coming parachute jump. Twenty parachutists would exit the aircraft at 1,500 feet above ground level (AGL). For today's jump, Sara had been assigned Lead for the exercise and responsible for any changes or adjustments in the order of the jumpers before they left the plane. The first fourteen jumpers were experienced smokejumpers. Sara assigned third year jumper Mike Wingate as number one to be followed by the rest of the jumpers. Jeff, her partner, would follow the four newly hired jumpers. As the team leader, Sara would be the last to jump after Jeff's newbies.

Sara leaned back and snuggled down and pushed against the seat's webbing. Her jumpsuit was unzipped to the belt line. She absent-mindedly fanned herself with her ball cap in the stifling heat of the plane's cabin. The football style helmet with the heavy cage wire face protector rested on the cargo deck held in place between Sara's booted feet. The heavy work boots showed below her frayed cuff-less denim Levi's. When she'd purchased the Levi's, she cut the pant legs off below the ankle and let them fray. If the pant leg snagged on a branch or other obstacle, the pants would rip free and release her.

Before Sara jumped, the ball cap would go into the large pocket on the right leg of the padded jump suit. The left leg pocket contained her lightweight duffle bag, her all-weather jacket and where she would stuff her baseball hat before the jump. She would exchange the helmet for the cap once safely on the ground. The parachute, padded suit and helmet would be left in her Forest Service bag to be picked up by a support crew. Her heavy denim pants and Pendleton wool shirt added to the oppressive heat. Once on the ground, each two-person team would travel cross county to a designated pick-up point and return to the Winthrop Forest Service Smokejumper Base.

Like Jeff said while they were suiting up, "A walk in the woods."

While they waited on the airfield runway for clearance to take off, the interior temperature rose fifteen degrees. Sara felt sweat run down the center of her back and pool at her belt before it leaked down to her underwear. The plane with its captive passengers continued to wait at the end of the runway for permission and clearance to take off. Each jumper looked forward to the cooler air at three thousand feet, AGL. The pilot shut down one engine to conserve fuel while they waited for clearance.

Sara tried to shift her thoughts to anything other than the coming qualification jump. She made similar parachute jumps many times during her time with the Forest Service. It was nothing new, but it was the first time she would be the lead for the entire twenty jumpers and follow them onto the LZ.

Sara shifted her weight and turned her body to ease the physical strain the web seat put on her back. She needed to keep her feet tight against the round helmet to keep it from rolling away on the tilted deck. The heat, the tilted floor of the cabin and the webbing made it difficult to relax. Sara, in her first year with the Forest Service, had learned quickly to relax and rest whenever the opportunity presented itself. The stress and hours of heavy physical work on a fire line led to exhaustion, so being able to relax during short breaks on the line was important.

Even after making more than two hundred jumps, Sara felt the stress of responsibility for the jumpers under her direction. If a jumper failed, the Forest Service would disqualify them and take them off the list of qualified smokejumpers and firefighters. Sara's sometimes jump partner Molly sat across the cabin, her helmet on her head, and appeared to be napping. Sara's mind flashed a memory of when the chute of one of the new firefighters failed and he'd been too close to the ground for his safety chute to open. She remembered the nightmare of the parachute streamer and the crash at the end of the spiraling fall, like a wounded duck, the jumper smashed into the trees and rocks. The primary danger of parachuting was the landing zone; it was sometimes small, merely yards across.

Sara forced her mind to think of things other than the upcoming jump. There were the stand-down periods when Sara's four-man fire team was not on the ready list. Stand-down periods were the only time smokejumpers could completely relax, go to town and have a couple of beers with friends. Each of the smokejumpers used his or her off time for mundane activities to relieve the stress of waiting for the fire bell, announcing another fire and a parachute jump into danger.

Sara's consciousness slipped and images of her life outside the Forest Service invaded her dreams, as she dozed.

Sara's mind drifted on the stream of dreams. She was a member of a local western team roping club where cowboys and cowgirls chased and roped fast running steers. Sara enjoyed her time alone with her horse and the peace it gave her when she rode the trails in the Winthrop area. She participated in the local team roping jackpots and practice sessions. Many of the local cowboys were members of her club and helped her improve her roping and riding skills. Each weekend, club members gathered at a local arena for jackpots and at the following social event at O'Reilly's Bar and Grill.

A couple of the club members were also tie-down ropers or calf ropers. They gathered for friendly competition after the team-event members were finished for the day. Sara wanted to try the tie-down roping but her skill with the rope wasn't up to the required level, and dismounting from a fast braking, but still moving horse wasn't a skill she possessed, yet.

Sara's other important activity was as an International and Olympic-level large bore marksman. In the fall, she was scheduled to compete at the National Rifle Matches at Camp Perry, Ohio. Sara was committed to compete in local matches at the Yakima Army Firing Range and at Fort Lewis near Tacoma, Washington. If she were successful at the local matches, her first national qualification match would be scheduled at Camp Pendleton, California, the large United States Marine Corps Base north of San Diego. The best shooters in the country would compete for slots on the National Shooting Team and represent the United States in world competitions.

To be competitive Sara followed a strict training program of conditioning, and marksmanship practice. Since her second year in high school, Sara had been an All-American shooter and one of the top competitors in the United States. She was defending National Champion in the women's large bore military competition.

Sara did not comport herself as a properly raised young woman was expected to behave. She engaged in games normally considered male-dominated. Her chosen profession was forest firefighter and parachutist. Sara liked men and she dated when the mood struck her. There were a number of suitors who wanted to be the other half of a couple containing Sara Bennett.

The men and women of the Winthrop Police Department and the county Sheriff's Department were some of her biggest boosters. She regularly practiced and competed on the range with them. Sara kept the bulk of her special match ammunition in the County Sheriff's Department ammunition storage locker. As a member of the National Team she received a monthly allowance of match ammunition for practice. Her ammunition was sent to her in care of the Okanogan County Sheriff's Department in Winthrop. One of the deputies was a Reserve Marine match shooter, and he saw to it Sara's ammunition was stored and secured properly and available to her when needed. The Sheriff's Deputies enjoyed shooting a friendly competition followed by a BBQ. Other police officers and invited local residents occasionally joined them.

Sara's thoughts whenever she was able to completely relax reverted either to her horse Buster and the team roping jackpots or to her marksmanship discipline. As she thought about shooting, her heartbeat slowed and her breathing became slow and steady. Everyone on the firefighter team could tell when Sara's mind was on shooting. She was in the zone alone accompanied only by images of her target, the sight picture, shooter position, and trigger squeeze. Sara was, as she described it, alone in a crowd.

When Sara first joined the Forest Service four years ago as a summer hire, she was already an established National Match rifle markswoman. During her high school years, she'd participated in several national and international matches. Sara had been one of the few civilian shooters who were invited to participate in the Marine Corps championships at Quantico, Virginia. She was especially expert at the longer ranges where many of the female shooters declined to compete. Sara competed against military men and women and consistently placed in the top five percent, only once placing below number five. Only one Woman Marine bested her at one thousand meters, both women shooting the modified M14 rifle or the M1A manufactured by Springfield Arms and tuned by the Springfield Armory. Sara loved to shoot at 1,000 meters, where a heartbeat can move the strike of the bullet by as much as twenty feet for a good but undisciplined marksman.

Sara competed at her first National Match when she was sixteen. She met a legend of the Marine Corps, Gunnery Sergeant Carlos Hathcock, a Marine sniper in Vietnam. Hathcock was known as White Feather and feared by the North Vietnamese and Viet Cong. A survivor, the Gunny encouraged Sara to keep practicing and honing her skills and to bring peace and stillness to both the firing line and to her daily life.

At twenty-three, Sara usually wore her dishwater blonde hair in a ponytail. At five feet seven inches, and one hundred thirty-five pounds, Sara was not a petite little girl. She was a "hard body" and lifted weights with the guys in the gym. When Sara first came into the base gym she raised the male hormones of her observers by several notches. Male eyes focused on her shapely figure, and her clear pale blue eyes became the subject of much male discussion and fantasy.

On Sara's first day at the gym, the activity slowed or stopped completely when she entered the weight room. She started her workout with moderate weight barbells. As Sara did reps the men returned to their own workouts but remained conscious of Sara sweating in the weight room with them. She wore one of her old college sweatshirts and a pair of black Marine Corps gym shorts, courtesy of her brother Phillip, a Marine F/A18 Hornet fighter pilot.

Sara walked and weaved her way around weights and benches to the barbell rack. She selected a moderate weight and began a series of reps. There was a sparkle in her eyes and a smile on her lips. Finished with the reps, she put the barbells back in the rack and walked toward a press bench. She wiggled her butt just a bit teasing the staring men. She spotted the only other female in the male-dominated gym.

Molly Thockmorton stood and watched the beautiful girl-woman walk toward her and licked her suddenly dry lips. Molly was the only female homosexual on the base and a smokejumper. Jeff Penworthy, Sara's team partner, was the only gay male. As she watched, Molly experienced a moment of raw lust.

Sara approached her as she stood, mouth open and holding a sixty-pound weight. Sara put out her hand. "Hi, I'm Sara Bennett." Sara smiled at Molly. "I heard there was another woman who worked out with the free weights, and I guess you're her." Sara waited while Molly slowly put the weight she was holding back in its rack. Molly clasped Sara's extended hand in a firm grip.

"I would assume you've heard about me?" Molly's voice hinted at a challenge. Molly sported freckles splashed across a plain and homely face done by a mad dabber. Short reddish hair topped her five-foot-five-inch body toned by years of lifting weights. Her bulky muscles surrounded her frame in lumps and ropes that bunched and rippled when she moved. Molly's weight pushed a hundred and sixty pounds without an ounce of fat.

Sara finished taking in the sight of Molly's physically powerful body and released her hand. "Yeah, I've heard about you. Just to let you know, I'm straight, love the male body. Now if I were inclined to swing the other way, you would definitely be at the top of my list."

Molly stood with her mouth open. She didn't know how to respond.

Sara shrugged. "While you're making up your mind, how about spotting for me on the bench press? I don't think any of these guys have enough blood left in their brains to spot."

Molly's mouth shut with a pop. She shook her head as if to clear the cobwebs. "Sure, why not." When they reached the bench, Molly asked shyly, "You think you could spot for me when you're finished?"

"Sure, would you rather go first? I could use a few minutes after my reps on the barbells."

"Yeah, okay. What weight do you use?" When Sara told her, Molly put that much iron on the bar. "It's pretty close to what I use too, a couple of pounds less but I think this weight will do." Molly lay back on the bench while Sara moved to the spot position ready to help with the weights when needed. Molly did three sets of ten reps shaking her arms out between reps. Finished with her reps, Molly wiped the bench with a towel and moved to the spot position while Sara took her place on the bench.

After the initial meeting and workout, the two women became good friends and rented an apartment together in town. The move started rumors, which the two women ignored. Each knew the boundaries of the other and gave space and when needed alone time. They were on different teams and only occasionally jumped or worked a fire together.

At the end of the first fire season, Sara returned to college. At the end of her third season Sara still hadn't decided on a career outside of firefighting. Molly planned to move to Los Angeles, California, and take the tests for the Los Angeles County Fire Department. The current season would be Molly's last as a smokejumper. She was hired by the Los Angeles County Fire Department with the condition she pass the required written and physical strength tests. Being a smokejumper was a huge plus on the LACFD firefighter's application. Molly expected to be assigned to the high-rise crew and work throughout LA County where she would fight high-rise building fires.

Sara's daydreaming ended when Jeff Penworthy bumped her as he shifted into a more comfortable position. Jeff had been Sara's normal jumping and working partner since her second year with the Forest Service. He sat next to her taking up the most parts of two of the web seats. The pair had teamed up during Sara's second year with the Forest Service. At the time, Jeff had been a senior smokejumper and firefighter and one of three smokejumpers assigned as lead trainer-guide for rookies. Currently, Sara was Jeff's training assistant for new jumpers. Jeff also inspected the chutes and worked as a rigger.

New smokejumpers were traditionally teamed with experienced personnel who mentored the rookies during their first year with the Forest Service. Jeff was twenty-nine and had been jumping smoke and fighting forest fires since joining the Forest Service shortly after his twentieth birthday. Jeff's six foot-four-inch stature and fit 250 pounds accompanied by his narrow waist, broad shoulders, curly light brown hair and hazel green eyes, turned the ladies' heads as he passed. Jeff's looks were something Sara teased him about. Jeff was gay but didn't bring his sexual preferences to work. Sara could be a little intense in her teasing, but Jeff took her in stride giving back as good as he got. His easy-going ways complemented Sara's intense machismo. Jeff wasn't above teasing Molly either, calling her the "macho bitch in the squatty body," but always with a smile from eleven inches above.

For the past four years, the supervisor had been using Jeff as a mentor and guide. Sara was Jeff's third first-year firefighter and smokejumper to train and look after while on the fire line. After Sara's first year, Jeff asked the supervisor boss for a break from mentoring and was teamed, for convenience with Sara. She was now in her fourth year jumping smoke and on her first assignment as the lead for a qualification jump. They both thought the assignment came because their immediate supervisor was still on vacation.

Sara Bennett was a fast learner, dedicated and loyal to her partner and the Forest Service. Jeff and Sara, as a team, were an asset to the Forest Service. Jeff's rugged good looks and being gay, was a source of envy and a waste in the eyes of some of his female friends.

Sara didn't know how long she had been dreaming. But shortly after being jostled awake, the pilot restarted the second engine and she felt the plane begin to move forward onto the active runway. The pilot held on the runway and revved the engines ready for takeoff. The change in vibration brought Sara back to focus on the upcoming jump. This jump was her qualification for the entire year. Subsequent jumps would be about the business of firefighting.

The landing zone was a small clearing and precision and accuracy with her new parasail chute would be measured and graded by observers on the ground. If she failed to satisfactorily complete the jump and associated map reading exercise, Sara would be placed on desk duty under the direct supervision of the man who had attempted to bed her last year. At least there were always the additional jumps to demonstrate techniques for visitors.

Sara zipped up her padded jump suit and set her helmet with its open hinged wire mask on the reserve parachute strapped to the front of her jump harness. She wondered why they carried a backup chute. Smokejumpers leave the plane so close to the ground there would never be enough time to deploy the second chute. In Sara's opinion, it was extra weight. Today the jumpers would jump into the landing zone without the usual bags of firefighting tools of chain saws, axes, and shovels. After gathering their chutes and stuffing the chutes, the padded jump suits, and helmets into duffle bags, the test would continue with a hike of eight miles cross country to a pickup point in teams of two. Each team would take a different path to their team's specific pickup point. Each pickup would be at a different location and the teams were expected to locate and move cross country within specific time limits based on the known terrain.

The drone of the DC 3's engines lulled Sara and she slipped back into her dream. The plane clawed its way to altitude and banked toward the training drop zone. The voice of Carl, the jumpmaster and onboard official observer, brought her back to the present. The door safety strap had been removed, and the warning light above the open door flickered red indicating they were approaching the DZ (Drop Zone) and the five minute warning. The next light would be yellow after the plane flew over the DZ and the jump master pushed out the "wind dummy". The plane would complete the circle with the jump master watching the wind dummy's descent and landing on the ground. One minute to jump, then the green light and out the door. Sara put on her helmet and closed the face shield. With two minutes to go, she signaled for the other jumpers to stand up and attach the hook of their ripcord to the steel cable that ran along the ceiling of the airplane. The ripcord was folded on the parachute backpack fastened by rubber bands and passed up from their shoulders and hooked onto the steel cable. Sara made sure each jumper's hook was firmly attached to the steel cable and would slide freely along the cable to the door. She made sure each hook was in its proper place in line to prevent fouling.

The jumpmaster's head was out the door in the slipstream. He looked forward toward the DZ. With one hand he held himself in position. In the other hand he held a second wind dummy which he threw from the plane to recheck the wind direction at the different levels of air currents. Carl noted the shifts in the wind directions but found nothing unsafe. He talked to the pilot on the intercom. The plane continued to fly forward then began a wide bank to the left. When the plane was lined up with the DZ it leveled off at fifteen hundred feet AGL. Sara glanced up at the lights and saw the red go off and the yellow light came on. At one minute to the DZ, the jumpers did a quick recheck of their gear and the gear of the person in front of them.

Sara stared at the yellow light. It blinked and went off and the green light came on. The first jumper was out the door with his partner a second behind him. The jumper in front of Sara left the plane with Sara a step behind her.

When Sara's chute opened, there was no opening shock with the new parachutes. She checked her canopy parasail and her risers. Next, she looked for Jeff and found him floating toward the ground to her left and five hundred feet below. As they neared the ground a fresh breeze swirled and caught Jeff's chute and caused him to twist around. Sara's chute, with its lesser weight, was swept to the side toward a large rock in the landing zone. She pulled her feet up but her right foot struck the rock and threw her to the side. When she hit the ground, she twisted and fell onto her left side. Her left arm struck a half buried rock and broke the upper arm bone and the radial bone in her left forearm. With two broken bones Sara had difficulty dumping the air from her chute and getting out of the chute's harness. She was able to unzip her protective padded suit and wiggle out of it before the pain of the broken bones reached her brain. Sara experienced the first stage of shock and knew full stress was seconds away and wanted to be prepared before she lost control of her body as it went into shock. She was standing holding her arm when her chute was caught by the wind and blown across the field where it caught on a rock and small bush. She looked down at her left arm and saw it had started to swell. The pain hadn't started yet but she knew it would come as the initial shock wore off.

Jeff ran up to her with his chute balled up under his arm. "Sara, are you all right?" Then his eyes locked onto her arm. "Oh God, you broke your arm."

"Yeah, tell me something I don't know." Sara sat down on the rock she had collided with. "Two hundred plus jumps without a scratch, sixteen into dangerous DZs and fires and I break my arm on a basic training, no-brainer qualification jump. Shit! Goddamn it! Now they'll put me at a desk all summer. This is going to ruin my chances at the Nationals too. I'll never be able to compete in the qualification matches. Crap!"

"I can't see you behind a desk, at least not for long." Jeff needed to keep Sara talking until the medics arrived. He was reminded he needed to call for a dust-off helicopter to get Sara to the Winthrop Clinic or to a hospital. Sara handed him her cell phone from her shirt pocket. He pushed the quick-dial button to call the base.

Sara could hear Kathy, the clerk in the Forest Service Headquarters office, answer the phone, but not the words. Jeff interrupted the clerk. "Sara Bennett has been injured in the jump at LZ Alpha. We need a dust-off. The injury is not life threatening." Jeff listened. "Okay, I'll wait for the call. This is Jeff Penworthy, and I'm on Sara's cell phone." He flipped the cell phone closed and dropped it into his shirt pocket. "Are you sure you're okay?" he asked Sara for the third time. Her complexion had grown pale during the short phone call as the pain reached her brain. Jeff saw the sweat forming on Sara's forehead. "Here, let me check you for any other injuries."

"I know you Jeff; you just want to see me with my shirt off," Sara tried to joke. Two seconds later she fainted and fell forward. Jeff caught her before she reached the ground. He held her, careful not to bump the injured arm.

Sara's phone buzzed in his pocket. "Yeah?" He listened. "Sara Bennett, she has a broken humerus and ulna, both in the left arm. She fainted and is still unconscious." Jeff paused and listened. "Yeah, the LZ is clear for a helicopter. Okay, hurry." Jeff flipped the cell closed again and returned it to his shirt, buttoning the flap.

A shadow attracted Jeff's attention. When he looked up he saw the entire plane load of jumpers surround him and Sara. "A dust-off is on its way. Jerry can you make sure the LZ is clear. Molly, would you mind accompanying Sara on the chopper to wherever they take her?"

Sara's phone buzzed again; it was Carl onboard the plane. "We just saw the chopper lift off from the base. Do we have an injury?"

"Yes sir, Sara Bennett broke her arm and she has gone into shock. I called for the dust-off." Jeff closed the phone for the third time and addressed the other jumpers. "The dust-off is in route, ETA five minutes. Molly will accompany Sara. John, you're my partner after Sara and Molly are out of here. The rest of you move out with your partners to the first checkpoint and continue with the exercise. The bus will begin pickups along the road starting at benchmark 5340 as briefed, questions?"

Everyone looked around at each other, no questions. They paired off into their assigned teams and started toward their first checkpoint as the helicopter came over the tree line, circled the LZ, and landed in a cloud of dust. Jeff carried Sara to the chopper and turned her over to the onboard medic. Molly climbed into the bird and said over her shoulder to the big smokejumper, "Don't worry, Jeff; I'll stay with her."

Jeff nodded and joined John to watch the chopper lift off and begin the climb over the ridge toward the nearest medical services at the Winthrop Clinic.

Chapter Two

The Clinic

Sara sat on the examination table; the paper cover crinkled and ripped along the table's edge. She still wore her Pendleton red plaid shirt. The medic on the helicopter had not removed the shirt, just immobilized the arm so Sara wouldn't try to move it. The medic put ice packs on each side of the breaks to help control the swelling while Molly watched. Luckily, the breaks were simple fractures and the bones had not pierced the skin.

While Sara waited for the doctor, Molly was sent by the nurse to wait in the lobby. Molly would wait for the decision on whether Sara would remain in Winthrop or be sent to the hospital in Spokane. The possibility she would be able to go home depended on the doctor's evaluation. Sara made it clear she wanted to go home and not to the hospital in Spokane or anywhere else.

To sit still and be unable to move around was nearly impossible for Sara. If the arm stayed still and was not bumped, the pain was more of an ache. The nurse returned and helped Sara remove her heavy wool shirt and bra to check for any additional bruising. The nurse gave her two aspirin and apologized because she was unable to give Sara more of a pain killer until after the doctor examined the injuries. Making sure Sara was comfortable, the nurse left her alone for a few minutes.

Sara draped her shirt on over her shoulders and was about asleep when a light knock on the door startled her awake. The door opened to admit a young man near Sara's age with a stethoscope hanging around his neck.

The man stopped while still in the doorway and introduced himself, "I'm Doctor Pat O'Hara. If you don't mind I would like to see what you've done to yourself. Then we'll decide if you need to go to Spokane." The nurse, with a clipboard, followed close behind the doctor into the room. She moved carefully around him in the small examination room and stood beside the table next to a supply cabinet.

Sara began to smile as she stared at the doctor: about six feet tall, dark blond hair a couple of shades darker than her own, freckles across his nose caused by too much time in the sun. His arms were dark in a farmer's tan below his light blue, short-sleeve shirt, no tie.

Sara with an effort raised her eyes to meet his smile. *Oh God, green eyes.* She was a pushover for green eyes and dark blond hair. *If he's six feet and unmarried I'll die.* Sara's eyes slipped to his belt and a bit lower before she caught herself. Embarrassed, Sara avoided meeting Doctor O'Hara's eyes. She did see the nurse roll her eyes and smother a grin. The doctor stood still and smiled. He was quiet when he should have been asking questions. The nurse interrupted both their thoughts by clearing her throat.

When the doctor moved close to Sara, she smelled his aftershave. *Manly, something like Stetson. Oh hell, I think I'm in love.* Sara could smell her own stale sweat. She completely forgot why she was there until O'Hara touched her arm to remove the ice pack and lift her shirt away. The pain was sharp and immediate and brought Sara quickly back to reality.

"What are you, who are you, what's your name again?" Sara stumbled over the words. Her thoughts were interrupted by a quiet cough from the nurse behind her. Sara ignored the other woman.

"My name is Patrick O'Hara and I'm the doctor on duty and the new director of the Winthrop Clinic, any other questions?"

"Ah yeah, but I don't think I can ask them." Sara laughed in spite of the pain in her arm.

"Listen, I have a patient in the other exam room bitten by a skunk. I need to take care of him and then I can give you my full attention. So, if you'll excuse me for a few minutes, I'll be right back. Jean, will you get the patient into a gown, just the upper body will be fine and give her a tetanus shot." He addressed Sara. "Are you allergic to any medications or pain killers?" He waited for Sara to shake her head. "Jean will need to ask you some questions about your medical history for your file." Doctor O'Hara grinned again and left the room.

Sara glanced down at the nurse's ring finger to see a gold wedding ring. "About the doctor, does he have a family?" Sara turned bright red.

"No, he isn't married and no he doesn't have a girlfriend right now. He's only been here a few weeks, not much time to get into any trouble." Jean smiled. "Just between you and me, he's hot, but so is my Bruce, so I'm not interested."

"Wow, I didn't know it showed. Talk about being swept off your feet. Wow, again." Sara and Jean shared a laugh.

"Sorry, this may hurt a bit." Jean stuck a needle in Sara's uninjured arm and then rubbed the puncture for a few seconds. "It will be a bit sore from the vaccine if you rub it, oops forgot." Jean rubbed the spot until the area turned red and the muscle relaxed. "Now let's fill out the family and personal medical history, but first I need to get that wounded wing unwrapped and you into a gown before Doc Hot gets back and I'm out of a job."

Sara sat still while Jean removed the wraps and cleaned the wounded area with rubbing alcohol. "What do you know about him?" Sara jerked her good arms thumb at the closed door.

"Well, according to rumor, he's single, finished his internship at the Medical Center in Spokane, twenty-six, a graduate of UW Medical School, six feet and a hair inches tall, green eyes, dirty blond hair, never been married, broke up with a girl about six months ago in Spokane. His family is from Spokane. He doesn't have a religion listed. He was going to go into the Navy Medical Corps, but after being sworn into the Navy Reserve he was put on a six-month delay. I think the delay is because of chronic motion sickness. He sees a boat and he's hanging over the side, even fishing boats on a still lake. The Navy can't have one of their doctors with chronic seasickness. But really, I think he's in a rotation system for duty with the Marines in Afghanistan or Iraq maybe. That's about it. Oh yeah, he thinks anyone who jumps out of a good airplane is absolutely, certifiably insane. He saw some of the new jumpers at the airport parachute down during an orientation day. When he came to work he was still shaking his head."

"I guess that lets me out, I'm nuts." Sara laughed then winced as Jean removed the last wrap from her forearm. The bone was pressed against the skin but hadn't broken though. While watching Jean work, Sara sized her up. About five foot four inches, soft dark brown hair, brown eyes and for the first time Sara noticed, Jean was pregnant, about four months.

"When's your baby due?"

"You noticed the baby bump? It's a girl and should be here near the end of August. We were hoping for an August baby. Both Bruce and I are Leos and it would be nice for our baby be a Leo too. But we'll love her regardless." Jean picked up the ice packs and dropped them in a waterproof bag. "Okay, my part is done except for the paperwork. I'll give your partner the ice packs, no sense buying more when these are perfectly fine. Stick them in the freezer until they are slushy inside and reuse them."

Jean asked about Sara's medical history for the record and filled out the forms on her clipboard. When finished, the two women talked about their jobs and the towns in West Central Washington State.

A knock and the door opened and interrupted the two women. Doctor O'Hara came into the examination room, a smile on his handsome face. "Sorry it took so long. Those rabies shots can be pretty painful and we had a little reaction to the serum. He's okay now. I think we'll keep him here overnight." He addressed Jean,

"Remind me, what time does Marilyn come on for the night shift when we have overnight patients?"

"Six p.m.. She usually gets here a bit early since Earl passed away."

"Yeah, okay I remember now. Remind me, we have to talk about getting another permanent nurse soon. Say Sara, you don't happen to know any nurses looking for a job?"

"No sorry." *More competition, shit, why did I think that?*

"Okay, I'm all yours. Let's see what you did to yourself." O'Hara gently probed the break in Sara's upper arm for any loose objects, did the same for her lower arm.

"We need to get some X-rays. Think you can walk across the hall or do you want a wheelchair? Let's use the wheelchair, Jean, please."

Jean left the room leaving the door open and returned with an old black wheelchair. The chair appeared to have seen better days from the tears patched with silver duck tape and the worn seat. Getting gingerly down from the exam table, Sara eased herself into the chair held steady by Jean. O'Hara was in the X-ray room when Jean wheeled Sara though the door. The table was already raised so Sara could lay her arm on the platform while she remained in the wheelchair. Jean excused herself and stepped behind the protective shield where she put on an additional lead apron around her waist and belly. The doctor placed Sara's arm in the position he wanted. Satisfied, he too stepped behind the heavy lead glass shield. There was a quick buzz and beep; O'Hara came out and repositioned the arm and took three more X-rays. O'Hara wheeled Sara back to the examination room while Jean processed the films.

While they waited for Jean to finish the X-ray films, Sara and the doctor small talked. Sara had a million questions, but didn't feel right about asking them. Patrick O'Hara had another million questions for the attractive blond woman who jumped out of airplanes. Together, none of the questions got asked or answered.

Jean came into the room and handed O'Hara four fifteen-by-twenty inch films of the fractures to Sara's arm. The doctor put the films on a wall-mounted light frame. "The breaks appear clean without any bone chips floating around to make things difficult. I'll set the bones and I recommend we wrap the arm up and use ice packs on it for tonight and tomorrow. After most of the initial swelling has gone down, we'll put a cast on."

"How much of a cast and how long?" Sara asked.

"We'll use a cast from the top of your shoulder to the bottom of the wrist and we'll use the thumb to anchor the bottom of the cast. Four to six weeks in the cast and another two to three weeks of very light use and physical therapy. After that you should be just as good as new."

"I can't do that. Two months is almost half the fire season. No, I can't do eight weeks, no."

"Look at it this way. You'll be coming here for the PT. I'll see you and can appraise how you're healing and maybe, just maybe, you'll be able to go back to work before then. You can do office work in a couple of days, but no jumping out of airplanes," he added.

"Oh my God, is Molly still waiting in the lobby?"

"You mean the woman who came in with you? Yes, she's still out there.," Jean answered.

"Could she come back here?"

Jean looked at the doctor. "Sure, I'll get her." The nurse left to return with Molly. Molly, who didn't miss a trick, watched Jean's butt and legs beneath the blue scrubs as Jean led her to the examination room.

When Molly entered and saw Sara, she rolled her eyes and flicked her head toward Jean.

Sara shook her head. "Sorry Molly, married, happily married."

"Nuts, all the good ones are taken, except you, my love." Molly was never embarrassed by her actions or words. Molly knew Sara and Jean were straight, but she always got in a word or two. Maybe that's why the guys liked her. She was just like them when it came to women. Molly wore a broad smile on her face as she took in the view of Sara naked to her waist, the nipples erect in the cool room.

The doctor introduced himself. "I'm Doctor O'Hara and our patient here will be ready to go home in a little while. I want her back here at 10 a.m.. tomorrow. You got that, Molly, whoever you are?"

Molly raised her eyebrows. "Yeah, I got it. She'll be here if I have to carry her."

"Good. Sara, here are some pills for pain. Take two and only one more after you wake up in the morning. I'm going to give you something now to ease the pain while I set your breaks." O'Hara removed a syringe from the cabinet and a small bottle from which he filled the syringe to about a quarter full.

Twenty minutes later, with the bones set and the arm wrapped, Sara felt like she was ten feet tall and was ready to leave with Molly. Before they could leave, O'Hara gave Sara additional instructions. "You can take the third pill after you get up, but no later than 8 a.m.. Remember: two, and one." He turned to Molly. "See that she follows my instructions. Now, do you have transportation?"

"No sir, but I can call the base. They'll send something." Molly wasn't sure how she felt about the doctor. He seemed like he knew what he was doing, but he also seemed a bit preoccupied with Sara. It caused Molly to frown, and then a grin spread over her homely face.

Sara sat in the wheelchair wearing her shirt. Molly started to wheel her out of the examination room when the doctor stopped them. "Here, you might want to take this with you." He held up Sara's bra.

"Shit." Sara started to reach with her left hand, winced and grabbed the bra from O'Hara's finger with her right hand.

Chapter Three:

Off the Schedule

Taken off jump status and danger pay, Sara was assigned clerical duties for the duration of her recuperation. She sat at the clerk's desk in the front office of the Forest Service and scanned the reports of the smokejumpers to satisfy her own curiosity and keep up with what was happening with the firefighter crews. The daily reports were done and submitted to the temporary district office in Brewster. Now all she had to do was to wait for the telephone to ring and monitor the fire control net on the radio. Two crews were currently dispatched on fire calls. Crew one reported their fire was out and were doing cleanup and looking for hot spots. When the hot spots were declared safe, Sara would close out the report. The other crew was working a fire on private land within the National Forest.

The Regional Forest Service Supervisor was due to fly into the Winthrop airfield. A scheduled meeting with the Winthrop supervisors would take up most of the morning tomorrow and Sara was expected to take notes and be available from 0800 to 1600 tomorrow. *Should never have taken that shorthand course in high school. Now they will never leave me alone.*

Sara was nervous because part of the purpose of his trip was to talk to her. She was sure the Regional Supervisor and her immediate supervisor wanted her to resign so they could hire someone to replace her.

Sara glanced up when the background hiss from the radio speaker broke indicating an incoming voice message. The radio in the office could pick up most of the fire control communications, but the transmissions were scratchy and weak. The strength of the signal depended on the terrain the fire crew was working in. By the weakness of the transmissions, Sara knew the firefighters were in rough country. She went to the large contour map of the Okanogan National Forest tacked to the wall. She studied the terrain and the blue pin indicating the number two, or Blue Crew's, location.

After making a note of the time of the radio break, Sara studied the map. Moments later, she heard the radio transmission over the air traffic net for one of the U.S. Forest Service jets on approach. She went outside and watched the small corporate jet land and taxi toward the aircraft parking area near the headquarters building. All three of the aircraft based at Winthrop were on assignments outside the area, so the jet was the only plane currently on the base.

Last night a tanker plane made an emergency landing at Winthrop when one of its engines caught fire. The modified B25 Mitchell WWII medium bomber landed with only one workable engine. Sara talked to the pilot, Ben Fisher. She knew the former Marine aviator from when she'd visited her brother at the Miramar Marine Corps Air Station prior to deployment on one of the mammoth nuclear aircraft carriers.

Sara and Ben went to dinner together at O'Reilly's Bar and Grill. Nearly all of the tanker pilots were former military and liked the excitement of bombing fires with fire retardant and "flying in the weeds," as the pilots called it. The heavy four-engine bombers and old passenger planes could dump water, but the smaller planes didn't have the lift capability to haul enough water to make a difference against a hot fire. The smaller B25s were used to drop fire retardant on small fires and hot spots.

Sara let Ben make a pass at her; she cheerfully turned him down, and he cheerfully accepted. They laughed over the half-hearted proposition. He said it was expected and it was his duty not to disappoint her. Sara lifted her broken wing as an excuse.

Over salad, Ben told her he was transferring out of the Forest Service and was going to fly for the Border Patrol. He said the Department of Homeland Security and the Border Patrol were looking for pilots and patrol agents. Border Patrol Agency work for the pilot would be mostly drug interdiction. Ben would train to fly the helicopters operated by the Patrol.

Ben told Sara the Federal Fish and Wildlife Law Enforcement Service of the Agriculture Department, FFWLES was currently hiring rangers to patrol the National Forests and Parks and to augment other Federal and State agencies when requested. The agents and rangers were armed, weapons qualified, and commissioned federal law enforcement officers. The rangers were empowered with arrest authority, and Ben thought Sara might like a change of pace. Chances were slim Sara would be allowed to return to firefighting with the attitude of the Regional Forest Service supervisors. She wouldn't be able to return to smokejumping until next year after she took another qualification parachute jump.

Ben and Sara talked about the FFWLES Rangers Program's plan to patrol the mountainous forests on horseback. Ben told Sara the Border Patrol and the Rangers were riding mustang horses gleaned from the herds on BLM land. Each year the Bureau of Land Management culled the wild horse herds so the horses wouldn't destroy their ranges by overgrazing. Sara knew one of the cowboys she team roped with rode a mustang he purchased at a BLM auction. The horse was a great heel horse. It wasn't very big, as horses go, but excellent as a heel horse in team roping. The mustang was barely a horse, but still not a pony at fourteen hands, two fingers.

Ben knew Sara was a National Match rifle champion and the conversation turned to guns. Ben said he was never very good with horses or military small arm weapons and just barely qualified with the M9 Beretta pistol pilots carried while deployed. He said being a shaky shooter was why he became a pilot. Besides, he felt better with his hands on the control stick of a plane and his feet on the rudder petals rather than in saddle stirrups.

After dinner, Sara dropped Ben off at his motel and promised to pick him up for breakfast and a ride back to the base. The problem with the engine on Ben's plane was a fuel line rupture and the line was easily replaced, about a ten-minute job. The damage to the engine was negligible, but he would fly back to his home base in Oregon. The engine would be replaced with another rebuilt motor and Ben would be back dropping fire retardant by the following day.

* * *

Sara thought a career change might be a good idea, especially after talking with the Regional Forest Service Supervisor. Sara looked up the Border Patrol on the Internet. She wasn't so sure she would like to do the Border Patrol work when she found out she would probably be sent to the southern border of Texas because she had taken two years of Spanish in high school and in college. After looking up the Department of Agriculture Forest and Park Ranger program, and the Federal Fish and Wildlife Law Enforcement Service, she decided a career change to the ranger program would be in her best interest. She printed the form to request a federal interdepartmental job transfer. Since she was already an employee of the Department of Agriculture she found she could change jobs as soon as the school of instruction opened and the orientation, job interviews and physical tests were completed.

Another two weeks in a cast and then a couple of weeks rehab and Sara would send the request for job change to the Headquarters of the Forest Service and the Federal Fish and Wildlife Law Enforcement Service, ranger program.

* * *

The day the cast came off, Sara submitted her request for transfer. A reply came immediately from both the Ranger Service and from the Forest Service. The Forest Service would release her at the end of the fire season, on the first of November.

The ranger training would start the middle of January, but after her release from the Forest Service. If she was available, she could work alongside a ranger currently working in the Mt. Baker National Forest and east through the Okanogan National Forest. FFWLES liked to have new rangers spend time with an experienced ranger before undertaking the formal professional training. The experience gained enhanced the training and influenced the attitude of the new ranger.

Sara knew if she did the occupational training with a current ranger, it would increase her chances of getting an assignment she favored. She hoped she would be assigned to the northern forests of Washington State. Meanwhile, she would keep her apartment in Winthrop and work for the Forest Service as a clerk. Because her arm wouldn't be healed enough to compete in the National Matches, Sara withdrew her name from the competition. There was always next year.

Chapter Four

The Date

Sara was reading the vitamin list on the side of a dry cereal box when she heard someone call her name. She looked down the aisle and her heart skipped a beat when she spotted Doctor Patrick O'Hara coming toward her pushing a grocery cart. He approached her, a grin on his sun-tanned face.

"What are you doing here?" Sara stammered: T*his is ridiculous, he's just a man.* Her attempt at rational thought was failing. *Oh God, he's seen me naked. Well, my boobs are my best part; even Molly thinks I have great boobs.*

"I shop here; even doctors have to eat." O'Hara stopped and put one hand on Sara's arm like he was holding her in place.

Sara stared down at his hand and then raised her gaze to meet his green, no gray, no, gray-green eyes.

"How's the arm?" he asked glancing down at his hand on Sara's left arm where the cast had been.

Sara dropped her eyes and stared at her arm where his hand rested; she was drawing a blank. Sara quickly raised her face to meet his eyes. "Fine, Doctor O'Hara, it's fine."

"Please call me Pat. Doctor O'Hara sounds so formal, and we aren't at the office."

"Okay, Pat." Sara felt like a high school freshman talking to the school's top jock.

"Say, I've got a few things to pick up yet. If you're not doing anything, would you join me for a cup of coffee or tea?" His eyes sparkled with boyish humor.

"I don't know; I should get this milk home."

"I don't see any ice cream in there, and the milk won't melt." O'Hara nodded at the cart. "The milk will be just fine for a few minutes outside the refrigerator, trust me, I know those things." He laughed.

"I bet you do." Sara sucked air though her teeth. *Now why did I say that?* She needed to get a better grip on her thoughts. "Sure, let me pay for these things and put them in the truck, and I'll meet you at the Starbucks Coffee counter."

"Fine, I'll do the same, see you there." O'Hara pushed his cart of groceries around her and left Sara to stare at his retreating back.

Sara watched the man go down the aisle toward the fruit displays. *Crap, my hair's a mess, no makeup and the same jeans and shirt I wore yesterday at the follow-up examination.* She took a deep breath and pushed her cart toward checkout.

"Do you want that, too?" The checkout clerk pointed at the cereal box still in Sara's hand.

"Sorry." She put the cereal on the wide black belt and watched it move toward the clerk. She took two twenty dollar bills from her pants pocket to pay for her groceries. *Get your shit together, girl.* After putting the groceries in her truck, she reentered the store and walked pass the Starbucks counter to the restroom.

O'Hara was waiting when Sara came out of the restroom. He waved, and she approached the table. "I'm glad we ran into each other like this. I can talk to you socially without office ethics getting in the way. Now, please call me Pat, or any other name you like." O'Hara held the chair for her. When she was seated, he asked, "What can I get you?"

"I'll have a decaf coffee, cream, no sugar, please." Sara was pleasantly surprised and pleased. No man had seated her in a long time. Actually, the last man who had was an uncle at a family wedding reception. "I've never seen you at the supermarket before. Do you shop here often?"

Patrick O'Hara was caught off guard by Sara's directness. "Well actually, I asked Jean what she knew about you."

"Why? You know just about everything about me there is to know." Sara was surprised and pleased Doctor O'Hara was interested in her.

"There is a difference between what I know from the office and what I would like to know. What foods do you like? Movies, books, everything. Not about you jumping out of perfectly good airplanes into fires. I think that's insane." O'Hara reached across the table and laid his hand next to Sara's. "I want to get to know you, the real you, not the macho chick."

"All you have to do is ask. I'm not a big secret." Sara was flustered. This was an entirely new line she hadn't experienced before. "Listen, if you want a date you can ask. I'm not saying yes. Depends on what your expectations are. I don't kiss on the first date." A smile spread across Sara's face. *Well, maybe a light peck on the cheek, if the gentleman deserves one.*

"Okay, how about dinner and a movie?" O'Hara interrupted her thoughts.

"I don't know of any movies playing around here and I'm on twenty-four hour call four nights a week. I have to be within one hour of the base. I monitor the emergency radio for the fire crews."

"How long does it take to get to a fire? Just curious." The doctor was interested. He was now a Naval Reserve medical doctor who had finished his indoctrination into the Navy Medical Corps and been commissioned a full lieutenant in the Navy Reserve. He was assigned to provide medical services to the Marine Reserve units in Spokane and Yakima four months ago, prior to taking over the clinic when the previous physician retired. He understood being on twenty-four hour recall and being on the duty roster from his time as an intern at the Spokane Medical Center emergency room.

Sara was proud of her firefighter crew and thought they were the best team in the Forest Service. "From the time the office receives the call, we want the on-call crew in the air within two hours." Sara caught herself. "Actually, I'm still on light duty, so I just sit by the radio and phones and relay messages. I've been thinking of transferring and applying to the U.S. Department of Agriculture, Federal Fish and Wildlife Law Enforcement Service Ranger Program. To answer your question about smokejumpers, most of the time we have been able to lift off with the whole team within one hour. It was actually fifty-eight minutes and fifty-two seconds for 'wheels up' on the last call. They beat the Winthrop Orbeck's team by three minutes and Missoula's best team by seventeen minutes." She sat straighter in her chair when she talked about her team of firefighters. She wore her pride and excitement on her face.

Pat listened politely. "Well, how about it, dinner and movie?"

"I'm off the watch schedule Wednesday, Thursday and Friday. I'm not eligible for the jump schedule with this newly mended wing unless some doctor at the local clinic clears me for full duty. But you knew that already?" She laughed.

"Yep, I did. I made sure they put you on the desk until that arm's one hundred percent. How does Friday sound?"

"Sound, oh yeah, the movie dinner thing. Yeah, I suppose so. You know where I live. You seem to know everything else."

"No, our files are confidential and some love-starved doctor isn't supposed to use them for his private, off-duty purposes." Pat found it difficult to keep a straight face.

"Well then, give me your hand." Sara ordered. When he put his hand over the table, she used a ball point pen to write her phone number and address on the inside of his palm.

"There. If you wash it off you won't know how to find me."

"I'll never wash that hand again. Well, only for emergencies of life or death." He took out a notepad and transcribed the information into his notebook. "Are you serious about quitting the smokejumping business?"

"Yep, I'm serious as a heart attack."

They spent an hour talking about nothing and everything. Pat told her about growing up in Spokane, and Sara told him about growing up in Bellingham. The highlights were enough to keep the conversation light with boy's adventures and the girl who wanted to play the boys games. During the process of growing up Sara had become a champion flag football player and rifle competition marksman.

* * *

When Sara arrived home there was a message on her recorder. Pat would pick her up at six o'clock Friday for their first date.

Molly looked up from the book she was reading. "Your phone has been ringing, and I let the answering machine get it. Sounds interesting. I suppose our Friday night at the pool hall is off?" she snorted. "You know I don't usually play pool with girls, you're the exception."

Sara popped Molly on the back of her head on the way to the kitchen. Her groceries put away, Sara listened to the recording and erased it from the machine. She plopped down on the couch and used the remote control to turn the TV on.

"Okay, give. What's going on? I let you go to the store and you meet some masher. I suppose he followed you home, too," Molly said with a grin, knowing Sara hadn't dated in months.

"I ran into Doctor O'Hara at the store and he invited me to the movies and dinner Friday night."

"Doctor O'Hara? Aren't you being a little formal with the name of somebody who's seen your pretty assets."

Sara tossed a paperback book at Molly. "It is going to be a very formal occasion, dinner at the Outback and a rerun of The Seven Samurai."

"Winthrop doesn't have a theatre or an Outback. Speaking of Outback, better stay out of the backseat or is he picking you up in the ambulance? That would be handy, don't you think?" Molly tossed the paperback book back.

"Molly, you should get out. Your team isn't on the schedule after tomorrow for two weeks. You can run over to Seattle or Spokane if you're desperate," Sara teased.

"Not to worry. You know that cute little waitress at the choke and puke. I think she's gay, or at least bi. I might give her a tumble while you're out making goo-goo eyes with the hunky doctor."

"You mean the little blonde with the large mammaries?"

"Yep, that's the one, cute huh? I'd like to get my hands on those. They're not as nice as yours of course, but beggars can't be choosy."

"Of course they're not as nice as mine, but hey, if you bring her home, use the towel on the doorknob thing, okay?" Sara was serious. She had walked in on Molly once and been embarrassed. It took an all-night session of explanations before the playing field was clear and their friendship safe. "I thought I'd teach him how to shoot. He's a Naval Reservist with the Marine Fourth Division and can be called to active duty with only a five-day notice. Now that would be my luck; get a decent boyfriend and he gets called away by Uncle Sam." Sara pursed her lips. "I could take him riding and maybe even teach him some roping."

"Don't bring kinky thoughts into this house Ms. Bennett," Molly admonished her room-mate. "Ropes indeed."

* * *

Friday, promptly at six o'clock, Pat O'Hara arrived in front of Sara's apartment. He was driving his tricked out ten-year-old greenish black F150 Ford pickup truck. Molly was at the window being nosy and watched the doctor get out of the truck and cross the wooden sidewalk to the stairs of their second-floor walkup apartment. O'Hara wore faded Levi's, a plaid green and blue Pendleton shirt with boots, old but clean. "Quick, get out of that dress and put on your jeans. He's dressed to kill, hunting deer kill. He's got a nice butt too." Molly laughed.

Sara quickly peeked out the window and saw O'Hara cross the walk. Yep, he was dressed as Molly described. "Answer the door and let him in while I change." Sara rushed into her bedroom ansd slammed close the door.

A minute later there was a knock on the door. "Who is it?" Molly asked sweetly through the door in a little-girl voice.

"It's the Big Bad Wolf, open up or I'll huff and puff until I faint," said a rough voice from the other side of the door.

Molly laughed and opened the door. "Why, if it isn't Doctor Big Bad Wolf himself. I suppose you're looking for Little Miss Riding Hood?"

"Yes, I am, do you know the damsel?"

"Most certainly, she's prepping her wolf-killing ensemble as we speak. Please do come in Doctor Wolf. Would you like a libation before dining with fair damsel?"

"No, I'm fine. Hey, this is a nice place you have here. It's a lot better than my digs. Do you have room for another room-mate? I have unlimited supplies of aspirin and Band-Aids."

"Aw, tempting, but sorry, we're full up at present."

Sara came into the room and looked first at Molly then O'Hara who was on the verge of laughter. "Okay, what is up with you two?"

"Only a small bit of patter. Please call me Doctor Pat, or Doctor Wolf as your charming room-mate does."

"So Doctor Pat, when will you have fair damsel back to her palace?" Molly asked like a concerned parent.

"Don't wait up." Sara smiled at Molly.

"Be off with you now. I have bridges to cross and a fair damsel of my own to conquer." Molly ushered them to the door with her hand on Pat's butt. "Nice buns!" she said in her best British accent.

"Is she always like that?" Pat asked once they were in the truck.

"No, are you?"

O'Hara rolled his eyes and leered at her. "Absolutely!"

Pat pulled the truck onto the highway toward Twisp. "I thought we would go to the new steakhouse in Brewster. Jean went there with her husband last week and thought it was worth the drive."

"I'm not much on steak. Not that I'm a vegetarian or anything. I suppose they would have fish." Sara restricted her intake of red meat to no more than once a week. She imagined a nice salmon filet with lemon sauce. Her mouth actually watered. Since leaving Seattle after college graduation, she missed the great seafood dining Seattle offered.

"I don't eat much red meat either. Red meat takes too long to digest. Since coming to Winthrop I've started running again and red meat doesn't fit into my diet. Now fish is a great substitute for steak, and any good steakhouse must serve a catch of the day." Pat kept up his side of the conversation.

Sara and Pat talked about their college days and life living in the dorm. It seemed a very short trip. They pulled into the restaurant parking lot before Sara realized they had arrived. "Must be a good place, the parking lot is almost full," Pat ventured.

"Yeah, that's kind of unusual for this far from the big city," Sara agreed.

The conversation over dinner was relaxed. Sara could feel a mild sexual attraction toward Pat and she was sure the feeling was mutual.

Pat had been engaged to one of his classmates at medical school. The engagement was broken when Pat came home to find his intended on the couch with another of their classmates. Pat moved out of the apartment and the other guy moved in. She mailed the engagement ring back to him and they never spoke to each other again.

Sara had a romantic fling. No engagement, but serious nonetheless.

The evening seemed too short. After dinner, coffee, and a shared chocolate mousse, Pat drove Sara home. He walked her to the stairs, gave her a chaste kiss on the cheek and asked if he could call her again.

Sara thought about it for a minute, just to keep him on his toes before she granted permission. She gave him the number to the desk at work. They made a tentative date for Sunday afternoon. Sara told him to wear old clothes and meet her at the rodeo grounds in Twisp no later than 1 p.m. Before he left, she put her hand on his shoulder, leaned in and kissed him quickly on the lips before she escaped up the stairs and into her apartment.

Pat sat still in front of the steering wheel for a minute before he started the engine and drove home.

Sara was relieved to find the apartment empty. Molly wasn't back from the pool hall. Sara turned out the lights but left the living room lamp on low. She took a shower and climbed into bed to read. Sara realized she read the same paragraph three times and still could not remember what it was about. She closed the book, set it on the night table and turned out the lamp. She turned onto her side and pulled the covers up to her shoulder and was quickly asleep. She dreamed of horses, cows, and a doctor as visions flashed through her mind.

Chapter Five

Revenge

Doctor O'Hara had been on Sara's mind a lot since their first meeting at the clinic. The cast was off and first dates out of the way. Another doctor was helping out at the clinic three days a week while O'Hara was at a Navy two-week medical orientation course to the Marine Corps at the Marine Corps Base, Camp Pendleton and the Naval Hospital and Medical Center at Lake O'Neill. The Spokane Marine Corps Reserve unit he supported was on the base for their annual training. Pat spent as much time as he could with the unit conducting physicals and tending to injuries the unit corpsmen were unable to handle.

* * *

Memories of an attempted sexual assault by her immediate supervisor invaded Sara's conscious thoughts. The memory popped into her mind as a primary reason for the transfer from the Forest Service. The incident happened toward the end of the previous year's fire season. The broken arm event this year was the icing on the cake, forcing a decision.

Sara remembered the confrontation with her boss while on a forest fire mission in Northern California near the Nevada border. Her crew had come off the fire line for crew rest. She was in the recreation room at a billeting hotel when her supervisor Edwin Johnston entered the room.

"Hi Ed, what can I get you? There are cold beers and wine in the cooler." Her hair was still wet from the shower. She wore a light blouse, an ankle length long Indian skirt, and no make-up. Sara leaned against the back of the room's bar, sipped on a Coke, and watched the news on TV.

Johnston moved up next to her and watched the news on the television for a couple of minutes before getting a beer out of the cooler. "It's been a long fight. The fire is ninety percent contained. We're done here and will return to Winthrop tomorrow. The plane will pick us up at the airport at noon." He stood close next to her, their shoulders nearly touching. "The only out-of-state firefighters scheduled to stay are the Indian Hot Shots from Nevada and New Mexico. The Hot Shots and the California crews will finish up. "

"It'll be nice to get home," Sara responded. "Bet your wife will be glad to see you."

"Yeah, well, we haven't been getting along for some time. She's going to visit her sister in Seattle for awhile." Johnston turned so he was facing her. He put his hand on her shoulder, and let it slide down across her breast as if by accident. "You know I've always thought a lot of you Sara. We could have a good thing going for both of us." He gazed into Sara's shocked face. "What do you think, maybe we get together?" His hand came up and brought the light-weight skirt's hem with it revealing Sara's leg and the bottom of her underwear.

Sara grabbed his hand in a wristlock and exerted enough pressure to cause pain. "Not on your best day, Asshole." She added a bit more pressure for emphasis and pushed him away. Sara picked up her soda and walked out of the recreation area to return to her room.

Sara slammed the door and went into the bathroom to wash her hands when a faint knock sounded on the door. Crossing the room, she looked out the peephole in the door and saw Johnston standing there with a sad look on his face. Thinking he was there to apologize, Sara opened the door. When it was open enough, Johnston pushed the door open knocking Sara back onto the bed of the small room. He kicked the door closed, crossed to the bed and grabbed Sara's legs, pushing them apart and the skirt up around her waist. Spittle struck Sara's face and one of Johnston's hands were on her breast the other at the waist band of her panties. He yanked, tearing the panties away dropping them on the floor.

"You want this. I can tell, bitch," Johnston said ripping her blouse. Sara was wearing only her bra and the skirt bunched at her waist.

"You're right, I've wanted to do this," Sara said huskily. Johnston grinned and eased back so he could see her. When his weight eased off, Sara moved a little to gain leverage and bucked him off her onto the floor. She jumped on him and open-handed slapped him like her brother taught her. She may have broken his nose. The power of the slap shocked Johnston and very nearly knocked him unconscious.

Sara stood over him wearing only the skirt and her sports bra. She grabbed the front of his shirt and hauled him to his feet. Slapping him again as hard as she could, Sara guided him toward the door, opened it and pushed him out into the hall. "I hope you got everything you came here for Mr. Johnston. If I can do it again, don't hesitate to ask." She slammed the door shut before the tears came.

One of her other crew members was in the hall and heard and saw Johnston pushed into the hall with blood on his face by a flattened nose. He heard Sara's words. "Hope I never make her mad," he mumbled as he let himself into his room.

The next morning, Johnston was noticeably absent. Someone heard he caught an early flight to Seattle to meet his wife for a holiday. Sara looked around the room, and some of the men wouldn't meet her eyes. Two of the female firefighters grinned and gave her thumbs up.

Johnston spent the next month on vacation. When he returned he stayed in his office leaving only when duties required. The following year when the parachutists returned for the fire season, Johnston spent nearly all the time in his office avoiding Sara.

Sara refused Johnston's suggestion that she transfer to Missoula citing personal reasons and family hardship. She would continue to jump into hazardous DZs and work as a firefighter. Johnston required her whole team to retake their qualification jump. He said there was a question whether the results of the original qualification jump had been tampered with, making the follow-up qualification jump required.

When Sara had gotten hurt, it had been a Godsend for him. Now he could get rid of the troublesome Sara Bennett. She would never jump again if he had any say in the matter. Maybe he could have her transferred to the Missoula, Montana, Forest Service Smokejumper Base.

* * *

Sara sat at her clerical desk in the supervisor's office at the airfield. Her arm was completely healed, but the supervisors still didn't want her to work fires. Sara had appealed the decision but she'd been unable to convince the three man supervisor's board she should be reinstated without restrictions. She knew why they kept her on limited-duty status: the incident with Johnston last year and her status with the National Shooting Team. Sara never told them she had taken her name off the National Team roster when she'd broken her arm.

Sara's supervisor Johnston was on the review board. She'd rejected his sexual advances and it had sealed her future with the Winthrop smokejumpers. When Sara called him a slug and pervert, it had doomed her career. *God damn it, the asshole is getting his revenge.* She'd never get back on jump status with him on the board; she knew the other two supervisors would back him.

The best option remaining was to transfer. Pat medically cleared her for full duty. She knew she could pass all the tests and physical requirements for work with the Federal Fish and Wildlife Law Enforcement Service. The ranger job was there waiting for her depending only on her passing the physical fitness test, the written test and the interviews. The FFWLES sent her the testing schedule for both physical and written exams. Next week she would go to Seattle and take the written examination. She could take the physical tests on any of six dates. Sara thought it was time she finished the transfer process. With seven vacation days due her she could take three and make the trip to Seattle. Sara got the telephone number out of her wallet and used her cell phone to make the appointment for the written test and the remaining portion of the physical test.

With all the tests completed, Sara would become a Federal Fish and Wildlife Law Enforcement Service probationary ranger. The rangers were required to be armed and possess arrest powers, which required weapons proficiency and formal training. Enforcing game and forest laws might be a little exciting and even dangerous; but smokejumping work was dangerous too and she'd survived that.

A week after returning from Seattle, Sara received an email that confirmed she had passed all the tests. She officially requested transfer the day she was released from the Forest Service. She asked to be notified of openings via email and snail mail.

Ken Behoney, FFWLES district supervisor, had been notified Sara Bennett requested a transfer to his agency. He asked she be assigned to his district. He knew all about Sara, how she'd been hurt and her recovery. He had no doubt she'd aced the physical and written examinations. A new Winthrop supervisor ranger would be taking over the northern area from Winthrop to the international border, east to Republic, and south to the edge of the Colville Indian Reservation and west back to Winthrop. Sara would be his rookie student for her orientation period.

* * *

Ken Behoney, the district supervisor of the Federal Fish and Wildlife Law Enforcement Service visited Johnston to inform him a ranger supervisor would be reporting to the Winthrop area before the end of fire season. Johnston was out of the office, so Sara took the message. The Federal Fish and Wildlife Law Enforcement Service headquarters wanted the ranger to go through the smokejumper parachute refresher training and make the required qualification jump. Taking advantage of the federally owned property, the ranger supervisor would use the spare office in the Forest Service building.

Chapter Six

Springer

The climb up the Loop Loop pass from Okanogan to Twisp was hard on the old green truck. The truck was old, a retired relic purchased at a Forest Service auction. Randy Springer spent many hours working on the motor until it ran smoothly. His clothing and other dry goods were double bagged in extra-strength black plastic garbage bags in the bed of the pickup truck. His personal pistol belt and the heavy .45 Caliber Long Colt revolver were on passenger's seat. The Government Sig Sauer 40 Caliber semiautomatic pistol was in its holster in the jockey box. Three rifles rode in hard plastic cases behind the seat with his briefcase containing official papers. Country music by Mary Kaye played on the state-of-the-art CD player.

A powerful multi-frequency radio was mounted on the dash tuned to the Forest Service Fire Control Net. The special radio allowed him to listen to both the administration net and the fire control net with a double receiver.

Last month, Randy had been transferred from the Kaniksu National Forest in northeastern Washington and panhandle of northern Idaho to the Winthrop office of the Federal Fish and Wildlife Law Enforcement Service. His new area of responsibility was in the Okanogan, Wenatchee and Mt. Baker National Forests and the Methow Valley, as a supervisory ranger.

Randy's three saddles and tack were packed in heavy canvas bags also in the truck bed. He was authorized to select three green-broke horses from the Bureau of Land Management roundup of mustang horses. Randy supported the mustang roundup to prevent the wild horses from overgrazing their ranges and starving during the winter months. When he reported to his boss, Ken Behoney via telephone, he was informed he would have the opportunity to select three mustangs for his official use and two additional mustangs for his own personal mounts prior to the BLM Mustang horse auction. He planned to buy two mustangs to train as team roping horses.

Randy was surprised when he was informed before he left Idaho, he would be the Winthrop area supervisor and liaison ranger assigned to work with the Forest Service smokejumpers and firefighters based at the Winthrop airport. He would also share office building space with the Forest Service supervisor. As an additional surprise, he was expected to make a qualification jump with the smokejumpers.

The current FFWLES Supervisor was stationed in Mazama a few miles northwest of Winthrop and was being transferred to the United States southern border in Texas. Three to five additional rangers would be assigned to the Winthrop office. Randy would be responsible for two experienced rangers, and two transfers from the Midwest and a new ranger transferred from a sister agency

Randy arrived in Winthrop in the early afternoon and rented a furnished apartment. He reported by telephone to the District Supervisor and was informed he was scheduled to accompany the ranger he was replacing on a five-week tour on horseback through the Methow Valley to the Canadian border, along the border with a Border Patrol agent and return to Winthrop. The planned orientation ride was a tad over three hundred miles.

Randy's two current rangers and six others who worked from offices in northeast Washington patrolled the international boundary with Canada and enforced Fish and Wildlife laws. His secondary job was to assist the Border Patrol and other agencies in law enforcement when they requested assistance. At the border north of the Methow Valley, on the first of the long orientation patrols, he was scheduled to meet with members of the Royal Canadian Mounted Police. The Mounties would accompany them on the patrol along the border from west to east. At Danville the RCMP would return to their headquarters and the FFWLES rangers would turn south and follow the District borders, terminating the patrol in Winthrop.

The day after he arrived in Winthrop, Randy drove to Brewster for a meeting with Ken Behoney, the District Supervisor. Before leaving Winthrop, Randy put his personal valuable possessions in secure storage. The rest he put into the apartment he'd rented via the Internet, and wouldn't move into except to sleep until he returned from his orientation patrol. The following morning Randy met with a new ranger from the Brewster office and together they trailered to Mazama where they would leave the truck and trailer. The Rangers would do a short week six-day patrol on the east slope of the Cascades. Randy planned to spend two days inspecting the service tack and assets in Winthrop in preparation for the five-week, three hundred mile orientation patrol.

On his first day without scheduled work, Randy went to the Forest Service building to introduce himself. He met a beautiful girl wearing snug, faded wranglers, a green cotton button-down collared shirt and worn roper cowboy boots with spur wear marks on the heels. A name tag above her left pocket gave her name as Sara Bennett. When he asked one of the off-duty smokejumpers about her, he was told she was a grounded smokejumper from an injury, and she was dating the doctor at the Winthrop Emergency Clinic. Randy, not one to give up easily, made a mental note to check on the progress of the doctor and Sara Bennett's relationship when he returned from the orientation tour.

There were two hundred and forty-five mustangs in the BLM corral in Spokane for the first public auction. Randy walked right into the arena where the mustangs were kept and stood quietly for more than an hour. First one then another mustang came to investigate this new addition to the herd. He selected the first five horses to come to him. After he checked them for injuries and health and was satisfied the five horses were injury free and healthy he bought the first two for himself and the next three mustangs for transfer to the rangers. Randy loaded the mustangs into the ranger seven-horse trailer and transported them to Winthrop.

Randy intended to train his personal mustangs as rope horses. Both were a hair over fifteen hands, well muscled and calm. When he walked into the corral the next morning both of his horses came to him when he caught their attention. The other three pool horses followed. Randy put halters on the horses and led them to a separate corral where he could spend some time with them. Gentle was the way Randy handled green-broke horses. Within the first week, he wanted to introduce them to trailers. By the second day he was riding the number one horse, and the following day his second horse. The third day he rode the other three horses. Randy trained them to cues and to ground tie. Randy had learned his horsemanship from his father and grandfather on the Rolling JH Ranch northwest of Missoula, Montana.

By the following Monday, Randy felt the pool horses were trained enough to take on a six-day trip. Randy planned to train the pool horses as the trip progressed. A local farrier put good shoes on the horses using the hot shoe technique, making sure the shoes fit properly and were well seated to the hoof's wall.

When Randy inspected his work, the farrier grinned. It was nice to see a horseman inspect his work and appreciate his craftsmanship. Randy ordered a second set of shoes for each horse. He would carry the spare shoes packed in the panniers carried by his pack horse. Each ranger had one pack animal assigned to him or her.

In the second week, Randy liked to spend an hour a day in the office. To get to his office, he had to pass through the Forest Service business office first and the blond clerk at her desk.

On the way to the office, he spotted Sara buying coffee from one of the local coffee shops. On the third day, he brought her a fresh cup of coffee accompanied by packets of creamer and sugar. When she put creamer and no sugar in her coffee, he grinned. It was the same way he drank his coffee, an omen. He accepted her nodded thanks, and went into his office, but left the door open.

The following day, Randy was busy with sorting and setting up his map stocks and wall-mounted his radio on a shelf next to his desk. He heard a faint cough.

Sara stood back from the open door and held two cups of coffee in her hands. When Randy smiled at her, Sara entered his office and set one coffee on the old gray metal desk. He invited her to sit but she excused herself, saying she needed to be close to the radio. A team of firefighters were in the field and she wanted to keep an ear out for them.

The following day, Randy again showed up with coffee for Sara. Sara followed him into his office and sat in his guest chair.

"Aren't you kind of young to be a section supervisor?" Sara opened.

"Hey, I've been cruising timber since college summers and full time the past five years." Randy couldn't help being a little defensive.

"I didn't mean anything by it. You can't be over, what twenty-two?"

"Nope, I'm an old man of twenty-five and you are?"

"A lady never tells." Sara laughed. She immediately felt comfortable with the six-foot two-inch ranger with the heavy automatic pistol on his hip. She noticed the locked horizontal rifle rack mounted on the wall behind his desk. The three weapons held in the rack impressed her. She spotted an antique M70 .30 Caliber Winchester with a Redfield scope, a .32 Caliber Winchester model 94 and a .45 Cal. Long Colt Winchester saddle ring carbine.

"Wow, I haven't seen one of those government M70s in a long time. Where did you find it?" Sara asked.

"My dad gave it to me when I accepted the ranger job. He carried it in the Marines for years. Said it was more reliable than the M40 once you got used to it. So you know guns?"

"Yeah, I do a little shooting from time to time," Sara admitted.

"Wait a minute, what was your last name?"

"Bennett, Sara Bennett."

"Hey, I know about you. Dad said you have more talent in one hand than most of those paper shooters will ever have. What are you doing here anyway?" Randy was impressed.

"What's your dad's name, maybe I know him."

"Hank Springer, Chief Warrant Officer Four retired USMC."

"Your dad is Hank Springer?"

"Yep!" Randy thought most people remembered Hank from his Marine days and cowboy work, not shooting. "Dad retired and now has a ranch in Montana and raises kids, horses, and cattle. I really don't usually do this, but if I invite you to visit the Rolling JH Ranch, it would make my dad's day, and Ralph's too. Course you'll have to bring your rifles for a little friendly shooting." Randy laughed, delighted with the growing friendship.

"Now that is an invitation I can't refuse. We'll talk later. I have to get back to work, got reports due." Sara stood, smiled and left Randy behind his desk wearing a crooked smile on his tanned face.

When Randy was leaving for the day, he stopped by Sara's desk. "Sara, I have a patrol coming up next week. I'll be gone about five weeks. Do you think you could find the time to kind of keep an eye on the place?"

"Sure Randy, my pleasure. Will you have your radios with you?"

"Yeah, I'll leave the frequency with you. We actually have three frequencies we monitor. Also, I have a sat-cell. I'll leave that number with you too. If there is anything we can do or check for you, give us a call." Randy tapped the counter and left. He could feel the flush the young woman brought out in him. *Damn, I'm in love.*

* * *

Randy spent the rest of the week working with the mustang horses. By Monday the ranger mounts were ready. The pack horses had been shod and vet checked along with the new horses. The vet found them to be sound and ready for the long trip. Randy decided they would leave the truck and trailer at the ranger station at Mazama. One of the new rangers could retrieve and return the truck and trailer to Winthrop. The new assigned rangers would report to the district office Monday morning for a welcome aboard meeting. Behoney planned to give the new rangers three days to find a place to live in Winthrop and get settled. He also planned for Sara to work in Brewster's District Office for the time the supervisory ranger would be on patrol before she reported to Winthrop and Randy.

* * *

At first light, rangers Martin Ortega, Ron, Zeke, and Randy started the trek patrol in a northwest direction. The four rangers each carried their personal sidearm and a heavy Caliber rifle in the saddle scabbard. Randy's Sig .40 Caliber automatic had been replaced by a .45 Caliber Long Colt pistol. The normal 30-30 carbine carried by most of the rangers was replaced by a Winchester Model 94 .45 Long Colt rifle. When Randy was on regular patrol he would replace the .45 Long Colt rifle for the longer shooting .32 Caliber model 94.

The Park Service informed the rangers, currently six groups of hikers were near their proposed route. The Forest Service would keep him informed as the patrol progressed. When encountered, the patrol would check on the groups for safety and proper equipment for the season.

Before he left the office, Randy handed Sara a copy of the patrol's planned route and radio frequencies. "Just so you know where I am," He teased. Sara surprised Randy and herself when she came around the counter and quickly kissed him on the cheek and admonished him to be careful. "There are druggies in them there hills," She warned.

Chapter Seven

Team Roping

Pat arrived at the Twisp Rodeo Grounds at half past noon to find the parking lot full of pickup trucks and horse trailers. He looked for and spotted Sara by a black and white two-horse slant trailer. She was talking to a tall man wearing half-length chaps, called chinks by cowboys, and a western straw hat. Pat hesitated and decided to wait and watch before letting Sara know he was there. He sat on the lowest bench of the small grandstand, not wanting to draw attention to himself. He saw Sara enter the tack room of the trailer and come out wearing a pair of buckskin colored chinks. She entered the back of the trailer and came out leading a light-colored buckskin horse. With his scant knowledge of horses Pat knew the horse was an American Quarterhorse. He could see the suppressed power in the wide chest and rear end of the horse. The breed was exceptionally fast, smart, and strong.

Sara tied her horse to the trailer and began brushing the horse. Pat watched from across the arena as she put a saddle blanket on the horse's back and ran her hand under the blanket to make sure there were no wrinkles to irritate the horse. At the tack room, she swung a saddle rack out and removed one of two saddles from the rack. The saddle horn was wrapped with what appeared to be rubber inner-tubing. The cinch, breast collar and back cinch were laid over the saddle's seat. He watched her use her knee to boost the saddle up onto the horse's back. She eased the saddle into place on the horse's back, then ran her hand between the saddle and the blanket to check for wrinkles.

As Pat watched, he recalled the time he took western riding lessons while still in elementary school. Memories returned and he understood most of what he was seeing. Sara pushed the cinches off the saddle seat to fall on the right side of the horse. She reached under the horse and grabbed the cinch to bring it up to the latego and D ring. Sara threaded the strap through the ring and cinched the straps snug. She adjusted and tightened the back cinch making sure it was in the correct position. A strap out of position might cause the horse to buck and result in the cowboy sitting in the dirt of the arena. She used a cowboy knot to lock the cinch and the breast collar and again checked the back cinch and made sure it was still in the correct position. Sara put a tie down on the horse's nose to keep his head down.

That was about the extent of Pat's knowledge of horse tack. He did know about the headstall, but the different types of bits left him confused.

Sara was inside the tack room when Pat approached her trailer. He kept a respectful distance from the horse. When Sara came out she found Pat waiting. "How long have you been here?"

"Just long enough to watch you saddle your horse. He's a Quarterhorse isn't he?"

"Yeah, his name is Buster, fifteen-three hands tall, good sized for a Quarterhorse. Buster is a head horse and runs like greased lightening. He's never had a steer get away from him. You know a head horse needs to be a bit bigger than a heel horses so they can take the hit when the steer reaches the end of the rope."

"What do you mean, a steer never getting away from him?" Pat asked. *What am I doing here?*

Sara hesitated and decided to explain about the horses in a little more detail. "A head horse must be quick out of the box but wait until the steer gets far enough out of the chute before leaving the box or he breaks the barrier, gaining a ten-second time penalty for him and his partner. He must be fast enough to get the roper to the left hip of the steer, ensuring a good position for the roper to throw and pull slack; to tighten the loop on the steer's horns. With a light touch of the rein or a foot cue, the head horse breaks to the left pulling the steer's head to follow."

"The heel horse doesn't have a barrier, but the horse must get quickly into position at the right side of the steer to haze so the steer runs straight. If the heeler gets too far forward, the steer may shut-down, that's stop. If the steer stops, it makes it impossible to get a good time." Sara stopped to make sure Pat was following what she was saying. Satisfied, she continued. "When the steer is pulled to the left, the heeler rides the corner and the horse puts the roper behind the steer's left hip, where he can throw a loop under the steer, what we call a trap, and catch the back feet in the loop. The heeler must throw, pull slack and dally in a split second. The header then faces the steer, and the flag comes down stopping the timer's watch. You'll be able to see it all; there are some good ropers here today."

Sara decided to explain further. "Some steers can run very fast and they do get an eight foot head start. With the head start, some steers are able to outrun some horses and get to the far end of the arena before the header can close the distance and throw a loop." Sara patted her horse's shoulder and rubbed his neck. "The Quarterhorse is the fastest of all the breeds and solidly built, perfect for cattle work. Some of the ropers ride mustangs, a wild horse long on brains and stamina. The drawback is they are normally smaller, but they are still nearly as fast as the Quarterhorse. I wouldn't be surprised if there isn't a relationship between the mustang and standard bred horse to get the Quarterhorse. Most breeders would argue, but they won't change my mind."

Pat was confused; Sara had given him a lot of information to absorb. "Okay, I think I've got the basics, or at least the theory."

Sara smiled. "This afternoon we have a jackpot team roping. We need someone to work the chutes, both the stripping chute and the box chute. I volunteered you." Sara smiled mischievously at Pat who wished he had been called into work. "I recommend you work the stripping chute, it's easier and less dangerous. The other chute you have to be in the heeler's box so you can see the header signal to release the steer. It can get a little crowded in the heel box with the horse and the cowboy operating the chute and keeping the steer pointed forward. If the steer's head is turned, the steer may miss the chute opening resulting in a broken barrier. Of course you can sit on top of the chute and let the other guys do all the work. Something to consider, if you're on top of the chute and you get a leg inside the chute, the steer might not like it, your choice." Sara smiled sweetly at the apprehensive man.

"Oh well, can't live forever and I do have Levi's on with my cowboy boots. Do I need a cowboy hat? I have one in the truck."

"No, you don't need a hat. Well maybe a give-me hat to keep the sun off your pointed little head." Sara laughed.

"Hey, don't laugh at me, I'm sensitive." Pat gave her a pouty look.

Sara looked at his boots. "You know what kind of boots you have on?"

"No, the guy who sold them said they were just low-heeled cowboy boots. I needed a pair to square dance in when I was dating Nancy. No more Nancy. Should I get rid of the boots too?" Pat said, teasing.

"No, those are actually roping boots, same as I'm wearing if you'd care to look." Sara lifted her Wrangler jeans up high enough to reveal the colorful tops of her boots and the low heels fitted with short roping spurs.

"How come everyone is wearing jeans six inches too long for them?"

"That's called stacking. The pant legs ride up when you're in the saddle and if the pants aren't longer, the top of the boots will show, uncool.," Sara explained. "You can ask questions, you're new. Next week no questions, so learn fast. Come on and meet Buster, he's really a sweetheart and the best header out here. If I was as good as Buster, we'd win it all."

Sara introduced Pat to her horse. After some coaxing, she was able to get Pat to actually pet her horse and feel his soft nose. "Horses are very trusting. Let him smell you and he won't forget, especially if you give him a treat, which you can't do. Treats spoil him and if he has some, he won't be worth a damn, and it makes him mouthy."

"Doesn't putting that steel thing in his mouth hurt?" Pat asked puzzled.

"No, here, stick your thumb in the side of his mouth, right here." She showed Pat where to put his thumb.

Pat was surprised when he couldn't feel teeth, only the horse's gums. "Where are his teeth?"

"Horses don't have teeth like humans; they have the chomping teeth in front, a gap and the grinding teeth in the back. Horses' teeth continue to grow their whole life, that's why we have them floated, or filed down every year or so. The choppers get long and you can tell the age of a horse by the length of the front teeth."

"Isn't it dangerous being around horses, especially riding and working from horseback?" Pat looked at Sara's horse; he could see the suppressed power. "Aren't a lot of people hurt? I had a man in the other day with a broken hip. He said his horse got pissed and threw him."

"Hey, shit happens. Every rider will get thrown. It's something you can count on happening, especially if the rider does something the horse doesn't like. Before we ride we also need to check his feet and be sure the shoes are still firmly in place and he hasn't picked up a stone." Sara had Pat pick up Buster's feet and check the shoes and the hoof walls for cracks and the frog for bruising. Pat was amazed the twelve-hundred pound horse let him walk around him and pick up his feet without a fuss.

Sara grinned as Pat moved around the horse and checked all four feet. "Now, let's get you where you have to be so we can get this jackpot started." Sara led Pat to a cowboy leaning on a fence by the chutes and introduced them. "George, here's your helper. You might consider putting him at the stripping chute so he's up out of the way until he figures out what's happening." Sara left Pat in George's hands. When she looked back, George was talking and gesturing with his hands as he led Pat toward the stripping chutes at the far end of the arena.

Sara finished saddling Buster by tightening the cinches and putting on the headstall and bit. She rode him into the arena to warm up with the other riders and horses. Sara walked Buster around the outside edge of the arena and then put him into a trot, followed by an easy lope for three circuits of the arena. After loping him in circles first to the left then right, she started him into a gallop and then put the brakes on. The horse dropped his rear and slid on his back feet as he came to an abrupt stop. She rewarded Buster with a pat on the neck. As Sara patted the horse, she could feel the heat come from Buster; he was warmed up and stretched out enough. Before loading him in the trailer this morning, she flexed him, stretching his legs front and back.

The timer called the teams; the heeler went into the right box and the header the left box. There were two ribbons staked eight feet from the front of the chute to mark when the header could leave the box. During rodeo events, a man tied a string to the steer's tail and other end to the barrier stretched across the header's box. The heeler shook out a loop and nodded to the header who had his loop ready. With a nod from the header, the chute operator released the lever which opened the chute with a bang, and the steer bolted out of the chute. The header gave the steer enough time so he wouldn't break the barrier and they were off; from zero to upward of twenty-five miles per hour plus in twelve feet.

The heeler moved up the right side of the steer to haze and keep the steer running straight and not turning into the fence. He needed to be careful. If he went too far toward the head of the steer, the steer would shut down and it would stop or turn back. The steer on the first run did shut down which resulted in a "no time" for the team.

During the second team's turn the header roped the horns and turned the steer to the left. The heeler rode the corner, spun a loop and threw a trap in front of the steer's hind legs and snared the legs in the loop as it pulled tight. The header turned and faced the steer while the heeler held the back feet together. Eight seconds was an okay time. World record time was under four seconds, but those times were for the professionals. Eight seconds was a good time for jackpots, depending on the steers.

The afternoon passed quickly for both Sara and Pat. She made twenty runs, catching seventeen of her steers while her heelers, a different heeler each go, caught nine. Not a bad day but not especially a good day either. She didn't get a paycheck but she had a lot of fun. The jackpot was worth the experience and the $20 entry fee.

Sara talked to some of the cowboys as they watered and let their horses cool down before putting them away in trailers. She noticed Pat limping toward her. "What happened to you, why are you limping? You're covered in green shit too." She couldn't help smiling. "What happened?"

Pat looked at her with a forlorn look. "I fell off the stripping chute when I was trying to get a twisted rope off one of the horns. I lost my balance and landed on top of the stupid critter and he kicked me. When I was trying to get out of the way, I tripped and fell in the shit. Don't laugh, it's not funny. Well, maybe a little funny." Pat noticed some of the cowboys were watching and listening.

Pat started to leave the arena when a half dozen of the ropers approached him and thanked him for helping and hoped to see him again, maybe on a horse next time. Sara could see Pat stood a little straighter as more of the ropers came by to thank him. By the time the cowboys had shaken his hand, Pat had forgotten his embarrassment and pain from being kicked, even the green stains on his shirt and Levi's.

On the way back to Sara's trailer, Pat asked her if she thought he could learn to do roping. "Are you serious?" She stopped and looked at the limping, vile-smelling man.

"Yep, I'd like to learn and how about your arm, isn't it sore?"

"No, the arm's okay. There is no stress on the left arm with the reins and holding the rope coils. The horse knows what to do. I'm more or less just along for the ride." Sara studied the man. "Can you ride a horse? Can you throw a rope? Have you ever done either of those things?"

Pat tilted his head to one side. "Nope, but you can teach me. I watched you making your runs, not just when you came by the stripping chute. You are very good."

"Actually, I'm not very good yet, but I can ride and do throw a pretty good loop most of the time. I'm not very fast compared to where I want to be. If you're serious, I'll help you but first you need to take some riding lessons and then find an older rope horse who knows everything so you don't have to worry about him doing his job. You need only worry about doing your job."

"Where can I get a horse like Buster? How much does a horse like him cost?"

"I bought Buster from a friend last year and he still cost me $7,500. Buster is seven years old and a fully trained gelding. I did need to take lessons in order to ride him properly. I've been riding for a lot of years, but each horse is different and you need to know those differences." She paused and watched Pat's expression. "First you need to learn to ride. You can take lessons and have a choice of five different places in Winthrop or Twisp. I'll get you the telephone numbers and go with you for your first lesson. Don't expect to be throwing loops at steers for awhile." Sara went into her tack room and came out with two of her old head ropes. "Here, use these to get started learning to twirl the rope, then just throw it at a spot on the ground until you can hit the spot nine out of ten times. These are head ropes; they are a few feet shorter than heel ropes. Heel ropes are softer. A heeler needs the softer rope so he can place the loop beneath the steer's belly in front of the rear legs. The steer's feet and legs snag the rope, the heeler pulls the slack, dallies, and the steer is caught. Here, let me put Buster away and I'll get you started with the ropes. There's a set of horns attached to a sled in the corner of the arena." She pointed to the near corner behind the arena gate. Pat saw what looked like a steer's head attached to a sawhorse mounted on slats so the sawhorse could be pulled.

With Buster in the trailer munching on a flake of hay, Sara went to where Pat was throwing his rope at the steer's head on the sawhorse. She watched him try to twirl the rope and throw it. "Here, let me show you how. First, you need a spoke, that's some rope between your hand and the honda where the rope passes through to make the loop. You also have to put a half twist so the loop opens properly. It will be second nature to you sooner than you think." She showed him how to establish enough spoke with the proper twist.

"The spoke and twist make it easier to throw the loop so the loop stays open and not twisted. Now, just twirl the rope around your head." Sara showed him how to take the spoke and how to hold the rope in his hand. Next, she showed him how to roll his hand so the rope spun around his head without dropping down on him.

Sara spun the rope and threw at the dummy's head to demonstrate. After removing the loop from the dummy's horns, she helped him with the spinning, throwing, catching and pulling slack. She watched him for a few minutes, and then did another half dozen tosses to show him again, catching each time. Sara could see he was analyzing her every move. She smiled to herself. *Maybe Pat is the man I've been waiting to meet.*

Chapter Eight

Ranger

Sara was at her desk when Randy Springer knocked, opened the door and stepped into the office. "Hi." She greeted him with a smile. Sara had been loaned back to the Forest Service to work in the office until Randy returned to take over training and supervision.

"Hi, is your boss in?" Randy couldn't keep the grin off his sun- browned face.

"Nope, he's taking some time off and won't be in the office all this week." Sara smiled as she subconsciously sized up the man on the other side of the counter. When they met two months ago, the two had seemed to get along well. Sara regretted the relationship with Pat O'Hara hadn't progressed one way or the other. Her mind was still up in the air about the doctor. Pat had been pushing her lightly as if he hadn't made up his mind to pursue her or keep the relationship on a friendly level. She smiled at Randy. Now here was a man who pleased her without ever having touched her. The thought brought up the memory of the kiss on the cheek before he'd left on his long patrol.

"Do you happen to have any messages for me? I'm looking for a message from my boss. He has a new hire supposed to be on an orientation program reporting here within the next couple of weeks."

Sara completely missed the reference to a new ranger, her mind on other things. She appraised the man with a smile on his tanned face. He needed a shave but his clear brown eyes mesmerized her and she was sure his smile would melt her heart given the chance. She guessed he was over six feet tall, wore his light brown hair cut on the short side, off the collar in back. He had a slight ruddy complexion, a result of years of exposure to the elements. Sara couldn't help notice the twinkle in his eyes as if he knew what she was thinking.

Sara watched his grin grow and gave her head a mental shake. "Is there something I can do for you?"

"Eh, no. He wanted me to meet with him after I got back from our ride. I made some notes about the forest condition and the amount of trash and slash. There were some campers and hikers on the more popular trails. The last heavy rain made a real difference in the fire danger. On our outbound leg, we patrolled south of the border using old logging roads; we crossed over the border occasionally, not much more than a mile at any time. I made a report for him on the health of the forest trees and an infestation of bark beetles. We saw a lot of dead or dying trees in patches. I marked them on a 1:50,000 map.

"The Okanogan Forest didn't get the amount of rain the western hills got. The forest will be a tinder box later in the fire season with dry trees and dry ground cover. You know seasonal summer rains drop a lot of water in a short time, but don't last long enough to really wet down the forest. My recommendation is to send crews to clear-cut the dead timber and clear slash." Randy reached into his small backpack and withdrew a Bureau of Land Management map of northern Washington and a folder of Defense Department maps issued by the Defense Mapping Agency.

"You want me to add the maps to a report for your boss, or leave them with you?"

Sara came around her desk, motioned to the map table below the window overlooking the airstrip. He put the map on the table and used large black paper clamps to hold the maps in place. They sat together on stools and Randy traced his patrol route. He explained how he had marked the maps and the margin notes. Sara noticed the legend marked on the maps were areas of top priority and dangerous drop zones for smokejumpers. She also noticed there were actually three sets of five maps rolled together.

Randy selected a roll of maps and started with the bottom map which showed the ranger's route marked in purple. Sara noted hot areas and drop zones were marked in red marked on a 1:250,000 scale map. "I marked in the best drop zones, highlighted in orange in each of the high danger areas we passed through. You can cross reference with each set of maps." Randy unfolded the next map and it showed the town of Winthrop in the lower left corner. "I thought 1:50,000 scale military topographical contour maps would be best to show the terrain smokejumpers would be jumping into. There are some additional notes on the DZs your team leaders may find useful." Randy pulled out the second and third roll of maps. "These are all 1:50,000 scale maps covering our area of responsibility."

Sara looked closely at the maps with small orange circles marking the drop zones. There were numbers at each site which corresponded with notes made in the map's margin. "Wow, this is better than the maps we've been using. The notes are really good and easy to understand. It'll make the jumps safer and easier for the pilots too."

"I thought you'd rather have too much information than not enough, so I added what I thought would help." Randy looked at Sara. "I've got a couple of questions you might be able to answer."

"Sure, if I can." Sara was curious. What would she know that a ranger might need?

"I was jump trained at Missoula but haven't jumped in almost three years. My boss doesn't think I need to take a full refresher course, just make a couple of jumps. Think I'd be able to jump with a training group to keep my qualifications up?"

"Sure, I don't think it would be a problem. We have a training jump scheduled for tomorrow. The plane's liftoff is scheduled for 1000 hours. If you want to jump, I'll get one of the team leaders to fix you up with a parachute and suit. Have you jumped with the parasail chute?"

"Yeah, that's what I trained with. They were brand new then and really easy to guide. You could put your feet into a washtub in a thirty-mile-an hour wind. They are a lot better than the old T10 chutes we got from the Army. Of course the T10 was a rugged chute but hard to steer. You never knew where you were going to end up. With the ram steerable chutes you can jump from higher up and still hit the center of the drop zone."

From the way he talked, Sara could tell Randy was an experienced jumper. She remembered a note requesting Randy be requalified. He was definitely not going to need the training course, just the jump. "Okay, what's the second question?"

"I bought a couple of mustang horses from the BLM for myself when I bought the horses for the job. I'd like to find a place I can board them that has an arena or at least a round pen where I can do some training away from the base. I left them here in the stable while I was gone and now I need to find them a home. I've ridden both mustangs on the trail and in the arena, but not enough to call them dead-broke. I've ridden them enough for them to be desensitized to people and tack, but they need a lot of arena work. If possible, I'd also like to find two or three steers. Corrientes, if possible to train them for work." Randy raised his eyebrows in question.

"That's more than a couple of questions but I might be able to help you out. You sound like a roper?"

"Yeah guilty, my family owns a ranch in Montana, northwest of Missoula a couple of hours, but you already know that. Team roping is kind of a family sport everyone does. My sisters compete, and Brent, my brother is on the circuit when he can get away from the ranch, and when Bev, his wife, lets him out on his own. He usually ropes with my dad and one or two of the kids."

Sara began to feel a little guilty, still dating Pat and conscious of a budding interest in Randy Springer. Sara made up her mind to settle the issue with Pat soon. "I do a little roping, started to get serious last year. One of the ranchers toward Twisp has an arena and keeps a fair-sized herd of Mexican steers. We have a jackpot twice a month and usually rope on weekends at the fairgrounds. Jim also has a great lead steer, if you're training a heel horse. I'm sure he would let you train with him. I board my horse at a stable just outside Winthrop. I know there are a couple of available stalls and a paddock where the horses can run."

"That sounds perfect. How much does he charge for board and feeding?" Randy was excited. It looked like he found a place for his horses, a place to rope and possibly a girl too. "Say, do you know where there's a good place to eat in Winthrop? I'm tired of fast food. How about joining me for dinner?" Nothing ventured, nothing gained. Sara reminded him of Sue. Sue was a couple of years younger and was his unofficial adopted sister.

Sara's face sobered, but she kept a smile for him. "Sorry about the dinner invitation, but I have sort of a boyfriend. Here, let me get you the name and telephone numbers for Jim and Larry. Jim has the arena and Larry owns the stables. I recommend them both." She went behind the desk, pulled a dark green backpack from under the desk, removed an address book and gave him the information. When Randy looked at the telephone, she nodded and put the phone on the counter.

"By the way, I've ordered the telephone service for my office. If you are available, would you let the installer in? He can put the phone anywhere on the desk."

"Sure, no problem. I'll be stuck behind this desk five days or more a week until I'm released from the Forest Service for a transfer to another job in the Department of Agriculture. I'll be going into the same business you're in. I took Spanish in high school and college, so expect I'll be sent south, although I would much rather stay in the Washington area." Sara smiled. "Maybe you can put a good word in for me."

The ranger grinned. "Sure, it would be my pleasure."

Randy made the telephone calls and arrangements to meet Jim and Larry. He turned back to the maps with Sara at his shoulder and explained each site on the larger scale map. He and his new ranger partner would be making another five-week tour taking a more southern route during the fall months. "I'll be making a lot of one and two-day patrols for the next few weeks. Except for one patrol, the long patrols won't start again in the spring. My boss, Ken Behoney, will be coming here in the next couple of weeks. I'll be sticking pretty close to Winthrop, maybe a couple of trips to the Chelan area."

When they were done with the maps Randy offered his hand to Sara. "Thanks for all your help with my horses. Does your boyfriend do any roping?" Randy hesitated. "Maybe after a roping we can all get together for a steak and fries."

"Sure, that would be great."

"I seem to be thanking you a lot, but thanks again for helping me with my horses and for setting up the jump. I'll bring you a coffee from Starbucks—white chocolate mocha I bet?"

"That would be great. See you tomorrow."

Randy left and climbed into his old green truck. Sara could still see where the Forest Service shield decal had been removed from the truck's door. *Damn, why didn't I tell him I was transferring to the ranger program and maybe we could work together?* Sara returned to her desk and put her head down on her folded arms. Her heart was beating a bit fast and confused. She was definitely attracted to the handsome ranger, but she was also attracted to the doctor, who she thought was a good match for her. Molly thought so, saying if she were straight she would steal the doctor away from her more attractive blonde room-mate.

Randy sat behind the wheel of the truck and thought about the blonde in the Forest Service office. After a minute, he leaned forward, turned the key, and started the truck. Maybe tomorrow he would have better luck.

Sara closed the office after Randy left and made her way to the parachute loft. She wanted to tell Jeff she was driving to Seattle Saturday if he wanted to join her. She also needed to tell Jeff she was leaving the Forest Service to become a Federal Fish and Wildlife Law Enforcement Ranger. Jeff would be the lead for the parachute jump tomorrow. Sara needed to tell him Randy Springer would be joining him and Randy's jump status and experience. Randy would need a parachute, helmet, and padded suit.

Jeff was at the parachute packing table repacking used chutes after checking for rips or frayed edges. Two stuff packed rejected chutes were in the "UNSERVICABLE" box ready to be shipped to the manufactor for exchange. Jeff studied the red and white parachute lying on the packing table. As Sara watched, Jeff ran his fingers along the seams stressing the material as he looked for signs of wear. He got a firm grip on one of the risers and tried to pull it away from the chute's edge. Sara could see the cord was slightly worn but appeared good for a few more jumps before being sent back to the manufacturer for repair or replacement.

Sara stood next to Jeff. The loud western music from his boom box had hidden the sound of her approach. "Hey, Jeff, you got a few minutes?"

"Sure, for you anytime, Sara." Jeff reached over and turned the radio down to a more reasonable level.

Sara told Jeff about Randy Springer, and said he would need a parachute and other equipment and would be jumping with the new hires tomorrow. Deciding it was time to tell him she was leaving the Forest Service, she hopped up on the packing table and told him her plans. "Besides the transfer, I'm driving to Seattle this weekend if you want to ride along."

"Sorry, I promised to take Steve Willis's place this weekend on the C crew. They're on the fire call roster this weekend. Why do you want to leave?"

"Look, the supervisors are never going to let me back on jump status. Not with Johnston on the qualification board. I can't live on the wages they're paying me to answer the phone and work in the office; so its time for me to change jobs."

"I thought they couldn't do that; I mean, cut your pay." Jeff looked confused.

"They could as soon as Pat O'Hara cleared me back to full duty. The board felt my arm would never be the same and would break again during the stress of a jump. You remember last year when Johnston made a pass and I slapped him around and told him to stick it?" Jeff nodded.

"Well, I think he is getting even. I've passed all the physical tests for a new jumper and they still won't clear me back to work. I'm going to take the transfer just as soon as I can get out of here. I left a copy of the approval for my transfer request on Johnston's desk. It looks like I'll be a ranger instead of firefighter."

"God, I hate to see you leave. What does Pat say about it?"

"I haven't told him. Pat and I are good friends, but not seriously dating, yet semi-exclusive. In fact, I just made my final decision a few minutes ago." She told Jeff about Pat O'Hara taking riding lessons at a local ranch and he had advanced much faster than she'd thought he would. Sara answered Jeff's implied question. "It's not like we're sleeping together or anything because we aren't." She squinted and chewed her lip. "I don't know why that is either. He's not gay, and I know he likes my boobs, in fact he can't keep his hands off them when we're alone."

"You don't suppose he's saving himself for his wedding night?" Jeff half joked.

"I don't think so," Sara said thoughtfully as she considered it. "I think he just doesn't want to screw things up, you know?"

"Well dear, knowing you, he had better shit or get off the pot, especially if you transfer to Fish and Wildlife."

"We're planning on a three-day trail ride to one of the lakes in a couple of weeks. I think maybe I'll push him a bit then." Sara kissed Jeff on the cheek and thanked him for getting Randy's equipment together, then left the building.

* * *

Sara thought about the different activities she and Pat were doing together. Sara was teaching him to throw a loop. A couple of days a week after work, she took him to the rifle range and taught him the proper way to shoot her large-bore rifles. Pat was improving much faster in both areas than she'd expected. Their dating seemed to be going nowhere. Sara knew he wanted to have sex with her, but something held them both back. She was determined to use the camp trip to find out if they were really suited for each other.

Molly was scheduled to leave Winthrop at the end of the fire season to work for the LA County Fire Department. But after an argument with one of the supervisors, Molly decided to leave early. It was a mutual decision between her and the supervisor.

The apartment was lonely without Molly's companionship. Sara even missed the snide remarks and jokes. She debated with herself whether to invite Pat to share the apartment. Sara knew she wasn't in love with Pat but there was a connection between them.

Chapter Nine

Hostages

The clinic parking lot was empty when Sara pulled into visitor parking. It was an hour before normal closing and she expected both Jean and Pat to be there. Even if Pat was on a house call, Jean should still be there. Jean was usually the last to leave on week days and her car wasn't in its usual parking place. Sara stopped and climbed out of her eight-year-old pickup and walked up the ramp beside the steps to the clinic door. The clinic door was locked, so she rang the night bell. She heard scuffling and faint arguing going on inside, and she rang the bell again. Still no one came to answer the door. Shading her eyes she looked through the reflections on the glass and saw a man's shadow pass across the hall beyond the reception desk.

Sara shrugged her shoulders; if anyone was watching they would think she was leaving because the clinic was closed. She drove out of the parking lot and down the road toward town. When Sara reached the Taylor Ranch turnoff a half mile from the clinic and screened from sight by thick woods, she made a U-turn and pulled off to the side of the road. She dug her cell phone out of her backpack and dialed 911. When the line was answered, she asked to be connected to the sheriff's office. Sara explained to the deputy on duty she thought there was some unusual activity at the clinic. Sara told the deputy sheriff the clinic had a police scanner and he should use land lines or cell phones for communications with other officers. She drove slowly back to where she could see the building without being seen from any of the windows.

Within five minutes Roy Danner in his sheriff's cruiser pulled up behind her pickup. Sara knew Danner from the base and team roping. He had been a smokejumper and firefighter before hiring on with the sheriff's office. Sara stepped down from her truck and went to the driver's window of the cruiser. She explained what she'd seen and heard through the clinic door. While Sara was explaining, an unmarked sheriff's car and a State Patrol cruiser pulled up without the light bars on. Sara explained all over again to the new arrivals what she had seen and pointed out Jean's car was not in the parking lot where her car should have been parked.

The deputy with the unmarked car volunteered to drive past the clinic and continue down the road about a mile on the lookout for Jean's car or Pat's truck. Sarah told them Jean drove a brown VW Beetle and described Pat's truck.

After the deputy with the unmarked car left, Sara, State Trooper Dave Spencer and Deputy Danner waited. Deputy Johnston, no relation to her boss, drove by the clinic without looking in or slowing. Two minutes later, Johnston called Danner's cell phone. "I found both the truck and the VW about three hundred yards down the road, parked in the driveway of a vacant house. Also parked in front of the house was a late-model Ford sedan. I think we need backup. I called the sheriff and he's on his way. We have to assume both the doctor and nurse are still in the building and are being held without their consent. We have another state trooper coming too."

Sara volunteered to help, but the sheriff on the telephone informed his deputies he wanted to be sure to keep Ms. Bennett out of harm's way.

Sara was disgusted. She was by far the best shot, and if Pat and Jean were in danger she could help. As she was trying to explain that to Danner, the cell phone rang again. It was the sheriff's office. A state trooper found an abandoned State of Washington corrections car beside the road on the east side of the North Cascade Pass. Seeing a blood trail, he found the Corrections officer shot dead hidden behind some bushes. A high-power rifle had been used, and the bullet that killed the officer had smashed through the driver's side window. The SOW Corrections office confirmed the corrections officer had been transporting a prisoner from the medium prison in Monroe to the high security prison in Walla Walla. The airplane usually used to transport prisoners was being used by the governor and was not available for prisoner transport. State troopers were being dispatched from Arlington and Concrete to the murder site. The sheriff was on his way from Twisp with the Twisp town marshal. SWAT support would not be available for two to three hours. The sheriff would take command upon arrival at the scene. The sheriff would make do with the assets on location and consider it a time critical hostage situation.

Sheriff Tomas Wilcox arrived six minutes later; all agencies maintained radio silence, using only cell phones for communications. The clinic did have a police scanner, and normal traffic stops and information continued as if everything were normal. Sara opened her truck and took out her M1A rifle from the locked rifle case behind the seat. An ammunition box held the magazines and the match ammunition she routinely practiced with. The scope usually used for long range shooting wasn't in the case, but the spotting-scope was in its box. Sara consulted her shooter's book for the M1A. The peep sight was zeroed for three hundred yards with known elevation clicks at fifty-meter increments from one hundred meters. The windage knob was set at zero. Sara took two twenty-round Lake City match ammo boxes and, along with one spare magazine, put them in a belly pack. The other magazine she loaded with twenty rounds and inserted the magazine into the rifle. Sara put the sling over her shoulder and confronted the sheriff.

"Sheriff, I don't know if you know who I am, but I keep some of my ammo in the police locker."

The sheriff didn't let her finish. "Yes, I know who you are. What do you propose to do with that rifle?"

"Well sir, you don't have a SWAT sniper; then I would guess I'm the next best shooter you have available. If you would just deputize me, I'll do your over-watch. You're going to have to go into the building to get the hostages if the hostage takers don't surrender. Judging from what I've heard so far, they've killed one corrections officer. I would say it's a safe bet they won't hesitate killing anyone else. Does that about sum things up?"

"I can't just let you shoot those people," The sheriff started.

"Sheriff, they are not just people. They have killed one man, and maybe the doctor and nurse. Just swear me in and I'll keep you safe, okay?" Sara's eyes pleaded with the man.

"Why are you so interested?"

"The doctor and the nurse are good friends of mine. I want to see them come out of this alive, and I know I can help. Now please swear me in and I'll function as a SWAT over-watch sniper. When I was at Quantico for a match I was invited to shoot at the SWAT sniper school. I attended and completed the two-week Sniper Course including the lectures on deadly force." Sara stepped back away from the sheriff, who wore a stressed, but thoughtful look.

Deputy Danner interrupted. "Sheriff, she is probably the best shot in the country, not just here. If she says she can help, let her."

The sheriff called the state troopers to join him, "Do you know of any reason I can't swear her in?" He jerked his thumb over his shoulder at Sara.

"Hey sheriff, it's your call. I don't know of any law that says you can't use her," the first trooper answered.

The Sheriff looked around at the men he had available: one man on the other side of the clinic, two state troopers, and three deputies but no sniper or other SWAT support.

"Okay, Ms. Bennett, raise your right hand." Sara was sworn into the Sheriff's Department as a Reserve Deputy. She went to her truck and loaded the second magazine with a full twenty rounds of Lake City Match ammunition. She engaged the safety and jacked one round into the chamber of the rifle. She put another fully loaded magazine into her belly pack.

"Sheriff, could I have one man to witness and observe for me?"

"Yeah, take one of the state people." He looked at Trooper Dave Spencer, who had his Mini 14 .223-Caliber rifle on a sling over his shoulder. "You go with her."

Sara had Spencer put his rifle back into his cruiser and get the spotting-scope from the truck. From the jockey box of the truck, she took a lighter and a coil of what looked like a fuse. She lit the end of the fuse and it gave off a black oily smoke. Sara blacked the rear and front sights of the rifle, put the fuse out, and returned the lighter and smoke rope to the jockey box.

Dave Spencer followed Sara across the street. She went to the back fence and yard of the first house and looked down the fence line. She spotted a child's treehouse in the corner of the backyard of the house across from the clinic. Sara pointed and Spencer followed her through the backyards of the houses to the treehouse. Only one neighbor came out and challenged them. Spencer told the woman to go into her house and for her and her children to go to the basement until a law enforcement officer told her the event was over and it was safe.

Sara and Spencer quickly climbed the ladder to the dark inside of the treehouse. While they were climbing up to the treehouse, the sheriff had one of the deputies tap on the clinic's side windows as a distraction so Sara and Spencer could get into the treehouse unobserved.

The treehouse's open entrance faced the clinic. The treehouse was about fifteen feet off the ground, a twelve-by-twelve foot square structure with solid side walls and a high window in the back wall. The front wall had a window installed to the left of the door about three feet up from the floor. The entrance and the single window faced the clinic. Sara set up her hide back in the shadows. She found and used an old fishing box for a rest covered by a towel from her truck. Sara helped Spencer set up the spotting scope. Using experience and the range finder built into the spotting-scope she determined it was one hundred twelve yards from her hide to the door of the clinic. The bullet fired from this position would drop less than an inch to cover the distance of the one hundred yards.

The wind sock on the roof of the clinic was hanging limp, not a breeze stirred the nylon. The Match boat-tail bullets would have almost zero drop and no influence by wind on the bullets' path to their target. Sara checked the zero clicks on her sights to the range of one hundred twelve yards. She lay down behind the fishing box to wait. The sight elevation knob was set at one click from base zero. The trooper sat behind and to her side with the spotting scope aimed at the clinic's front door through the treehouse window. Spencer was surprised when he looked through the scope and could see a fly resting on the side of the door. At first he'd thought it was a speck of dirt until it flew away.

Sara peeked through the spotting scope and saw she had limited vision into the clinic through the reflection on the glass door. She declined to use her usual shooting glasses to avoid any chance of reflection from the lens. As she watched, the sheriff drove his car into the parking lot, got out, went up the steps, and walked toward the clinic door. Sara went back to the rifle sight and watched. She asked Spencer to describe what was happening as she maintained a perfect sight picture.

The sheriff rang the bell and stepped to the side of the door out of the sight of anyone looking out from the interior.

"There's a man in a white doctor's shirt or smock coming to the door. He's opening it." Sara could see Pat's face as he opened the door about three inches and talked to the sheriff. She could also see the shadow of another man behind him with something in his hand.

"There's a man behind the doc. He's got a gun to the back of the Doc's head. I can see a nurse by the desk and another man behind her," Spencer said.

"I can't see the nurse or the man by the desk clearly. I can see their shadows. I can see the gun and the face of the man behind the doctor. He has a bandage on his forehead, and over his right eye. I don't see any other injuries. There is a pistol and a rifle with a scope. The rifle is on the desk, the second man's right hand is on the rifle, and it's pointed at the man in the white smock. The second man moved behind the desk with the nurse standing in front of him." The trooper gave a continuous update of what he saw. "By the way, my name is Dave Spencer; call me Dave if you need to use my name. Can the guy with the rifle see us up here?" Spencer said nervously.

"I don't think so, that's why we're in the shadows. If I do take a shot I'm sure he'll know where it came from. Dave, if I shoot and he lifts that rifle, I want you to get over there against the wall because it will be just him and me."

"Isn't that a flash suppressor on your rifle? Won't it hide the flash?" Dave asked.

"Yeah, it's a flash suppressor, but don't count on it hiding a flash. I'm using 7.62mm Lake City Match boat-tail ammo, and it will flash. If you see either of them lift their weapons and look like they are going to shoot, tell me. I really would like to get that glass out of the way."

Sara heard Dave speak to one of the deputies. She watched the sheriff still beside the door as he listened to his cell phone. Then the sheriff took his pistol and smashed it against the door window. She saw the pieces of glass turn to granules and fall to the cement walkway. The man with the gun yanked Pat back into the room while the other man got down behind the desk. Both Pat and Jean stood alone in the reception area the two bad guys were hidden from view.

Minutes passed with no shots taken; the sheriff retreated to his car. Sara could see into the clinic without the reflection. She determined the biggest threat was the man with the rifle. He was probably the one who had killed the corrections officer. Sara zeroed in on the man's nose. She saw the other man drag Jean toward the door and as he raised a handgun to her head, Sara watched closely, thinking about what kind of shot she could take without hitting either Jean or Pat.

"The hammer's back on the pistol, he's put the barrel on the top of her head. I can see about half of his face," Dave reported.

Sara saw the pistol and about two inches of the man's face. "If he moves or looks like he is going to shoot, tell me, don't hesitate."

"He's pointing the gun, finger on the trigger." The report of the high-power rifle in Sara's hands was deafening in the small, enclosed tree house and made Dave's ears ring. "He's down. The nurse dropped to the floor. I can't see if she is hit. I don't think so."

The second man with the rifle stood up straight as the first man snapped back, blood sprayed, and the shot man fell back to the floor. For just a second Sara saw the second man clearly. She wanted him alive and shot the rifle at the grip. The weapon spun around and broke into two pieces. "Tell them now, get in there now." Sara shouted at Spencer. He spoke into his cell phone and out of the corner of her eye she saw the sheriff start toward the door. The deputies and the state trooper ran toward the clinic. She saw the second man reach for the dropped pistol on the floor and shot him in the hand. He dropped back on his butt and held his smashed hand against his chest as the sheriff charged through the door. Seconds later, Sara saw Pat and Jean come out and down the walk toward the parking lot.

"We're done here." Sara gathered up her spare magazine and broke down the spotting-scope. Sara and Spencer climbed down from the tree house and walked around the house and out across the street to put her rifle and the spotting-scope away. Spencer stopped long enough to knock on the door of the house and tell the lady he'd told to go to the basement, the event was over.

When Sara arrived at the parking lot, the second man was handcuffed laying on his face next to the State Patrol car. The first man was obviously dead with most of his face missing. But the sheriff had handcuffed him until he'd been declared dead by a doctor. Pat didn't look like he wanted to see the dead man or treat the other man's hand. Jean put a bandage on the hand and gave him a tetanus shot from the clinic first aid kit.

Sara approached Jean, who sat on the steps of the clinic. "Having a rough day?"

"Don't be a smart ass, Sara. You know, it's been rough. How would you like to be assaulted by two nasty men and then have them shot right in front of you?"

Jean drew in a deep breath and scooted over as she made room for Sara. "I didn't even hear the gun go off. Just as the first guy told me he was going to kill me and Pat, his head exploded. They were going to shoot Pat before going out in a Butch Cassidy, Sundance Kid exit. Shit, Sara, I thought we were dead." Tears leaked from Jean's eyes. "He said if I hadn't been eight months pregnant he would have fucked me. He was going to make me give him a blowjob when you came knocking on the door. It really spooked them when they saw you look through the door window." Sara noticed Jean wasn't wearing her bra and some of the buttons on her dress were undone.

"You sure you're okay?" Sara tugged the blanket together around Jean's shoulders to cover her.

"No, no I'm okay. Thanks." Jean pulled the blanket tighter. "Whoever did the shooting was really good."

"I happen to know the shooter; pretty good shot I've heard." Sara leaned around so she could see into Jean's eyes. "Are you sure you're okay? Maybe you should go to the hospital? I'm sure the sheriff can get a helicopter here to fly you to Moses Lake or Spokane."

"I think I'm okay, Bruce is on his way. The sheriff called him as soon as we were safe." Jean put her hand on Sara's arm. "I saw you come to the door. I hoped you wouldn't make a pest of yourself but go call the police. The one guy, the leader in prison clothes wanted to let you in so you could be his toy. But when you left, I thought you'd figure it out and get help. Christ, this has been one hell of a day and now I've got to explain everything to Bruce. He's never going to let me work again."

"Oh sure he will. Maybe now he'll appreciate you more. Listen, I've got to give a statement to the sheriff. I'll stop by tomorrow. Are you going to work tomorrow?" Sara asked, frowning.

"Oh yeah sure, can't leave the doctor in there by himself. He'll just make a mess out of everything. Besides, I have to clean up the mess." Jean looked over her shoulder at the broken door and the blood splashed over the reception room.

"Listen Jean, the sheriff's office can have somebody clean up the mess and just bill the clinic's insurance company. I bet they won't mind." Sara put her hand on her friend's shoulder and rose to walk back to her truck. Trooper Dave Spencer was waiting and watched her approach.

"Miss Bennett, I've been waiting for you. I gave the sheriff a statement. I saw everything through the spotting-scope. In my opinion, the bad guy with the gun at the nurse's head was going to shoot and you just beat him to it. By the way, those were great shots. I hope I never make you mad. Where did you learn to shoot like that?"

"I'm on the National Match Shooting Team. I've been practicing for the Nationals at Camp Perry and carry my weapons so if I get a chance to practice I can take advantage. Maybe you'd like to come out and shoot with me sometime?"

"No, I don't think I'm anywhere close to your league. You are definitely one cool lady. Thanks."

Sara was confused. "Thanks for what?"

"For the lesson." Dave put out his hand. "I'd like to shake your hand. I saw you with the nurse; she's one cool customer. She married?"

"Yep, she's married." Sara laughed. "She's real married. You should have noticed she's eight months pregnant too. Here comes her husband now." She nodded at a blue Datsun sedan pulling up next to the trooper's cruiser. Bruce bolted out of the car and ran to Jean still on the steps. She threw her arms around his neck. Sara could see her body racked by sobs and the tears from forty feet away. She watched for a couple of minutes, popped Dave on the arm and went to wait in her truck until the sheriff came for her statement.

Sara watched the Emergency Medical Technicians carry a body bag from the clinic. They loaded the bag into the ambulance and with lights on but no siren, the ambulance left for the morgue in Wenatchee. The man Sara shot in the hand was now in the deputy's car with the light bar sending out its blue and red flashes. As if he knew she was watching, he lifted his head and glared at her. The hatred his eyes unleashed, would have intimidated a lesser person. Sara smiled and made like shooting a gun as she pointed her index finger at him. Then she made a motion like she had just made a shot. She grinned at him again and then made a motion like sticking a needle in her arm and pointed at him again. He had killed a law enforcement officer in a premeditated murder; his future was limited.

Pat sat in the deputy's cruiser as he gave a statement for the sheriff's office when he saw Sara's truck leave. He wasn't positive who had made those shots taking out the two gunmen, but he was pretty sure it had been Sara. He needed to see her and thank her for saving his life.

He promised himself he would call as soon as he got home. As many good intentions go astray, his did too. He did call the next morning, but her phone went unanswered.

Chapter Ten

The Arena

A week passed since Sara and Roy Danner, who had accompanied her to Seattle, returned to Winthrop. Roy visited relatives while Sara was busy with follow-up interviews. They decided to stay an extra day to visit the Pike Street Market and buy some spices and odds and ends not available elsewhere. They enjoyed dinner with wine at Anthony's Homeport on Shilshore Bay and strolled the beach under a star-filled sky.

Back in Winthrop, Sara waited a day before she called Pat to tell him she was home. She wanted time to herself to think through their relationship. Sara enjoyed Pat's company and his attention, but there was something missing. Sara could feel the emptiness of a space between them even when they were together.

Pat wasn't pushy and gave her plenty of alone time to make up her mind about her priorities and future. She thought of Pat and herself as individuals not as a couple and it confused her. In a couple of days it would be Saturday and she would see him at roping practice. She was not anxious see or be with him and she felt she should be excited to see him.

* * *

Twenty-six teams of ropers were waiting their turn when Pat O'Hara entered the arena. Before Seattle, Sara had helped Pat find a well-trained rope horse. She introduced Pat to a horse breeder and trainer and Pat was able to buy a good fully trained ten-year-old gelding who knew both heading and heeling. The horse's previous owner had retired from competition and didn't want to keep the horse as a pet. The trainer thought the gelding had many good years left and the horse loved to compete. The horse was fifteen two hands, buffed out with a deep chest and was sound with strong, well-muscled butt and legs. The horse was not exceptionally big, but he was powerful enough to work as a header. Pat promptly named his new mount Butch. The trainer taught Pat the cues to communicate his desires to the horse. Pat with Sara's help learned to guide the horse with a minimum of rein direction, to use his legs and feet to communicate with his mount. Pat had gentle hands and quiet legs and feet, a must for a good horseman.

As team roping heelers progressed their skill level, they learned to catch both feet as part of the throw. Air catches were much faster than using a trap. The best heel horses are quite small, around fourteen hands at the withers. The heel horses didn't take the hit a head horse had to endure.

Sara waved as Pat rode Butch to where Sara waited in the mix of horses and riders. Pat watched a header throw his rope up in the air to get the rope away from him and his horse to prevent a wreck between the steer, rope, horse, and rider. A small mistake handling a rope could cost the roper a thumb or a couple of fingers. Even world- class ropers have lost fingers and thumbs when as little as a hand movement put the thumb against the horn as the rope tightened.

Pat watched the ropers from a distance. He still didn't feel 100 percent accepted and didn't want to intrude where he wasn't welcome. Sara backed Buster so she and Pat could talk. Pat saw a rider heel a steer and thought he was very good. He pointed it out to Sara. She shrugged and said the man was a two and a half, not all that good, but a little above average. Sara was a number one and a half header and hadn't tried her hand at heeling yet.

"Maybe next season," was her reply when asked if she wanted to try to catch a running steer's hind legs. "I will have to buy another horse, a heeler, if I want to do much heeling. Heeling is a whole new ballgame. I don't know if Buster would like another horse around. At times he appears to be a bit jealous when I'm around horses and riders he doesn't know." Sara tilted her head forward to hide her grin and her eyes looked up coyly at Pat. "Are you jealous when I'm around these other cowboys?" She smiled at Pat's embarrassed expression.

When it was Sara's turn, she glanced at Pat before riding into the header's box. Thirty seconds later Sara and Buster were in hot pursuit of a 650-pound steer. She threw her loop and caught the horns perfectly. Buster pulled the steer into position for the heeler. The heeler rode the corner, threw, and legged, catching only one back leg. Sara was quick with her loop and showed she was ready to move up to a number two header.

After her run, Sara joined Pat in the group of waiting ropers. He touched her on the arm. "That was a great run, you were perfect." Pat waited a couple of heartbeats. "I tried to call," he said a hurt tone with a quiver in his voice.

"I know. I'm sorry. I've been kind of busy last couple of weeks. I made a trip to Seattle and did the final employment hiring interview for the Fish and Wildlife Ranger Program. I have final approval for transfer and will probably change jobs within the next few weeks. Roy went along to visit his relatives who live in Burien."

"Oh, you were in Seattle, with Roy Danner?" Pat felt the pang of jealousy drop into his stomach like a bag full of ball bearings.

Sara heard her name—it was her turn again. "Hey, I've got to go, talk to you later." She rode into the head box. Pat noticed Roy Danner enter the heel box. Sara watched Roy, and when he was settled she checked the steer and nodded. The steer broke from the chute and she followed, swung her rope twice around her head and threw. Sara caught the horns and turned the steer. Roy caught both feet.

When Sara returned to her place in line Pat was waiting. "You guys did pretty good; has Roy been roping a long time?"

"Nope, he's has been heeling about a year. His horse is really cow'y and Roy sent him to a professional trainer for a couple of months. The trainer told him the horse was plenty good enough to win in most of the events on the Northwest Circuit. The horse puts Roy in the sweet spot every time. Now if he can just learn to throw the heel loop as good as he throws a head loop, maybe we can win some beer money." Sara glanced at the jealous doctor. "Are you going to rope or just sit there like an eye on a spud? Ask Roy, he'll rope with you."

Pat looked around for Danner and saw him looking in his direction. He squeezed Butch forward. "Think you could go out with me?"

"Sure Pat, not on a date you understand but I'll rope with you," Roy teased. "I think it would be easier if you shook out a loop from the rope tied to your saddle." Danner grinned. "Go ahead, and we'll take a turn. I watched you chase some steers, and you've got a good horse there. Just ride him and he'll put you where you need to be. A couple of suggestions: point your toes down, not up with heels down and when you are in the sweet spot pull the trigger, it won't get any better. If you wait too long the odds of missing increase."

"Yeah, okay," Pat said, embarrassed as he untied his rope and shook out a loop. He took plenty of spoke. Pat knew Roy was just trying to help, but he still resented it.

Pat walked his horse into the head box. He watched Danner settle his horse in the back of the heel box. He waited until Danner was set then looked at the steer and nodded. He wasn't quite ready for the acceleration of Butch. It was the first time he had actually ridden out of a box after a steer. The horse just wanted to do his job and Pat almost went off the back before he grabbed the horn to stay in the saddle.

The end of the arena was coming up fast before Pat threw the loop and missed by a wide margin, but he was still on horseback, an accomplishment in itself. Sara told him the acceleration of the horse from standing still to leaving the box was greater than a fuel dragster. The trick for the new guy was to hang on or he might get the seat of his pants dirty when the horse surged out from under him.

Pat returned to where the other ropers waited their turn and was greeted with back slaps and advice. The ropers compete among themselves, but they always welcome a new roper, another cowboy willing to put his entry money down.

Sara grinned at the newest member of the roping club and contributed her own backslap as she moved Buster next to Butch. "You did good there cowboy. You didn't fall off like many of these guys you see here on their first time out of the box. It won't be long, and you'll be competitive. You've got a good horse and he'll keep you honest. Just ride."

At the end of the day, Pat helped remove the horn wraps when the roping was done and released the steers to pass through the stripping chute to the holding pen and on into the pasture where two of the men spread hay out for feed. He took Butch to his new two-horse slant trailer and tied him to the trailer before he removed the saddle and brushed him. Pat led the horse to the water trough for a drink. One of the ropers walked up to Pat with a beer and handed it to him, another sign of acceptance.

Sara watched Pat put his tack away and brush his horse. Butch would teach Pat a lot about roping and cattle. Sara showed Pat how to put the horse into the two-horse slant without getting kicked or stepped on. He put a half flake of alfalfa mix in the feeder for Butch to munch on.

Sara put her arm around the new roper. "Come on, there's a couple of cases of beer in the cooler. You look like you could use another." She led him to where the other ropers with their beers talked about jackpots scheduled and jackpots past, steers caught and steers missed.

Some of the ropers planned to meet at O'Reilly's Bar and Grill in Winthrop for a steak dinner after the horses were back home. Sara waved and said she would meet them there. Pat really wanted to talk about dating, a subject Sara wanted to avoid. She liked the young doctor, a lot, but didn't want a commitment from him nor to make one. Her life was unsettled. She would be officially transferred to the Federal Fish and Wildlife Law Enforcement Rangers in the Chelan National Forest and the Mt. Baker National Forest within in the next two weeks.

* * *

While sharing a steak dinner at O'Reilly's, Pat asked Sara to go on a weekend ride up in the wilderness area northeast of Winthrop. They would take the horses and camp out at Eureka Lake, a primitive area accessible only by hiking or on horseback. The small lake had a private and seldom used campground. He challenged her to find out if they were suitable for each other.

Since Randy Springer's arrival and during the setup of his office in the Forest Service Building, Sara's thoughts had been filled with questions concerning the ranger. It bothered her that she was still dating Pat, but thinking about Randy.

What the hell! she figured, and agreed to the outing. They planned to leave early Friday for a three or four-day weekend.

At home, Sara sat at the kitchen table with a notebook and listed all the good things she felt about Pat and all the not-so-good things. The list on the good side was extensive, affirming she needed to at least attempt to find out if there were romantic feelings between them. Sara knew she didn't love Pat like she should if they were to establish a relationship together.

The list lay on the table when Sara finished her shower and was ready for bed. She stood staring at the list, but the face in her mind wasn't Pat's, it was Randy Springer's. The ranger had done nothing, but she could feel him and read his body language. Deep in her subconscious mind, Sara knew Randy was the man for her and felt she was the woman for him. Sara went to bed early, more confused than before. She dreamed about the tall ranger and woke with a damp nightgown and a feeling of frustration.

Chapter Eleven

The Lake and A Tryout

It was mid September and the days were becoming shorter. Sara drove toward the stable to ready Buster for the planned camping trip. A light mist and low clouds covered the valley. The air smelled clean and crisp with the bite of autumn in the air. It was the kind of day when mist and clouds burned off early to reveal the day to be warm and sunny. Sara could smell the soil after last night's light late- summer rain. The moisture was just enough to remove the dust from the air.

The month of September brought with it the last of the summer rains. Raindrops were cool and refreshed hot, overworked bodies. The roads steamed and mist rose from the earth in the warming air.

Sara arrived at the stables to find Pat there with a cup of Starbucks coffee for her. Butch was tied to the side of Pat's trailer. She noticed a three-man tent and oversized saddlebags loaded to the bursting point. Two boxes of groceries were in the bed of his new F250 pickup truck. The two-horse slant bumper pull trailer was still wet from having been washed.

"You must have slept here all night." Sara teased him as she accepted the coffee, with lots of cream and no sugar. Sara went to get Buster from his stall; the horse didn't want to leave his breakfast, but reluctantly followed her when she put a halter with lead rope on him. After tying Buster to the trailer, she took two extra full flakes of alfalfa-grass mix from her stack of hay and put them in Buster's and Butch's feeders. She threw a bale of hay into the back of the pickup and retrieved her saddle and tack from her tack shed.

A standing water tap supplied water for the horses and for cleaning her trailer. Her own hose was coiled on a wheel rack beside the cement slab and cross ties. Sara shared the cost with other boarders for the laying of a cement slab and the gravel for drainage from the wash-rack.

Horses loaded in the trailer and ready to go, Pat climbed into his new F250 pickup truck beside Sara and started the diesel engine. After a warm up, he put the truck in gear and drove out onto the highway north. Sara put her heavy brown Cathartt coat on the floor at her feet and leaned back into the seat. The sound of the tires on the asphalt road lulled her and she slept.

Pat planned to leave the truck and trailer with the Marcs family who lived about a mile off the rural macadam road where it ended in a dirt trail. From there it was an easy half-day ride to the lake. The Marcs also volunteered a pack horse and panniers for the outing.

Sara discovered she also knew the Marcs family from when she and Randy Springer met them during an orientation ride a few days after her return from Seattle and her transfer to the rangers. There would be plenty of green grass around the lake, so horse feed wouldn't be a problem; only people food needed to be hauled to the camp grounds. To be on the safe side, Sara put a bale of hay in the back of the truck. Sara's father taught her it never hurt to put extra horse feed into the panniers as padding and for emergencies when natural feed wasn't available. He taught her to always use some horse hay to pack panniers. The rest of the bale would be stored in the trailer.

"I haven't packed in a few years. My dad, brother, and I used to pack into the Bob Marshall in Montana or into the primitive area near Mr. Baker each summer until Phil joined the Marines and I went away to college. I think I remember how to use a pack horse."

"The Marcs said we could use their pack horse, frame and the panniers. I don't know what all the stuff is, but I'm sure you will enlighten me," Pat said with a smile.

"This is going to be an interesting weekend. I can read the newspaper headlines now. Campers lost for six months mysteriously reappear in the town of Twisp."

"Aw come on Sara, it isn't that bad, is it?"

"No, at least you did make arrangements for packing. I don't think all the stuff you brought will fit into a couple of sets of saddlebags." Sara leaned back into the backrest of her seat and closed her eyes. "Where are we going anyway?"

"Eureka Lake is about six miles from where we'll leave the truck and trailer. The place has a good campground on the north end near where two creeks come together and empty into the lake. I got permission to fish for food only from the Federal Park Service, actually the Fish and Wildlife people. I thought we could fish for breakfast. I love fresh trout from cold waters."

"Yeah, who do you know who would issue you a license to fish out of season?" Sara sat up in her seat.

"I did a bit of work for the Park Supervisor when I was still an emergency room intern in Spokane. When one of his rangers came down with appendicitis, they couldn't move him, and I dropped from a helicopter and performed emergency surgery in the field. Since then all I have to do is ask and I get special consideration. An out of season fishing license is actually the only special deal I've asked for." Pat drove in silence on the two-lane macadam road until it changed to dirt and gravel.

Pat turned off the road onto a dirt and gravel narrow road. The dirt tracks disappeared into the forest. Pat followed the tracks until they came out into a large meadow with a small ranch house and barn. Sara saw a horse in a round pen. A set of panniers leaned against the pen. Pat pulled the truck into the ranch yard; a man and woman came out of the house and waved.

With the driver's window down, Pat waved back. The man pointed to a spot near the barn for Pat to park the truck and trailer. Sara climbed out of the truck and went to greet the couple, reintroducing herself to Rowdy and Penny Marcs. Pat finished with the truck and trailer, and joined them.

"I would guess you want to get on your way. Don't want to be wandering around these woods in the dark, don't you know." Rowdy had a country way about him and a quaint regional accent. Penny stood quietly letting Rowdy do the talking.

While Sara listened to Rowdy Marcs, the image of the tall ranger invaded her thoughts. She quickly repressed the image. "This is really out of the way." Sara looked at the surrounding forest. It was then she noticed Penny was pregnant, about five months

"Penny, if you have a few minutes, I'd like to take a look at you to make sure the pregnancy is progressing well," Pat said. Penny looked at Rowdy who nodded. Pat retrieved his medical bag from the back seat of the truck and he and Penny walked toward the house, while Rowdy led Sara to the round pen.

The pack horse was named Flower. Rowdy didn't know where or when the name was tacked onto the horse, but Penny liked it, so the name stayed. Rowdy explained the good points and bad about the horse, who belied his name by being a bit of a handful.

"He takes a good hand to handle him at times. If you stay off his face as much as you can, I think he'll be okay. Pat said you were a good hand, so I'm not going to worry. I remember you and the ranger stopped by a bit ago." Sara nodded and Rowdy opened the gate and brought the horse out and tied him to the pen rails. While Sara watched, Rowdy put the pack frame on the horse, and strapped and tied the panniers to the frame. He checked the cinch and declared the horse ready to be loaded. Within ten minutes, everything was gathered near the horse and ready to be loaded into the panniers.

Sara lined the bottoms of the panniers with flakes of hay from the back of the pickup, while Rowdy nodded approval. She, with Rowdy's help, finished the loading. Sara got Buster and Butch out of the trailer and tied them to the trailer's rings. She was about finished with saddling Pat's horse when Pat, followed by Penny came across the yard.

"Penny is doing well," Pat said to Rowdy. "I would like to see her get a little more rest. Don't let her throw around those 90-pound hay bales. If Penny spots, I want her in bed until I can get out here. If it is more than spotting, call me, and we'll decide how best to handle the situation. But I want you to call me weekly, Rowdy. The baby appears healthy with a strong heartbeat." Pat shook Rowdy's hand and gave him his cell number on a business card.

While Pat was talking to Rowdy, Sara took the halter lead rope and led Butch to the pen and tied him to a rail close by Flower. Close enough for the horses to get used to each other but not close enough for one to bite or kick the other.

Sara got the two headstalls from the trailer and looped them on the horn of their saddles and tied a sixty foot ranch rope to her saddle. She didn't like to put the bit into Buster's mouth until she was ready to mount.

Thirty minutes later they said goodbye to Rowdy and Penny and began the six-mile horse trek to the campground at Eureka Lake. Pat led after consulting a map and Sara held the rope to the pack horse. Flower was a bit barn sour, and didn't want to leave the farm and he balked at the gate. Sara backed Buster to stand beside Flower, and they stood together for a couple of minutes. Sara again started Buster forward through the gate and Flower followed without a backward glance. Flower and Buster had bonded.

They exited the forest through a cedar grove and saw Eureka Lake a half mile ahead when it started to rain: not a heavy rain but a light summer rain with large, warm raindrops. A mist formed over the lake. Sunlight penetrated the thin clouds and painted the surroundings in indigo, lending vibrant colors to the trees and surroundings. Natural features became sharp and clear. A rainbow arched near the shore of the lake. A grove of aspen trees anchored one end of the rainbow and a meadow the other. A double rainbow formed and anchored one end near the campground easily seen on the far side of the lake.

"Do you think we'll find a pot of gold under the rainbow?" Pat joked. "I am an O'Hara, you know, and am an acquaintance of the Great King Ralph of the Leprechauns. Actually, the King is my cousin."

"So that's where you get all the blarney I've been hearing the past few miles. I thought it was the rain speaking to me."

Pat sat up straighter in the saddle. "You know Summer Rain is the name of a Fairy Princess."

"Yes, and she paints the forest glens with indigo to entrance and capture humans so she can have her way with them." Sara joined in the storytelling. The rain brought a warm breeze, and although wet, the riders were still warm. Sara took the lead and trotted the horses to the campsite. She spotted a fire-ring of stones and a level spot for the tent at the edge of the forest. It appeared to be an excellent spot to set up camp five feet above the water level with fresh running water thirty feet away. The ground was firm with good drainage in case of heavy rain, a must for a comfortable camp.

Sara turned Buster loose to graze on the green grass on the west side of the campsite after taking his saddle off and putting on a halter with a hanging lead rope. Pat watched her and followed her example with Butch. Sara tied Flower to a tree limb and removed the tent from the pack. Five minutes later she had the tent laid out on the canvas ground cloth and was ready to hook the tent to the free-standing frame. Pat helped her. When the tent was up, Sara staked the tent to the ground and placed the rain-cover over the tent and tied it to the tent stakes. Pat dug a shallow drainage trench around the edge of the tent to keep water from pooling and leaking under and into the tent. As soon as the tent was up, Sara hobbled Flower and let the horse graze with Buster and Butch. Sara took the hobbles from the pannier and put them on both Buster and Butch and removed the halter. The horses were set for the night with plenty of good grazing available.

Sara was sitting in the tent on her sleeping bag when Pat crawled in carrying his own sleeping bag. "What are you doing?" Sara asked.

Pat stopped half in half out of the tent and stared into Sara's blue eyes. He stuttered, "I, ah, am just getting my sleeping bag out of the rain. I'll put up the other tent as soon as the rain lets up a little."

"What, you're letting a little mist stop you from putting up that little tent you brought? I'm surprised your mother let you cross the street alone," Sara said without cracking a smile. "You think I should help you? You need a girl's help?"

"God damn it, Sara, I thought…"

"You thought? What makes you think you have the right to think?" Sara couldn't take it any longer and broke into a fit of laughter. The look on Pat's face made her laugh harder. "Come in here, you poor baby. Here, let me fix your tidy little sleeping bag so you won't freeze your little bottom off."

"You know you can be a witch." Pat laughed, but he passed his bag to her and watched as she unrolled it next to hers. "Are we just going to let the horses wander around all night?"

"No, I was about to check on the hobbles to make sure they are fitted properly and let them forage all night. They won't go very far from the camp. You'd be surprised how reliant the horses are on human company, especially Buster." She pulled on her boots, which she had left close to the entrance to the three-man tent. The tent slept three comfortably and two with plenty of room.

Pat followed, as Sara checked the hobbles on Buster and Butch and then readjusted Flower's hobble. She took the halters off Butch and Flower. Next she got the food out of the pannier and put it into two large double-strength plastic bags. Everything not in cans or sealed in heavy plastic went into the bag; bacon, lunch meat, bread and anything else that might tempt the forest critters, bears, and raccoons. She walked along the lakeshore until she spotted a suitable tree with a limb sticking out over the lake twelve feet above the water. She tossed a rope over the limb and tied the end to the bag after putting on a slick plastic ring above the bag so it covered the width of the whole bag. If a critter tried to drop from the limb to the bag it would slip on the plastic and fall into the lake. Sara hauled the bag up to hang two feet below the limb but still ten feet above the water. She tied the other end of the rope to the tree so the bag was left hanging where the critters couldn't reach it and far enough from the camp not to bother the humans or the horses.

Finished safeguarding the food, Sara returned to the tent. "Hey, I thought you were going to catch some fish for our supper and breakfast? Don't you think you should get started?"

"Have a heart Sara, it's raining."

"Well, you're already pretty wet, so a little more water won't hurt you,—get to your work caveman." A minute later, she heard him rummaging around looking for his fishing gear.

Feeling sorry for him, Sara stuck her head out through the entrance and called, "Didn't your mother teach you to come in out of the rain? Get your wet little buns in here."

Pat didn't waste time; he was in the tent seconds after Sara got out of his way and sat on the end of his sleeping bag to get his wet boots off. Sara sat cross legged on her sleeping bag and watched him. "Don't you think you should take those wet clothes off and put something dry on.? We don't want you catching cold and having to go to the doctor now, do we?" She teased him mercilessly. Sara realized she was doing it but was unwilling to stop. Sara felt a little uncomfortable, knowing what both she and Pat expected to happen during this camping trip. Now she was feeling shy and hoped Pat wouldn't push her too far too fast.

Pat was having similar feelings. He wanted to have sex with Sara but had been getting mixed feelings about her. "I have to get the grill out of the panniers and put the steaks on. I nuked the potatoes before I packed them. They just need to be warmed." Pat pulled on his boots and his rain slicker before he crawled out of the tent.

Sara heard him banging things around in the panniers. Ten minutes later Pat returned and found Sara sitting as he had left her, except she now wore only her sweatshirt and white half panties. Pat stopped half in and half out of the tent. "Ah, I got the fire going and as soon as the grill is hot I'll put the meat on to cook."

Sara was silent. She looked directly into his gray-green eyes. "Come here."

"Sara, we don't have to do this if you don't want to."

"I think we do need to do this." Sara pulled her sweatshirt up over her head. She sat wearing only the white panties. "Are you going to keep wearing all those wet clothes, or are you going to join me?"

He set a record getting out of his clothes. When he was wearing only his gray jockey shorts he moved closer to Sara. He tentatively put out his hand and gently touched her left breast. He found the nipple hard against the palm of his hand. Sara closed her eyes and felt his lips surround her nipple as he sucked. When he drew back, the wet he left was chilled by the cool mountain air. Her nipples were erect and ready for his touch and attention.

Sara opened her eyes and noticed his erection constrained in his shorts. She reached down with one hand while the other pushed him onto his back. She used both hands to pull his shorts off, took his erection into her hand, and held him as she looked into his eyes.

Pat was surprised by Sara's forwardness. With her holding him in her hand, he leaned forward and gently pulled her panties down and off over her feet. They were both completely naked in front of each other. Sara lay back on her sleeping bag still holding him. She rubbed him gently and felt him get even harder.

"I think you like me," she teased as she pulled him toward her and kissed him.

Pat groaned. A beautiful woman held his dick in her hands and all he could do was groan. He licked her nipples and suckled first one and then the other. He put his hand on her, pushing the light brown-blonde pubic hair aside to find her wet and ready for him.

They remained holding each other long after the love making was over. Pat pulled his open sleeping bag over them to keep warm. The cook fire had long gone cold. The steaks, still in plastic wrappers, were forgotten lying next to their boots.

"Pat?" Sara said softly. "You awake?"

"Yeah."

Sara took a deep breath. "I don't know what it is. The sex was great, but something was missing."

"Yeah, I know. I could feel it too. God, Sara, I think the world of you and enjoy your company, but there is just something missing. It was almost like I was making love to my sister or cousin, you know?"

"Yes, that's the way I felt too. Shit Pat, I think of you more as my brother. What a shitty thing to say about a lover. God, I'm sorry, Pat. I can't help it." She rolled up on an elbow to look into his eyes. "I don't know if I can do this again."

"Yeah Sara, I know. I feel the same way." Saying it out loud instead of thinking it helped Pat relax. He felt Sara relax beside him. "I think of you as my sister. I hope you don't think I don't love you because I do, but not as a lover. I bet if you made love to Roy Danner it would be different."

"I did and it was a lot different. I felt freer and enjoyed the sex more. I think you're more lovable than Roy, but it was different. I don't want to lose you as a friend." She stared into his eyes. "Have I lost you, Pat?"

"No, I think the brother and sister thing is the way to go for us. Shit, if it weren't for this summer rain keeping us cooped up in this tent, I bet we would never have discovered or told each other the way we feel." Pat leaned over and kissed Sara lightly on the lips, a brotherly kiss. Still naked, the two ex-lovers lay together, touching, but not touching. Sleep found them and they slept chastely in each other's arms.

A scratching sound woke Pat during the night; he looked around in the bright moonlight but didn't see anything out of place and went back to sleep. In the morning, the steaks were gone. Only the plastic wrappers were left scattered around the campsite.

Pat and Sara knelt at the entrance of the tent and looked at the mess left by the night raider. "Looks like somebody enjoyed the steaks," Pat ventured.

"Yeah, red meat isn't good for us humans, so I guess the little bandit did us a favor. Would you care for some oatmeal, or mush, if you prefer?" Sara giggled and sat naked with the naked man next to her, as they talked about mush.

"Do you want to go back?" Pat looked at Sara, clearly giving her the decision whether to return to Winthrop of stay until Monday.

"Let's stay. I brought a couple of books I've been meaning to read if the rain keeps up. If the clouds lift, I'd like to ride up the ridge and take some pictures."

The remainder of the day was rainy and turned cold. They stayed in the tent bundled up in their sleeping bags. Later, Sara led the horses to another grassy area within sight of the tent. They horses appeared perfectly content to graze all day and sleep lying in the wet grass. Toward evening, the clouds disappeared and the stars of the Milky Way crossed the sky. The half moon rose in the early morning hours and bathed the mountain lake in its weak, pale light.

Sara and Pat were sitting next to the fire pit when the call of a wolf pierced the night. The wolf's howl was answered by another wolf miles away. The answering call echoed off the mountain walls and soon there were a number of howls searching the night. A mountain lion screamed from the other end of the lake. Sara brought the horses closer to the camp, putting them on a picket line. The big cats rarely attacked horses especially near humans. The forest was filled with the cougar's natural food. The wolves would take only the easy to catch, the infirm, the older deer and elk. The Methow Valley wolf pack usually patrolled the northern parts of the forest. Their calls could be heard miles from where the wolf who made them sat and surveyed his domain by moonlight.

Sara stood and grabbed her towel from where she'd put it that morning after washing. She moved to the shoreline, took off her clothes, and placed them folded on a large rock and waded into the cold water to dive under the surface. Her head broke the surface thirty feet from shore where she treaded water. "Aren't you going to wash? You smell," She called.

Pat rolled his eyes, grabbed his own towel, stripped, and ran into the water, diving below the surface to come up beside her. He put his hand on her head and pushed her below the surface and then swam quickly to the rocky beach. Sara was right behind him. Laughing, they toweled each other dry and rubbed some warmth back into their chilled bodies.

Dressed once more in their sweats, they lay in their sleeping bags content with the other's company. "You know this is strange for me," Pat ventured.

"Yeah I know. I don't think I've ever had a man friend who I've made love with and am completely comfortable, even naked. Are we strange or what?"

"No, I like being friends with you." Pat sat up. "You are still going to keep roping with me, right?"

"Oh yeah, training another guy takes too much time and effort. You should think about getting a heeler to enter the jackpots. By next year you'll be ready for some of the small ProWest rodeos around here." Sara rested her head on the palm of her hand, weight on her elbow. "I've been thinking about trying my hand at heeling. If I get good enough, you can rope with me."

The rest of the evening was made up of small talk about rodeo and the clinic. The topic of the incident at the clinic came up. Sara admitted she'd been the one who made the shots. The state trooper had been on the spotting-scope, and he had told her when the first man was about to shoot Jean.

"You know that bullet didn't miss Jean by more than an inch, or maybe two. She told me she felt it snap past. He'd started to shoot her, and then the guy just wasn't there anymore." Pat was silent for a long time. Sara thought he had fallen asleep. "I meant to thank you before now and I just didn't seem to have the opportunity. It's the first time I've been that close to death. It's sobering."

Sara didn't answer, but laid her hand on his arm and gave a gentle squeeze before she slid down into her bag and fell asleep.

They woke to birds calling to each other and flitting from tree to tree. A bald eagle was perched in a tree not far from the camp. An osprey circled over the water. Sara tapped Pat awake and pointed to the hunting bird. The eagle watched the smaller fish hawk. In an instant, the osprey dove toward the water, and swooped across the still surface, dipped its talons into the water, and came up with a fish that had been feeding near the surface. As the hawk circled to gain height, the eagle left its perch and dove at the smaller raptor, which dropped the fish. The eagle twisted in midair and dove after the falling fish and caught it before it hit the water. The eagle returned to its perch with its breakfast where it proceeded to rip the fish apart and swallow the chunks. The osprey returned to its hunting as if nothing had happened. Within minutes the gray and white hawk had another catch. This time the bird stayed close to the surface of the water. The eagle let the osprey escape, and return to its nest to feed its one or two chicks.

The day promised to be sunny and warm. Sara saddled Buster after she gave him a good brushing. Pat followed her example and brushed Butch before he saddled him. Sara put a couple of sandwiches, two bottles of water and a few pieces of elk jerky in her saddlebags. She left a flake of hay for Flower to keep him content until their return. The two riders set off up the trail toward the ridge that bordered the east side of the valley.

Two hours into the ride they were on a high ridge above the lake. They could see miles up the valley and back toward where they left the truck and trailer. "God, it's beautiful up here." Sara dismounted hanging onto one of Buster's reins. She selected a large rock and sat to admire the view. Pat joined her; there was no need for words to enjoy the view and companionship.

Pat led Butch and walked along the ridge trail. He stopped the horse and looked down onto a steaming pile of scat. "Hey Sara, what's that?" He pointed at the small pile.

Sara squeezed Buster forward and stopped beside Pat. "Bear scat, we had better keep an eye out. The bears are feeding almost constantly now, with the weather cooler they can feel the winter coming on. The bears can be aggressive this time of year. They need a thick layer of fat to make it through the winter, especially if it's cold and long." She reached up and removed her Winchester 25-35 from the scabbard. "This rifle isn't really much of a bear gun, but the noise might scare a bear away."

Pat pointed down the trail and there, about a hundred yards away was a cougar watching them. Sara cocked the Winchester. "It is however plenty big enough against a pesky cat." Sara removed a pair of binoculars from the saddlebags and looked at the mountain cat through the glasses. "It's a male, and he appears to be well fed. He'll leave if we start riding toward him. Just remember to keep a tight rein on Butch. I don't know how he'll react to the cat's smell. Buster doesn't mind unless we get too close or the cat is aggressive." Sara mounted and waited until Pat was ready. She squeezed Buster into a slow walk and Butch followed. They moved toward the cat.

In the blink of an eye, the cougar disappeared. Pat was able to see only a small dust cloud slip away on the freshening breeze where the cat had leapt over a log.

"We had better head back to camp. The weather can change quickly this high up. The breeze you're feeling is coming from the north off the mountain snow fields." Sara looked up toward the northern mountains, and untied her coat from behind the cantle, and put it on. Thick dark clouds gathered in the fading light of late afternoon. "It's not unheard of for snow to fall early. I'd rather be down at the camp if the weather gets serious."

"You're trail boss, whatever you think." Pat let Butch follow Buster down the ridge trail. Butch was not only an accomplished team roping horse, but good on the trail. Taking horses who worked mostly in an arena out on trails was good for their minds and helped keep them calm. The horses came to trust their riders and didn't let the little things spook them.

They rode into camp and Sara walked Buster into the water below the suspended bag with the groceries. She stood on the saddle and swung the bag over the ground. Climbing off the horse, she lowered the bag and removed the food for their dinner. She removed a package of sausages and a bowl of fresh-cut veggies. Closing up the bag, she climbed up on Buster again and pulled the bag over the water. Buster moved toward the bowl, and Sara rushed to save their dinner. Buster nosed over it ready to have the veggies for a snack. Sara grabbed the bowl and led Buster back to the camp. She handed the food to Pat.

"Dinner—you'll be glad for the hot stew. I expect the temperature will drop tonight. Would you get the stew stock pot out of the pannier while I take care of Buster. I think we had better use a picket line again tonight."

When Sara returned to the tent, she found Pat had a fire going and a generous pile of semi-dry fire-wood stacked within reach. She took the stew pot, rinsed it out in the lake, and filled the bottom with a few inches of water then put the pot on the fire to boil. Sara dumped the precut, seasoned veggies into the boiling water with a packet of spices. She took both links of the sausage and cut them up, adding them into the pot to cook.

A drop of rain splashed onto Sara's head and she looked up to see a solid overcast sky as the rain began to fall. The campers hastened into the tent and watched as the rain poured across the lake and created the music of falling rain into the lake water.

"We could take a shower and rinse in the lake," Pat suggested.

"You just want to look at my body." Sara laughed. "It is a good idea and the lake water should be warmer than last night."

"Hey, it isn't just your body; however it is very nice to look at. I smell a bit like my horse, stinky." Pat began to take off his clothes, grabbed the bar of biodegradable soap and went down to the tiny beach and began soaping himself in the rain.

Sara watched for a moment and decided to join him. Stripping off her clothes, she joined Pat. They soaped each other teasing. Pat dropped the soap and Sara accused him of having done it on purpose. When she picked up the soap it had sand and grit embedded on one side. She picked out most of the sand and carefully placed the soap on a clean flat rock.

Although the water wasn't as cold as before, it was still too cold to be comfortable. Sara dove under the surface and swam out toward the lake's middle. When all the soap was rinsed off, Sara began to casually swim back to shore, passing Pat who was on his way out toward the center. As he swam by, she dunked his head and initiated a playful dunking game until she tired and broke off to swim back to shore. Pat followed her up onto the beach. He ran to the tent, and got their towels, and handed Sara her towel.

Pat watched Sara dry herself. "Damn Sara, this is the first time I've been alone with a beautiful woman and not made a nuisance or ass of myself. You are one of the most pretty, sexy women I've met, and yet…" Pat shook his head, looked down at himself.

"It's all right Pat, you're sexy too, but you are just not for me. Don't take this wrong, but you just don't turn me on. For awhile I thought you did, but I was wrong."

Sara stood fully exposed to Pat's view. He looked at her, legs slightly apart, the dark blonde patch of her pubic hair still wet showing drops of water, her breasts large, firm with her nipples erect in the cool mountain air, her blonde hair darkened by the water. "God Sara, you are gorgeous, a fifteen on a scale of one to ten. I think I love you, but like a sister, you know?"

"Yeah Pat, I do. You had better stop thinking about it. Part of you has a mind of its own." She pointed at him. He was nearly fully erect.

"Shit, I'm sorry. It appears it does have a mind of its own."

When they finished dressing, Sara checked the stew. "About another half hour and the veggies should be tender. The sausage was precooked so it'll be ready when the veggies are done. There's a loaf of French bread wrapped in tin foil in my saddle bags. If you'll get it we'll be ready to eat when the stew's done." The rain had stopped and the forest brought out all its best aromas of evergreen, damp earth and fresh air.

They ate in silence and enjoyed being together without the stress love and sex often brought. Rain from passing clouds hissed into the lake in sheets and swept across the surface. The rain created ripples as heavy rain drops splashed on the lake's surface.

Sara checked the horses while Pat washed the dishes in the lake, scouring the metal bowls with sand. Sara gave each horse a flake of the hay from the bottom of the panniers. Buster and Butch were gentle nosing their flakes so the hay was spread out but still near enough to reach. Flower flipped his flake up into the air and it fell out of his reach. He made a noisy fuss, and Sara kicked it back so he could get it. When all three horses were munching and satisfied, she returned to the tent.

"I think we'd better call someone and tell them we'll be back Monday instead of Sunday," Pat said. "I'll call Jean and let her know so she won't worry. Since you're still on terminal vacation from the Forest Service, you can stay as long as you want."

The weak sun disappeared behind the hills and darkness came fast to the lake and the hidden valley. Sara placed a small candle lantern near the head of the tent. The sky was filled with clouds, layer upon layer. Not a single star or ray of moonlight would penetrate them tonight. The two campers snuggled down into their sleeping bags, Sara blew out the candle and they lay back and listened to the forest and the frogs as they croaked to each other. On cue, a wolf howled and was answered. Sara smiled as sleep claimed her.

Pat remained awake for a few more minutes thinking about the changes this camping trip had witnessed. He'd found he wasn't attracted to Sara in a sexual way, but had strong feelings for her. He had a twin brother and was surprised he felt the same love for Sara he did for his twin: protection, companionship and the freedom to talk and confided in one another. At first he'd been confused by this strange feeling, but now he found he was warm and comfortable with his feelings for Sara. *Nobody will believe it, I don't believe it.* Sleep came and found a smile on Pat's relaxed face.

On the fourth day, Sara gave the last of the hay to the horses while Pat made breakfast. He used the remainder of the eggs. Chopping up the last bit of onion and celery he combined them with the eggs and ham to make an omelet. "There anything else we can put in the eggs?" Pat asked.

"I think you've put just about everything left in the food bag in there. I'm going to hate leaving. It's been so nice up here, even with the rain. After breakfast, I'll saddle the horses if you clean up the dishes." Sara retreated into the tent and rolled up both sleeping bags. When the tent was down and the panniers loaded, she would use the ground cloth to cover the panniers. She put her small knapsack and the two sleeping bags near the entrance. Pat put the omelet on their plates with the balance of the bacon he'd fried earlier. "We can take the tent down last, after the pack frame and the panniers are on Flower," Sara explained.

Sara accepted the plate and sat on her sleeping bag near the tent entrance away from the drizzle of the misty rain. "Summer rains are awesome; the air is crystal clear, and the forest smells so clean afterward, she said before shoveling omelet into her mouth with the spoon. "I think we should do this again. Maybe next time I'd like to bring someone up here with us. You had better find yourself a girlfriend, because I'm not sleeping with you in the tent with us." She laughed.

"Yeah, I thought you were the one for me, but it just wasn't meant to be. I'm not sorry because I now have a special friend. A friend I can trust and that isn't as common as you might think," Pat said as he sat beside Sara. They watched the fog lift and drift through the tree tops. The first ray of sunshine struck the lake's far end. A rainbow arched over the water, its anchor hidden by trees. "Come on, finish up, I've got dishes to wash and you've got horses to get ready."

"Before you do the dishes, help me break down the tent. When we get home I'll have to set it out to dry properly. I hate the smell of mildew."

"Where can you set up the tent at home? You live in an apartment." The tent would need at least four hours to dry properly, even in full sun.

"The apartment building has a small yard in back where we have BBQs sometimes. I've set up there before, so not a problem. My storage locker is just off the yard too." Sara started to laugh. "Molly used to sunbathe in the nude back there. Nobody ever bothered her. I don't know why, but nobody did."

"Knowing Molly, I can understand why everyone would keep their distance." Pat saw the cloud spread over Sara's face. "You miss her, don't you?"

"Yeah I do, I miss her friendship." Sara's face brightened. "But I've got you now, and no, you can't move in. It might be a bit crowded if I find a boyfriend to move in. I know Roy wants to date, and not just for the ropings. We've had sex once. I can tell he wants more. I realize I want that too, but maybe not with him." Sara sighed. "I think everything will work out. God, I feel relieved. I didn't realize I was so uptight." She placed her arm around Pat's shoulders and hugged him. "I know you'll be a good friend and I'll always be here for you when you need me."

"Sara, I've been meaning to tell you, I'm a Naval Reserve Medical Officer, and I will probably be activated in the next few months for duty in Afghanistan with the Marines. The Spokane Reserve unit returned over a year ago. I expect them to be put on active duty within the next year. I might be going with them. I do their medical stuff, like physicals once a month as one of my required drill weekends. Medical personnel are usually activated for one year; occasionally some specialists are kept for up to two years." Pat looked down at Sara, shook himself, and took the plate from Sara's hands. He pushed himself to his feet, turned and offered his free hand, and pulled Sara to her feet.

It took only a few minutes to collapse the tent and pack it away in its bag. Sara let Pat help her with the panniers and then he went about cleaning up the camp while she saddled the horses.

Pat led on the way back to pick up the truck and trailer. Flower knew when they were close to home and tried to push the horses in front of him to walk faster. When they arrived at the small ranch, they found nobody home. Sara wrote a note for their friends and loaded the horses into the trailer. She put Flower into the round pen with a small flake of hay after brushing him and checking his feet for bruises or cracks in the hoof walls. Finished, she climbed into the truck with Pat and together they returned to Winthrop.

Chapter Twelve

Changing Jobs

When Sara reported to her new boss, District Supervisor Ken Behoney, after leaving the Forest Service, she received her orientation speech to the Winthrop area. Since she had worked as a smokejumper there, it was a short orientation. She was sent to the Winthrop office to work with Ranger Randy Springer. Randy and Sara traveled to Burns, Oregon, to the Bureau of Land Management's wild horse stables to select two mustang horses and a pack horse for her use during the course of her Fish and Wildlife orientation. It was an all-day drive to Burns from Winthrop pulling a seven-horse trailer.

During the drive, Randy and Sara completed the extensive employment interview and the supervisor's interview. They took turns driving with Sara napping when Randy drove, and vice versa. The Service made reservations for them at the Burns Motor Lodge. Both parties were tired from the trip and after a light dinner went to their rooms. Sara lay awake until after midnight, thinking she should take advantage of the alone time to get to know Randy. Randy also lay awake, his mind in turmoil knowing he was developing feelings for his new ranger.

They shared a breakfast and drove to the BLM office to view the mustangs in the corrals. Randy told Sara to walk calmly into the corral and squat down and wait until the animals came to her. Sara had been squatting for nearly an hour when the first gelding came to her and nuzzled her hair. Sara stood up slowly and calmly patted the horse on the neck and let him smell her. After fifteen minutes another mustang came to her, and he too smelled her. She stood quietly, and both horses stayed with her. She calmly patted the horses until they let her touch their heads. Sara walked to the gate of the corral and Randy handed her two halters. She put the first halter on the first mustang and the other on the second. Randy opened the gate, and Sara led the mustangs out.

Randy, with a halter on each shoulder, entered the corral. Within ten minutes, he was leading two more of the mustangs. Sara was impressed with how the horses came to Randy and smelled him. Randy led the four horses to two round pens. He winked at Sara, took the lead rope for the first horse she had selected and led him into the pen. Within minutes, he had the horse responding to signals to go right or left around the pen. At first Randy would not let the horse into his space. After another ten minutes Randy had the horse follow him around the pen. He tied the lead rope around the horse's neck loosely. Randy led the horse to the side of the pen, climbed up the rails, and leaned on the horse. The horse calmly leaned back while Randy petted and rubbed the shoulders and neck.

Before Sara knew what Randy was going to do next, he was sitting on the horse while rubbing the neck and shoulders. Randy and the horse had been together for fifteen minutes, and Randy squeezed with his knees. When the horse stepped forward, Randy took the pressure off. At the end of an hour with the horse, Randy rode him around the outer edge of the pen, first in one direction, then the other.

Randy slid off the horse and walked to the gate and the horse followed. He opened the gate, and he and the horse walked to where Sara sat marveling at the man's skill. Randy led the horse to the other pen and turned him loose. He turned out the other three horses into the pen; then he threw four flakes of alfalfa, spacing them apart into the pen.

"Okay, so much for showing off. The first two horses if they pass the vet-check, will be yours to train and use on patrols. You may select one more for a just-in-case horse. We need to go to another corral where the pack animals are. It's about a ten-minute drive." He smiled. "Unless you want to go to lunch first?"

"I'm not hungry. I want you to teach me how to do what you did with the first horse. I want to ride the second horse. I'll call him Curley today."

"Let's find you a pack animal first. The vet is due here around three-thirty, and we'll get all the horses checked at the same time. The office said there aren't very many pack animals; so we should be back here, even with lunch by two o'clock."

Randy drove ten miles down State Highway 20 to another pair of corrals where a dozen larger horses were milling around. Randy walked to the corral, put his foot on the rail, and studied the animals.

Finally, he pointed at a larger dun-colored horse. "There's your pack horse. Go get him." Randy handed her a halter.

Sara entered the corral, went to the center of the pen and stood quietly for ten minutes, until she felt breathing on the back of her neck. She slowly turned around, and the dun horse was two feet away looking at her. Sara stood quietly, then reached out with her hand and let the horse smell her. After a minute, she turned and walked back toward the gate. The horse followed, his nose almost touching her back.

"Come on Pat," Sara said and put the halter on the horse. She led the horse out the gate, and after Randy closed it, introduced Randy to her pack horse Pat.

Randy borrowed one of the BLM horse trailers and transported Pat to where the other horses were and added Pat to the mix.

The vet called Randy's cell and explained he was held up and would be at the corral by 7:30 the next morning. Sara made sure the horses had water and added an additional half flake of hay for each horse. When Randy and Sara were leaving to return to the motel, the horses were in a bunch watching them drive away.

The vet was already at the corral when Randy and Sara arrived at 7:15. The vet made sure he was inspecting the right horses and checked each for any lameness or bad feet. He inoculated them for West Nile and gave them each a four-way shot. Randy signed the papers transferring the horses from the BLM to the Fish and Wildlife Law Enforcement Service. Sara named her second horse Moe.

The mustangs would be Sara's upon completion of the scheduled twelve weeks of formal classes. After a probationary period, Sara would then begin the extended patrolling of the hundreds of square miles of the National Forest within the Brewster-Winthrop Ranger District.

* * *

In the Ranger Office at the Winthrop airport, Sara found an envelope for her on her office desk. Opening it, she found a welcoming note for her personnel file from Ken Behoney. In the envelope were the instructions to report for training and orientation in Colorado for the first class after the first of the year. She was expected to attend the orientation training in Colorado for four weeks and another eight weeks in law enforcement training at Quantico, Virginia, and in Brunswick, Georgia. At the completion of training, she would be commissioned a Ranger and Federal Law Enforcement Officer.

For her first assignment, Sara would be assigned and report to the District Ranger for duties in the Mt. Baker and Okanogan National Forests with a base at Winthrop, Washington. She would share an office with the current supervisor ranger. Sara could appreciate the irony. In the scheme of things, other than fire fighting, she would have a General Services rating one half step above the Forest Service supervisor. Her time as a smokejumper and firefighter counted for seniority. Johnston had two years service compared to Sara's four years. Sara's starting General Services rating was a half step above his. *Won't have to put up with his crap anymore.* At the completion of training she would receive the other half step on the GS scale.

* * *

Deputy Sheriff Roy Danner and the newly hired Fish and Wildlife Probationary Ranger Sara Bennett had become an item since her return from the weekend spent with Pat O'Hara. Sara knew she didn't love Roy, but she enjoyed his company. She didn't think dating her supervisor was in the best interest of the Service and avoided talking to Randy other than on professional business.

Sara's new job limited the time she and Roy spent together. She knew Roy wanted a commitment from her. Sara didn't react well to the pressure and their relationship became strained.

Roy and his new team roping partner, Pat O'Hara began to make regular trips to the jackpot pay window at ropings around Central Washington. Sara was busy getting to know her job, and elected not to accompany them. She continued to make short patrols to familiarize herself with her new territory. Occasionally Randy accompanied her, teaching her to look for signs of conflict and aggression from individuals she met on the trail. Sara lobbied Ken Behoney to allow her to make overnight patrols, but he would not authorize a probationary ranger the freedom to make longer patrols and restricted her to daylight patrols around Winthrop unless accompanied by another regular ranger. When she found time, Sara worked in a little roping during practice sessions at the local arena, and spent a few hours a week on the shooting range.

Roy continued to push her to spend more time with him, and Sara resented his intrusion into her life and his demands on her time. At first she'd thought Roy would be a nice diversion until Mister Right came along. Her supervisor Randy Springer had been on a series of long patrols and meetings with other supervisors in sister law enforcement agencies. The patrols into the forest for up to five weeks were stressing. He wasn't able to spend as much time with the new ranger as he should. Springer was technically her partner and she rarely saw him except to say "Hi" and "See you later." Sara looked forward to the rare patrols together with Randy. They had dinner together a couple of times when they were both in Winthrop at the same time and Roy was on duty. Sara had pretty much made up her mind to end the affair with Roy and to concentrate on her new career and her competition shooting.

Sara spent many hours working with her new horses, Pat, Curley and Moe. When she was comfortable, she followed Randy's methods and rode them for the first time.

When Randy was on patrol, Behoney watched his new ranger and was pleased with her progress with the mustangs and with her own awareness of her job, its rewards and dangers.

Chapter Thirteen

Roper Watching

Randy sat on the top rail of the arena far enough away from the boxes and chute so he wouldn't bother the horses or the ropers. He watched the tall blonde, her hair in a French braid as she warmed up her horse doing figure eights at the far end of the arena. Sara was a natural rider, smooth in the saddle, both her hands and legs quiet. He saw her cue the horse to do a flying lead change as she approached the corner of the arena. After a hard left they continued along the fence. Randy watched her give the horse his head with a light squeeze of her knees and the horse transitioned into a full sprint. Sara sat back in the saddle and Buster came to a sliding stop.

Randy and Sara's contact with each other was kept strictly professional, after the trip to the BLM stables at Burns, Oregon. Randy was smitten and he was definitely interested in Sara romantically. It was difficult, but he worked hard at keeping their time together to subjects surrounding their jobs.

Sara noticed the cowboy on the fence was her ranger boss. She was sure he watched her as she warmed-up Buster. Sara was scheduled for sixteen weeks of training with law enforcement agencies she might be required to work with and classes on deadly force and enforcement. She would attend the normal twelve weeks of training, and an additional four weeks of training in drug interdiction with the Drug Enforcement Agency, the Border Patrol and Task Force Six at El Paso, Texas. Yesterday, she had finally finished the multi-page questionnaire for security clearances for the Justice Department and the Department of Defense (DOD). Tomorrow she would drive to Seattle and submit the papers at the Federal Building and be interviewed by the Defense Investigative Service. All law enforcement officers who may use government assets on the job were required to be vetted by the Departments of Justice and Defense.

At the end of the training period she would receive her Smoky Bear hat, her Federal Law Enforcement credentials and her government weapon. Sara was officially a probationary ranger and would be until after her return from the formal training and completed a probationary period set by her district supervisor.

Memory of when she met Randy Springer and the quick kiss popped into her mind every time she saw him at work or away. The image of the smile on his face as he left the office was as vivid today as the moment the kiss happened. She remembered when she'd helped him get his personal horses settled at the same stable she boarded Buster. Sara was still confused by her feelings and wondered what she would do if he made a pass at her. She didn't know if she would reject him or would jump into his arms.

Subconsciously she altered her warm-up routine to end fifteen feet from where Randy sat on the top of the five-bar steel fence. Sara dismounted, loosened the cinch, and used one end of the roping reins to lead the horse to the water trough where she allowed him to drink. As soon as the horse lifted his head from the water, she led him back to the spot where they had stopped. She used a halter and lead rope to tie him to the rail to rest for a few minutes before the team roping began.

"Hi, Randy, I didn't know you were still interested in team roping. I know you train horses but didn't do any roping since you left the family ranch. I was going back over the past year's patrol record and noticed you've been on patrol almost since you arrived here. Nearly every time I think we might have a chance for a longer patrol together, you disappear into the wilderness."

"Yeah, the phantom Randy Springer, that's me." Randy hopped down and shook hands with her. "You ride well,. Do you throw a loop as good as you ride?"

"Not yet. I've been riding for years. I started roping last summer during down times. How about you? Do you remember how to ride and rope?" After the words were out of her mouth she thought how lame they seemed. She knew he was an accomplished horseman and had witnessed his way around horses.

"I've been known to fall off a horse or two." Randy coughed and grinned.

Embarrassed, Sara joined in the humor. "Somehow I don't see that happening very often. Do you do any roping?"

"I've done some. Mostly on the family ranch, you know friendly stuff against my brother and my dad," Randy answered. "I think we've had this conversation before."

Sara grinned and felt there was more than a little friendly competition within the Springer family. "I know you have horses. Did you bring them with you?" she asked. "You know you're welcome to join us. We're pretty much weekend ropers. During the spring, summer, and early fall we practice on Tuesdays and Thursdays after work and on most Saturdays and some Sundays. We've got another few weeks of good weather before the snow flies. You should join us."

"Yeah, I remember. I've still got the horses I picked up from the BLM. I've brought them along as far as I can without working them on cattle in the arena. I'd like to train here. Do you think the other ropers would mind if I brought my green rope horses?"

"I don't think they'd mind. Some of them started their horses here. How green are they? Geldings, right? Wait, they probably don't know you're one of the horse patrol Fish and Wildlife guys?"

"Yeah, I don't think I know any of these guys. I requested a transfer to the Methow. I heard there were a couple of openings and here I am. Of course, you know all that."

"I put in a transfer from fighting fires to Fish and Wildlife Enforcement. I received a letter of conditional acceptance the same day you reported in and I met you at the office. We haven't had much of a chance to talk since the first patrol and the drive to Burns. You don't talk much when you're working except to explain the job. You know, I was listening like a good little probationary ranger." Sara leaned back against the fence beside Randy.

"Mr. Behoney did tell me the Service sometimes lets rookies do patrols with a training ranger before they are sent to school. As soon as I could find and buy my mustangs I trained them a bit beyond the green broke and took them on that first patrol. When I got back I spent most of my time with the new service mustangs. I'm sorry we only had limited opportunity for training." Randy paused, while he wiped the inside of his straw hat. "You'll be leaving for formal training in a few weeks." Randy was a bit nervous. He put his hands in his back pockets after he set his hat back on his head. "I have been rather busy, but I think I'm ready to get into a routine." Randy spoke softly. "These extended patrols are nice but can be restrictive too. I've got my feet wet and feel I'm ready to actually be your orientation training officer. I'm sorry it has taken so long. Behoney has some long- range plans and you are a part of the personnel package of who will be involved. I look forward to working with you when you return."

Sara was excited. "That would be great." She looked at her boss. "You know because I'm only probationary, I am not armed and my patrolling is restricted to close in, mostly between here and Mazama along the river. No overnight stuff. I've been restricted to observations only and not able to confront anyone. I report seeing any laws broken and another ranger is sent to correct the situation."

Randy changed the subject. "Say, do you think the other ropers would like me to work the chute?" He smiled down at Sara.

"Yeah, that would be great. We won't have to take a team out of the rotation then. We've got a new guy who is still learning to be around steers. He's got another couple of practice sessions before the boss will let him throw a loop at a steer. We don't want him losing a couple of fingers or thumb. Henry works the stripping chute and at the end of practice he chases the critters back to the pasture after the wraps are off. You sure you don't mind working the chutes?"

"You know if I work the chutes, it's going to cost you."

"What do you mean?" Sara looked up into his youthful grin.

"Dinner—let me take you to O'Reilly's for a steak dinner. You might even meet one of the steers you've been chasing."

"We'll see how you do on the chute before I commit to your price." Sara laughed; she enjoyed the verbal patter. He was good looking and she could tell well educated and intelligent. Pat was now a friend and not a suitor. Besides, Pat was at Camp Pendleton with the Marines and maybe on his way to Afghanistan at the end of his orientation and training period or sent home until needed. Sara remembered she would be going to a big West Coast large bore shoot in June of next year. Maybe things were beginning to swing around to the plus side for her.

Sara led Randy to where Art, the roping club's unofficial leader, was talking to the ropers and assigning jobs to support the day's practice roping. "Hey Art. We've got a volunteer to work the chute." She turned Randy over to Art who introduced him to the other ropers.

When the pre-practice warm-up session was over, Randy went to the holding pen and pushed the steers into the return alley and helped put on the protective horn wraps.

Sara watched Randy and could see he knew his way around the boxes, the chute and the steers. Art told Randy not to bother setting the barrier. They would use a marker instead of a barrier. Randy slipped into the heel box and urged the first steer into the chute. He nodded to the first team and watched the heeler ride into the box while he leaned on the chute. When the heeler was in position, Randy shifted his attention to the header. The header nodded, Randy released the steer and immediately closed the gate and urged the next steer into the now-vacant chute to be ready for the next team.

When it was Sara's turn in the head box, Randy watched and almost missed her nod to release the steer by opening the spring-loaded gate. He watched her catch the horns a jump late but a good turn for the heeler. He smiled as he reloaded the chute with the next steer.

The next team asked for a score before their run. When the team was set and ready, he opened the chute and let the steer out. The riders kept their horses in the box and Randy loaded the next steer.

The practice went by quickly. At the end, Randy helped remove the horn wraps, then released the steers into the arena to run free. Henry, a new roper and his horse chased the steers to the stripping chute where the steers went directly into the holding pen. When all the steers were ready to be turned out, Randy opened the gate to the pasture. Art and two other ropers checked the feed and water and left the steers to themselves, their work done.

Randy returned to the gate where Sara met him with a beer. He took the beer, grinned, and used his thumb to remove a bit of steer poop from her cheek.

"Now, how about that steak; come on, its only dinner, not a proposition."

"Why not?" Sara surprised herself.

Caught off guard, Randy was slow to respond. "Well, it certainly could be, but I think slower is better. I don't want to screw up." Randy had already made up his mind about Sara Bennett. She was far above any woman he had ever met: smart, sexy, talented, and strong minded, and not afraid to take chances. Besides, he could see the relationship with Roy was already over in her mind. She just hadn't ended it yet. Randy knew Sara dated Pat O'Hara and could see they were best friends. He was pretty good at reading people and saw where the two were not sexually attracted to each other. Randy wasn't one to cut into another man's love life, but Sara and Roy's affair wasn't hitting on all cylinders.

Sara studied the man in front of her. "You just aren't going to take no for an answer, are you?"

"Nope!" Randy grinned. "What time do I meet you?"

"Seven-thirty at O'Reilly's. You know the place?" Sara noticed Roy stood by his trailer and watched the interaction between Sara and Randy. Sara made up her mind to tell Roy their relationship was over. There was no time like the present. She knew it wouldn't be a surprise to Roy.

"Look, I have something to take care of before I leave here. So, if you will excuse me, I'll get to it." Sara smiled and walked toward where Roy waited.

Roy Danner watched Sara approach. He knew what was on her mind and had accepted it. "I can see you've got something on your mind." Roy greeted Sara.

"Yeah Roy, I've been invited to dinner by Randy and I've accepted." She looked down at her boots and then up into his eyes. "You know we've been through for awhile. I like you Roy, but I don't love you and never did. We had some good times together, but now it's over. I'll put your things in a bag and you'll be able to pick them up at the apartment. Leave my apartment key on the table. I hope we can still remain friends and continue to rope together."

Roy interrupted, "I know we're done and I'm sorry it didn't work out for either of us. Maybe we can share a lunch sandwich sometime. I'm not heart broken. I think this is for the best. I knew going in that you were never going to stay with me." Roy leaned forward and kissed Sara on the cheek. He turned his attention to his horse and stuffed a half flake of hay into the feeder. When he stepped down, Sara was gone. He saw her check on Buster, climb into her truck and drive out onto the highway.

Randy watched the interplay between Sara and Roy. When she turned her back and walked quickly to her truck and drove away, he knew the affair between Sara and Roy Danner was over. It made him sad to see a relationship end, but his heart was growing lighter and more excited as it looked forward to dinner with Sara Bennett.

Chapter Fourteen

The Roper and the Breakup

Doctor Patrick O'Hara was single and not seeing anyone. Jean constantly tried to set him up with some of her visiting friends from Seattle where Jean had attended nursing school before marrying Bruce. All attempts found little success. Since the affair with Sara hadn't worked out, Pat tended to the medical business. The town's single ladies thought he was wonderful, but he wasn't interested. He still roped with Sara and her former boyfriend Roy Danner. Pat and Roy became friends as well as roping partners. Pat had repeatedly warned Roy not to push too hard on Sara. Roy was stuck in his own ways of courting and Pat could see when Sara became stressed. Pat wasn't surprised when the relationship ended. Sara began to date Randy Springer and Pat thought Sara had found a partner at last.

Roy was a number two and a half heeler while Pat was rated as a number one header. Occasionally, they broke the eight-second time. Roy didn't come up empty often. He might catch one leg, but even with the penalty it was still good for a time. On a four-steer go, a single leg and three good catches without penalty was usually good for a trip to the pay window.

Randy started to train his mustangs in earnest after working the chutes for the Methow Roping Club. He spent the next two weeks working with three new BLM mustangs purchased for the new rangers. Ken Behoney expected a new ranger to report within the next month. The Winthrop Station would need at least three additional horses. Behoney liked to keep at least two trained spare horses. The horses were kept at Mazama, but were easily accessible when needed. Every day Randy worked each new horse for at least one hour plus the brushing and handling before and after the training session. He fed each mustang as a group and then individually. He loaded the horses into the seven-horse trailer and drove them around on paved highways and bad country dirt roads. Randy varied the position of the horses in the trailer but used each horse's personal feedbag and feeder. The horses became accustomed to riding in the trailer and used to the smell of their own feedbag and eventually ignored the other horses' feed and hay. At the end of the two weeks of intensive training, the horses looked forward to Randy and actually seemed to enjoy the outings in the trailer. Each mustang would follow him into the trailer without the requirement of a lead rope, but Randy always put a halter on them when he trained.

At the end of the second week Randy tied them all night to a picket line and then varied the picket line with hobbles. By the end of the second week, he could leave the mustangs on the line all day without them complaining. As long as they had water, they were content. During the second week of training, each mustang was sensitive to foot and leg cues and would respond without a bit or headstall.

Randy introduced his mustangs to cattle. The horses trusted him and were not afraid of the smelly creatures. They were curious and would walk around the cattle. When Randy left a mustang alone with the cattle, the bored horse would begin to play by getting all the cattle together into a corner and keeping them there. The horse would go to the other end of the arena and wait quietly until the cattle began to spread out. Then the mustang would calmly gather the herd back into their corner of the arena. Randy worked on cues and introduced verbal commands. Randy patiently taught the mustangs their job.

Late each afternoon, Randy worked with his mustangs. At the next roping after the dinner with Sara, Randy took his mustangs to the roping practice and club jackpot. He scored each horse three times before letting the mustang chase a steer. The horses put him in the sweet spot each time. Randy used light contact to tell the horse what he wanted. By the fifth run by each horse, the mustangs were doing their job like seasoned rope horses. Randy temporarily named them Frick and Frack.

Art approached Randy and waited until the rider acknowledged him. "Those are mustangs, right?"

"Yes sir."

"Where did you find trained mustang rope horses? I've never seen any at the sales, at least young horses. What are those two, about five?"

"Actually I bought them at a BLM sale a few months ago. I never had time to train them until recently. They've got about a month under saddle. The breed is underrated. I think Frick here is maybe four years and Frack is three. That's a guess you understand."

"You mean you broke and trained them in just a few weeks?" Art was amazed.

"No, actually they were green broke when I bought them. I know the wrangler who gentles and gives the horse their first ride, and he's very good with young horses."

"Who trained them on cattle?"

"I did. They are just naturally curious and love to please, so it was easy bringing them along. It only took a day to get them used to the rope. They like to be handled; maybe a bit too much." Randy put his arm around Frick's neck and the mustang actually lightly leaned into him until Randy pushed back. "I don't know if they will ever be NFR Caliber, but they're good for jackpots and most of the PRCA events in the Northwest."

"You wouldn't consider selling them?" Art asked hopefully.

"No, I like these boys."

"Say, how much roping and training have you done Randy?"

"I was raised on a Montana ranch. My dad and brother are ropers. Dad taught me how to rope and train horses. You never give them enough time to forget what they've learned," Randy explained.

"You a rated roper?"

"Yes sir, I was a four and a half header and number four heeler. When I was last rated. My brother is a four each end, but he's sandbagging. I think he's at least a five. My dad's a solid four."

"Have I heard of them?"

"Maybe, Hank and Brent Springer."

"They own a ranch in Western Montana?" Art was truly impressed. A small crowd formed around the two men. "There is one horse trainer, a girl who is rated as a number three and a half header and a great horse trainer. Her dad's Ben Withrow, you happen to know them too?"

"Yeah, Ben and Sue work for my dad at the Rolling JH ranch. Sue's been at Washington State University Vet School and when home, works on rope and ranch horses. Ben's been training mostly cutters the last couple of years. My sisters Margie and Gail do a lot of general ranch and exercise horses working with Ben." Randy was pleased the men had heard of his family.

"Why aren't you working for your dad? You're very good." Art slowly shook his head.

"I really enjoy my job. I meet great people." Randy made a hand gesture indicating the men surrounding him. "Some are a bit prettier than others." Randy laughed, joined by the other cowboys and the three cowgirls. They all knew whom he was referring to. "I don't know how much I can help but I'd be happy to help with any problems with the horses," Randy offered.

The questions came fast and furious. Randy agreed to help all who asked. He noticed Sara stayed on the edge of the crowd and listened to every word Randy said.

When the group broke up and got down to the practice, Sara approached him. "Why didn't you tell me you were a rated roper? You never told me you knew anything about rope horses or team roping."

"Well, I didn't want to toot my own horn and there are some good ropers with a lot of talent here. With a little help they could become great ropers. By the way, you're one of those I'm talking about." Randy smiled. "You throw a good loop and ride well. With a change or two, you could knock a couple of seconds off your average times."

"Really, you're not just saying that to get into my knickers are you?"

"No, the knickers might come in time. I am certainly interested in those too."

"That why you took me to dinner a couple of weeks ago?" Sara squinted at him. "And why haven't you called me since?"

"I've been a bit busy. Ken wants the mustangs from the BLM ready when the new transfer ranger gets here next week. Besides you've been on day patrols and working with your own mustangs."

"You can't tell me you've been working all night."

"No ma'am, but I have been busy, and you didn't indicate you wanted me to call. I didn't have your telephone number either." Randy smiled.

"You didn't ask." Sara was having a hard time keeping the smile off her face. Finally she said, "555-9737, any time. How about dinner tonight, my treat?"

"That would be great." Randy was surprised at the invitation.

"You're on. 7:30, same place? Yeah, now I've got some roping to do. Would you watch me and give me some pointers?"

"Sure. Tell you what, I'll be your heeler for your first couple of runs. Art asked me to heel a couple for him too." Randy nodded. Sara returned his nod and went to get Buster warmed up.

While Sara and Randy were waiting their turn in the box, he told her what he intended to do and what she should do. When it was their turn, Randy moved his mustang into the heel box and waited until Sara was settled. He smiled and Sara returned the smile and nodded to turn the steer loose. Randy wanted Sara to throw her loop at the first opportunity she had. She came out of the box, went twice around with her loop and tossed to catch the horns quickly. Sara pulled slack, turned the steer and before she had a chance to look over her shoulder, Randy had both back legs in his loop. Sara almost lost her dally when the rope went tight, and she attempted to face the steer.

Sara sat on Buster, her mouth open in shock. Randy held the steer with his rope and grinned at her.

Art rode up while they still held the steer. He was staring at his stopwatch. "5.1 seconds, that's the fastest time this season. Sara, you were amazing." They both looked at Randy who put his hand out and wiggled it palm down in a so-so gesture.

Randy stepped his horse forward, releasing the steer's back legs, and Sara followed the steer to the stripping chute. Randy watched her direct her horse with her feet and legs.

Sara was a very good rider and not a bad roper either. With a bit of help learning to read the intentions of the pursued steer, and getting a little quicker out of the box, Sara would be a top competitor.

When Sara first heard the rumor about her and Randy being an item, she was surprised the rumor made her feel warm and wanted. Even when Randy attempted to explain, Sara just smiled and invited him to take her to dinner and Randy jumped to comply.

Chapter Fifteen

Training

The following weeks were busy for both Sara and Randy. She dropped into a physical training program of running, free weights and yoga and continued her marksmanship training. Sara concentrated on the longer shooting distances and used "Able" targets which consisted of a ten-inch black bull's-eye, rather than the standard twenty-inch bull's-eye with a ten inch X ring used to break ties in points. She primarily used her M1A military match rifle. Twice a week she drove to the Army Yakima Firing Center to use their known distance course and the variable distance course.

* * *

On a Saturday afternoon in late January, Sara left for her formal training period, subletting her apartment to one of the new girls who worked for O'Reilly's Bar and Grill. She was given a bus ticket to SeaTac, overnight lodging at a local hotel and plane tickets to Colorado to arrive Sunday afternoon. Her initial training would take place in Colorado followed by Virginia and Georgia. After she completed the initial eight weeks of formal training for new Federal Law Enforcement employees, she went to Quantico, Virginia, for weapons training with the FBI on the application of deadly force. She would go to Brunswick for cross training with the U.S. Marshal's Service for two weeks. During the weeks of instruction, Sara was kept so busy she didn't have time except for the classroom, study, and sleep. Sara was sent to El Paso, Texas, for drug interdiction training where she made patrols with members of Joint Task Force Six. JTF6 was a joint multiagency unit responsible for the southern border from California to the Florida Keys.

It was mid May when Sara completed all the training cycles Behoney could send her to. She returned to the U.S. Marshal's training facility at Brunswick for an additional week. At the end of her extra training with the Marshals she returned to the Colorado headquarters for her commissioning ceremony and was presented with her Smokey Bear hat. Sara was issued a large Sig Sauer 10mm semiautomatic pistol and her Federal Law Enforcement Shield and credentials.

When she left the Colorado Headquarters for Seattle, she boarded the airplane after her identification was checked and rode as the Air Marshal on the flight. Her carryon baggage consisted of a hatbox for her Smoky Bear hat. Her pistol was concealed in a shoulder holster, her Federal Shield pinned to her belt hidden by her civilian North Face jacket. It felt strange for her to climb onto the plane with the heavy pistol on her person. The flight crew knew who she was and she was given a special aisle seat chosen at random for the Air Marshals. She was expected to refrain from consuming any alcoholic beverages. Sara smiled at the stewardess when she declined a lunch sandwich on the flight.

* * *

After she retrieved her hat box from the flight attendant, Sara stepped onto the ramp from the Boeing 757 into the terminal; Randy Springer was there to welcome his newest commissioned ranger. She was surprised to see Randy wearing his Sig Sauer 10mm pistol strapped to his belt. His shield was pinned to the left breast of his brown jacket. It was unusual for a federal officer to wear a sidearm into an airport terminal unless on duty or traveling under specific orders to carry. But here was Randy armed, wearing his brown Stetson hat, and a uniform of a brown shirt, brown jacket and pressed jeans.

"What are you doing here?"

"Now don't start our official relationship with dumb questions. I'm here to pick you up and take you to dinner and then drive you to Winthrop," Randy responded with a grin. "You have to go with me because I'm your boss, but if you put up too much of a fuss I'll let you walk home."

"I guess I'd better do what you say Mr. Boss." Sara laughed.

Over dinner, Randy brought Sara up to date with the situation in Behoney's District. Her horses were in the corral behind the headquarters. Her not-so-new truck and trailer were there after Randy picked them up from the Oregon Regional Headquarters and drove them to Winthrop.

"I didn't think you'd mind, so I exercised your horse Buster when I had spare time. I've been kept pretty much in Winthrop." Randy brought her up to date on the area patrols and into the world of being a ranger. He explained when she could expect to begin her independent patrolling after three to five patrols with her supervisor.

Randy reached to the inside pocket of his jacket and withdrew an envelope addressed to her from the National Rifle Association. Sara knew it was the National Competitive Match schedule. He handed her the envelope and watched while she tore it open and read.

"I've been confirmed to compete in the Western Division Matches at Camp Pendleton, California in June." She looked up at him. "That's not even two months from now. Do you think I'll have enough time off to practice?"

"I'm sure Sara, the District Director is behind you and so is your supervisor. I don't think you'll have any trouble getting some time to practice." Randy smiled. "Now if you're ready we can start for home. The North Cascade Pass opened a couple of weeks ago and is in pretty good shape. Snow's melted below 3,500 feet, so there might be a bit of snow at the highway summit. If it doesn't snow on us over the summit, we should be in Winthrop inside of three hours. Actually the time for the trip depends on traffic between here and Arlington on I-5."

"When do you want me to start patrolling?"

"I think the lower trails off the main highways would be a good place to start. Fishing season opened last month and I'd like to check the lakes. The lakes will probably be your first few patrols. Most of them you can drive to, do an overnighter and move to the next lake. Let's say four overnight day patrols to start. Your schedule will be four days on and three days off for five weeks then three days on patrol, two days in the office and two days off. That sound okay with you?"

"Fine, great, I'll get time to practice. What about the longer patrols?"

"Let's not consider them until you get back from California. We have another new ranger, actually not a new ranger, but one who has been with the Service for three years in the Midwest. I'll expect you to train her with weapons. She's from an area with not a lot of poaching." Randy saw surprise in Sara's eyes when he said she would be the training officer for the new arrival.

"Okay, anything else?"

"Nope, we might as well get on the road and get you home." Randy stood after paying the tab with cash. He saw the surprise in Sara's eyes and explained. "I don't like those credit cards—to easy to get in trouble with them," He grinned.

On the way Sara asked if he knew why her training had been extended by four weeks. A new investigative class was available and she had received a message she would be attending, but that class was canceled. He shook his head meaning wait until they were on the highway back to Winthrop.

Once in the truck Sara again asked if he knew why she was back and why her investigation class was cancelled.

"I got lonely and couldn't wait any longer to see your beautiful face," Randy teased, but didn't answer her question.

"Come on give, I know you know what's going on."

"Well, the Border Patrol intercepted some really bad drugs and we have been assigned as an additional federal agency along with DEA to look for them," He paused. "The FBI has also taken an interest but Homeland Security has challenged them; so Homeland Security will be the lead agency on the task force. It's really a gaggle. Ken has brought all the supervisory rangers in his extended district to Winthrop for an organizational meeting scheduled for tomorrow afternoon. I want you to sit in on the meeting. Most of the supervisory rangers have been assigned to special patrol areas leaving the newbies to take care of the routine patrols, meaning you and the new girl ranger. Three supervisory rangers' teams have been stretched from Winthrop to the Idaho border and south to Highway Two. I have been assigned to administer to the needs of the new people." Randy's eyes took on a mischievous shine., "She's pretty too. Our new ranger."

Sara slugged Randy on the shoulder. "Pretty as me?" Sara batted her eyes at him until he laughed.

"Nobody is as pretty or as beautiful as you, nobody!" Randy grinned.

Sara scooted over next to Randy, leaned her head on his shoulder and promptly fell asleep. She woke when Randy stopped in front of her apartment. He helped carry her baggage upstairs and left, claiming an early meeting with the Northwest Area Manager and the District Boss as the reason.

Chapter Sixteen

The New Ranger

For the next few weeks, Randy was kept busy training new horses. Of the six new horses five were mustangs, and the sixth was a young quarterhorse gelding whose former owner could not afford to feed him any longer. The new ranger, Janet Awel, returned from vacation and moved her personal effects cross-country and reported to her immediate supervisor Randy Springer and the District Supervisor Ken Behoney. The attractive brunette possessed some experience with horses, and Behoney assigned her to assist Randy with mounted training. Randy at the same time would conduct the local area orientation.

The first two weeks, Janet spent half of each day working with Randy in the mornings. Janet rode her new horses and assisted in their training. Randy taught her the art of packing both for herself and the pack animal using panniers. In the afternoon, she worked with Sara on marksmanship and to zero the sights on her Marlin lever action 30-30 rifle.

Janet's previous post was in Ohio where mounted patrols were handled by one rural ranger. All other patrols were by four-wheel drive in three-quarter ton trucks and Jeeps. She came to Winthrop with only 4 by 4 patrol and water patrol experience. Behoney made it Sara and Randy's responsibility to bring the three new rangers assigned to his district up to Winthrop standards. Randy taught advanced riding, packing and land navigation. Sara taught threat identification, marksmanship, and the use of deadly force. Janet patrolled with Sara on close-in patrols and two-day patrols with Randy.

After her first two-day patrol, it was clear Janet idolized the tall, good-looking ranger. She only let up on her hang-dog expression and attitude when Randy told Janet, he and Sara were an item. Sara passed her probationary period and all restrictions on her patrolling were lifted. She could now patrol by herself without a second ranger as backup.

* * *

Sara was assigned a green 3500 Dodge diesel pickup truck and a bumper-pull three-horse trailer as her personal work vehicles. The truck was a five-year-old dual cab pickup and possessed a solid diesel engine, a good strong transmission and 4 by 4 drive. A camper shell covered the truck's pickup bed. The rumor was the Service was to be equipped with new 4 by 4 SUVs complete with light bar mounted on each vehicles roof.

The Forest Service smokejumpers were always bumming rides after the firefighting was over. Sara continued to keep track of firefighters in the forest. When possible she would drive and pick up the crews and give them a ride back to Winthrop. The only items they needed to take to a fire were the parachutes and firefighting gear: axes, chainsaws, shovels and other tools to fight forest fires. The parachutes and padded jump suits were packed in waterproof bags and left where they could be retrieved later. Most of the padded suits jumpers wore to protect them during descent through trees were hand-me-down suits. Many of the suits were older than the jumpers who used them.

With her own truck and horse trailer, Sara would be free to plan her own patrols subject to the approval of her immediate supervisor. Currently she was restricted to the area of Mt. Baker National Forest. At Winthrop, Randy gave her a box of the plastic ties many law enforcement agencies used in lieu of handcuffs. The Smokey bear hat she received at the graduation from the training courses would go on a peg in her apartment replaced by her comfortable brown, beaver felt Stetson. She was required to wear the brown jacket and tan colored shirt, but was allowed to wear Levi's or Wrangler jeans. The shirts and jackets were made specifically for the Forest Service and rangers. She wore her Federal Shield pinned above the left pocket of the jacket or on her tan shirt. When not in uniform and depending on the assignment, she would wear the badge on her belt, but it must always be in view whenever she confronted people in the woods.

* * *

Sara named her new horses Larry, Moe and Curley after the three Stooges. Moe and Curley were the mustangs, Pat being her assigned pack horse, a Morgan-Quarterhorse cross. The Ranger Service with assistance of the Border Patrol constructed a double stable, two arenas and a round pen during the months the construction trades were short on work opportunities. A hay barn was built with left- over materials. It was spacious enough to store feed for twenty-five horses for eight months. Randy was kept busy training horses assigned to new rangers. Sara, with Randy's assistance, trained her own Service horses. The number of horses in the Winthrop ranger herd had more than tripled since Randy assumed duties at

Winthrop. Randy's personal mustang rope horses were still at his original boarding stable. Pat O'Hara and Sara still boarded Butch and Buster at the same stable.

During the spring weather, Sara spent many hours riding to keep Buster and the Service horses legged up and ready for the trail. Only one Border Patrol agent, Jim Hookstra was assigned to the Mt. Baker common border with Canada on a permanent basis. Hookstra was the only Border Patrol Agent assigned permanently to the Mt. Baker National Forest at Oroville, Washington, and he patrolled the border. The Border Patrol did have other agents at border crossings, but they did not patrol except occasionally using 4 by 4 vehicles for specific missions.

With her District Supervisor Ken Behoney's concurrence, Sara was able to keep up with her shooting practice. When time and work schedules permitted, she taught Pat how to shoot military large bore rifles with accuracy and precision. Pat was a natural marksman, who only needed to practice to reach a competitive level. Behoney thought it was great having Sara, a national shooter, represent his district in national and international events.

Sara was scheduled to compete at the Western Regional Championship at Camp Pendleton. She was the defending Women's large bore champion on the military known-distance course of 200, 300, 500, and the 1,000 meter ranges. She looked forward to seeing old friends. Molly Throckmorton was off probation with the LACFD and planned to put in for some vacation to watch the week- long competition. Gunnery Sergeant Nancy Clark had been promoted to Chief Warrant Officer 2. Nancy was the best woman shooter in the Marine Corps and would be competing against Sara. Nancy was the absolute best for a military shooter. Nancy's only real competition was in the men's and open events, where she excelled.

Nancy and Sara became friends when they were the only women shooting against the men at the Camp Perry Nationals three years before. Over dinner one evening after an afternoon of shooting practice, Nancy confided, she always wanted to visit Washington State, but Marine Corps commitments interfered. Nancy was a Marine first and foremost always ready to step forward. Nancy didn't look much like a competitive rifle shooter or a Marine for that matter. She could have been the model for Snow White in Disney's classic film. Her short dark hair, erect stature, and feminine figure left a backwash of romantic suitors behind her as she went about her Marine Corps business.

Nancy joined the Marine Corps on her eighteenth birthday. She had worked in supply until the opportunity to shoot competitively was offered. She was the first woman to graduate from the Marine Corps Scout Sniper Course at Camp Pendleton. A match rifle in her hands was a finely turned instrument. Nancy completed a tour in Afghanistan, where she worked as a sniper with the Surveillance, Target Acquisition (STA) platoon. Nancy and Sara knew and respected each other for their skills and knowledge.

Sara continually teased Nancy with an invitation to visit Washington, where Sara would teach her to ride horses and become a team roper. Nancy always said she would think it over. In another two years, she would be eligible to retire from the Marine Corps and was still young enough to join one of the numerous outdoor occupations offered by the government in the Northwest.

* * *

Sara spent one week on patrol with another ranger and one week working in the office. With the added poaching due to the economy, two more rangers were assigned to the Winthrop office. So far Randy Springer was the only ranger who consistently patrolled in the more remote areas. Other rangers rarely patrolled for more than a week and never in the more remote areas. In May, Behoney ordered his supervisory rangers to patrols no longer than one week unless assigned longer patrols by the district office. Randy's normal patrol time was cut. Sara was assigned two, three and four-day patrols, but she was restricted to the Winthrop area. Her first solo four-day patrol was scheduled around the four lakes area. Ferguson Lake was the first of the four lakes on her schedule.

During the fishing and tourist season Randy assigned five rangers to be in the field, another ranger to work in the office to issue licenses and operate as an information source, and two rangers on off days. In addition, there were three probationary rangers in Randy's section. Sara was scheduled to leave the station after two days off and a day in the office when she received a call from Pat at the clinic. He would like to see her today if possible.

Sara called Ken Behoney to let him know she was closing the office early since Randy Springer was trail-training a new ranger. She would check into the office before going on patrol tomorrow. Behoney changed her patrol to two days at Ferguson Lake campground Thursday night and return Friday to Winthrop to man the office. Ken also promoted her to Assistant Supervisor of the Winthrop office. When Randy was unavailable she would see the patrols were conducted and confirm the routes to be covered. The new job didn't add any money to her wallet, but did give her additional flexibility to set her hours of work.

Sara drove her green truck to the Winthrop clinic, and parked in the space for official vehicles. Sara locked the truck. Her Winchester 30-30 rifle was in the rack behind the seat. She skipped up the steps and entered the lobby. The bullet hole left from the shot that had killed one of the hostage takers last year was still behind the lobby desk. It was a reminder of the event and still a major topic of conversation.

"Hi Jean, Pat called and wanted to see me. Is he in?"

"Sure Sara, I'll get him—or do you want to go to his office? You know the way."

"I'll just mosey back and surprise him. How have you been, and how's that new daughter of yours?"

"Growing like a weed. Her christening is next month, and Bruce and I would like you and Pat to be her Godparents, if it's not an imposition,. If it wasn't for you, we wouldn't be here." Pat had told Jean who saved her life.

"Gosh Jean, I would be honored. Have you asked Pat?"

"Yes, he's agreed. He said you would too. I just didn't want to take advantage you know?" Jean came around the desk and put her arms around Sara's neck. Sara could feel the tears touch her cheek as the other woman drew a deep breath and gathered her emotions before she stepped back. Jean palmed a tear from her cheek and walked behind the desk. "I didn't mean to embarrass you. I'm just so grateful for you saving us, your Goddaughter and me. It's been so long since you've been here. I know you've been busy with your new job and all and I thought I'd better ask as soon as I saw you."

"I'm truly honored Jean, you tell Bruce that too and give my future Goddaughter a hug from her God-mommy." Sara felt her eyes pool with tears. She turned and walked briskly down the hall to Pat's office. "You called?"

"Oh hi Sara, yeah I got a notice I've been assigned to the 1st Marine Expeditionary Force (IMEF) for duty in Afghanistan. I have seven days to report to the Lake O'Neill Hospital at Camp Pendleton. Looks like I won't be going with the reserves from Spokane. They haven't received a Warning Order yet and it takes forty-five days after notification for the transition to active duty for training and overseas deployment."

"I am sorry to see you go. It's only a year, right?" Sara plopped down in the side chair.

"Yeah, but they can extend it to two years depending on the requirements for medical personnel. I don't expect it to be more than a year, but one never knows." Pat opened his middle desk drawer and took out a brown envelope. Sara could see her name written in Pat's neat script across the front. "Sara, you are my best friend. My brother Daniel is pretty much irresponsible living in San Francisco at the moment. In a year he could be anywhere." He handed the envelope to Sara. "That is a copy of my will, and all the necessary documents should something happen in Afghanistan. I've given you power of attorney over my estate and Butch. I don't have much. Both parents are deceased."

"I don't know about this Pat. Are you sure you want to appoint me power of attorney?" She held the unopened envelop gingerly in her hands as if it would break. Looking down at it again, her hands tightened on the brown paper. She clinched and stared at the envelope like it was a poisonous snake.

"Please Sara, you are the only one I can trust, except for Bruce and Jean and I don't want to burden them."

"No you'd rather burden me." Sara felt her eyes tear up again. "Of course Pat, I'm pleased you thought of me and trust me with this. Look, when you get back, this envelope will still be unopened and I'll sit right here and hand it back to you." She sat up straight. "I hear you and I are going to be Godparents."

Pat laughed. "Yeah, Jean and Bruce asked me a couple of days ago. Jean really wanted you but was afraid to ask. They didn't want to impose. I told Jean you'd be honored to be a Godparent. They will have the christening next Saturday. I called your office and they said you'd be back on Friday."

Sara stood up, "Yep, true. Is this it for now?"

"Yeah, that's it." Pat gave her a weak smile. "Will I see you before I leave?"

"Sure, I will be on patrol two days at a time for the next couple weeks. After that I don't know what the schedule is. The schedule has been changed so much in the past month. Randy isn't back until later this week to let me know what he wants for the next patrol assignments. I'll be taking Pat, Moe, and Curley for this weeks patrol. Buster might need a ride if you wouldn't mind. He likes you. Your hands are softer than mine." She smiled at her friend and reached out to ruffle his short blonde hair. "Later." Sara stopped in the lobby, only long enough to kiss a surprised Jean on the cheek. Sara sat in her truck for a few minutes waiting for her nerves to settle, and thought of the friends she'd made since she came to Winthrop.

Chapter Seventeen

Murder at the Lake

The three-horse trailer tracked well even when the horses were restless and shifted their weight. Sara drove her truck through the small settlement of Mazama and on toward Ferguson Lake. She planned to stay one night at the lake depending on the number of hikers and fishermen. Sara planned to return to Winthrop the following afternoon.

Although still early in the season, fly fishing was in full swing with fishermen hiking to some of the higher lakes. At the higher elevations, she would be the only ranger on horseback available to check licenses and boats for safety equipment. Less than a dozen lakes had some limited vehicle access. Randy planned to have his less experienced new rangers drive their vehicles to the accessible lakes, leaving the mounted patrol to his more experienced rangers. It was important the rangers made sure the people who camped at the lakes obeyed the rules for the primitive areas. Citations and warnings issued required the violator to visit the District Ranger Station in Brewster within thirty days or a non-compliance citation would be issued, doubling any fines.

The drive up the road toward Ferguson Lake was especially pleasant. The weather was warming and many of the snowfields in the lower elevations to the west had already melted. In the higher hanging valleys, the snow might last through the summer in shady isolated places. The snow pack was good this year and the runoff slow because of lower average temperatures.

Parking the truck and trailer at Ferguson Lake's south end campground, Sara unloaded the horses. The pack horse Pat didn't have much of a load to carry; Sara had elected to use the two-man tent. The one-man tent issued by the Service was too small and uncomfortable for Sara. In the pannier were freeze dried food, a camp pot, and Sara's sleeping bag, plus some incidentals and a half bale of hay. There were two rural stores a short distance away where she could restock her consumables should her patrol be extended. The citation book, the required extra ammo for the 30-30 rifle and the Sig Sauer 10mm automatic pistol were carried in her saddle bags. Sara wore the pistol in plain view. She was required to wear the pistol for the duration of the patrol. Sara slid the Winchester into the scabbard. The scabbard was strapped to the saddle between the saddle blanket and the saddle fender.

Sara saddled Moe and tied Curley to Pat with a longer lead rope. The horses were bonded to each other, and she didn't worry about one of them wandering off. The bright yellow slicker and her heavy coat were rolled together and tied behind the cantle of her saddle.

Sara planned to patrol up the east side of the lake and camp at the far end. She sat on Moe and shifted the pistol to a more comfortable position and set off on the east trail as soon as the horses were lined up in trace to follow Moe. She estimated they would arrive at the far end of the lake before nightfall, still more than six hours away. Sara rolled the edges of her Stetson and settled it on her head. She adjusted her stirrups a little long so her legs could stretch and settled into the saddle. After an initial snort from Curley, the three horses with their human boss strolled along the well-worn bark covered trail.

Coming over a small rise in the trail, Sara found herself face to face with a man with a fly rod in his hand. He wore a set of waders and a fish creel balanced on his left hip.

"Hello, how's the fishing?" Sara smiled and dismounted.

"Not too bad, rainbows mostly, a little small, but I kept enough for dinner." The fisherman watched Sara dismount. He noticed the flash of her shield attached to her shirt. There was no doubt Sara was a ranger by her tan shirt and the pistol on her hip. "I suppose you'd like to see my fish and my license?"

"Yes sir, please." Sara put out her hand when the man took a folded piece of paper from his shirt pocket and handed it to her. It was his license issued in the Winthrop office, which surprised her. Only a dozen licenses were issued there. She checked the date and the signature and found everything correct. The man started to open the creel, but Sara waved him off. "No need, you seem like an honest man. The license is valid for rainbows and cuts. The rest are catch and release, any questions?"

"No ma'am. Nice doing business with you." He folded the license and returned it to his shirt pocket.

"Have you seen anyone else up this way?"

"No I haven't seen anyone. Wait, there was a guy with fishing gear on this side yesterday. He had one of those little short casting rods and hip waders. We just said howdy and that's about it."

"Okay thanks, you have a good day. You do have a cell phone with you?"

The man patted his other shirt pocket and smiled.

"Good, stay safe." Sara climbed back into the saddle and led the horses past the man who tipped his hat. Sara tipped her hat in return and continued up the trail.

Just before midnight, Sara heard two shots a minute apart echo off the lake. She couldn't tell the location of the shots, but thought they were on the opposite side of the lake from where she had checked the fisherman. She made a note in her logbook about the shots and noted the shots were the flat report of a pistol, not the crack of a high-power rifle. She would investigate tomorrow if she had to travel completely around the lake. Sara had tied her horses on a picket line and gave each a handful of oats. Tomorrow she would find a place where the horses could graze for a couple of hours. She liked to give the horses grazing time when she couldn't let them graze all night. There was the light of a small fire about a half mile away on the west side of the lake.

First light found Sara eating a plate of powered eggs and dried bacon. Thirty minutes later she was on the trail. She left Pat and Moe on the picket line and rode Curley to investigate the shots she heard the previous night. When she approached the location of the camp, a man and woman greeted her.

"Morning ranger, we've got coffee on if you'd like a cup," the woman offered.

Sara accepted the offer of a cup of coffee, refusing to share breakfast with the couple. "Did you hear any shots last night?" she asked.

The man who sat on a folding camp stool looked up. "Yeah, I didn't think guns were allowed up here outside of hunting season."

"You can carry if you declare at the ranger office you have a hand-gun with you and have a permit from the state to carry. Many folks carry either a heavy handgun or a rifle for protection from animals or to scare them away." Sara smiled at the man and asked, "Where do you think the shots came from?"

"I think they were down that way." The man pointed down the west side of the lake. The woman nodded in agreement.

"Thanks, I'll be heading down that way myself. Thanks for the coffee. You do have a cell phone with you?" Sara asked.

The man went into the tent and came out with a cell phone and a folded piece of paper. He handed the fishing license to Sara who checked the date, noting the license had been issued by the Everett office. "I only catch a couple of fish for breakfast or dinner. About the cell phone, it doesn't work here, but if I go over there," he pointed to a small point of land, "It works fine. We called home last night; it is kind of a second honeymoon for us, ten years."

"Congratulations, continued happiness." Sara shook both their hands and mounted Curley. She tipped her hat and started down the west side trail.

After a forty-five minute ride, Curley began to jig around, not a good sign. Sara rode along the trail toward the south end of Ferguson Lake. Curley smelled something he didn't like. Sara slipped the Winchester out of the scabbard and levered a round into the chamber. She let the hammer down gently but kept her thumb on it, prepared to thumb it back. Then she smelled it. Sara smelled the odor of a human body that had voided itself in death. Sara dismounted, and tied Curley to a tree with a lead rope.

Sara walked down the trail toward the source of the odor. She came to a ruined camp. The tent was trashed, everything was dumped on the ground, and even the sleeping bag was ripped open. Sara backed away but kept the barrel of the rifle in a search pattern left and right as she looked for a target. The odor of death was strong. She returned to Curley, opened her saddle bag and retrieved the extra ammo box and camera and dropped them into her pocket. She next cocked a round in her pistol, letting the hammer ease down.

Sara made a trip completely around the campsite. She saw signs indicating someone on horseback had come into the camp and then left. The tracks were fresh, made after the brief rain of last night. An animal had left faint tracks and the horse had stepped on the animal track and completely destroyed it, which told Sara the second person had left after the rain and shots. Sara's mind was eased a little but not enough to let her guard down; she continued to search.

Sara approached the camp from the south until the smell was so strong she covered her mouth and nose with a damp handkerchief. She entered the campsite and saw the bottom of a foot. The rest of the body lay hidden behind a bunch of huckleberry bushes. Still she searched around and kept the rifle barrel moving. Sara inspected the body. The man's body was naked, with two bullet holes, one in the chest, the other in the back of the head. Sara thought back to when she heard the shots, about a minute apart, enough time to shoot, turn the body over and put a round in the back of the head.

Per the standard procedures, Sara began to take pictures of the campsite and body. It appeared the body had been tortured; a rag or sock had been shoved into the man's mouth far enough to keep him from spitting it out. There were marks on the wrists indicating the man had been tied up when he was tortured and killed. Sara found footprints around the tent: a large, boot print with a built-up heel, like a logger or rancher, not a particularly good walking boot.

She stood close to the shore and was able to get cell service; Sara used her cell phone to call the office and was surprised when Ken Behoney answered. Sara reported the murder and the location of the campsite. Ken said he would notify the sheriff's office and use the Forest Service helicopter to fly to the site. He asked her to mark the nearest place a helicopter could land safely. Ken would send the Forest Service copter back to make room for the FBI's copter which would undoubtedly arrive from Spokane.

Securing the area, she marked a sandy patch of land not far from the camp as the landing zone. Sara pulled out one of the five red smoke grenades she carried in her saddlebags. She sat down to wait upwind from the camp, knowing she would probably be at the site for the next few hours. She took the saddle off Curley. Sara found an open area with grass not far away and hobbled the horse there.

She kept the rifle with her; the murderer couldn't be too far away. Even on horseback it was some distance to a major road, a trip of at least five hours on horseback. The closest access road was at the south end of the lake at the small campground and parking area. She didn't remember having seen any trucks or trailers parked there when she had arrived yesterday. Getting out her maps, she studied them and found there was an improved macadam road about a twelve-mile ride over the ridge to the west. She looked closer and saw there was a hiking trail up over the ridge and it crossed a Forest Service fire road. The fire road intersected a north-south improved road. From the campsite to the improved road over the ridge and with the twists and turns of the trail and the fire road it was at least fourteen miles, about a twelve-hour ride. She remembered the road being well maintained. Sara bet it was the way the murderer had come and gone. Sara used the map and measured distance and the terrain. She thought a man on horseback might be able to make it to the road in ten hours depending on the condition of the horse and the hiking portion of the trail.

Sara called the Sheriff's office and Roy answered. "It's me, and there has been a murder at Ferguson Lake. I think the murderer is on horseback and going over a hiking trail west of the lake to intersect a fire road and then to the improved road up the valley to Canada or south to join the traffic on Highway Two or the interstate. Can you call the helicopter and have the pilot check the trail and the fire road as soon as they drop off my boss?"

"Yeah sure Sara, I'll take care of it. Give me the grids of the trail and road you think the killer is using." Roy had a topographical 1:100,000 scale map in his office. Sara read the grid and dropped the call and left the rest to Roy.

In the distance, Sara heard a helicopter beating the air. She moved to the improvised landing zone ready to pop the red smoke grenade. She called Ken's cell phone and asked him to drop a deputy at her campsite and bring Pat and Moe to the murder site. When the plane came up the lake, she pulled the pin and tossed the smoke into the center of the LZ. The helicopter pilot saw the smoke and pulled a hard left bank and lined up on the small LZ. As soon as the skids touched the ground, Ken was out of the bird followed by one of the sheriff's deputies.

Sara explained what she had done to secure the site. The deputy surrounded the area with bright yellow crime scene tape twice around the campsite. A second helicopter, this one black with FBI markings, came from the east. It must have been on the Colville Indian Reservation to get there so fast. Sara used a second grenade and popped the smoke as soon as she saw the helicopter. This one would probably be staying.

To make room, The FS helicopter lifted off and went to drop the second deputy at Sara's camp to bring her gear and two horses to the murder site.

The helicopter landed and the pilot immediately shut down the engine. The main rotor slowly spun to a stop. A man wearing a red Pendleton shirt and gray-green wool trousers climbed out followed by a second man.

The agent introduced himself and his partner. "Special Agent Edward Pena and this is Special Agent Marc Bennet, from the Spokane office. We just happened to be returning to Spokane from the reservation when your call came in to our office. We diverted to here. We had enough gas to come here and get to Winthrop with a bit to spare, so here we are. Who found the body?"

Sara stepped forward. "I found it about two hours ten minutes ago. I got to the site at 0911. I checked the time so I could make an accurate entry in my logbook. I could tell the camp wasn't trashed by animals because food was littered on the ground. I wanted to make sure the killer wasn't still in the area. I didn't find the body for another thirty minutes when I approached the camp from the south."

"Ranger," Agent Pena questioned, "could you run your activities since you arrived at the lake?"

Sara related her activities since leaving Winthrop. When she was through the two agents were staring at her. "The pilot just reported he has a request from the sheriff's office to fly over a trail and road on his way to Winthrop to refuel. Do you know anything about that request?"

"Yes sir, I suggested the sheriff's office make the request." Sara waited for the agents to ask why. She didn't care much for Pena but Bennet seemed to be an okay cop. She addressed Bennet. "Agent, I did a quick map survey on how someone could get out of this area without being seen."

"How do you know it's a man?" Pena interrupted.

"Well sir, judging by the size of the footprints, before they got messed up. I would say the feet are a little large for a female. A woman with a size twelve would be noticeable."

"You're kind of a smart ass aren't you ranger?" Pena turned to ignore Sara.

Agent Bennet stepped forward. "Ranger, can I call you Sara?" He received a small smile from Sara. "Sara, could you show us what you mean by a map survey."

"Sure Agent Bennet, mind if I call you Marc? Well Marc, I didn't see any trace of our man's vehicle which he would have had to stash; a truck and horse trailer are pretty hard to hide up here near the lake. Since he left on horseback, he must be taking a trail out of the lake area to intersect a road where his truck and trailer could have been left without attracting a lot of attention. According to the map, there is a trail, a pretty good horse trail over that ridge there." Sara pointed to a ridge seven miles to the west. "Without pushing, he could ride from here to the road on the other side of that ridge in about ten to twelve hours depending on the trail condition and the condition of his animal. It was dark so that would slow him down some too. I think it is worth the gas to fly the trail and road and look for a truck and horse trailer."

"Not bad reasoning Sara. How would we identify the truck if we did see it?"

"I would guess it's a two-horse standard trailer being pulled by a F150 or a truck of that type and size. The exit to the north is the border crossing, which has both Border Patrol and RCMP facilities. My guess he doesn't think we'd figure he would go over the ridge. I think he would drive south and try to join the usual traffic on the way to Moses Lake, Yakima, or over the hill to the Seattle area. I would guess he thinks he has a ten to twelve-hour head start. By using the helicopter we can cut that lead to a couple of hours. Of course that's just a guess, you understand."

Bennet walked away, deep in thought. Sara saw him put his hand over his head and spin his hand around, signaling the pilot of the helicopter to start the engine. Bennent returned to where Sara and Agent Pena waited. "Pena, you stay with the ranger here and the deputy bringing the horses. I'm taking the helicopter and fly the trail and the road on the other side of the ridge. We'll gas up before coming back here. You may have to ride out with the ranger or deputy. You can ride can't you?"

Embarrassed, Pena shook his head negatively. He glanced over at the horse that stood quietly on the short picket line.

"Hey, I only have the one saddle and these mustangs are pretty rough to ride bareback," she said coming to the defense of the agent. "Of course it's only about a four-mile ride to my truck." Sara smiled at Pena, who returned it with a weak smile of his own.

"My other two horses are at my camp from last night about two miles from here. Ken had a deputy dropped off and he will bring the horses here," she said and confirmed Bennet's plan. "Listen, I should wait until the sheriff says we can leave and the coroner declares the body. I know the deputy would feel better if there were at least two people here, besides the DB. I know my boss has to get back to Winthrop; there is going to be a load of paperwork and the media's going to be a pest."

Bennet turned to Sara's District Supervisor. "Listen, I'd like to have Sara ride with me in the helicopter. She is the expert on what we are looking for. Agent Pena can stay with the deputy. I think we'd better get moving or the killer is going to get away." Marc turned to Sara. "Will your horses be all right until you return? I guess it is going to be about three to four hours before we get you back here."

"Oh sure." Ken answered for her. "Gene is on his way here with the horses and can take care of them. Another ranger came in this morning and he can ride out here and take the horses back to Sara's trailer." Ken said, "Gene should be here within a few minutes. Agent Bennet, you take Sara and check that trail. I'll wait until Gene gets here before leaving. My helicopter is on the way to pick up the coroner. I'll ride back with him."

Sara addressed Ken, "Just give the horses some water and there are a few flakes of hay in the bottom of the pack panniers." As they were talking, the deputy rode into the site and ground tied the horses near Curley. Sara repeated her instructions for the deputy.

"Sure Sara, no problem." The deputy lifted the cover over the small pack panniers Sara used. As Sara followed Marc toward the helicopter, she saw Gene removing the panniers from Pat.

"I forgot to ask, Sara, are you commissioned as a Federal Officer?" Bennet asked.

"Yes, I was commissioned a few months ago." She patted the pistol on her hip. "Wait here." She turned and ran to where her saddle now rested on the canvas pack after the panniers were removed from Curley. She retrieved her rifle from where she had put it back in the scabbard. She checked her pocket for the spare box of cartridges and ran to climb aboard the helicopter, taking a back seat. A minute later, they were roaring out over the lake. The pilot followed Sara's directions and picked up the trail over the ridge.

Fifteen minutes later, the helicopter dropped down the west slope of the ridge. They could see the road in the distance. Marc told the pilot to swing around in a circle. Sara spotted a dark-colored truck with a brown horse trailer. A man was loading a horse; he glanced up at the helicopter, swatted the horse on the butt and slammed the back closed. In less than a minute, he was in the truck and driving fast down the road before the helicopter could land to cut him off.

The pilot flew the chopper up the road behind the truck and trailer. Trees on each side made it difficult to stay low. Marc had the pilot move in front of the truck to block the road.

The truck slowed and stopped about a hundred yards from where the chopper hovered. The driver's door opened and the barrel of a rifle appeared. A second later, the Plexiglas bubble in front of the pilot spider-webbed, the pilot grunted and the chopper landed hard. The chopper's blades hit the ground and the aircraft went from a flying machine to a wreck in half a second. Marc was busy unbuckling when a second spider-web appeared and Marc let out a loud "woof" and slumped over in his seat. The pilot moaned. Marc was silent. Sara in the back apparently hadn't been seen by the shooter; no more holes appeared in the windshield.

Sara could see the shooter walk around the open truck door and start toward the crashed helicopter. Her rifle was on the helicopter's floor. She eased down and retrieved it. Sara thumbed the hammer back. She knew a bullet was in the chamber; the rear sight was bent off to one side. *No matter*. Sara released her seat belt and let herself fall out of the helicopter onto the ground. She kept the rifle at her side out of the shooter's line of sight. She watched the man walk toward her with the bolt action rifle at first pointing at her; then the barrel lifted and pointed up and away to her right.

"Well, well. What do we have here; if it isn't a little girly ranger? Do you want to have some fun before I kill you little girl?" the man asked and laughed. His eyes were fixed on the pistol on her hip, still in the holster. He dismissed the pistol as a threat knowing he could shoot her before she could get the pistol out and cocked. The Winchester was on her right side hidden by her body, and the man did not see it.

Sara watched as the man walked up to the wrecked helicopter, the rifle again pointed at her. She watched him swing the rifle to shoot the moaning pilot. "I wouldn't do that if you want to live," Sara said in a voice a little above a whisper. The man clearly heard her and turned to see Sara holding the Winchester in her right hand like a pistol. He laughed and started to swing the rifle toward her. Sara squeezed the trigger and her bullet nearly ripped the man's shoulder off. The rifle he was holding dropped to the ground. One handed, Sara levered another round into the chamber of the Winchester. The man had been knocked backward, sat on the ground and stared at her. "Would you like to try for the other shoulder, asshole?"

The man flopped back into the dirt of the road. Sara got to her feet, removed the plastic flexi-cuffs from the pouch on her pistol belt. She exchanged the Winchester for the Sig and approached the man; he was unconscious, a pasty color, clearly in shock. The 164 grain slow-moving bullet from Sara's rifle had done major damage to the man's shoulder. Not caring, Sara pulled his arms around his back and cuffed him. She pulled him away from where he fell, did a quick search. She found a small automatic pistol in an ankle holster and left him lying on his face in the dirt.

Sara returned to the wreck and pulled the pilot out of the cockpit to the side of the road. She checked his wound which had not started bleeding yet. Sara unbuckled Marc and pulled him from the wreck. Marc was breathing, but he had a bullet hole in his upper right chest. She checked the exit wound which was large and beginning to seriously bleed. Sara did a quick first aid check to see if he was bleeding from the mouth; he wasn't. She stuffed her handkerchief into the exit wound. Sara went to the helicopter and found the first aid kit. Sara applied first aid to Marc and the pilot doing what she could for them.

Sara moved them further away from the wreaked helicopter which was leaking fuel. In Marc's shirt pocket she found a cell phone. She checked the phone menu and found a number for the dispatcher in the Spokane FBI office. She pushed the speed dial, and reported the incident to the FBI operator. Next she dialed the sheriff's office. Roy answered on the first ring. She reported everything to him with their location.

Roy finished taking Sara's short report. He called all the agencies that might have interest in the shootings. Fifteen minutes later Sara heard sirens in the distance echoing through the valley. A vehicle was coming up the road and Sara saw the reflection of red and blue lights. A WSP vehicle with the light bar on and siren wailing appeared from the dust and slid to a stop twenty feet from where she sat holding Marc Bennet's hand as he struggled to talk.

Dave Spencer jumped out of the car and quickly looked over the situation. He checked the prisoner, who was still unconscious, or maybe faking it. Sara didn't care—if he made a threatening move she would shoot him again. The pilot was conscious and in quite a bit of pain. The bullet had hit him after passing through the plastic windshield, where it lost most of its power, high on the hip and broke the pelvic bone.

Sara used the suspect's shirt to bandage his ruined shoulder. She hadn't bothered with the truck. It was obvious he was alone. With Dave watching the prisoner, Sara went to the man's trailer to check on the horse. She gave the horse some hay she found in the tack room and a drink of water from a bucket and five-gallon water can.

After checking all the injured and the prisoner, Dave searched the truck and found the registration. Behind the back of the driver's seat he found ten kilos of Mexican brown heroin, probably the motive for the murder at the lake.

Dave returned to relieve Sara, and finished searching the prisoner. He found a knife on the inside of his boot. Just to be safe, he pulled the man's pants down to his ankles and pushed what was left of his undershirt up around his neck. The man moaned and regained consciousness as Dave was searching him. When the man looked up at the trooper, Dave said, "You are a lucky man. None of the victims, two federal officers, will die which would have earned you the needle. We may still try for the death penalty. We hang people here in Washington you know." Dave read the man his Miranda Rights.

Dave got his victim box out of the cruiser's trunk and put a blanket around the injured. He sat down next to Sara to wait for the next responder. "Sara, we have got to quit meeting like this. People are going to think you enjoy shooting people. That guy makes three that I know of."

"Well, they all deserved it." She smiled at the tall trooper. "How's everything in your life?"

"It's going okay, actually better than okay. Shelly had a little girl a couple of months ago. We got married the day after she told me she was pregnant. I never thought I'd be a father. You want to see her picture?" Before Sara could answer, Dave had his wallet out and was thumbing through a series of pictures of a smiling Shelly holding a tiny baby wrapped in pink.

"They are beautiful, just beautiful Dave. You are a lucky man." She punched her friend on the arm.

The sound of an approaching helicopter interrupted them. She recognized the sound of a Huey as the blades beat the air into submission. It's the only way a helicopter flies, according to the men who fly them; a million pieces and parts all flying in different directions. The sound got louder and up the road came the olive drab helicopter of the Air National Guard rescue unit. The chopper landed in a cloud of dust and the pilot put the rotor blades in idle. The sounds didn't go away; another chopper followed the first to land on the road. Dave got up and moved his cruiser down the road to the curve with his light bar flashing to warn any approaching vehicles. No vehicles had passed in the hour they had been there. A deputy sheriff's car came up the road with lights flashing and parked at the other end, effectively blocking both approaches to the scene.

Roy Danner ran up the road and went directly to Sara. "Are you okay, anything broken, shot, what?"

"Nope sorry, you can't be a nurse this trip." Sara leaned into Roy's arms and he kissed the top of her head, holding her wrapped in his arms. After a minute he said, "Sara, I've got work to do. I'll be back, don't let those hugs get away." Roy left to talk to Dave and the medic from the first helicopter. The first bird would take the pilot and Marc to a Spokane hospital. The second bird would transport the prisoner to Seattle where he would be held in a Federal hospital facility. A third helicopter from the Forest Service was assigned to pick up Ken Behoney and Agent Pena from Ferguson Lake, taking them to Winthrop. The deputy would use Sara's truck and trailer to bring her horses to Winthrop.

The Winthrop clinic had been notified and Pat O'Hara would check Sara for injuries from the helicopter crash. The Regional Fish and Wildlife Law Enforcement Service Director was flying in from San Francisco to conduct interviews and the investigation of the shooting of a criminal by one of his rangers. The Secretary of Agriculture had been notified and a statement would be issued by him about the use of firearms by the rangers and the shooting following the downing of an FBI helicopter.

The Secretary was not a happy camper. He was an anti-gun, anti-deadly force advocate. Rumor was, he wanted to fire Sara for shooting the criminal before warning him. The Secretary discounted the warning she gave him when he was about to shoot the pilot. When he tried to take all the weapons away from Fish and Wildlife Law Enforcement Rangers, he found their mandate had been set forth by Congress and he didn't have the power to disarm the rangers.

Only the President can issue an Executive Order to disarm commissioned officers and that would be political suicide, disarming one of the Federal Law Enforcement agencies.

Since Dave was required to be checked also, he drove Sara back to the Winthrop Ranger Headquarters where she would meet the deputy bringing her truck, trailer and horses back from Ferguson Lake. Behoney left orders for Sara to immediately go to the Winthrop clinic.

The clinic was closed when Sara drove her truck into the parking lot. She saw a light on in the lobby. Looking closely, she saw reflected light in back where the examination rooms were located. Reluctantly she climbed the steps, opened the door and walked in. Jean was in her private office behind the desk doing paper work and looked up. Jean jumped out of her chair, raced around the desk and hugged Sara. A word did not pass between the two women. Jean looked her friend in the eyes; tears pooled in the nurse's. Still without a word, Jean went back behind her desk, put her head down and started reading a chart.

Sara stared at the nurse shocked at the expression of affection. A little confused, Sara continued back toward Pat's office. The door was open. She stood in the doorway and knocked lightly. Pat looked up and stared at her. The expression on his face told her he'd heard the story about the shooting on the road and the murder at Ferguson Lake. Pat was still on pre-deployment leave and was only working to give the replacement doctor some time off.

"Take your clothes off. I need to check you for unidentified injuries. God damn it Sara, when are you going to quit looking for trouble? I don't know what we would do around here if something happened to you. Go into the exam room one. Do you want Jean to stay?"

"No, it's okay. I trust you," Sara said speaking contritely, but not knowing why. She was the one who'd almost been killed. She went into the examination room with the large 1 painted on the door. She closed it, and began to take her clothes off. A paper gown was on the exam table, so she put it on and sat down on the table trying not to tear the paper covering.

A knock on the door announced Pat; he entered followed by Jean. "I thought Jean might as well listen and learn about everything without having to put two and two together like I've had to lately." Pat sat down on the examination room rolling stool while Jean sat in the chair.

"First, I need to check you over, top to bottom. It's a nice bottom too.," he said over his shoulder to Jean, who chuckled.

Jean opened a folder and a chart of the human body was fastened by clips to the inside flap. "Ready."

"Okay, let me check your eyes and ears." Pat was thorough; he looked under each eyelid and for any foreign objects in her ears, under her fingernails. He pushed the gown down around her waist. The doctor examined her back from the hair line to her waist. He found a bruise below her right breast tender to the touch. Sara hadn't even noticed it before. There was a tiny puncture in the bruise center. Getting a magnifying glass, Pat found a plastic sliver imbedded just below the skin. He used tweezers and removed a half inch long plastic sliver. Shaking his head, he dropped the sliver of plastic into a glass bowl. The sliver could have caused serious infection if it had gone undetected and untreated. When he pulled out the stirrups, Sara started to protest, but a look on Jean's face told her to keep the comments to herself, this was serious.

Gritting her teeth, Sara looked first at Pat and then Jean. Shaking her head she removed the paper gown, crumpled it up and tossed it in the waste basket. "Now, let's just get this over with."

"I'm sorry Sara, the sheriff's office and the Feds ordered this physical exam. I'm glad they did, because we found that piece of plastic and it could have been serious if it didn't work itself out." Pat scooted his stool back. "Look Sara, I don't know what's going on, but I have to do everything including the pelvic exam. Who did you piss off this time?"

"I don't know, one FBI agent, I think his name is Pena didn't like me very much. Now that his partner is in the hospital and rehab for the next six months, I bet he's just pissed."

"Yeah, that could be. I've got to ask these questions."

"Go ahead, you've seen all of me and know all my deepest secrets." Sara shook her head slowly from side to side. She watched as Pat took a blood sample and sealed one capsule into an envelope and a second capsule he handed to Jean to run tests.

"Pat, do we have to do all this? We've never done anything like this before after a shooting incident." Jean stood up and started for the door.

"Jean, sit down. You know we have to do the physical, set up the X-ray. We need a urine sample too. Get Sara a cup. You need to be in here to witness. Either that or I witness." Pat looked at Sara.

"Whatever. Give me the damn cup. I'm getting pretty good at this. Hand me that bedpan." She pointed at a bedpan sitting on the counter next to the sink.

Finished, Sara handed the sample to Pat. When Jean returned he handed the sample to her to run the tests. "Sara, I have to ask. Are you sexually active? And with whom?"

"Pat, you know I am but not with Roy anymore. You do know Roy, your team roping partner." Sara was pissed.

"Okay, lay back, feet in the stirrups please. Excuse the fingers." He pulled on a pair of rubber gloves.

"Don't worry about it, you've been in there before."

After Jean returned with the results of the urine sample, Pat took three X-ray pictures.

"Just what the hell are you looking for, Pat?" Sara challenged. "I've never had a physical like this one and with you and Jean being friends, and at least I think we are friends I don't know what to think."

Jean met them in Pat's office. "Everything normal: urine, blood, X-rays; nothing unusual. Can we tell her now?"

"Sara, the reason the Feds gave us for doing the physical and not telling you anything about it until all the tests were completed was because of who you captured and what he was carrying. The heroin you and Dave found is laced with a very toxic poison. The drugs destination were the colleges and universities around the state. Free heroin—it would have wiped out a major portion of the users. The man you captured is one of the domestic terrorists who want to make a large terrorist impact and publicity by targeting college and even high-school students. The toxin is a time-release poison carried by bacteria and released into the bloodstream. It is possible there could be a lethal infection up to five persons away from the initial human carrier. It is transmitted like Ebola, by body fluids. Once the virus got started it would be hell to stop. You're smart, do the math. Oh yeah, the five persons is just a guess, it could go much further."

"You're kidding, right?"

"Sadly no, the Mexican brown heroin is the best carrier outside of the body. The shelf life of the virus is so far undetermined in the medium of the Mexican brown. It's possible the poison could infect ten persons away from the initial carrier's infection just through bodily contact. It wouldn't be lethal, but it might be incapacitating a long way down-stream. That's why we needed to give you a physical. Don't worry, all the folks that were there are going through the same procedure. I bet Dave Spencer and Roy are livid. Oh yeah, the guy you shot is a carrier and infected. He probably won't live to see a trial."

"Well then, I guess this has been a good thing. Why didn't somebody just tell me?"

"They couldn't. The government put a secret classification on the information. I'm taking a chance telling you. They came and scared the hell out of Jean; Bruce was here and they just took him outside without telling him anything. Jean, when she goes home still won't be able to tell him." The doctor leaned back in his chair. "My leave has been cancelled effective tonight, or tomorrow. I have to return to California tomorrow before 2400 hours. The verbal notice from the medical folks at the Pentagon said I can expect to be deployed within the next few weeks. The First Marine Division is deploying in the next couple of months. I've been assigned as a Medical Officer Forward with the lead surgeon for further assignment to the 1st Marines. The deployment is for one year. I suppose the drug thing will be over by then."

"What about the clinic? What about Jean?"

"There is a temporary doctor on call here now and another coming from Spokane to take care of the clinic. I expect to be back here about the first of May next year. Don't get married until I get back; I want to give the bride away. That is if your brother can't make it and is deployed. I've heard the F/A18 squadrons are doing quick turn around with the deployed carriers." He grinned at the two women. Most of the tension left the room. "Why don't you go home, I'll see you in a year. Take care of Jean for me. When you see Roy, tell him, I'm holding him to the promise he will rope with me." Pat stood up and gathered Sara into his arms, joined by Jean a heartbeat later. The three friends held each other, and let the news sink in. "Try not to shoot anyone while I'm away, okay?"

Chapter Eighteen

Love Found

It was the second month of Sara and Randy's on-again, off-again dating and a month after the shootout at Ferguson Lake. After steak, baked potato, steamed veggies, a tossed salad and a half bottle of wine, the couple sat at the table talking, telling stories of childhood adventures. The following morning, Sara was to leave for Camp Pendleton and the West Coast Invitational qualification match for the National Match Shooting Team. Sara had invited Randy to take her to dinner.

After Randy drove Sara home, she invited him for coffee and some conversation and maybe to watch a movie.

"Sara, don't get the wrong idea, but you may have noticed I don't drink much coffee and it's a little late for a movie. I'm excited to come in, but I won't unless you're prepared to have breakfast with me."

Randy's statement stopped her for about ten seconds. She stared into his eyes. When Randy turned to leave, Sara put her hand on his arm and gently pulled him back.

"Are you sure Sara? I don't take much to casual sex. I find it cheap and degrading."

"I'm sure Randy, I think it's right. Are you sure?"

He leaned down and kissed her for the first time as a lover would. "God Sara, I've wanted you from the first time I saw you in the office."

"It took me awhile, but I'm here now. I want this with you more than anything I've ever wanted." Sara turned her face up for him; her eyelids slowly closed over her sparkling eyes as she leaned into the kiss.

Randy kissed her again with feeling and passion. Sara melted into his arms.

"I think we had better go in before the town gets a new show." Sara pulled him by the hand up the steps to her apartment.

As soon as he was inside and the door closed, Sara was in his arms again. Her arms went around his neck to pull his lips to hers. When they came up for air, she pushed his jacket off his shoulders and let it fall to the floor. She took his hand and pulled him toward the bedroom.

Sara stood in front of Randy and stared into his eyes, a question unasked.

"Sara, you are the most beautiful, intelligent and talented woman I have ever met. You own my heart." He kissed her gently. His hands unbuttoned her Pendleton plaid shirt and pulled the shirt from her jeans, but he left it on her. She faced him, and the brown bra cupped the swell of her breasts. Her nipples pushed against the silken material and were clearly visible. He glanced around the small room. A braided throw rug was beside the bed; an LED alarm clock on the nightstand cast a faint glow about the room.

Randy moved her until the edge of the bed touched the back of her knees. He gently removed the shirt and lightly brushed her breasts confined by the bra with the back of his fingers. Sara shivered at his touch, her eyes closed. Randy unbuckled her belt, unzipped her jeans and pulled them down to her ankles. A pair of bikini panties matching the bra did little to hide her. He helped her remove her boots and step out of the jeans.

Randy stood unmoving in front of her. Sara opened her eyes and saw a softness reflected in his eyes and a serious smile on his face. She reached out and unbuttoned his shirt. He shrugged it off as Sara unbuckled his belt and unzipped his jeans. He toed off his boots and his socks and stepped out of the jeans and kicked them toward the foot of the bed. Randy stood before Sara wearing only his white jockey shorts. Sara reached behind her and unhooked the bra. She let the bra slide down her arms and drop to the floor.

Randy leaned down and kissed and licked her nipples. When he lightly blew on them the nipples grew hard and protruded, begging for attention. Randy spent minutes attending to Sara's breasts. She shivered and he dropped to the floor and kissed her through the cotton fabric and breathed on her as he shared his warmth. He hooked his thumbs in the sides of the panties and pulled them down.

Randy stared at Sara. Her brownish, blonde pubic hair was trimmed short and he could see her clearly. He put his arms around her and pulled her against him. His lips kissed her and she moaned as her legs threatened to collapse from under her.

"I want you in me. Make love to me, Randy." Sara gasped, and drew back from him. Randy pushed her back onto the bed and slid his length into her. He held himself still until she began to move beneath him. A minute later both were sated for the moment. They made love twice more before falling asleep in each other's arms.

Randy woke first. He supported his head on his hand and studied the beautiful woman's body next to him. He kissed the back of her neck. Sara moaned and turned toward him. An eye studied him through a small slit. A smile slowly spread over her face.

"Does this make us an item?" she asked sleepily.

"You bet it does, that is if you still want me?" Randy said softly.

Sara's eyes snapped opened wide. "Want you, I'm never going to let you out of this bed. Want you, are you insane? Just try to get away." She reached under the covers and took him in her hand. With her other hand she threw the covers away from them, leaned down and kissed him and brought that certain part of him fully alive. "My God man, are you for real?"

"Yeah, do you want to use that or put it back to sleep?" He laughed as he took her breast and brought the nipple to his mouth and pushed her back onto the pillows to admire her with his eyes, lips, and tongue.

It was an hour later when they stumbled into the bathroom and took a shower together. While he was drying her, he brought up the question again. "Are we an item now?"

"After last night you can ask me that. Damn straight we're an item. I just can't believe it took me so long to realize the man of my dreams was right in front of me. If you'll still have me, I'm all yours Mr. Springer."

Sara glanced at the clock beside the bed. "Oh my God, I've got to get to Seattle. I've got a 1400 flight to San Diego. The rifles are already on their way overnight delivery so I don't have to worry about them. God, Randy, I hate to leave just when we are getting started. I'll be back in ten days and I want you here in my bed when I get home."

"Sara, you know I've got a two-week patrol I'm supposed to take Janet on beginning tomorrow. I think I'll just turn your order around and say, I want you in your bed, naked, waiting for me when I get back."

Randy kissed her and touched her. She broke away stomped to her dresser and took out another pair of panties. "Damn you Springer, you touch me and I get wet." Sara took off her jeans, went into the bathroom and came out wearing the new panties. "You stay away from me, damn it." Sara quickly kissed him on the lips and was out the door before he could touch her again. He found a spare key on the kitchen table with a love note explaining the key and saying she would call his cell that evening. Randy grinned and cleaned up the apartment before he locked the door and went to check on the horses.

Chapter Nineteen

Camp Pendleton

The afternoon sun began its long drop into the Pacific Ocean. Sara enjoyed the warm sunshine on the BOQ patio when a shadow passed over the book she was reading. She looked up and saw the outline of a man standing with the sunlight at his back surrounded by a golden halo.

"You're in my light."

"I think I've always been in your light Sara."

She recognized the voice and jumped to her feet and threw her arms around Doctor Pat O'Hara. "I didn't know you were staying here." Sara dropped back onto her lounger and pointed to the lounge next to her. "Jean told me you had left for Camp Pendleton after your leave was canceled. She blamed it on the murder at Ferguson Lake and the tainted drugs."

Pat sat and pulled his lounge chair closer to Sara. "Yeah, I've finished my orientation and have been assigned as the primary doctor for the 2nd Battalion of the 1st Marines. I'm going home in a couple of days to finish my pre-deployment leave. We have a new doc at the clinic who will take my place while I'm gone. If he works out, we'll ask him to stay on. We need three doctors really, especially if you keep shooting potential patients. I only have six days of leave left so I will only be gone a week."

"How did you end up in this establishment?" Sara asked.

"It was the only BOQ with rooms available. I'm scheduled to deploy with the advance party of the MEF. The actual date is restricted information right now, but if you read the papers it will be in six weeks or maybe two or three months. II MEF has three months left in country before we relieve them. The medical rotation is a bit different and a lot depends on the availability of personnel and overseas control dates for the Navy's full time Docs." Pat smiled at his best friend. "Okay, tell me what I've missed."

"It turns out Ranger Randy Springer is the best roper in the whole east side of the state, both as a header and heeler. He's been giving me lessons and teaching the other ropers. As you know, he also trained his own mustang horses and is helping other ropers train mustangs he helped them buy at the BLM sales. When Randy showed up with the mustangs he'd trained, everyone wanted one. Spokane was having a big show and sale with over 150 mustangs available. Randy went to Spokane with those who were interested in the wild horses and helped them select the best of the stock available. I've been advanced a whole number as a header. I'm now a solid two, thanks to Randy."

"That's nice to know Sara, but what about your love life?" Pat knew Sara ended the affair with Roy some time ago.

"You know Roy and I broke up before you came down here the first time. I didn't date at all for awhile and started dating Randy Springer off and on. He's been busy with patrols and I've been out by myself on patrols. Right now he's on a two or three week patrol with a new ranger transfer from Ohio. It's her first longer orientation patrol for the Central Washington area. Randy has been giving her riding and horsemanship lessons. I was assigned her instructor in weapons and threat recognition. It seems only Washington, Idaho, Oregon, Northern California and Montana use regular mounted patrols. The rest of the country is patrolled with 4 by 4 vehicles." Sara grinned. "Let me tell you the new ranger has been in culture shock since she arrived in Winthrop." Sara put her forgotten book in her large beach bag after she dog-eared her place in the novel.

Pat sat in the lounge chair beside Sara so the sun wouldn't be in her eyes. "I thought you would be at the range or the gun-smith's instead of lazing in the afternoon sun. Better still, why aren't you on the beach?"

"What beach? I thought this was a harbor where big landing ships come to dock." Sara looked toward the harbor where one of the Air Cushion Amphibious Crafts (LCAC) was off-loading vehicles. She watched as one of the huge desert painted tanks clanked ashore. The tank drove up the beach and was met by a group of Marines with hoses to wash the corrosive seawater from the tank. Four Marines each carrying a buckets of suds and water scrubbed the tank with a brush then wrapped a towel around a thin pole and swabbed the main gun before rinsing the gun and the tank with the hose.

"Do the Marines always wash the tanks and Jeeps when they come back from wherever they've been?" Sara was fascinated by how the Marines took care of their equipment.

"Yeah, every Marine who is part of the tank's crew or driver of one of the other vehicles stays working on their equipment until it is ready for inspection. I've sat where you are and watched them work for hours on one piece of gear." By Pat's tone, Sara could tell Pat was proud of his Marines and his association with them.

"Back to your orientation to the harbor, there is a very nice beach a fifteen minute walk from here. It has tables, shade and fire pits for weenie roasts. You can get special permission from MWR to use the beach after hours."

"What's MWR?"

"I don't know the whole thing, but Welfare and Recreation are part of it. I think, think mind you, the M stands for Morale or Manpower, but I'm not positive about that." He hesitated before asking. "How about joining me or us for dinner? I'm meeting some of the medical people at a fish place at the harbor."

"I don't want to intrude Pat. That's your time with the people you work with."

"You wouldn't be intruding. I'd like you to meet my boss and the people I spend a lot of time with at work. You'd like them and my boss. She's a lot like you, stubborn." Pat's boyish smile washed over his face. "Come on, you'll have fun and I have a surprise for you."

"I don't know, my rifles are supposed to be delivered to the range armory tonight and I sort of wanted to be there when they came in." Sara was making excuses, weak excuses. She wanted to call Randy before he left on patrol. The more she thought about Randy the stronger the attraction became. She could call him later and wake him up. She would get back at him for keeping her awake last night making love. "Okay, but I need to change. I don't think shorts and a T-shirt would be appropriate wear to meet your boss."

At 1900 hours, Sara met Pat in the BOQ lobby. Together they walked out through the Del Mar gate and the mile to the harbor restaurant. Pat led her to a small group of men and women sharing the large table in the restaurant bar.

"Ladies, gentlemen and boss, I would like you to meet my friend, ex-girlfriend, team roping partner and life saver, Sara Bennett of the United States Rifle and Pistol team." Pat started with the three nurses, another doctor and finished by introducing her to his boss. "Sara this is Lieutenant Commander Sabrina Springer, the heart and soul of this team." Pat wore a huge grin plastered on his face.

Sara was dumbstruck. "Oh my God, you're Randy's sister Sabrina."

"How do you know my retarded baby brother?" Sabrina smiled.

Sara was at a loss for words. "Ah, Randy and I work together for the Fish and Wildlife Law Enforcement Service."

"So you're the one he's been waiting for? I think I should warn you. Whatever he says you can take it to the bank. He speaks with his heart and not always his brain." Sabrina smiled then stepped forward and hugged Sara. Sabrina glanced at those watching. "Come on people, it's time for food." Holding Sara by the arm Sabrina led them into the dining room where an extra long table had been set for them. She seated Sara next to her so they could talk.

It was over coffee and dessert when Sara leaned over to Sabrina after glancing at her watch. "I want to call Randy tonight before it gets too late. I think I should go."

Sabrina smiled at Sara. "Don't worry, we'll call him later." Sabrina watched the disappointment come over Sara's face. "I call him a lot later than this and it's good to make him wait awhile." Sabrina sighed. "You're sleeping with him."

Sara looked away at first, then said, "Yes, the first time was last night. I don't know if I should tell his sister, but he is an awesome lover. God, he brought me up as least three levels; way beyond anything I ever experienced before."

Sabrina smiled and her face brightened. "Bess says the same thing about Dad and Bev about Brent. You have got to get Randy to take you to the ranch. He's never brought a girl home. Even in high school and college he never did. There was a time we all thought he and Sue were going to become an item. Instead they found a different kind of relationship, like brother and sister. Even today, they are defensive and selfish of the time they have together." Sabrina sat back and stared at Sara. "Oh God, you're a natural blonde. Dad is going to have a fit, a good fit but a fit just the same."

"What's he got against blondes?" Sara was confused.

"Dad said, if another blonde showed up he was going to move and live in the line shack. Bess and Bev are both blondes. Mary Ann, Sue and Gail are blondes and No-see-em, that's my baby sister Lori, four years old, is a towhead. Wilma, Ben's wife is blonde too. The only brunettes are Charlene and Margie on the whole ranch except for Charlene's kids, Bea, Jessie and Cassie. You would think the ranch people were transplanted from Sweden or Norway."

Sara and Sabrina excused themselves, said good night and walked back to the BOQ and Sara's room to call Randy. Sara handed Sabrina her cell phone with a mischievous grin matched by Sabrina. Using Sara's phone she dialed Randy's number.

The phone rang and was answered on the second ring. "I've been waiting, thinking you've found another lover down there in sunny Southern California."

"Now why would I want another lover, Randy?"

"Sabrina? Damn it put Sara on—no wait. Send her to the bathroom, I've got some questions for you."

"Okay, just a minute." Sabrina motioned she wanted some alone time with the phone and sent Sara out onto the balcony. "Okay, Sara's on the balcony, what's on your feeble little mind?"

Randy waited a full minute organizing his thoughts before beginning to question his sister. "Sabrina, this is serious. I'm almost sure I love Sara. I've never been in love before, so I'm not sure my feelings are really love."

"Why are you asking me? I've never been in love either." Sabrina said just above a whisper.

"Brie, I'm confused. Sara has dated a bit since I've been at Winthrop. I don't think I could handle her rejection. I want to be with her all the time. She's smart, courageous and beautiful. Did you know she shot a criminal who was about to kill Pat and his nurse?"

'She did that?" Sabrina said impressed.

"Yeah and she was a smokejumper too."

"Are you going to take her to the ranch? You should. Dad and Bess need to meet her. Let them know you are human and can fall in love like the rest of us mortals."

"Yeah, what about you; are you in love?"

"We're not talking about me. I knew you'd twist this around to me. I just knew it," Sabrina snapped.

"You know it's only because we love you. Now will you let me talk dirty to my squeeze?" He laughed into the phone. "I assume you approve of Sara, yes-no?"

"Yeah, I do Randy. For what it is worth you have my blessing and support."

"Thanks Brie, that means a lot to me. Now, please let me talk to Sara so I can tell her I miss her. Love you too Brie."

"Okay, I love you too Bro, hang on." Sabrina opened the balcony door and handed the phone to Sara.

"Sara?" Randy asked when he heard a soft "Hi" from the phone. "I hope you and Brie had a good talk at dinner. Just so you know, she approves of you and thinks you're great too." Randy hesitated. "I'm just going to say one thing then I'm going to hang up. If you have questions Brie can answer them." He waited for Sara to say something. When she didn't, he said, "I miss you Sara Bennett." The phone went dead.

Sara stared at the phone. Tears came unbidden and spilled down her cheeks. Sabrina opened the door, took one look at Sara and rushed across the room.

"Did he tell you he loved you or something else?"

"No, yes, he said he missed me. Oh God Sabrina, what am I to do?"

"Do you think you love him? Can you feel it? Come on Sara, you know. Randy's been around you for some time. You know if you love him. It's in your eyes and I'm sure your heart knows one way or the other. Do you love him?"

"God Sabrina, I do. I really do but what about my time with Pat and Roy? Won't he be upset about that?"

"Not unless you make a big deal out of those affairs. You have an opportunity to start fresh with Randy. He probably does love you or at least considers you a possible life partner. He told me months ago when he met you, you might be the one. Of course it's your decision."

Sabrina stayed with Sara and they talked about Randy until Sabrina had to return to her own BOQ room. She had an early meeting with the hospital's commanding officer and another staff meeting with the commander of the MEF's forward deploying units. Sara was the senior medical officer who would deploy with the forward unit. Pat would transfer to the 1st Marine Regiment for assignment to the 2nd Infantry Battalion. Pat had trained with the 2nd Battalion, 1st Marines during most of the training exercises. He had been issued an M9 pistol as his personal weapon and qualified expert with the M4 rifle. Headquarters, Marine Corps and the Navy's Senior Medical Officer with the Office of the Chief of Naval Operations had extended his one-year tour to two years, hence the extended training period prior to deployment and the pre-deployment leave. Pat was actually looking forward to the adventure in Afghanistan.

Sabrina was getting another reservist, a trauma nurse who deployed six months before with the Army and volunteered for another tour when asked by the Navy due to the limited number of qualified surgery and trauma care nurses.

* * *

For the next two days, Sara practiced on the known distance targets, refining the dope on each of her rifles. The Marine match weapons specialist tightened her trigger pull and she needed to practice and get used to the new trigger break. During a practice round shooting the competitive course, Sara scored high in the long distance known range but finished third behind Marine Chief Warrant Officer Nancy Clark and an Air Force security sniper, Staff Sergeant Joyce Olson. Sara competed in the open 1,000 meter shoot and finished fifth overall. The Air Force shooter was disqualified in one match due to an equipment malfunction. The Marine Chief Warrant Officer in charge of the armory worked with a Marine Master Gunnery Sergeant weapon's specialist most of the night rebuilding her rifle to specifications. At 0515, as the sun crested the Ortega hills she sent the first rounds down range from the 300 meter firing line on the practice range. Forty minutes later she was on the 1,000 meter line zeroing her rifle. Satisfied with what the Marines had accomplished with her match rifle, she fired a qualification string and was allowed to return to the competition. The Air Force Staff Sergeant finished in the top five, a remarkable comeback.

Sara and Nancy took their new friend and fellow shooter to the Del Mar Officer's Club for a celebration drink and then to the seafood restaurant for dinner. Sabrina joined them for baked salmon and drinks. Sabrina wanted to spend more time with Sara before Sara returned to Washington. Sara missed qualification for the National Match and the subsequent International Match at Camp Perry, Ohio, by one place but both of the other women qualified for their respective service teams.

After dinner, Sara and Sabrina excused themselves and went to Sara's room to call Randy. They knew he was on patrol and Sara was familiar with the campgrounds and where he would be camping. His government-issue cell phone would be able to receive calls at his first three camp grounds using normal telecommunication facilities. After tomorrow to contact him she would have to rely on the government facilities.

Sabrina listened to Sara's half of the conversation. "Hi Randy, it's me." She listened, then in a soft voice said, "I miss you too. Sabrina is here and wanted to talk to you." Sara handed the cell phone to Sabrina.

"Hi Randy, just wanted to talk in case I have to leave early for the Stans. The advance party will be deploying soon. If I don't have to leave with the lead element of the advance party, I should be able to get a two-week leave and make it home for a few days. I was wondering if you knew if Jeff is coming to the ranch for a vacation. I'll call the ranch before I leave but wanted to say I think you and Sara are a good match. You treat her right or I'll come back and whomp your butt." Sara listened then said, "I love you too Bro and yeah, I'll take care. Bye."

Sabrina handed the phone back to Sara. Tears glistened in her eyes and she turned away embarrassed. Sabrina went to the refrigerator and retrieved a bottle of water. She sat in her chair and stared out at the harbor.

Sara and Sabrina talked until Sabrina needed to get some rest. She had a minor procedure scheduled for the next day at 0600 hours. Sabrina knew she was assigned to the advance party and the exact deployment date for the medical element hadn't been set or it was still classified.

Sara was scheduled to leave Camp Pendleton for the San Diego airport at 0600 for a 9 a.m. flight to SeaTac airport. She had left her truck at the long-term airport parking so transportation to Winthrop wouldn't be a problem. Sara hoped to be home in time for dinner and looked forward to one of the famous steaks served at O'Reilly's Bar and Grill. A sharp feeling of loneliness seized her but passed quickly. She smiled at the memory of Randy and their time together before she left for California. Guilt still lingered as she recalled her two previous lovers, Pat and Roy. Both affairs occurred after Randy's arrival at Winthrop. Sabrina's words helped as Sara recalled their conversation about Randy and his personal philosophy and attitude about Sara's life before him. Unless Sara made a big deal about her affairs, Randy would let her previous life affairs be as if they never occurred.

Sara climbed the steps to her apartment, opened the door and spotted only one added item to her digs. There on the hat rack beside her Smokey Bear ranger hat was Randy's own ranger hat. In her bedroom she noticed the bed was made with fresh sheets and the bathroom cleaned, new towels on the towel racks. In the bedroom, Sara found her clothes neatly folded on the corner of her dresser with a note from Randy.

"I didn't feel right about pawing through your things, so I'll let you put them away. Will see you in about three weeks the patrol was extended one week. Janet is doing well but still a bit skittish about being on horseback with a loaded rifle under her knee. If you would, could you make out a training schedule for her that includes shooting from horseback both rifle and pistol. Thanks, miss you. Randy"

Sara sat down on the bed in the place Randy slept. She lay down and the long day caught up with her. She woke only to take a quick shower and return to bed. Sara was saddened he had washed the bedding; only a faint smell of him remained.

Chapter Twenty

Home

Late spring and summer in the Methow Valley and across the upper half of Washington was expected to be warm and dry. Occasional summer rains passed from the mountains and crossed the dry lands turning the flora green and brought the smells of freshness and moist soil. In September the smell of winter would invade the hills and mountains surrounding Winthrop. The bite of winter was easily felt with the night chill and the day's air slow to warm. Weather in the lower elevations with the first frost brought redness to the apples of the orchards throughout the valley and along the Columbia and Yakima rivers.

Summer days were hot and dry with the occasional summer rain to cool the earth. After the rebirth of spring, summer in the forests was enchanting. The gnarled mass of the ponderosa pine, red and white fir and the colorful larch shaded the hikers and horsemen who traveled the trails and roads of the back-country. The wildlife adults trained their offspring for survival. Deer and elk grazed in the meadows and bears fed on the mountain huckleberries. Hawks and the occasional eagle soared on the updrafts and surveyed their kingdom. Small animals scurried about gathering food for winter, ever mindful of the birds of prey, especially the hawks and owls. A family of wolves moved about in their established range. Life in the National Forests was varied and fruitful.

Chapter Twenty-One

The Bear

It was a warm day as Randy led the horses and pack mule along the narrow trail to traverse the side of the isolated mountain. Janet Awel followed twenty feet behind Randy's pack mule and led her own spare horse and pack horse. Randy's job besides enforcing the Fish and Wildlife laws was to see Janet learned what she needed to know to be safe while on patrol. He insisted she have her own pack horse, pack her own supplies and shelter as if she were alone. Randy also insisted Janet lead at least half of the patrol. He required her to plan their route using only the maps provided by the Service.

The cell phone rang as Randy was leading the string of animals and Janet across a wide, shallow fast-flowing stream. He didn't try to answer until Janet and the animals were safely across the stream and resting in a small open meadow.

Randy took the cell phone from the chest pocket of his jacket. "Hey boss, you called?"

Behoney's voice came through the cell loud enough for Janet to hear. "Yeah Randy, are you near the campground at Salmon Lake?"

"Not too far—we are up the north fork heading toward Eight Mile Ridge and Lamb Butte. Why?"

"We have a report of a bear mauling at the Salmon Lake campground. The report indicates the bear left the area after some idiot shot him with a .38 Caliber pistol."

"Oh shit!" Randy dismounted and sat down on a fallen tree. "How bad was the bear wounded?"

Behoney's feelings were clear how he felt about the shooter. "The man shot six times and reported he hit the bear each time. A witness said the bear was hit five times, which is bad enough but each hit was in a place where the wound would fester. One shot was in the lower chest which may kill the bear eventually if it becomes infected. Until then, we have a wounded rogue bear. The description indicates an older grizzly. The witness, who appeared to know what he was talking about said the bear was 8 feet to 9 feet tall. He used a tree for comparison and measured size that way."

"So we've got a grizzly, wounded and not afraid of humans, right?"

"Yeah Randy, I want you to track the bear down and put an end to this before he kills somebody. I'll send a helicopter to meet you at the Salmon Lake campgrounds tomorrow morning. Do you need anything special?"

"No. What do you want Janet to do?"

"Take her with you, it's good experience for her. I'll send one of my newbies, names Milton, to take care of the livestock. I don't suppose you want to drag all the horses and pack gear with you on a bear hunt? Milton can stay at the campground until you tell him otherwise."

"Okay, have Milton bring his own gear, tent, and food. We could use some eggs and fresh fruit if you've a mind. I'll take one pack animal and two spare horses. What do you want to do about the bear?"

"Bring the hide back with you if you can. If not, bring the right paw."

"Okay, we'll leave here in the next few minutes. Right now we are at the lower meadow east side of Salmon Creek." Randy read the location grid from the topographical map. "I'll plan to start the hunt tomorrow morning after the copter leaves."

"Randy, we really need to get this bear, sooner the better."

"Got it boss, talk to you later, out here." Randy dropped the call.

After explaining the changes to their routine patrol, Randy selected the most direct route to the campground at Salmon Lake. It was late afternoon when they arrived at the campground. They cleaned two of the pipe stalls for horses and put the pack animals in one and the mustangs in the other. The stalls were large enough for four horses and the mustangs fit with room to spare. Randy and Janet spent the rest of the afternoon talking to the campers who were present when the bear incident occurred.

Before the sun set, Randy used the information gleaned from the witnesses to locate the bear's trail. He followed the trace out a quarter mile. The signs indicated the bear was headed away from the campground.

The two rangers sat around the campfire, cooked dinner and Randy cleaned and inspected his .32 Caliber Winchester Model 94. He also traded his 10mm Sig Sauer pistol for the heavy .45 Caliber Long Colt revolver. He inspected Janet's 30-30 Marlin lever action saddle rifle. He didn't want any misfires or other preventable malfunctions with the weapons. Their guns might be the only thing between the bear, humans and the horses.

The cell phone rang, it was Sara. Twenty minutes later when he finished the call he was all smiles. *She missed me!*

Randy crawled out of his tent at 0530; Janet was already bent over the campfire. The sizzle and smell of the last of the bacon reminded Randy he was hungry. Red hot coals were pushed aside for the coffee pot. Janet wiped out the large iron fry pan with an oil cloth she kept in a plastic sandwich bag. A large prebaked potato was diced and eggs from the ice chest were on the nearby picnic table still in the blue plastic hard case. A thermos of orange juice sat on the table with two cups. Randy poured the juice into the cups and handed one to Janet.

"Morning Randy, coffee will be ready in a few minutes. Thought we'd finish the last of the eggs. I diced up the spud with some onion and will fry them together with the eggs."

"Sounds good to me." Randy belted on his .45 Long Colt pistol.

"Looks like you're loaded for bear." Janet joked. "I'm stuck with my piddly 9mm Beretta, but I've got fifteen bullets to your six. You think I should exchange the Beretta for the 10mm Sig?"

"Yeah, good idea. With your mini gun you can miss more than me." Randy laughed. He could feel the pressure of the coming hunt ease as they joked and teased each other. Janet would make a good ranger when she gained more experience and confidence.

"How did Sara do in the matches?" Janet asked.

"She did better than she thought she would. Didn't make the National Team but came in as runner up in the 1,000 meters. I wish I could shoot like that." They finished the juice, rinsed the cups and Randy poured himself and Janet cups of the fresh brewed coffee. "Since you're cooking I suppose you expect me to do the dishes?"

"Nah, I thought you'd like to cruise the camp while I clean up. How soon do you want to leave?"

"The chopper is due by 0700 and I'd like to leave as soon as our horse and camp sitter is settled. Behoney wants the chopper back so it will be a drop and go for the bird. The new guy is bringing a new set of radios. I suspect Ken will send more groceries, eggs and other eats too. He's good when it concerns the comfort and safety of his rangers."

"Who is coming out to watch the camp?" Janet asked.

"I don't know him, a new ranger named Milton. Another ranger reported in yesterday too, but the boss didn't give his name. Unless Ken decides different, I'm thinking you can catch a ride back to the base after we get the bear and the new ranger can relieve you and bring your horses back to Winthrop. When you get back, I'd like you to work with new horses and be ready to patrol with Sara. You might do some close-in solo patrolling from the base along the river."

"Jeeze Randy, I've got more time in the service than Sara."

Randy interrupted her complaint. "Yeah I know you're senior but Sara has more real experience than you and she can teach you a lot." He squinted at his partner. "Don't get an attitude. Sara is exceptional at her job. As your immediate supervisor I'm assigning you to Sara for training." He thought for a few seconds, "With Sara's Forest Service time I think she has more total service than any of the new rangers, including you."

After he toured around the campground, Randy returned to the camp and was having a cup of coffee with Janet when they heard the sound of a helicopter echo from the hills. The helicopter passed over the campground twenty feet above the trees, circled the camp and settled onto the playing field landing zone. First off the plane was Ken Behoney followed by a short stocky man wearing the forest green of the US Forest Service. The stranger carried a long hard case for a rifle. Randy didn't recognize the man but could make a pretty good guess what he wanted; to take the grizzly alive, judging from the rifle case.

Janet and Randy met the new arrivals at the edge of the LZ playfield. Behoney introduced Jake Hurley of the USFS. "Jake has a special task for you. He needs to have the bear alive. It seems one of our three-letter agencies has done some experiments with this bear. It's all classified so don't ask and I suppose you've guessed Jake really doesn't work for the Forest Service." Ken introduced Milton who immediately left to retrieve his gear and a large ice chest. Randy watched Milton; despite the name, the new ranger looked competent, about six foot, 220 pounds not much fat. Randy noticed Milton wore comfortable-looking roper boots and a pair of faded Wranglers.

"I recognize the case for the new dart guns. Come over to the camp and we'll have some coffee and you can explain what Jake here wants me and Janet to do." Randy led them to the camp's picnic table. Behoney started to excuse himself but Randy stopped him. "Ken, you stay until we leave or Mr. Jake here can go out and get his own bear. I thought about sending Janet back with the helicopter, but now I think it would be best if she stays here. You know hunting a rogue wounded bear is a two man job."

While they were talking Milton came up with his pack and tent. Randy pointed to an empty tent space where Milton could dump his gear before he joined them at the table.

An hour after the helicopter arrived, it lifted off with Jake and Ken. Milton stayed with Randy and Janet. They helped him set up his camp, secured their spare weapons in the mobile lock box Ken brought. Everything not going along on the hunt was put in the box and placed in Milton's tent for safe keeping. There were four new radios belonging to the Fish and Wildlife Law Enforcement Service and two radios that belonged to the agency Jake worked for. Special instructions would come over the special radio and Behoney instructed his rangers to follow Jake's instructions within safety boundaries. Jake's radios were the new satellite frequency hopping encrypted type. Randy couldn't help but be impressed. Each of the Fish and Wildlife radios had two-way communications with limited range. The radios provided by Jake's agency would work anywhere in the world with completely safe communications.

* * *

Janet cleaned up the camp while Randy checked and fed the horses. He found one bent and loose shoe on the pack horse. Randy was surprised the animal hadn't gone lame. He would have preferred to hot shoe. Without an oven and anvil to shape the shoe properly he would have to wait until they returned to Winthrop.

When he loaded the rifles he added two speed loaders for his Colt pistol and put the remainder of the .45 Caliber ammunition in his saddlebags, except for twelve rounds in his jacket pocket along with the speed loaders. He fully loaded his .32 Caliber Winchester with one round in the chamber, four rounds in the tube and another ten rounds in his other jacket pocket.

"Randy, would you mind checking my Marlin?" Janet asked on her way to put the trash bag in the camp garbage can.

"No problem. I'll put one in the chamber and four in the tube. All you have to do is thumb the hammer and flip up the safety." Randy put the remainder of the box in Janet's saddlebags. He set aside five rounds for Janet to put in her jacket pocket. He placed the dart rifle to hang down from the saddle horn on his horse with his own scabbard and rifle beneath the fender of his saddle with the stock buttplate to the rear.

Janet finished loading the supplies onto the pack mule and covered the supplies with a tarp in case of rain. Randy checked the pack, the ropes and knots. He saddled his and Janet's horses while she told Milton they were leaving and traced their basic route on his map. They would take only one spare horse each and the pack mule.

Randy led Janet and the animals to the farthest point he had tracked the bear last night. From there he had to track and look for blood sign. Janet kept her head turning watching the surrounding forest. He found a place where the bear rested. By the spacing of the tracks, Randy could tell the bear was moving slowly.

The trackers followed the trace until late afternoon. Randy found a spot where the animal crossed a stream and sunned on a large granite ledge. The blood on the rock was still wet and sticky. He didn't want to meet the bear in the dark and the sun rapidly sank toward the western ridgeline. Randy decided they would make camp and continue the hunt in the morning.

The second day of the hunt was a repeat of the first. The bear's wounds had stopped bleeding except for the right shoulder. The blood trace from the other wounds left on leaves and where the bear rested had disappeared. The foot wound track appeared to have a small scab which the bear knocked off or licked off so it bled lightly. Randy continued to track the bear toward evening. He used one of the radios to report their progress and location. The bear's track made an arc and appeared to be heading back toward the Salmon Lake campground. The rangers decided they could cut the arc and intercept the bear.

They cut the bear's track early. The horses were nervous but trusted the humans to keep them safe. The breeze was in their face as they continued the hunt. Janet dismounted, handed the reins to Randy and went to a grove of trees to relieve herself.

Randy heard a scream which was cut off abruptly. He could hear the grunt and growl of a bear. He grabbed his rifle, jumped down from his horse and rushed to the grove.

Janet was on the ground while the bear held her unconscious body against the ground. The bear set his teeth into her shoulder as he prepared to rip the shoulder from Janet's body. The bear spotted Randy, roared defiance and sank his teeth into Janet's shoulder again. The bear rose to a height and the ranger's feet dangled three feet above the ground. The bear stood on his hind legs: paws with six inch claws waved in the air and snarled at the new threat to take his food away. It was the largest bear Randy had ever seen. The hump on the bear's back was nearly all white. The animal held Janet's shoulder in his mouth and faced Randy. Janet's was in front, her body held against the bear's chest. Randy knew the bear claimed Janet as food and would kill her while protecting his food from the man standing in front of him.

'Screw the darts.' Randy thought and aimed his rifle at the bear's head. The way Janet's unconscious body was in front of the grizzly, Randy didn't have a safe shot.

He had to get the bear to drop Janet. Randy took careful aim and fired but the bullet skipped off the bear's thick skull. He made a decision and he put his rifle on the ground and drew his pistol. It wasn't exactly a bear gun but the large bullets might stop the bear. Randy charged the bear and it dropped Janet and swiped her back between his legs. The bear charged, Randy aimed at the bear's neck below the chin and fired. The bullet hit the bear and he stopped the charge. On his hind legs the bear attacked again. Randy picked his aiming point and fired three quick rounds into the chest above the heart. The bear seemed to shake off the bullet impacts. With only two bullets left he had to pick his target carefully. The grizzly roared, his mouth open showing all this teeth and Randy fired his last two bullets into the bear's mouth. He aimed for the spine at the back of the throat.

The bear stopped, and stood still less than ten feet in front of Randy while the ranger reloaded with the speed loader. He pulled back the hammer ready to fire another six bullets into the bear. Randy stared at the bear as it stood still and then slowly toppled forward and landed with the chin two inches in front of Randy's left foot. The man stared at the bear, stepped to the side and put the pistol against the bear's spine and fired again. Except for the impact of the bullet, the bear didn't move or make a sound.

The ranger stared down at the bear and looked for any sign of life. He holstered his pistol and rushed to Janet. Her shoulder was torn and her jacket and shirt ripped and covered with her blood. He quickly removed her torn jacket and shirt. He set her bra aside to be used as a sling. Randy applied the bandages from the first aid kit. When he had the bleeding under control and her wound bandaged, he covered her with one of his sweatshirts from his saddlebags and used her bra to hold her arm against her chest. Finished with first aid, he called the base for a medevac dust-off.

When the dispatcher asked for his location, Randy just yelled to get the helicopter in the air while he looked up the coordinates. He got the 1:50,000 scale map from his saddlebags thankful the horses had remained ground tied where he left them during the altercation with the bear. Randy put the radio frequency on the Guard emergency channel and was able to talk with the helicopter pilot. The nearest clearing was a quarter mile away. Randy didn't want to move Janet and asked if the paramedic could come to his location with a stretcher. While he waited, Randy called his own office hoping Ken Behoney was there. When he heard the helicopter fly over the trees not far away he popped a red smoke grenade to mark his position. The pilot could then pick his own landing zone.

* * *

Sara was in Randy's office with Ken Behoney when the call from Randy came in with the report of Janet Awel's mauling by a grizzly bear. Ken put the call on the speaker so Sara could listen to Randy's report. When she started to speak Behoney put up his hand to stop her. After Randy finished his report and hung up, Sara asked Ken what happened and if Randy had been hurt. She was relieved when Ken explained this was Randy's follow up report and everything was in the hands of a Federal Agency and he wasn't free to discuss the incident with her at this time.

After she listened to what Ken could tell her, Sara said she had already ended her assignment with the rifle matches for the year.

"Do you want me to go out and meet Randy and help him bring in the horses or finish up the patrol with him?" Sara's attitude indicated she was ready to leave now if Ken would let her.

"Sara, I was at the campground and I left Ranger Milton Stomeyer with Randy to help. I haven't decided yet whether to end the patrol a week early and have Randy return now or finish the loop. If he finishes the patrol he will be back here in ten or eleven days and Milton will gain valuable experience being with Springer." Ken sat back in his chair. "Excuse me Sara, I have some reports to submit; you can wait if you think you need to or I'll see you tomorrow morning."

Sara decided to leave and return to work in the morning. On the way to her truck it began to rain large warm drops. It refreshed and removed the dust from the air. Sara watched the little puffs of dust from the ground caused by the large drops. The rain stopped as quickly as it started. The air smelled fresh and alive. The day was warm and the breaks in the scattered clouds allowed the sun to shine through in golden beams. The forecast for tomorrow promised more of the same. The air appeared to shine and a double rainbow arched across the sky. The vibrant colors of the day matched Sara's inner feelings. She was sorry Randy wasn't there when she got home but thankful he hadn't been hurt. Sara went home for the rest of the day. There was her laundry from the trip for the dry cleaners and the apartment needed dusting.

* * *

Thirty minutes later Randy heard the helicopter land and directed the two on-board medics to follow the red smoke to his location. Randy was talking to Janet when the medics stepped out of the trees. She was slipping in and out of consciousness. The medic stabilized her and started an IV per instructions from the doctor at the emergency room at the Spokane Hospital which was the closest major medical facility.

After Janet was put on the helicopter, Randy pulled the bear up into a tree with the help of the mule. He skinned the animal and scraped the hide, salted it and rolled it into a large double plastic garbage bag. He put the head into a second large plastic bag on the mule. As the sun was setting, Randy entered the campground.

Milton helped him care for the horses after Randy used the satellite phone from his saddlebags and called Ken Behoney's office, getting no answer. He pulled the bear's two garbage bags into the trees high enough above the ground to prevent the night raiders from getting a free meal.

Milton fed and bedded the horses and mule in the pipe stalls,. Randy sat with Milton at the picnic table and called his boss again on his cell phone. When Ken answered, Randy asked about Janet's condition. The hospital report said Janet's condition was non-life threatening—the surgeons were able to save her arm and the shoulder. She was still serious but the doctors expected a full recovery.

Finished with Ken Behoney, Randy called the special number and reported the bear had been killed. Randy was told to remain on the line. After ten minutes Randy dropped the call. Within five minutes the phone rang. Randy pushed the receive button, and the angry voice started immediately.

"Listen asshole, you don't hang up on this line ever." Randy pushed the end call.

The phone rang again. Randy pushed the receive button only to hear. "All right asshole you made your point and don't piss me off again."

Randy pushed the end call button again.

The phone rang again and Randy accepted the call. "Sorry we got off on the wrong foot. Can you tell me what happened and where the bear is now?"

Randy could tell the spook was having a difficult time controlling his voice and temper. "Okay, now you sound like you're ready to listen."

"Listen asshole, don't push it!"

Randy again pushed the end call button. The cell rang again and Randy pushed the receive call button. The caller was quiet for perhaps a full minute before a calm voice came from the tiny speaker. "I'm sorry kid, I think this job is getting to me. First, is your partner okay? I understand she was mauled and has some severe bites to her shoulder and arm. I'm really sorry she was hurt. I'm going to tell you a little about this bear before I ask you any questions, okay?"

"Sure." Randy could understand this man was under considerable pressure.

"The bear was captured in Alaska and was given a special diet, a major part being steroids. The more steroids the meaner it got. The service was having trouble with large cats in the Southern California Ortega Mountains and another agency's scientists thought a super bear would kill off the cats. It didn't happen the way it was planned. It appeared the bear and cats teamed up. The bear didn't become meaner and dumber, it became meaner all right and definitely smarter. That's when my agency became involved and I was assigned to the Bear Project. That was two years ago. The bear killed a ranger in the Shasta area last year and we moved him to the area east of the Methow Valley where there are a couple of cougars moved up from the Ortega Mountainss in California. Tracking indicates the cougars are currently in the area north of Concunnully. The cougars are each responsible for a human attack resulting in a death. The grizzly has killed at least one human." The G-man paused and Randy waited for him to continue.

"Randy, it is Randy Springer right?"

"Yeah, I'm Springer. What do you need to know?"

"Can you tell me how the bear was killed?"

"Sure." Randy paused to organize his thoughts. "My partner surprised the bear and it attacked. I didn't witness the attack but from the tracks that's my best guess. I first saw the bear with my partner's shoulder in his mouth. There was no way I could use the dart gun and I did try my rifle but the bullet bounced off the bear's skull. To get the bear to release Janet, I charged it in a threat mode as if to take his meal away. The bear dropped Janet and charged me. I shot it once in the area below the jaw. When the bear reacted it stood up and I shot it three times in the heart area. It stood and roared at me, opening his mouth. I used my last two rounds and shot twice and hit it pretty much within a six inch area in the back of the throat and took out the spine. The bear dropped while I reloaded. I checked the bear: dead."

"Christ, what did you shoot it with?"

"I used my .45 Caliber Long Colt pistol. Each bullet took out a pretty good chunk from the neck and chest. I figure the bear was pretty much done by the second shot but it doesn't hurt to make sure." Randy gave a short laugh.

"Anything else you can tell me?"

"I figured you'd want the head and skin, so I cleaned and skinned him. The skin is in one bag the head another. If there are any extra holes I didn't put them there."

"Thanks ranger, you did good. Can you get the remains to Winthrop?"

"I'm at least six days away from the base. I can meet you along the way."

"That would be great. I want to apologize for my conduct before. You've done more than I could expect. I'll get back to you on a location or if I can get the helo I'll meet you at the campground if you can delay your departure a day."

"No problem, I'll wait here. I don't have any ice and do recommend you pick up the bear remains ASAP."

"I'll see you tomorrow and Randy, thanks." The call ended.

Randy used what was left of the night to clean his rifle and pistol. He called Behoney and asked to keep Milton to help bring the stock back to Winthrop.

Randy called Sara and told her about Janet and the bear and said he would be back in Winthrop in about a week. Sara said she was going to be on a series of overnight patrols over the next couple of weeks. If he had a chance, could he ride Butch. They ended the call with, ""I missed you." Sara went to bed feeling warm, knowing Randy missed her and maybe even loved her. Randy crawled into his tent and fell asleep thinking of Sara.

* * *

It was afternoon when Randy heard the helicopter approach the field. He stood on the edge of the grassy area as the helicopter settled on the ground. He recognized the government man when he climbed down from the HU1 Huey helicopter with U.S. Army markings. As soon as the man cleared the rotor disc the helicopter lifted and left to the east. "Don't worry, the bird has a drop off at Republic and will be back for me later." The G-man shook Randy's hand. "Meanwhile I recommend we get rid of this contraband." The man produced two six packs of icy beer from his canvas bag. "You got a place we can sit out of the sun?"

The ranger grinned and led the way to his tent and the picnic area. Randy pointed to the black plastic bags hanging twenty feet above the ground. "That's your bear. You can have him anytime you want."

"Let it hang there," the G-man said and twisted the cap from a Coor's Light beer and handed it to Randy. "You look like a cowboy beer man." The man twisted off another cap and dropped the caps into his bag. Milton joined them and was handed a beer.

* * *

Sara was at her kitchen table cleaning her service pistol. Randy was due back at the end of the following week. On his nightly call he asked Sara to go with him to Spokane to visit Janet in the hospital.

Finished with her pistol, she wrote a note to Sabrina. She hoped she and Sabrina would become good friends and Sara promised Sabrina she would take good care of her baby brother.

Sara was putting Sabrina's envelop in the mail box when she noticed a delivery man at her door. "Can I help you?"

"I have a delivery for Ms. Sara Bennett. Do you know if she's home or when she is usually home?"

"I'm Sara Bennett."

"Yes ma'am." He set a long box down on the porch. "Please sign— you are over twenty-one?"

"Yes, and then a little bit," Sara joked and signed for the delivery. She took the oddly balanced box into her apartment and set it on the table next to the metal ammo box containing her gun cleaning kit.

Sara opened the box and didn't know whether to laugh or cry. In the box was a small bottle of her favorite wine, a stuffed mustang horse, a girl rider with a rope and a dozen roses. The note said, "Couldn't think of anything smart or witty to say so, miss you, Randy'"

Sara cried and laughed and hiccupped. It was the first time she had ever received a dozen roses. The macho guys she knew wouldn't think of roses. Now here was the most macho man she ever met and he not only gave her roses, but included thoughtful tokens of humor and said he missed her.

She put the roses in water and when she went to bed, she brought them into the bedroom along with the stuffed mementos. She slept smelling roses.

Chapter Twenty-Two

Sara and Trouble

At Ken's suggestion, Sara planned a series of short two day patrols around Ferguson and Eureka lakes and some of the higher-elevation lakes. Each two days she would be at a different lake. She would not return to Winthrop until she had visited each of the lakes. The total duration of the combined patrols would be twenty-four days. Ken would give her four days off plus she would work in the office for the following two weeks. Sara planned to leave in two days. She would take one of the new probationary rangers for orientation. There were three small villages along their planned route and Sara planned to restock supplies at the general stores.

Ken wanted Sara to pay a visit to the RCMP post on the Canada side of the border and introduce Probationary Ranger Ed Lowell to the Border Patrol agent and the customs people at the crossing. Ken wanted to establish a connection with the other agencies his rangers might be required to work with. He also wanted to keep Sara away from the headquarters and the Drug Task Force operated by the Department of Homeland Security. The Homeland Security agents had been a pain in his butt since the first day they were organized;—if how they operated could be called organized.

Pat was released from active duty, granted an extended unpaid leave for personal reasons. He returned to his practice at the Winthrop clinic. He and Sara dined together and talked about Sabrina's and Pat's upcoming deployment. Sara told him if they could get together, he and Randy should rope together before he left to join the 1st Marines prior to deployment. Pat received a note from the 2nd Battalion, 1st Marines Commanding Officer. The battalion would be the last unit of the 1st Marines to deploy. That would give Pat an extra month before leaving.

At the end of the evening, Sara went home to pack for her patrols. She would take all three of her horses, Pat, Moe and Curley. Her patrol partner would take two of the new mustangs and a pack horse Randy had trained. With six horses Sara would take the seven-horse trailer and enough horse hay and feed so the animals would not have to eat the new growing grass and other fodder. Randy would exercise Buster for her to keep him legged up and in shape to compete in the arena.

In the morning she decided to take the panniers to get Pat used to carrying them instead of only the pack on its frame. She loaded hay into the front of the horse trailer and put grain feed in the dressing room. Sara checked the pack Ed's pack animal would carry and recommended he take a two-man tent instead of the one man tent he planned on taking. Sara would take the other two-man tent which was easier to set up than the one-man or the three-man tents. The forging for the horses at Ferguson Lake and some of the higher lakes might be a bit sparse and six horses could damage an acre of new grasses midway through the growing season in a short time.

* * *

Sara and Ed left on the scheduled patrol the next morning; she thought: out early, back early. Except for two locations, Sara and Randy could continue their nightly talks. He was on the homeward leg of his patrol but would still not return to Winthrop for another ten days. He decided to use the time with Milton to do some extra training on tracking and map orientation and extended his patrol a few days. Janet would be in the hospital at least a month. Doctors were concerned about an infection in her shoulder and the bites weren't healing quite as fast as they thought they should. The doctors wouldn't release her to go home until the infection was completely cured. Randy talked to Janet on the phone when he stopped for supplies at a small town northeast of Omak. Ken was bringing another new ranger to spend the last days of the patrol with Randy and Milton.

The Fish and Wildlife Law Enforcement Service was expanding and Ken was getting three more rangers for his district, which now included the mountain slopes northwest of Wenatchee to the crest of the Cascades. It added another few hundred square miles to Ken's district. He wanted Randy to select eighteen more mustangs and oversee the rangers in the training of their horses. Ken was having another stable built in Winthrop and one in Brewster to house the new horses. Randy was now the District Training Officer, area supervisor and horse manager. Ken assigned Sara as Randy's administrative and scheduling officer. The jobs would reduce the patrol time of both of his top rangers but the payoff was a dozen well-trained rangers to cover the northern part of his district. The district built an office building for the rangers and they had moved out of the Forest Service office building. The rangers were now separated from the Forest Service by a walkway and located on the other side of the flag pole. Sara had her own office, and Randy's, the supervisor's office was twice as large as his former office.

* * *

It was four months after the incident at Ferguson Lake. The government Gulf Stream V corporate jet lined up on approach to the small runway at the Winthrop Forest Service base. Sara Bennett sat on a stool in front of the drafting table the rangers used as a map board. Alerted by the sound of the jets approach, she watched the sleek airplane land with a chirp and puff of smoke from the tires. Sara knew she was in trouble with the higher ups in the Department of Agriculture and the Federal Fish and Wildlife Law Enforcement Service. She didn't understand what the problem; was, she had solved a murder and prevented the murder of two Federal Bureau of Investigation agents and assisted in the recovery of a lethal recreational drug, possibly saving multiple lives. Ken Behoney came out of Randy Springer's office. Randy and Ed Lowell were on an unscheduled patrol to investigate malicious vandalism at three isolated campgrounds and wouldn't return for another two days.

Ken leaned over and patted Sara's shoulder. "I don't know what their problem is, but I think they're nuts. You did an outstanding job with the Ferguson Lake and helicopter problem. You should be getting an award, not this bullshit."

"Damn Ken, I thought I did it pretty much by the book. I warned the guy before I shot him. If I'd have stopped and read him his rights, I'd be dead along with Marc and the pilot. Worse, the drugs may have made it to the college campuses."

"Yeah, I know. You did good Sara. I'm with you all the way. I'm glad Randy isn't here. He would probably explode and assault one of these assholes."

Together, the two watched the jet come to a stop next to the Forest Service Headquarters building. The jet engines wound down and came to a stop. The steps under the door folded out and dropped to the asphalt. When the door opened, two men is business suits deplaned and walked up the white gravel path to the rangers' office door.

Sara recognized both men; their pictures were on the wall over the window overlooking the airfield. Ken stepped out of the office to welcome the two men. Sara went into Randy's office. There were only two chairs, Randy's chair behind the desk and a side chair. She went into the ranger conference room and brought in two additional chairs. She waited, and could see the three men as they talked on the small raised wooden porch. Ken gestured and appeared to be in an argument, talking first to one then the other executive.

Ken turned his back on the two men and entered the office, letting the door swing shut. He ignored both men and let them open the door themselves. Ken stormed into the ranger office, went behind the desk and sat in Randy's chair, or his chair when he was in the Winthrop office. *I need to get another desk for me., I hate using Randy's desk when he's here.,* Ken thought.

The two men in suits came into the office, and glanced at Sara who sat in the desk's side chair. The Director of the Fish and Wildlife Law Enforcement Service started around the desk to have Ken move, but one look at Ken's face told him it would be better if he sought another seat. The secretary sat down and opened his briefcase to remove a folder that contained a thick number of pages.

The director sat, opened his briefcase and removed a similar folder to the one held by the secretary. He scowled at Ken and sat down in the chair closest to the front of the desk. The director started to put his briefcase on the desk, but again one look at Ken's face changed his mind.

"I suppose everyone knows one another, but for the record, I am James Durham, Secretary of Agriculture. To my right is Mr. Thomas Kroeber, Director of the Federal Fish and Wildlife Law Enforcement Service. I am addressing Kenneth Behoney, District Supervisor of North Central Washington District and Ranger Sara Bennett of the Winthrop, Washington, office. Absent is Randal Springer, Supervising Ranger, Winthrop office. Mr. Korber and I are here to discuss the charges brought against Ms. Bennett by the man she shot during an altercation in the vicinity of Ferguson Lake, Washington."

Behoney nodded as did Sara, but Ken followed up the nod with a snort, a blatant show of disrespect. Ken didn't care what these two political appointees thought of him but wanted them to know what he thought of them.

The secretary ignored Ken's insult. "I have a list of the charges filed in the United States District Court in Denver." Ken started to say something, but Durham held up his hand. "Wait until I've read the charges."

Durham removed a file of papers held together by a blue cover. "First, wait until I have read all the charges before you begin your rebuttals. Now, for the first charge: unauthorized use of deadly force. Second: illegal search of subject's vehicle. Third: civil rights violation and racial profiling; subject is of American Indian descent. Fourth: subject was not Mirandized. Fifth: attempted homicide. Sixth: use of an unauthorized weapon. Seven: Violation of written protocols; a list shall be provided at a later date. Do you understand these charges? Please indicate your understanding vocally. These proceedings are being recorded." Durham removed a small recorder from his briefcase.

"Yeah, I understand," Ken stated.

"Please state your name before stating your understanding." Durham smiled at Behoney.

"Yeah, I'm Kenneth Behoney and I understand the bullshit charges."

"Please refrain from your added vulgarities," Krober interrupted.

Durham turned to Sara. "Do you understand these charges?"

"Yeah, I'm Sara Bennett and I understand the bullshit charges too."

"Now, would you make a statement for the record?" Durham continued and checked the recorder.

"No ,I do not wish to answer these charges at this time. When I do it will be with the advice of my lawyer." Sara was ready to shoot these two assholes. She noticed Krober glance at the automatic pistol on her hip.

Krober was red faced. "I notice your are armed Miss Bennett. Now that charges have been read, please remove the weapon from your belt. District Supervisor Behoney can hold it for you until disposition of these charges is completed."

Sara removed the pistol from its holster, removed the magazine and the bullet from the chamber. She made a point by thumbing each round onto Randy's desk in front of Durham and Krober. Krober winced as each bullet dropped onto the desk with a loud bang. Finished, she gathered up the bullets and handed the pistol and bullets to Behoney.

Ken grinned. "Thank you Sara. I'll hold the pistol and of course the bullets until you need them again." He stared at the two men opposite him until they nervously began stuffing papers back into their briefcases.

"Don't you want a statement from me?" Ken asked politely.

Durham answered, "Of course, please."

"Well, I think the two of you coming here and making these unfounded accusations is a waste of time and resources. Each one of those charges will fall apart and I'm sure your bosses will be amused. Yours Mr. Secretary will be especially interested in how the Department and the Fish and Wildlife Law Enforcement Service treats their employees and must determine which side your are on. When I heard there were charges, I immediately filed for the venue to be transferred to the United States District Court in Seattle. United States District Judge Herman Fullworth has granted the request. I suppose we will be seeing you in court. By the way, the court date is next month for the grand jury in Seattle. I suspect we will see you two gentlemen there. The judge faxed two subpoenas, one for each of you to appear before the grand jury." Behoney handed each man the subpoena with his name prominently on the cover sheet.

Director Krober appeared panicky and looked at Durham for guidance. Durham slowly extended his hand and took the papers held out to him by Behoney. He slowly read the document after he handed Krober his subpoena. "This is most irregular. I'm not sure this is entirely legal."

"Oh I assure you, it is perfectly legal. Judge Fullworth checked the subpoenas personally. The District Court in Denver also agreed the case should be heard in

Seattle and not in Denver." Behoney took the pistol out of his desk drawer and handed it back to Sara with a handful of bullets. "I am returning Ranger Bennett to full duty until told otherwise by the District Court in Seattle. I checked with the judge and was informed that was a decision within my purview. So, if there is nothing else on your minds, we both have work to do. Oh, by the way, the judge also said any further actions by you would be considered contempt of court. It seems the judge has some prior knowledge of how both of you conduct yourselves." Ken waited until Sara reloaded her magazine with bullets and holstered her pistol. "Sara, would you please escort these gentlemen to their ride and see they leave, immediately?"

"Yes sir, my pleasure."

Durham and Krober rose to their feet and without another word left the office and building, followed by Sara with her hand on her pistol as incentive. She escorted them to their plane and signaled the pilot to start his engines by twirling her index finger over her head. Sara could see the grin on the pilots' faces as they started the engines, let the jet warm up for a couple of minutes while the passengers entered the jet. He gave Sara thumbs up then taxied to the main runway and jammed the throttles forward for a short-field takeoff.

Sara returned to the office where Ken waited for her. "When you and Randy are ready, I want both of you to take a couple of weeks off and disappear. Go camping." Ken laughed and left the office to return to his own office in Brewster.

Chapter Twenty-Three

Together

Randy led the string of horses into the small round pen at the Fish and Wildlife Ranger Station. Milton, riding drag, led the mule. Randy turned his attention to the riding horses, all mustangs trained by him. When all the horses were in the pen, Randy, Ed Lowell and Milton started with the pack animals and checked for injuries, sore legs, backs, and hooves for cracks, bruises and soft spots. Randy turned the mustangs out into the arena to run and roll before brushing them and turning them out into the second pasture to graze.

Randy threw flakes of hay over the fence and turned his attention to cleaning the truck and trailer. The mustangs ate and ran as a group. The two rangers wrote up their patrol reports and went home.

* * *

Sara was on a patrol to check on reports of poaching along the Chemack River. Ken Behoney wanted her away from Winthrop and decided a patrol would be a good way to make her scarce around the office.

Sara was disappointed Randy didn't wait for her and wasn't in a hurry to get home to her empty apartment. When she entered her two-bedroom apartment, she went to the kitchen and poured herself a glass of milk. She spun around when she heard the sound of the shower running. At first she was puzzled and then she rushed across the room to the bathroom. The door was slightly ajar. Sara pushed it open and could see a man's shadow behind the shower curtain. She pulled the curtain aside and found a naked Randy with soap on his chest wearing only a grin.

"Well, what are you waiting for? Get those smelly clothes off and rinse this soap off me."

Sara squealed like a young girl as her clothes starting dropping on the bathroom floor. Randy watched, a smile on his face and love in his eyes. "Are you going to move and let me in?" Sara giggled. Sara never giggled; she thought girls who giggled were dunces.

Once in the shower with water running over her face, head and shoulders, Sara pushed herself against Randy, her arms around his neck. "Where have you been all my life? I waited and waited for you. I've missed you." Sara looked down and then up into his eyes. "I see someone else missed me too." She took him in her hand and gently pulled him to her.

"Wow girl, I think you missed me too." Randy kissed her; his tongue searched against her lips until her mouth opened and their tongues met.

The kiss made both lovers dizzy. Sara stepped back. "Wash me and make love to me." Sara stood on tip toes to whisper into his ear. Her warm breath teased him. His erection swelled to fill her hand. Sara began to sink to her knees but he caught her and held her to him. She tried to bring him to her, but again Randy held her still.

"It's time I welcomed you back properly. First, I think I love you and I don't want you to ever hear it too much or too little." He smiled down at her.

They stood in the shower and held each other as the warm water cascaded over their bodies. Sara felt like she was home in Randy's arms. She didn't want to let go but she could feel her need for him grow.

As the water flowed over their bodies, Randy held Sara close until she leaned back so she could look into his eyes. "Randy, you don't have to tell me you love me. I'll be happy with any time you care to share with me. Do you understand what I'm saying?"

Randy looked into Sara's blue eyes; he could see the love there and the choice she offered him. "You know Sara the offer you just made only makes me love you more if that's possible. It isn't the time we've spent together but the meeting of two mates, soul mates some people would say. You are the one woman my heart has searched for all my years, since puberty at least." He grinned and Sara couldn't help herself as she grinned back at him.

"Don't you think we should find out if our first time wasn't a fluke or real?" Sara smiled sheepishly.

"Now that you mentioned it, yeah I do." Randy's smile matched hers. "You want to get out from under the water and move to the workbench?"

"No, you haven't finished washing me yet. Don't you think you should get started?"

"You know, I could have said the same thing." He returned Sara's mischievous grin and wiggled his eyebrows at her.

"Wooooeee, you are so scary. Are you going to rope me and tie me to the railroad tracks?" Sara lifted her breasts and teased him. "My, what are these for?" She put her hands behind her head and posed. Then she brought her hands down, looked into his eyes and put her hands behind his neck and pulled his lips to hers. They kissed and held each other until Randy lowered his head to her nipples. "Maybe you are just going to eat me up?" Sara laughed lightly, still in the moment.

"Aw fair damsel, don't tempt this mere mortal with such delectable feminine charms. I surrender and fall to my knees before such beauty." Randy dropped to his knees. He put his arms around her and before she could respond he pulled her to him.

* * *

The spring and early summer were especially good to the newly coupled Randy Springer and Sara Bennett. The charges against Sara were dropped without prejudice. The District Court Judge in Seattle looked over the charges and found them unfounded.

Ken Behoney teamed them together. They didn't get their vacation but camped together on three and four-week patrols. Sara received an e-mail from Pat. He was in Afghanistan assigned to the 2nd Battalion of the 1st Marines as the medical officer. Sabrina Springer was in charge of the surgery unit at Camp Leatherneck and was the senior medical officer promoted to full commander with connex box quarters she shared with a Woman Marine Lieutenant Colonel. It appeared Pat was enjoying himself being with the Marines and the twelve Navy Corpsmen assigned to him, not including the corpsmen assigned to each platoon and company. Time was flying past and Pat would be back in the States in another seven months. Pat was notified from Navy Headquarters, that his active duty was officially extended to two years with the possibility of a third year if he volunteered. It didn't come as a surprise; he expected the extension after seeing how short of professional medical personnel the Marines were.

On company-size patrols, Pat volunteered to accompany the Marines, leaving the other two doctors both doing their internship with the 1st and 3rd Battalions of the 1st Marines to tend to the sick calls and accidents that occurred around weapons and heavy equipment.

Sara answered his e-mail and told him she and Randy were officially together. Randy bought her an emerald friendship ring and she wore it every day. Randy asked her to visit the Montana ranch with him and she was looking forward to meeting Randy's family in the fall.

Chapter Twenty-Four

The Task Force and the Search

The telephone rang and insisted on being answered by consistently ringing every five seconds. Sara reached across the sleeping Randy.

"Hello, this better be good!"

"Sara, it's Ken. I need you and Randy in the office. Do you happen to know where he is? Anyway, find him and get in here ASAP." Behoney paused. "Did your weapons get back here from your last recreational match? I know they were on the way, you might need one of them."

"Yeah, they're here. Why? What's happened?" Sara was wide awake. She shook Randy awake and signaled for him to be quiet and listen.

"I don't want to talk about it on the phone. I need your input on a problem that started last night—actually early this morning."

"Ken, I know where Randy is and we'll be there in an hour. Anything besides my guns needed?"

"Bring your ""Go Bag"". Have Randy bring his Winchester, the .32 Caliber rifle and his own "Go Bag." He does have one, right?"

"Yeah, Randy has a 'Go Bag" too'"

"Okay, have him bring his too." Behoney ended the call.

"Randy did you hear all that?"

"Yeah, I've got my bag at home and my guns too. We had better get a move on if we're going to be in Ken's office in an hour. I'll shave while I watch you shower." He laughed. "Watching you has become my favorite pastime." He smiled and it turned into a wide grin. He reached out to grab her but she scooted out of his reach and escaped to the bathroom.

The couple ended up together in the shower. Randy shaved while Sara applied soap and washrag to appropriate places. Finished with shaving, Randy watched while she rinsed the soap off. He stopped her and held her against him for a few seconds, kissed her and left the shower. "I need to pick up my gear. I'll meet you in the boss's office." He dressed and left the apartment.

Forty minutes later Ken sat in Randy's office when Sara came in without knocking. "Now that you are both here I'll brief you." Ken began, "This is all close hold information, consider it classified at the secret level. You two have been loaned to

Homeland Security for the duration of this crisis. You have been requested specifically and the Service in general by Homeland Security to plug some of the holes in their web to capture a five-member team of terrorists. Go ahead and jump to conclusions and you would probably be right." Ken wasn't happy about losing his two best rangers.

Ken could feel the dynamics between Randy and Sara had changed since about the time she went to California for the National Matches. Ken enjoyed playing Cupid with his two favorite people. He could guess what happened between them by the way Randy and Sara looked at each other.

Behoney sat quiet for a couple of minutes, took a deep breath before he began to explain the specifics of the Task Force. "This morning I received a telephone call from the FBI office in Spokane and another from the FBI office in Seattle. It seems the person Sara shot was part of a terrorism cell associated with a brother cell comprised of five Middle Eastern Arab terrorists here on student visas. The FBI has been watching the group until a week ago, when they disappeared. The drugs recovered from the pickup truck at the Ferguson Lake incident were only a small part of the original shipment of over two hundred kilos of the contaminated drugs. The dead man was a courier of one shipment of the tainted heroin. He had already made three major drops of ten kilos each around this area. DEA intercepted the three drops and the fourth was to be distributed on the college campuses in Seattle. DEA had him under surveillance for the two weeks prior to his murder, when he dropped out of site camping at Ferguson Lake. Our murderer was sent by the Arabs to find the courier, recover the remaining drugs and eliminate what the Arabs thought was a leak in their security. The Arab terrorists regained control of the heroin here in Washington. One hundred kilos were put in a locker in the bus depot in Seattle. It was recovered by DEA this morning from the locker. There is still fifty kilos of tainted heroin in the possession of the Arabs when they disappeared after being traced to Spokane. They were spotted by a State Patrol trooper on Highway Two four days ago in Davenport. It is thought the terrorist's are moving toward the Canadian border. They can move around easier in Canada. The Mounties have some people available but the FBI fears if the Arabs reach the border, we'll lose the heroin." Ken paused and retrieved a notebook from his desk drawer. "What the Feds want is to establish a blocking force across the major trails north of the Colville Reservation to the border." Ken paused and consulted some notes. "I have two teams on likely routes. You two are the third team but I'm keeping you as a reaction force. Now you know as much as I do. Questions?"

"What the hell do the Feds want us to do? There must be a couple of hundred trails from almost anywhere in Washington to the Canadian border." Sara stared at Behoney. "Just where do you want us to set up?"

"My feeling is you stay right here until there is some indication where the terrorists are or were so we can pick up their trail. If you have any suggestions, now is the time." Ken sighed, looked at the wall map of central Washington and shook his head. The relationship between his two best rangers could complicate things.

He thought, *We're all adults here and can handle it.* "Sara, Randy, the Feds want you to establish a blocking force ahead of the Tangos somehow. I disagree with them so you are my reaction force. There is satellite coverage and as soon as they are sighted we'll know where to set up to intercept them."

"How many teams are there going to be, total? It sounds like kind of hit or miss operation to me. Are we taking the horses or do we get an airborne ride?" Randy asked.

"You and Sara may be transported by helicopter to your position as soon as it's known. Your horses and pack animals will be brought by another ranger after you are in place. I am keeping Ed and Milton as go-fers and general work around here. All the other rangers are either on their way to blocking positions or already there. You'll have five animals total—that's two horses apiece plus one pack mule. If anyone should ask, your camouflage cover is to check for poaching. Sara, one of your rifles is a M70 Winchester sniper rifle; looks like a hunting rifle?" Ken looked at Sara for confirmation.

"Yeah, you can't tell the difference without an in-depth inspection. It is accurate out to about 1,200 meters but only a sniper would know its capability."

"Okay, take any weapon you want. Randy, you have your .32 Caliber Winchester lever action, iron sights and I guess about a 300 meter max effective range."

"Good guess except I've shot at 500 meters and it's not bad, better than throwing rocks." Randy laughed. "Yeah, but it is a close in weapon, say up to 200 meters." He knew the rifle made in 1938 was a lot better than originally advertised, especially with modern powder and bullets.

Ken had his two rangers look over the series of 1:50,000 scale maps. They spent two hours over the maps and talked about various options the Tangos could take.

"Randy, do you still have those phones the three letter agency guy loaned you?"

"Yeah, they're in the locker behind you. They will need to be charged." Randy opened the gun safe and removed the radio telephones and their chargers. He plugged them into the power socket and returned to his chair.

"Take them with you. Will they match frequencies?"

" I think so. They are the same make and model. What's on your mind?"

"If they match then the one they loaned me should also match and we can use them for communications and will be able to talk securely between us."

"I know they have the guard frequency programmed as station 'E' on both of the phones I still have," Randy volunteered.

"That matches mine. We'll keep the 'E' frequency as emergency. If we can pull it off, you take your horses and truck. I'd rather you had all your gear with you with options open. Stage everything you think you would need on a long patrol with a real threat. Use the conference room—the only room more secure is your office." Ken rubbed his chin before continuing. "I don't know if this is the right thing to tell you, but the Special Agent In-Charge (SAIC) for the Homeland Security folks is a real prick with a capital P. Personally I wouldn't trust him with a bag of horseshit. But he is in charge. Try to play nice with the new kids; it's their ball, but it's our sandbox. Try to keep me in the loop. I wouldn't be surprised if the prick isn't playing for the other side from some of the decisions and practices he has implemented. Keep in mind it is our responsibility to keep everyone safe."

* * *

For the next two days Randy worked with the horses. The Homeland Security SAIC hadn't called or briefed them since a phone call the first day of Operation Warlord, as the SAIC called it. Randy put new shoes on the pack animals and led them on trails around the airport. Mostly he stayed close to the base headquarters. Randy and Sara each carried one of the secure cell telephones. Ken returned to the Brewster District Office. Sara spent an afternoon cleaning her weapons including the rifles in Randy's office and checking all the ammunition and other equipment they would take with them. She decided to take both the M70 Winchester and the Springfield M1A military match rifle. She knew she could hit a quarter with the M70 at two hundred meters, but she could hit a half dollar with the M1A and the 25 cents didn't make much difference to the target.

On the third day the SAIC arrived in an Army HU1 (Huey) helicopter and gave Ken and the rangers a brief on Operation Warlord. (Randy had started referring to the operation as Operation GeeWhiz.). It was a counter-terrorist operation in the area starting in the west at the base of the Cascades near Ross Lake. The search area would cross northern Washington to Danville and the town of Republic with Moses Lake anchoring the southern extent of Behoney's area of operation. The border with Canada would be the northern edge of the Area of Operations (AO). When asked if the RCMP were involved, the SAIC said that information was classified and Fish and Wildlife didn't need to know. After Ken came down from hitting the ceiling, he was told to mind his own business and leave the big stuff to Homeland Security or he would be relieved for the duration of the operation. He wouldn't even tell them his name. The SAIC finally relented and gave them his name, Duane T. Dewar and he was appointed by the Director of Homeland Security personally to conduct Operation Warlord. When Ken asked about helicopter support, Dewar said only he could authorize use of the helicopters assigned to the operation. The helicopters belonged to the Spokane Sheriff's Office, the Moses Lake Sheriff's Office and two Army HU1s assigned to Operation Warlord. Dewar said he wanted to have them available if the terrorists were spotted.

Ken called the Director of the Fish and Wildlife Law Enforcement Service and was told in no uncertain terms that Dewar was in charge and not to call him again. The next morning as a show of disrespect toward Dewar, Ken brought his wife's clothes line to work so Ken would have a place to be when he was hung out to dry. Dewar didn't think it was funny and left immediately for Seattle in one of the Army helicopters.

The reports sent to Fish and Wildlife indicated the terrorists were already across the Canadian border and were now a Canadian problem. Randy, Sara and Ken did a map analysis of the terrorists' last suspected position and were of the opinion the terrorist team was hiding in one of the hundreds of cabins a hundred miles from the border.

Ken thought the terrorists were close to one of five projected routes. The Feds, who worked for Duane Dewar, were convinced the Tangos were gone and wanted to close up Operation Warlord. What confused Ken, Randy and Sara was if the terrorists were gone, why was Operation Warlord not closed down and why were the air assets still attached to Homeland Security. Somebody disagreed with Dewar and kept the air assets attached to the operation.

Randy thought the terrorists were not only still in the area, but may have taken hostages from one of the outlying ranches and the horses if the ranch had any.

Randy stepped away and stared at the map, his eyes unfocused. "What do you see?" Ken asked when Randy's mind released his body.

The young ranger tapped some black spots on the map which indicated houses and cabins. "Has anyone contacted any of the people who live in this area?"

"I don't know," Ken answered. "Why?"

"Can you get someone to check with the BLM map sales offices and see if any of these terrorist guys bought any maps?"

"Sure." Ken picked up the phone and called the special Task Force for Homeland Security. Randy heard Ken argue with someone on the other end of the phone. "Just have someone check, okay. If that's a positive have the hardware and general stores checked for ammunition sales and any explosives. Oh yeah, have them check for camping gear too."

Forty minutes later the phone rang and Agent Dewar was on the line yelling at Behoney to stay out of Homeland Security's business if he knew what was good for him. Ken grinned at Randy who was in his office, a map spread out in front of him. A lined tablet held down one side of the map and was covered with notes and a list of items folks unfamiliar with mountain camping might buy. On top of the list was ammunition, specifically 7.62X39 cartridges used by AK47 assault rifles, the weapon of choice for terrorists.

"Well, I guess you heard. I don't think anyone has checked any of those items you came up with. I'll call the sheriff of Okanogan County and see if he has a deputy who can check the general stores and other places that sell hunting gear and ammo. I have a friend at the Bureau of Land Management Map Sales in Spokane. He can check map sales since all the records have been converted to computer files." Ken picked up the tablet and scanned the list. "You think checking on maps of the area north of Concunnully, east to Republic and west to Winthrop will cover the area the terrorists are in. Hell, I'll just have him check on all map sales especially of the Okanogan Forest from the Colville Reservation to Mazama."

Randy took the tablet and added the stores and places ammunition and trail food could be purchased. Ken shook his head. "Do you think we'll find them?"

"Yeah, I do, especially if we find ammo and food with no pork products purchased." Randy grinned and went back to study the map.

Ken sat on the edge of Randy's desk and rubbed his chin which had three days' growth of beard. "We need the telephone numbers for the general stores in the forest too. Why don't you get with Sara and put together some action plan if we get a hit from the map folks or one of the stores. Your gear is still in the conference room. Bring the horses and pack animals and stage the horse trailer here at the stable. Be able to move from here within an hour and don't call me to let me know you're leaving. If Dewar has other ideas, I want to be able to say I don't know exactly where you are. Oh yeah, don't count on the helicopter flying you anywhere." Ken thumped the map with his finger over the group of houses two hours east of Winthrop. "Here's my guess where we'll pick up their trail."

Ken passed his and Randy's suspicions to the sheriffs' offices in three counties. They each agreed to put a man or team out to check the stores.

It was after 2100 hours when a call from a deputy sheriff came in with some interesting information. None of the terrorists were directly involved but the wife of one of the local people who lived ten miles from a small town came into the general outfitting store and bought five sleeping bags, five back packs and all the 7.62X39 ammunition in the store. She also bought ten boxes of 9mm parabellium ammo. The store owner knew the family of four; wife, husband and two children, a seventeen-year-old boy and his sixteen- year-old sister. The family trained pack and saddle horses. The store owner thought they had about fifteen horses at their small ranch. It was a guess, but at this time of year they would normally have about ten horses in training plus their own personal horses.

Randy interrupted the sheriff. "How did she appear and act: scared, calm what?"

"The store owner said she was nervous and she had a large bruise on her arm."

"Where is the deputy right now?"

"He is still at the general store."

"Stay right there in your office so we can contact you. What's the deputy's name and cell number?" When he had the sheriff's deputy's contact information he turned to Ken who was talking to the task force agent in charge again. Randy listened to Ken's explanation to the agent and saw the surprise on Ken's face as it turned red; he slammed the phone down.

Ken was so mad he couldn't talk until he regained his composure. "That stupid jackass doesn't think it's worth investigating since it's over forty miles from where the asshole thinks the terrorists were and they've already crossed the border. He did let us keep the deputy. He said the cop was probably new and dumb and didn't know how to spot threats." Ken fought to remain calm. "What do you two think?" he asked Randy and Sara.

Sara sat on the stool at the map table. "The place is sixty air miles from here about eighty miles plus a few by what looks like a macadam paved road." Sara grinned at the two men. "Looks like we're on our own." She sobered. "We need the deputy to check out the cabin. He needs to be a good actor because only bluff is going to keep him alive if it's where the Tangos are."

"Get him on the phone," Ken said and Randy dialed the number and the phone was immediately answered.

"What's your first name?" Randy listened. "Okay Andy, we've got something for you to do, but it's dangerous and strictly voluntary." Randy smiled when he heard the man's answer. "Airborne ranger, wow, I'm impressed. Does your boss know you were a ranger? Didn't tell him huh? Well, that's good for us." Randy gave the phone to Ken who explained the situation and the agent in charge's attitude.

When Ken was done, Sara took the phone and explained the plan the three rangers thought was the best and safest way for Andy to get his part of the plan done. Randy went to get the mustangs and the pack mule loaded in the trailer. Ken joined him and helped with the animals. Randy loaded the light pack frame on the mule to keep it out of the way. The panniers were put in the back of the pickup truck along with the saddles and other tack. Next Sara and Randy set the emergency packs into the pickup and personal supplies and clothing they brought from home. Randy slid the weapons box into the back seat and checked each rifle to see it was properly secure. The rifle scabbards were already tied to the saddles and only needed the rifles to be slipped into them.

Sara joined the men and personally checked her M1A without the scope and the M70 with a scope. She put her rolled up ghillie suit in its butt pack on the floor of the back seat. Sara added a box of 250 rounds of Lake City 7.62 US match boat-tail ammunition for the M1A and fifty rounds of .30 Caliber Lake City match rounds for the M70. The spotting scope box went into position behind the seat of the boss's new F350 dually. It looked like they were going to war.

Except for the guns and Sara's ghillie suit, they were only taking what they would normally take on a two-week-long patrol. The rangers left Winthrop with Randy driving. Sara was on the cell phone talking to Deputy Andy. He was at the suspect cabin's location and ready to climb up the steps and knock on the door. She ended the call to let Andy get to his part of the job. Sara called the owner of the general store who agreed to wait for them to arrive. There was a small box of sandwiches and sodas on the seat should they need a snack. Five minutes later they were on the road toward the east and a meeting with the general store owner and a deputy sheriff.

* * *

Deputy Sheriff Andy drove his cruiser up the drive and parked in front of the five-bedroom split log house. He saw several horses in the arena. A stable for about twenty horses was between the house and a large arena. Somebody had thrown a flake of hay to each of the horses. He could see the horses were happy and he shifted his attention back to the house. Andy limped up the steps to the broad porch and knocked on the door.

A woman in her mid-thirties answered with fear in her eyes. "Can I help you sheriff?"

"Yes ma'am, we're going around to folks who live away from town asking if you've noticed any strangers or anything strange in the past couple of weeks."

"No, nothing around here. Everything's just like always, nothing new. Thanks for your concern sheriff."

"You're welcome ma'am, have a good evening." Andy turned and limped down the steps and drove away. When he was a couple of miles down the road he called the number Sara had given him.

Sara answered on the first ring. "Yeah Andy, what did you see—are they okay?" Before the deputy could report, she said "Wait one minute Andy." Sara hit conference and brought Ken onto the call. "Go ahead Andy. Randy and Ken are on the line with us."

"Yeah Sara, you guys nailed this one. The lady is scared spitless. There were plates on the table but she was the only person I saw. I smelled Hoppe's gun bore cleaner but stayed in the doorway. I bet the lady is cussing me out for being a dumb cop."

"Andy, you did great and everyone is still alive, as far as we know."

"Yeah, I didn't smell any nitrate so at least a gun hasn't been fired where I could smell it."

"You did great. Randy and I are about an hour or a little less from the general store. We'll meet you there."

"Roger that." Andy dropped off the call.

"Ken, you want to pass the info to the Task Force? I personally don't know if I would tell them anything," Randy said loud enough for Ken to hear while he concentrated on the road.

* * *

Deputy Sheriff Andy Carter sat in his cruiser and waited for the two federal rangers to arrive and listened to the dispatch radio. Andy noticed the headlights of a pickup and horse trailer pull off the main road and enter the one street town.

Randy pulled the truck and horse trailer to a stop on the opposite side of the road from the sheriff's cruiser. No Name town was a real one-street town. All the businesses were compressed into one block on one side of the street.

Randy dismounted the truck and stood by the front bumper. Per instructions from Ken, Sara reported their location to the task force clerk. After giving the clerk her information, she asked if Dewar was in the area. Sara could hear the disgust in the clerk's voice. She informed Sara, Dewar had taken one of the Army helicopters and flown to Seattle again. He was probably still in the air, as he left an hour before. There were a dozen Homeland Security agents in Winthrop but their instructions were not to leave the town of Winthrop without checking with Dewar first. When the clerk attempted to contact Dewar, his phone appeared to be switched off. The ping by the cellular operator indicated he was out of the calling area. The operator said she would have Dewar call if he contacted her.

Randy checked on the animals and found them quiet; the mustangs munched on leftover hay and the pack mule was asleep and faced the back, leaning against the trailer wall. Randy made a decision for the future; he would load the mule last so it could lean against the last panel which would give the horses more room.

"Think that's our cop?" Sara stood beside Randy and pointed across the street toward the cruiser.

"Yeah, since he's the only cop I see, it should be a safe bet. You wait here and cover me." At that instant, Randy's cell phone buzzed.

"Are you two just going to stand in the street or do you want me to join you? I suggest we go into the store."

Randy laughed. "Yeah, that's Carter." He said aside to Sara, "Let's meet inside." Randy closed the phone. After he locked the truck, Randy followed Sara across the street and into the general store. The deputy followed them through the store's front door. They were met by the store owner, Ronald Bratman. Bratman offered them the use of a round table in the back of the store. There was a coffee pot under a sign: "coffee .25 cents, stale pastry .50 cents, large coffee to go $1. Don't laugh, make your own change or pay up front." Randy dropped two dollar bills into the canning jar that contained a couple of bills and some change. He poured a cup of coffee and grabbed a maple bar before Sara could. She poured a cup of coffee while Randy cut the maple bar in half.

"How about you Andy? " Randy asked, indicating the coffee.

"Sure, you know us cops, can't pass a cup of coffee or a doughnut." This brought a laugh from Randy, Sara and Mr. Bratman who had joined them. Bratman took the empty coffee pot and made the fixings for a new pot before sitting down with the rangers and the deputy. Mrs. Bratman came out from the back, put a huckleberry pie on the table with four plates. She had cut the pie into four pieces and left a quart brick of vanilla ice cream.

"Well, the Misses has concluded you all ain't customers so must be friends." Bratman scooped a quarter piece of pie onto a plate and scooted it in front of Sara. When everyone had a wedge of pie with a slab of ice cream on top, Bratman asked, "Okay, how can I help? You know Willa saw Mrs. Jacobsen too. You want her here?"

"No, we'll start with you and then talk to Mrs. Bratman." Sara took the initiative and asked questions.

"How well do you know the Jacobsens and did Mrs. Jacobsen look stressed or different when she was here?" Sara asked and waited while Bratman thought about his answer.

"My wife knows the Jacobsens better than I do. She and Mrs. Jacobsen are in some clubs together, like quilting and books. Things like that. While she was here Mrs. Jacobsen looked stressed and nervous. She used a credit card to buy the camping gear and the Jacobsens never as far as I know used credit cards. Clem and the Mrs. always pay cash. If they can't pay cash they wouldn't buy things." Bratman paused to think. "You know she didn't stop to chat like she usually does. She said hello like we were strangers and she has always been polite and interested in things around town and the families. In a small town it's like we're all related, you know?"

"Anything else you can think of?" Sara asked.

"Well, it did look like she had been crying and she had bruises on her wrists and a large bruise on her upper arm. Now that I think about it, the bruises on her wrists looked like rope burns, not like the ones you get working around horses. I bet her wrists had been tied together. She acted calm, but I think she was really scared."

Sara turned her attention to Mrs. Bratman, who had joined them. "Is there anything you can add?"

"I saw pretty much what Mr. Bratman saw. But when she bought the ammunition she looked at it like she had never seen stuff like it before."

Mr. Bratman interrupted, "When she bought the ammo, she asked if it came in bigger boxes than the twenty-round boxes we had."

"Thank you both, you've been a big help." Sara sipped her coffee. "How well do you know the Jacobsen ranch?"

"I've been out there quite a bit. My grandson took riding lessons and did trail riding with the boy and a bit of team and calf roping. I've been in the stable and the house some. Yeah, I guess I know the ranch pretty good." Bratman grinned.

"Could you draw us a map of the ranch, especially the buildings and their locations with distances between them? A sketch of the inside of the house would help."

"Yeah, I suppose I can do that." Mr. Bratman picked a tablet from the shelf of school supplies and a pencil from his apron pocket.

Twenty minutes later, the three cops had a detailed map of the Jacobsen ranch complete with the inside floor plan of the ranch house and stable.

"Thank you, you've been a great help." Sara smiled and the Bratmans left the table.

Chapter Twenty-Five

The Jacobsen Ranch

The two rangers and the deputy sheriff studied the sketch and made a plan to keep the terrorists at the Jacobsen ranch and the Jacobsens alive until help arrived. The primary concern was the safety of the Jacobsen family. Randy and Andy were concerned about the weapons the terrorists had. They knew the 7.62 X39 shells were made for use in the AK47 assault rifle. It was easy to gain possession of the cheap but reliable weapon.

Sara interrupted them saying the AK47 was a good weapon but still needed to be aimed. Most terrorists just pointed the rifle in the general direction of the target and pulled the trigger. If the terrorists were properly trained they would aim.

Andy added they should consider each Tango had a AK47 and also a 9mm pistol which meant you had to be sure the target was down before exposing themselves.

Sara asked about their weapons. Andy had a 10mm Glock pistol and a Mini 14 semi-automatic .223 Caliber rifle. He also had a 12- gauge pump shotgun with slugs instead of BBs. Sara had her 10mm Sig Sauer automatic pistol and her two match rifles: the M1A 7.62mm semi-automatic with twenty-round magazines. Her best weapon, the one she was most comfortable with was her M70 Winchester bolt action. She had 250 rounds of 7.62 match and 50 rounds of the .30 Caliber match for the M70. She also had 100 rounds for her 10mm Sig Sauer; her 9mm Beretta 92SF match pistol was in a box behind the truck seat. Randy had his .32 Caliber Winchester lever action with 140 rounds and an additional 100 rounds for his Sig Sauer 10mm automatic pistol. Andy had a box of 12-gauge shotgun shells, three thirty round magazines for the Mini 14, and 121 rounds for his 10mm automatic pistol. They considered themselves relatively well armed.

They studied the 1:25,000 scale topographical map of the area surrounding the Jacobsen ranch. Bratman had sets of maps from the Defense Mapping Agency's online outlet. Mr. Bratman gave them two sets of maps: 1:250,000 scale, 1:50,000 scale and the 1:25,000 scale series of the area north of Conconnully to the Canadian border. Randy folded the maps he thought they needed and put them in a map case Mr. Bratman gave them from his stock.

After the map survey of the area north of the No Name town and the Jacobsen Ranch, they agreed a small knoll 300 meters from the house's porch was a good place for a sniper. Andy got his black tactical suit from the cruiser. Randy borrowed some camouflage paint from Mr. Bratman and blackened the POLICE letters on the back of Andy's suit. Andy used the black and tan cami paint to break up the outline of Randy and Sara's ranger uniforms. The former Army Ranger showed her how to apply the face paint. With the face and uniform camouflage the two rangers would be invisible unless they moved. They went outside to the cruiser and laid the weapons on the hood. Five minutes later the hand weapons had disappeared and were secreted on the persons of the two rangers and the deputy.

Sara called the task force dispatch and Dewar still hadn't called in to the operator. There was a message that all calls from Behoney's people were to be ignored. Ken Behoney had received a message from Dewar he wanted Sara and Randy to meet an agent on the highway at the southern limits of Conconnully.

"That guy's crazy." Randy kicked a rock off the roadway. "Shit, we're going to do what we planned. You with us Andy?"

"Hell yes, I'm with you. Where do the Feds get those brain-dead people?" He laughed.

"They find the least competent people and put them in charge. This idiot thinks anyone with an idea other than his is absolutely wrong—not just a little wrong but not worth the energy of a thought. Yeah, this guy is really on a power trip," Randy agreed. "Sara, you ready?"

"Yep, ready. You want me on the knoll? We can use the radios or our cell phones."

"Let's use the cell phones, put them on vibrate. We don't want to let these guys know we're here."

Sara put her ammo in the pockets of her jacket and her small backpack. She attached the ghillie suit to the ties of the pack. The rifle she slung on her shoulder and back. Randy unhitched the horse trailer from the truck. They put the rifles in the back seat except for Sara's M1A with the twenty-round magazine. Sara sat in the middle with the M1A between her knees. Due to the diesel noise, Randy drove far enough past the ranch the truck motor couldn't be heard at the ranch house before turning to drop Andy and Sara off.

Randy taped the switch for the door lights and when Andy dropped away from the truck he disappeared almost immediately. Sara dropped away next and when Randy looked, Sara too had already disappeared.

Randy drove down the road and met a logging truck coming down from higher up in the mountains. He did a quick U-turn and turned his lights off and followed the logger. The giant diesel of the logging truck masked the motor noise of Randy's truck.

Andy was already on the edge of the trees and watching the house, yard and stable. He would go to the stable first and then the house. It was about two hundred yards from his position to the stable. The former Army Ranger took advantage of every shadow and moved like a whisper. He stood in a shadow at the corner of the stable and listened for noise. It was quiet; he should have been able to hear the horses. On the way from the trees to the stable, Andy passed the arena where horses had been earlier and it was empty.

Andy was about to begin his low crawl to the house when he heard a soft moan come from inside the stable. He slipped into the breezeway and passed the tack room. He noticed eight of the saddle racks were empty. He looked at the pegs where head stalls and tie downs were and eight more pegs were empty.

A quiet whimper of pain stopped Andy and he silently worked his way toward the sound, which came from a horse stall. He did a quick peek and saw a boy huddled against the back of the stall. He quickly moved to the boy and immediately noticed the leg was bent at an unnatural angle. In addition to the broken leg the boy had what appeared to be a knife wound to his stomach. Andy was able to make the boy aware of him and cognizant enough to answer questions.

"The men who took your family, where are they?"

The boy answered in a whisper. "They took the horses, my mom and dad and sister. They left a couple of hours ago, I think."

"There's no one left at the ranch but you?"

"No, just me. When the horse kicked me and broke my leg, the leader told one of them to knife me and make it so when I was found the knife stab wound would have killed me."

"Okay kid, I'm going to get you some help. Hold on."

Andy went outside, aimed his shielded flashlight toward Sara's position and flicked it on and off, then dialed her number. "You need to call for a dust-off, we have a wounded boy here. Everyone else is gone. Come on in." Andy pushed Randy's number and relayed the information. The deputy called the general store and asked Mr. Bratman to come to the Jacobsen ranch and bring a good first aid kit and if Mrs. Bratman could come along too.

Sara jogged up toward the stable with the M70 across her back and the M1A ready at the port. "Where are you?"

"Right here in the stall." Andy turned on his flashlight to shine on a wall which reflected the light so he could see as he worked to stop the bleeding on the boy.

"Did you call for a dust-off?"

"Yeah, you aren't going to believe this. Dewar had the other helicopters fly the rest of the agents to Seattle for a meeting with the task force brass. It just landed at Boeing Field. Dewar won't release it until after the meeting and then only after it brings him back to Winthrop where he is setting up his new headquarters in the conference room of the Bar and Grill."

"So no dust-off?"

"Right. Ken might be able to get a bird from either Moses Lake, Spokane or Yakima. The Spokane medical bird would probably be the fastest unless the Army has a bird in the air."

"Try all three, starting with the Army. You have the number?"

"Yeah, it's programmed in our cell phones." Sara pushed the number and was connected to the duty officer at the emergency airfield. Sara explained she was a federal officer and needed a medical evacuation for a causality of the terrorist operation. The duty officer was aware of the terrorist task force and on his own dispatched a medevac from the old Larson Air Force Base north of Moses Lake. The bird was about forty minutes out. Sara gave him the coordinates and would light the landing zone.

Randy drove the truck up to the front of the house and joined Sara. Together they went into the house to search for more causalities. Andy met them as they came out onto the porch. He had stopped the bleeding on the boy's wound and would wait for the helicopter. Andy would have to go with the boy to the hospital as the law enforcement officer who found him. Mr. and Mrs. Bratman arrived as Randy and Andy were talking on the porch. Andy asked Mrs. Bratman if she would stay with the boy at least until the medevac helicopter arrived.

"Listen, I know you and Sara are going after these guys. I'm not much of a horse person and would probably slow you down so I'll go with the boy to the hospital. If I can get a return trip from the helicopter folks I'll stay here and see what I can do about Dewar. My sheriff is pretty good at backing us and isn't afraid of the Home Security Agency. He think's most of them are idiots."

Randy and Sara laughed their agreement with that assessment of Dewar and the Department of Homeland Security. "Good deal Andy. If you can't get back right away, leave a message with Ken." Randy asked the deputy to try and keep Ken Behoney updated.

Sara nodded and bent over the maps. Randy said, "Andy, let's look at the maps and pick a place where we might be able to intercept these guys. Maybe take a short cut." Sara shrugged and left to check on the Jacobsen boy and talk to Mrs. Bratman.

"Maybe we should wait until Sara gets back." Sara had been a firefighter in the area between the Jacobsen ranch and the border. The two men walked toward the stable. They met Mr. Bratman.

"You find anything we should be aware of?" Andy asked.

"No sir, the place is like I remember but no livestock."

Randy returned to the house. The map was spread on the table.

After studying the maps for a few minutes, Randy suggested they take a break and bring their resources to the Jacobson ranch. Sara offered to straighten and clean the kitchen. Andy volunteered to help her. Randy went on a walk around the ranch buildings and found the trail where the terrorists with their hostages left on horseback.

Randy drove back to town and brought the horse trailer to the Jacobsen ranch. He put the horses in the arena along with the mule after he removed the pack. With Andy's help, Randy staged the panniers and other items they would take with them.. He cleaned and set the panniers next to the arena fence, ready to be loaded on the mule and put hay into the bottom of the panniers. Randy fed and watered the horses and mule, then put the saddles on the hitching post and wiped off the dust and dirt from the road. He put the saddles in the trailer dressing room and closed and locked the door.

Sara prepared the added provisions they would take with them on the hunt for the terrorists.

The helicopter came low over the tree tops, circled once and settled onto the front yard as Andy guided it to a landing with a flashlight. A medic was the first off the bird, and left with Mr. Bratman toward the stable. Randy and Andy signaled the pilot to join them.

"Major, I'm Randy Springer, a Fish and Wildlife Law Enforcement Service Ranger, and this is Deputy Sheriff Andy Carter. He will be riding with you to accompany the boy. Mrs. Bratman is taking care of the Jacobsen boy and he knows her. We didn't want to move the boy until a medic checked him. About Mrs. Bratman—can she ride along with the boy to the hospital?"

"I don't see why not. This is kind of unusual for me, so sure. Where do you want him taken? Spokane is the best medical center and its only twenty minutes longer flight time than Moses Lake or Yakima."

"Make it Spokane. Andy, the deputy, will ride along too. My partner and I will be following the terrorists, but we will be on horseback."

The two medics brought the boy on a stretcher, followed by Mrs. Bratman. The Major returned to his seat. Randy approached Mrs. Bratman. "Ma'am, since you know the boy, we've asked the Air Force to take you along to Spokane. He knows you and I'm sure would feel better with you along. Andy, the deputy sheriff will also go along and get any statements from you and the boy we may need later. Sara and I are going after the terrorists on horseback. I think our chances are good. We know them and they don't know us or that we're on their trail."

"Is Mr. Bratman going to be staying here?"

"Yes ma'am, we need to talk to him a bit more, than we'll be leaving here too. I see the major is signaling he is ready. Can I help you to the helicopter?"

"No, I can make it. This is the first time I've ever been in an airplane. I'm glad I wore my best jeans." She grinned at Randy and walked toward the helicopter where she was met by the crew chief.

Randy watched Mrs. Bratman helped to climb aboard and she sat next to Andy. He saw Andy say something to her and she patted him on the knee. The crew chief put a pair of earphones on Mrs. Bratman. When she looked out the open door at Randy as the helicopter lifted off the ground, her eyes appeared the size of dinner plates.

* * *

"The horses could use a flake of good hay before we leave. I broke up a bale and put it in the panniers." Randy spoke in a soft voice. "You know the odds are against us getting all the Jacobsens back alive? I don't want any argument so let's have it out now. When I say you stay hidden and work as a sniper, you do it." He sat down on the house porch steps. "You know in a hostage situation you either take the hostage out of the equation or the Tango, right?"

"Yes Randy, I understand. I hope you don't mind if I shoot the Tango first." Sara grinned; she knew the danger they were riding into. "You know the Tangos probably heard the chopper and know we've found the Jacobsen boy. Or they may think it's just a search flight. They won't be able to get a direction of the chopper noise because of the hills."

Sara went into the house to fix a snack while Randy checked the horses and watered them. He wanted to rest the horses before taking them out on a long rough ride. The mustangs came through the hours in the trailer better than Randy had hoped. The mule, well, he was a mule. Randy wanted to rest them for three or four hours before leaving. The humans could use a break too.

When Randy entered the house he found Sara frying up two steaks on the air grill of the modern stove. "I found these already thawed and still in the butcher's wrapper. I put potatoes in the microwave and they should be done in a few minutes. There was lettuce and a couple of tomatoes in the crisper so we have a salad. I looked but couldn't find a bottle of wine—I bet those terrorists drank it. You know most of them drink wine and a lot of them drink whiskey. I don't know what Allah would say about that, but I say drink a lot and pass out. A hangover will slow them down, but the down side, it would also make them meaner than they already are." Sara smiled. "We can kill them awake or in a drunken stupor."

"You sure you didn't find the wine?" Randy teased and knew Sara was talking off anxiety. This hunt could go either way and he needn't worry about Sara, but he knew he would.

Chapter Twenty-Six

Pursuit

After five hours of sleep, Randy and Sara sat at the kitchen table and ate a sparse breakfast of eggs, potatoes and toast. The sun was just breaking the eastern horizon. They ate in silence. Sara rinsed the dishes and left them with the other dirty dishes the terrorists left. She found a quart thermos and filled it with coffee and set it on the table so she wouldn't forget it. It promised to be a long night. They changed the plan to leave at daybreak. Sara pointed out a Forest Service trail on the 1:50,000 scale map. Randy remembered one of his first patrols was over part of the trail and the first section could be dangerous in places where it was cut into the side of steep hills. After the hills, the trail wandered through the forest passing through old growth cedar groves beside one of the numerous streams.

After some discussion, they agreed the terrorists would travel all night and put as much distance between them and the ranch as possible. If they pushed the horses too hard, it would slow them down instead of saving them time.

Together, Sara and Randy decided to cut cross country in an attempt to intercept the terrorists. The terrorists already had a ten- hour head start but didn't know the trail and Mr. Jacobsen would probably be leading and sticking to marked trails. If they got ahead of the group without knowing, they would have to double back. Both rangers thought it was worth the added risk. They knew the last thing the terrorists would do before leaving the United States was to kill all the hostages: the terrorists did not want to commit a crime in neutral Canadian territory. Obtaining permission to pursue into Canada would be difficult and time consuming; time, Randy and Sara and the Jacobsens didn't have.

Sara spent a few minutes with her mustangs while Randy was on the cell phone with Ken. He was camped in Randy's office for the duration. Randy briefed him on what had taken place at the ranch. While Randy and Sara were busy at the ranch, Ken had been on the phone with the Homeland Security office and wanted to know why the helicopter assigned to the task force as a support asset was not available for a medical emergency.

Randy was a silent listener on the telephone conversation. Ken swore, the first time Randy had ever heard him use a swear word stronger than "damn." Ken wasn't happy his rangers were going after the terrorists and hostages without some direct support. It had been refused by Dewar.

Ken gave Randy a set block of time to check in and wished them good hunting and ended the call leaving Randy listening to a dial tone.

"The boss's last words were, 'Good hunting."

Randy loaded the food and sleeping bags from the truck into the panniers. Sara stored the extra ammo and tied the M70 rifle case onto the pack. She put the M1A with one round in the chamber on her saddle and the magazines in a ready access pocket on her jacket. Sara put Randy's rifle into his scabbard, tied his non-reflecting poncho behind the saddle, then tied the ghillie suit pack and her poncho behind the cantle of her saddle.

With one last look at the map, Randy wanted to measure some distances. He laid out the 1:100,000 scale map on a nearby picnic table. Sara joined him as he traced the trail he thought the Jacobsens would try to guide the terrorists onto. Randy took out a green lead pencil and traced with it. Each time he came to a piece of terrain or stream he placed a hard line across it. He continued the line until it reached the border with Canada. He traced from the border back to the start point at the Jacobsen ranch. He figured each mark would take an average of 45 minutes to cross. Using the slow average rate of travel for a horse, he thought they were less than ten hours behind and by using the Forest Service shortcut they only had four hours of actual travel time to make up. He counted on Jacobsen to drag his feet and travel as slow as possible without getting killed.

"That could be dangerous as long as they don't think Mrs. Jacobsen can do whatever her husband can do. Then they wouldn't need both of them and might get rid of the man. I'm sure they will use the girl as a tool to get the most out of her parents." Randy thought for a minute, then went to the sheriff's cruiser and retrieved the Mini 14 from the trunk.

"Why are you taking the Mini 14?" Sara asked.

"The Mini is light and has good firepower and I want to carry it across the saddle where I can get it fast. It's a good weapon; I've used one before as a varmint gun."

"Yeah, the M1A is a bit heavy to carry all the time especially with the full twenty-round magazine. Now are we going to stay here jawing all day or hit the trail?" Sara teased Randy but reminded him each minute the terrorists were getting farther away and closer to Canada.

Randy and Sara mounted and turned toward the trail.. Randy led the way from the Jacobsen ranch and after two hours they found the forest trail used by the rangers during patrols. The two made good time and camped for the night. Randy didn't want to stumble into the terrorists by accident. With first light, they would continue the hunt.

* * *

On day two, Randy woke and found Sara already up. Water for tea was coming to a boil on thc small gas camp stove.

"Randy, can you smell the smoke?" Sara asked.

"Yeah, I bet Jacobsen put some green fuel and dried larch on a campfire. Not enough to smoke badly but enough to send the smell through the forest. How far do you think?" Randy took a deep breath through his nose and Sara did the same and shrugged her shoulders. "It could be a mile or ten miles, anybody's guess."

"There is a knoll not far from here where we can see most of the area to the northwest and southwest. I worked a fire line through here a couple of years ago. Take us about an hour to get there." Sara poured the water into camp cups and spooned in tea leaves.

"How long will it take us with only the two horses? We can leave the mule and the spare horses here."

"We could make it in twenty minutes or less if we leave everything we don't need."

"We could be there and back in less than an hour?" Randy had his map out. "Show me on the map."

Sara scanned the map and pointed to a spot about a mile from their present position.

"That's doable. We'll leave the mule on watch and go for speed. When we get back we can change horses." Randy collected two of the mustangs and saddled them. By the time Sara put away the stove and sleeping bags, Randy had both horses saddled and ready to mount. He put his binoculars in his saddle bags. "Check the cinch, I left it loose and the horses are hobbled., he told Sara before she mounted. "You lead!" When Sara was in the saddle she nodded and rode out of the camp at a trot with Randy twenty feet behind her.

Thirteen minutes later, Sara led Randy onto a pronounced knoll covered with burned trees, and stumps. The Forest Service had planted young trees and the new trees and underbrush were well rooted. An open space on the knoll's top provided a good view of the forest Randy suspected the terrorists and hostages were passing through.

Using the binoculars, Randy sectioned off the forest and spent a few minutes as he studied the terrorists' suspected route to Canada. He spotted a wisp of smoke and called Sara's attention to it. They agreed the smoke was from the terrorist camp. "We need to get in front of them today. They could make Canada by tomorrow afternoon if they pushed hard."

The rangers returned to camp and found it as they left it. They decided to make a fast trip to get in front of the terrorists. Once there, they could pick an ambush site and have time to set up. Sara suggested they get far enough ahead to spring an ambush in the morning as the sun came up. They would keep the sun at their back so it would shine in the terrorists eyes.

Tomorrow they would challenge the terrorists when and where the sun would be at Sara and his back. Sara would find a hide and be able to take two or three terrorists from ambush. Randy would challenge them and try to take the terrorists captive. The key to success was surprise and getting the hostages out of harm's way as quickly as possible.

"What about the chance to surrender? Do we want to offer one?" Sara asked.

"I know we should, but not if it endangers the Jacobsens. At the first aggressive action, take them out," Randy said. "I'll challenge them to surrender if the opportunity presents itself. Don't wait if you have a good shot and they make an aggressive move. You take the shot."

They changed horses after two hours and picked up the pace. Sara thought they were ahead of the terrorists and Randy agreed, only not far enough. "Let's keep up this pace for a couple of more hours."

* * *

The morning birds began their calls to one another as the sun reflected on the clouds above the eastern ridge. The forest and surrounding hills were still in shadow and colors were just beginning to emerge. Randy woke to the chattering forest as the birds welcomed the sun of a new day. Randy pointed out a doe and her fawn grazing in a meadow 50 yards down slope from their camp.

Last night, Randy left Sara at a small clearing and went back trail until he spotted the group coming uphill toward him. He counted the terrorists, paying special attention to where they were in the line and where they carried their weapons. He estimated how long it would take each man to get his weapon into action.

While he watched, three of the five terrorists nearly fell out of the saddle. They were exhausted and the horses were sweated up and needed attention. Mr. Jacobsen was first in line with one of the terrorists within twenty feet of him with an AK47 across the saddle, and he appeared alert. Jacobsen turned and said something and the line of riders stopped. The man who appeared to be in charge rode up to Jacobsen and began yelling at him. Jacobsen pointed at the animals with their heads down, more than one in distress. Finally the terrorist nodded and Jacobsen dismounted and led his horse toward a clearing on the far side of a hundred yards from where Randy lay hidden behind a log and bushes.

All the riders dismounted and followed Jacobsen, who took the heavy saddle off his mount. He hobbled his horse on the far side of the clearing and rigged a picket line. The terrorists took their sleeping bags from the pack horse, but left the other horses for Jacobsen to attend to. The woman and her daughter were allowed to relieve themselves but stayed in sight of their guard who watched them as they cleaned themselves with leaves from a pair of broadleaf trees. He laughed at them and struck the older woman for not being faster. A small stream flowed not far from where Randy lay and the woman and girl with a camp bucket were able to clean themselves before Jacobsen started a small fire to cook a pot of rice with chunks of some kind of meat.

Mrs. Jacobsen passed close to where Randy hid. He was able to see bruises on her face and arms not covered by sleeves and rope burns around her neck. He suspected the girl also bore the bruises inflicted by her captors. Mr. Jacobsen was tied at the edge of the camp and a sack was put over this head so he was unable to see or hear what was happening around him.

When the food was cooked, the mother and daughter were made to strip away all their clothing to insure they had no weapons. Naked, they served the men. While serving the leader, the girl was slapped hard on her breast. Randy could see the pain on her face, but she didn't cry out. Tears cut a line in the dirt down her face and dripped off her chin. The woman closed her eyes while the terrorist abused her daughter. Tired of the game, the man let the girl go and motioned to the woman to attend to him. It was difficult for Randy not to kill the man where he lay on his back. The woman administered to him as he twisted her nipples. Finished, he slapped the woman's face and pushed her away with his foot. Mrs. Jacobsen glanced at where her husband sat tied and blindfolded. Her face was red with shame, but if she hadn't done what she did her daughter would have had to.

Chapter Twenty-Seven

The Ambush

Randy had seen enough. He slipped quietly downhill and made his way back to where Sara waited a mile uphill from the terrorist camp. He whistled softly before he stepped out of the trees. Sara could be a little trigger friendly and he didn't want to get shot by accident.

After describing to Sara what he had seen, the two rangers firmed a plan to stop the terrorists in a clearing Randy found on the way down trail. Sara would wear her ghillie suit and they would not shoot until all the terrorists were inside the kill zone. Randy would conceal himself uphill and ahead of the line of riders. He would yell for them to surrender and give up. At the first movement toward weapons he would shoot the leader or the man behind Jacobsen. Randy would take as many as he could before Sara would begin to shoot taking the last man in line and working forward until all the terrorists were down. Hopefully, Randy would take down at least two with his Winchester before Sara had to fire her first shot.

Randy and Sara cleaned and oiled their weapons, not using bore cleaner. The odor of bore cleaner could be detected from a long distance. Weapons clean, they laid on their sleeping bags completely dressed, weapons beside them. The horses were on a picket line or hobbled. Mustangs made little noise and they were asleep as soon as they ate their half flake of hay from the pack mule.

* * *

Randy rolled up his sleeping bag and started the small white gas camp stove to boil water as the light in the forest brightened. He added four eggs, two apiece to the hard boil and then used the hot water to make tea. It was still two hours before the sunlight would actually crested the ridge. Morning twilight lasts a long time in the forest and then break into bright sunlight in a flash. There were still stars visible as the two rangers sipped their tea in silence, each lost in their own thoughts about the coming encounter with the terrorists. Randy wanted them to be in position an hour before the sun crested the eastern hills. He fed the horses another half flake of hay and checked them by rubbing his hands over every inch of their hide for any unwanted hitchhiking critters. He did find a tick on the mule and removed it. He moved calmly among the horses in the dark. The horses accepted him and welcomed him with a woof. While the horses ate he lifted each foot and checked for cracks in the hoof wall and bruises with his small hooded red lens flashlight. He did a second rub down of the mule and looked for any sore spots caused by the pack frame.

While Randy looked after the animals, Sara began to break camp. The night had been clear and they didn't want to chance the tent. Both Sara and Randy were experienced in movement in the forest and moved so not to raise dust. Sara rolled up her bedding and staged everything they used last night ready for packing. They would hike downhill to the ambush site.

"Today after the ambush, we'll use the horses that rested yesterday." Randy grinned at her. "We could use a break too. Maybe a little physical exercise might be called for. Don't want to get fat and lazy you know." Randy did the thing with his eyebrows to tease Sara.

"Speak for yourself Mountain Man." Sara teased right back. Randy was actually on the slim side of the men Sara associated with in the Forest Service. Not meaning he was skinny, he was strong and wiry with large shoulders and narrow waist. She sometimes wondered how he kept his pants from slipping off. "I did bring some natural soap I found in the Jacobsen's cabin. I didn't think they'd mine. Do you think the boy will be all right. The knife wound looked pretty bad."

"I've seen worse and it looked a lot worse than it is. He would have bled out within a couple more hours if he hadn't been found." Randy sipped his tea, put his arm around Sara and pulled her close. "Don't you ever get hurt; I don't think I could handle it. Let's get the rest of the gear staged."

Sara brushed and checked her two horses while Randy hobbled the mule and the horses. He finished before her and checked the camp for anything they have left. The last thing was the sack containing all the trash they compiled since leaving the Jacobsen ranch.

Before leaving, Randy pulled out his map and Sara joined him as he ran through their plan for the last time. "It's all downhill from here to the site and we should make it a bit faster than I did yesterday. There anything you want to add?"

"No, I think you've covered everything. I'll wait until we're closer before putting on my ghillie suit. It gets hot if I have to move around much. If we've timed it right, we should hit them where they are looking into the sun coming over the ridge. I would think they'll break camp at daybreak and be on the trail after eating. I'm going to try and get as much of a level shot as possible—a downhill shot is harder and each shot is going to be critical."

"What rifle are you going to use?" Randy had watched her clean both of the rifles she brought last night.

"I think the Springfield would be the best for this situation. It's semiautomatic if I need a second shot. I've been using it a lot the past year. Any shot from less than 300 meters should be dead on."

"That sounds good Sara. I'd like to be completely set up by 0600."

"No problem. How fast do you think they will be moving?" Sara asked.

"Judging by what Jacobsen did with the smoke., I'd say he's going as slow as he can without getting himself shot or his family hurt." Randy pointed at a small stream on the map. "They're probably already on the move and if he can get away with it, he'll try to have them cross this stream twice. That should slow them down quite a bit and have them moving uphill still looking into the morning sun when they reach us. The down side for him is he'll have them cross in daylight. If they figure out what he was doing, they could kill him on the spot."

"You really think he will do that?"

"Yeah, if the Tangos aren't trail wise or know the forest. It's pretty thick in there and he should be able to sell the idea of hiding from aircraft if the Feds are looking for them. If they heard the helicopter when the boy was sent to Spokane, they'll be a bit wired. That's one of the reasons I picked the ambush spot where it is." Randy grinned. "I think we've got a pretty smart guy out there helping us."

"Okay Ranger Rick, we're wasting daylight." Sara picked up her rifle, slipping a full magazine of twenty rounds into the well. She released the bolt putting the first round into the chamber. She picked up the ghillie suit by its straps and settled it on her shoulders.

Randy checked the horses and mule one last time, then led Sara downhill to the kill zone.

"I think Jacobsen is using the most predicable route. My guess, he knows someone is on his trail. It's the only real hope he has. My bet, they will approach from right out of there." He pointed to an opening in the trees where the trail turned uphill. Randy sat on a rock quiet with his thoughts. "You have everything you need?"

"Yes, no wait." Sara pulled a belly pack around her waist and put the spare fifty rounds of ammo for the Springfield in the pocket of her ghillie suit with the two spare magazines. Before leaving Winthrop, she had removed the Redfield scope from the rifle and would rely on the standard peep sight. "I'll be scouting around until you get back. Still think we have plenty of time?"

"Yeah, I'll be back as soon as I can." Randy climbed uphill and walked into the slight breeze. With the breeze at the Tangos' back there wasn't much of a chance they would smell or hear anything. Randy was confident the mustangs wouldn't make a sound with no humans around to protect them from the dangers of the forest. The mule didn't care and rarely made any noise.

Randy picked a position that offered him protection if a firefight erupted. The tree he hid behind had a large rock beside it Randy could use for both protection and a rest for the Winchester. He returned to find Sara where he left her.

"You find a hide?" he asked.

"Yeah, I need your help with the suit. I haven't had it on so the ties are not set and I could use help there."

"Where did you ever get a the suit? It looks brand new." Actually the suit looked like a bundle of rags and when Sara put it on, she could lie down on the ground and disappear unless you knew she was there. The suits were made for the sniper teams used by the Army and Marine Corps.

"A friend thought I might be able to use a little extra something someday. The Gunner got it for me at the Sniper School at Camp Pendleton after I did a class on long range marksmanship, timing and drift. I think they consider me a mascot or something." Sara laughed.

Sara pulled the suit from the bag. "Here, help me with the pants." She sat on a rock and pulled up the pants which tightened to her jeans with ties. The jacket was covered by hanging pieces of burlap in ground colors and a wrap-around hood went around the face so only the eyes were visible. With a little cami paint on the eyelids, Sara's face disappeared when she closed her eyes. Her rifle was also wrapped in burlap. She made sure the operating rod could move freely. The rifle blended in so well it was invisible in the half light of the morning. Sara's brown boots were covered with dirt, scuffed and matched the suit.

Sara pointed out where she would set in, kissed him quickly and left. Randy watched her walk away, then turned and went to his own hide. When he looked for Sara, she had disappeared completely. He used his binoculars to look and still couldn't find her and he knew within a few feet of where she was.

"You set?" Randy called on his cell.

"Yes, now don't call me again unless you tell me you love me."

"I love you."

"I love you too. Now quite pestering me. I've got a squirrel nosing around and he's doing a fine job."

With his rifle and a pocket full of spare .32 Caliber Winchester shells, Randy applied some cami stick to his hands and face. He wrapped a strip of burlap around the rifle barrel then settled down to wait. His hide was up slope and about 60 meters from where he wanted the lead Tango stopped. It was almost two hours before Randy heard the sounds of horses on a trail. For the past two hours he had tried unsuccessfully to find where Sara lay hidden. He tried once more to locate her, failed and turned his attention to the approach of the Tangos and hostages.

The first to appear from the forest was a large man, Clem Jacobsen. The man was a horseman and used his feet to guide the horse. He matched the description of Jacobsen Mr. Bratman gave them at the general store. He rode a large sorrel horse and was followed by a dark-skinned man on a smaller dun horse. The man carried an AK47 assault rifle across the saddle in front of him. Randy studied Clem Jacobsen and could see the man held his left arm as still as he could. The hand was inside his shirt to work like a sling. The assault rifle was pointed in the general direction of Jacobsen. The second Tango rode behind the first, his eyes shifting from side to side. Behind the second Tango was Mrs. Jacobsen, her eyes downcast. Another terrorist with an AK47 rode a few paces behind the woman. The last hostage appeared riding her horse followed by the fourth terrorist. The girl rode a dark Quarterhorse, her hands tied together in front of her. In the drag position was the last terrorist and he too carried an AK47. Each assault weapon had a banana magazine inserted in the rifle. Randy studied the second man and that's when he spotted the rope around each of the women's necks. Each rope led from the woman's neck to the saddle horns of the terrorists who rode in front and behind them.

Mrs. Jacobsen looked back at her daughter to make sure she was still there. Randy guessed the last terrorist had taken the girl off the trail a time or two. The girl's face was set in a permanent sneer except when she saw her mother look at her and she smiled. The mother's eyes slipped past her daughter and glared at the terrorist behind her. The third terrorist behind Mrs. Jacobsen yanked on the rope and nearly pulled the woman off her horse.

The binoculars revealed the bruising on the girl's face and the blood on the girl's pants. There was no doubt in Randy's mind what had occurred. It would account for Clem Jacobsen's broken arm. From 75 meters away, Randy could see the hate in the mother's eyes and the resigned posture in the girls.

Mrs. Jacobsen blood on the front of her shirt and the crotch of her pants and her nose looked like it may be broken.

As Randy watched from his place of concealment, all five Tango's entered the kill zone of the ambush. They were in the open and it was time to spring the trap.

Randy stood and peered around the large ponderosa pine. "Federal Officers, drop your weapons and put your hands in the air." The lead terrorist fired his weapon in Randy's direction.. Randy fired once and saw dust from the Tango's jacket puff out as the bullet hit the center of the his chest. The heavy .32 Caliber bullet drove the terrorist backward and over the butt of the horse.

"Give it up, drop your weapons." Randy yelled again with his sights on the second terrorist who held Mrs. Jacobsen's neck rope. The terrorist started to swing the AK47 toward his captive when Randy squeezed the trigger a second time with much the same results. When slack came into the rope around her neck, Mrs. Jacobsen snatched it up and over her head. She started to turn her horse back toward her daughter but the remaining three terrorists closed to within feet of the Jacobsens.

"Drop you guns or we kill the girl," the number four terrorist yelled.

"Surrender, drop your guns. Turn the girl loose," Randy commanded.

"We kill girl now then mother," the third terrorist screamed.

"Look, you don't have to die. Turn the girl loose." Randy tried again.

The terrorist grabbed the girl's shirt and pulled her in front of him as a shield.

Randy didn't have a shot. "Look you don't have to die. Drop your weapons or I'll kill you and bury you in pig guts." Randy was getting pissed as he watched the terrorist rip the shirt from the girl.

"This is my slave, you drop your gun or I kill her. I have pardon from Imam, so swine blood can't hurt me," he screamed.

Clem Jacobsen had his horse turned around and was urging it toward the terrorist. A savage yell came from him. But he only distracted Randy from his rifle sights. Mrs. Jacobsen had gotten loose and rode toward her daughter. Two terrorists had her daughter and she knew it was suicide to charge the men with the assault rifles.

The terrorist grabbed the girl's neck rope and pulled her closer to him and put the AK47 next to her face. Randy didn't have a shot, but Sara did. The sound of the shot followed the terrorist's head as it exploded and covered the girl with blood and gore. The last terrorist in the line started to point his weapon at the girl when his head too exploded followed by the rifle's report. The sound came back over and over as it echoed off the steep hills.

Thanks to the excellent training Clem Jacobsen had done with the horses, they stood quietly while the girl lifted the noose from around her neck.

Randy stepped away from the tree and yelled at the Jacobsens. "How many were there?"

"Five," came the answer immediately from Clem as he rode toward his wife, who ran toward the girl. Mrs. Jacobsen, the first to reach her daughter, pulled her from her saddle and had her arms around her to comfort her. Randy ran toward the family. He knew there was one Tango left. Randy skidded to a stop in front of Jacobsen. He gave Mrs. Jacobsen his handkerchief to wipe the blood off her daughter's face.

The last terrorist stepped from behind a tree and pointed the AK47 at the group. A shot rang out and the terrorist was thrown backward against a rock where his body remained, the weapon still in his hands, unfired. The girl screamed and pointed at a bush that appeared to rise from the bare ground and advance toward them. Sara pushed the hood back to reveal her blonde hair and her face.

The girl closed her eyes, but her breath still came rapidly and the ranger could see the girl was close to retreating into shock. Both women hung onto their husband and father.

Randy realized he didn't even know the women's first names. Clem Jacobsen didn't smile as he introduced his wife and daughter to the rangers who saved his family's lives. Mother Amy and daughter Denise tried to smile but started crying.

"They killed Danny. Did you find his body?" Clem asked.

"Yes sir, we found the boy and he's been flown to a Spokane hospital and is expected to recover according to our boss. Mrs. Bratman went to Spokane with him. Now if you'll excuse me I'm going to try to get a dust-off to take you all to Spokane and rejoin Danny." Randy took the cell phone and called the office in Winthrop.

Sara smiled at the Jacobsens, "Everyone good here?"

Randy answered for everyone. "Yeah, I think so. Remind me never to get you mad at me."

The Jacobsens stared at the crazy rangers who had just saved them. The first to recover was Mrs. Jacobsen who smiled and hugged her daughter, fearing to let go of her. Clem next hugged his daughter then noticed she was nude from the waist up and painfully took off his shirt and covered her. The family gathered in a group hug with their heads together.

Sara took Mrs. Jacobsen by the hand and led her and her daughter away from the bodies of the terrorists. Sara had her rifle in hand and still wore her ghillie suit. Randy checked each of the dead men, and put plastic handcuffs on each per procedure. He left to get the horses and mule. An hour later, Randy sat with the Jacobsens and shared some bottled water. Sara and Mrs. Jacobsen washed the bit and pieces of the terrorist from the girl's body. The mother and daughter were each given one of Sara's spare sweatshirts to wear.

Sara inspected Clem's arm and with Randy's help reset it and rigged a sling from his shirt ,returned from Denise. Clem wore one of Randy's sweatshirts. After a brief interview while everything was fresh in the Jacobsen minds, Randy called the base and reported their location and the Jacobsens were safe and all the terrorists were dead. He was informed a helicopter was being dispatched with Dewar on board.

The rangers thought the helicopter would pick up the Jacobsens and take them to a medical facility but Dewar spent fifteen minutes on the ground, took pictures of the bodies, picked up one of the AK47s and got back in the helicopter and left. Randy and Sara couldn't believe Dewar left injured people behind. Randy called Behoney and said they still needed a medevac. Randy was told the Homeland Security people took all the helicopters and left. The message from Dewar to Ken Behoney was, they should ride out using the horses. The most serious injury was Clem Jacobsen's broken arm. The women would recover without immediate medical treatment.

Ken said Dewar called the Tangos suspected terrorists. Ranger Randy Springer's reaction was, "He did what? He said what? You're joking right?"

"No sir, the SAIC took all four helicopters, including the two Army choppers from the Yakima Firing Center. He said the Homeland Security people needed to report the rescue of the hostages and the killing of the suspected terrorists."

Randy couldn't believe what he was hearing. He motioned for Jacobsen and Sara to join him and put the phone on speaker. "Would you say all that again?"

"Sure Ranger, the SAIC took all four helicopters to Seattle to report the rescue of the Jacobsen family and the killing of the suspected terrorists. He wanted all of the Homeland Security people there to make the report."

"Okay, who are you and who do you normally work for?"

"I'm Bob Madsen and I work for the Forest Service on loan from the Spokane office. I also work for the Bureau of Land Management."

"Well Bob, it looks like they left you and us holding the bag. Did Dewar actually use the words, 'suspected terrorists?"

"Yeah Ranger, those are the words he used." Randy started to drop the call but held the contact. "Bob, do you know if there is any helicopter support available in the Spokane area, or in Eastern Washington?"

"The Spokane Sheriff's office has one Ranger helicopter that can be used as an ambulance. The Air Force at Fairchild Survival School have a couple of Huey's we might be able to get if it's an actual emergency."

"Okay Bob, try to get the Air Force for a dust-off and to pick up five bodies."

"Sure, I'll try. I've got your number—be right back." Bob disconnected.

Randy looked at Jacobsen and Sara. "Can you believe that asshole took the only air support we had for an admin flight to Seattle?" Randy kicked a pine cone in frustration. "Mr. Jacobsen, he took all four birds. Who is that guy anyway. I wonder if the idiot is an American."

"Ranger, maybe you should be calling me Clem and not Mister. It looks like we might be together for a while and I owe you my life and the lives of my wife and daughter. Sara told me my son was rescued and taken to a Spokane hospital by a county deputy sheriff. Thank you for that too. I'd like you to meet my wife Amy and my daughter Denise. Denise is my youngest. Call her Deni, she doesn't like Denise." Clem laughed and held his broken arm up against his chest.

"Clem, I'm Randy Springer and this beautiful partner is Sara Bennett." They were interrupted by the phone signal. Springer answered.

"It's Bob, I talked to the sheriff's office and their bird is committed. He called the Air Force with me on the line and asked for a medevac and a way to get some dead people away from the forest."

"Thanks Bob, you did good, anything else?"

"Yeah, they'll contact you on Guard and are sending two Huey's. The lead pilot is Colonel Wilson and is the Survival School commander and Blue Flight One." Bob was interrupted by a background voice. "I was just informed both Huey's have departed Fairchild Air Force Base and will call you on Guard in about thirty mikes, eh minutes."

"I know about 'mikes' Bob. You've done a good job for us. I look forward to meeting you. Take care Buddy." Randy dropped the call.

Sara and Randy removed the pack from the mule and tied all the bodies onto the pack frame. They put sacks over the head-shot terrorists. Randy led the mule up to an open area and dumped the bodies in a pile there. He returned to find Sara had each of the Jacobsens mounted and waiting for him.

The five riders were coming out of the trees when the cell phone signaled an incoming call on the Guard frequency. "Springer," Randy answered.

"This is Blue Flight with two chicks. We are about fifteen mikes from your last position report."

"Roger Blue Flight. We have moved to an open hilltop. When I see you I'll pop smoke to mark the Landing Zone."

"Roger Ranger, you will mark LZ with smoke."

"Roger out." Randy left the cell phone on monitor and removed a red smoke grenade from his saddlebags. He and Clem stood together while Sara moved the horses out of the landing area and tied them on a picket line in the trees. Sara was walking up the hill to the LZ when the unique whopping sound of Huey helicopters echoed off the surrounding mountains. When Randy was sure the helicopters were close, he pulled the pin from the smoke grenade.

The speaker of the cell phone immediately sounded. "I see red smoke."

"Roger red smoke, wind about three knots from the southwest. The LZ is covered with huckleberry bushes, should not be a problem, the LZ is clear."

"Roger copy." The lead Huey circled the LZ one time and landed nearest to the group on the ground. As soon as the Huey was on the ground about 100 feet away, the crew chief was out of the chopper doing his safety checks. The second Huey landed about 100 feet up the hillside. The pilot's door opened on the first bird and the pilot approached. "You Springer?"

"Yes sir." Randy introduced Sara and the Jacobsens to the colonel.

"Say, you don't happen to be related to an old Marine named Hank Springer?" the Colonel asked.

"Yes sir, my father. You know him?" Randy was always meeting people who knew one of the Springers.

"Now there is a solid citizen. I met your dad right after I crashed a Huey as a lieutenant on my first deployment in Thailand. We dropped right on top of a group of Muslims who took us captive. Somehow your dad knew and about three hours later a Marine Warrant Officer with a gunnery sergeant carrying some huge automatic weapon walked into the camp right down the main drag and went right to the headman said something then walked over to us and cut us loose. The headman started dancing around and yelling, your dad said something in his radio and the next thing I knew an F18 Hornet came over us at treetop level, busted the sound barrier right on top of the camp. After the Hornet passed the only two still standing were your dad and the Gunny. The Gunner took me by the arm, the Gunny took my copilot's arm and my crew-chief followed us to the end of the village as a Marine Sea Knight helicopter landed on the headman's goats. We just walked up the ramp and the Sea Knight took off. As we departed the area, two Hornets crossed the village, did a pull and climbed straight up to twenty thousand feet." The Colonel paused. "We had lunch on the ship and an Air Force helo picked us up and I was in the club for happy hour. Before we left the ship I asked the Gunny about the Warrant Officer. He told me and I quote, "The Gunner does that shit all the time." I heard later his wife was killed in a car wreck and he retired."

"When my mom died, Dad went into a dark place but he pulled himself back. We moved to Montana. He lives just north of Missoula a couple of hours." Randy took out his notebook, wrote a note and handed it to the Colonel. "He would like to hear from you. If you can find the time give him a shout." Randy shook the Colonel's hand. "I suppose we'd better get these folks out before dark."

"Yeah, we can talk later. How do you want to load? I understand we'll be taking the dead terrorists out too."

"I've got a strange request, Colonel. Could you take the Jacobsens to a hospital in Spokane? The man has a broken arm. The mother appears okay but I have some doubts. The girl's behavior tells me, and I think Sara agrees, that both the mother and the girl were assaulted and sexually abused." Randy talked softly, and the colonel had to lean close to hear. "I noticed some blood on both the females. If I didn't need Sara, I'd have her travel with them."

"Don't worry, the crew chief on the other chopper is a woman, young but a solid NCO. We'll use the second bird as the ambulance. I'll take the dead. Where do you want them?"

"I have a feeling both the Fish and Wildlife and Homeland Security are not happy with the outcome of this Op. Could you hide the bodies for a couple of days or maybe a week or so? We need to have somebody other than those government agencies take charge of the bodies. We need a complete medical workup. I think there's more going on here. The Task Force SAIC for this area did a lot to interfere with us and was definitely unhappy the terrorists died. Colonel, I don't want you to get into trouble, but I need as much information about these guys as I can get."

The Jacobsens climbed aboard the second Huey while the bodies were dumped aboard the Colonel's plane. When the last Huey left the LZ, Randy turned his attention to the horses and the terrorist equipment. There were four AK47s and the ammo plus the camping gear Mrs. Jacobsen bought from the general store. Tied behind each of the terrorists' saddles was a bag containing $50,000, three passports, one a United States Passport. There were some papers with Arabic writing and a sealed two-kilo plastic bag containing a brown granulated powder in two separate bags. Sara had seen packages like the bags before and guessed it was Mexican brown heroin and Randy agreed.

"We need to get this stuff to a safe place," Sara suggested, "but first let's go home."

Chapter Twenty-Eight

The Homeland Security Agent

Three days after the ambush, Randy and Sara pulled the truck and horse trailer into the Winthrop Fish and Wildlife compound. Inside the trailer were four tired horses and one mule. The past days on the trail had been hard. A summer rain came down and continuously soaked and chilled them. On the first night they had to set up the tent as the rain fell heavy. Jacobsen's horses were spooky, but the mustangs remained calm which had a good influence on the other horses. The mule didn't seem to mind one way or the other. On the way to pick up the truck and trailer, they had dropped by the Jacobsen ranch and found Clem Jacobsen home. Mrs. Jacobsen stayed in Spokane with their son and daughter. Both Amy Jacobsen and Deni were in therapy and doing better than expected after at first denying the assaults and rapes by the terrorists. Deni was still in denial, but was making headway into accepting what had happened to her. At sixteen, Deni had to grow up fast. Both mother and daughter were seeing a personal counselor.

At the ranch, the two rangers helped Clem Jacobsen put the horses away and feed them. Randy and Sara were both near exhaustion after leading a thirteen-animal string for three days from the ambush site to the ranch. While Sara fixed Clem some dinner, Randy loaded the four horses and mule into the trailer and topped off the truck with diesel fuel from two five-gallon jerry cans. Randy just happened to drop the cash found on the terrorists in the stable. He told Clem whatever was left by the terrorists the family should keep to pay for the therapy and hospital bills. Clem walked with them to the truck and thanked them again for saving his wife and children.

Three hours later, Ken Behoney met the two tired rangers at the compound arena next to the stables. "Glad you're back but I've got some bad news. Our glorious director has brought charges against you and Sara for unauthorized use of deadly force among other charges. The charges start with unauthorized use of government assets including the horses. The use of personal weapons not authorized, putting civilians in a deadly situation where they could have been injured or killed. Unauthorized use of military assets; i.e. the Army and the Air Force helicopters." Behoney paused. "Now for the worse part. There is a Homeland Security Agent with an arrest warrant with your names on it. You're being charged with the premeditated murder of five foreign students. I assume that's the terrorists."

"You've got to be shitting me!" Randy was stunned by the charges and the arrest warrant. "What do you want us to do?" asked Behoney.

"One thing we are not going to do is go to jail!" Sara said loudly.

Behoney smiled for the first time. "I called the Federal Judge in Seattle and he cancelled the arrest warrant, but couldn't do anything about the charges. They are still pending."

"What about the agent here to arrest us?" Sara asked.

"Tell you what. I'll bet the Homeland Security office hasn't told him about the warrant yet. He's going to try and arrest you." Behoney actually smiled. "I'll tell him the warrant is no good and has been cancelled and he won't believe me. I'm authorizing you to resist arrest and if necessary arrest him for assault on federal officers should the opportunity arise."

"Great. This should be fun., Randy said to Sara.

"If we have to take him down, what do we do with the agent?"

"I'll send him back to Seattle with the reference the judge gave me. If he actually pulls a weapon, you have my permission to take him down without deadly force, right?" He waited for both his rangers to acknowledge his instructions. "Put him in handcuffs and I'll have him delivered to the U.S. District Court in Seattle; of course by the slowest conveyance I have other than the horses. All this was really the judge's idea. The judge has had some contact with the Task Force and that asshole Dewar."

Randy interrupted his boss. "Ken, we turned the terrorists' bodies over to the Air Force for safe-keeping along with four of the AK47s and other weapons. There were five total AK's one was taken by Dewer. Can you ask the judge what we should do with the bodies and the other stuff? Specifically the dope, weapons and passports." Off the record Randy explained what he did with the money. Ken shrugged and appeared uninterested with the money.

"The bodies and stuff, why did you do that?" Behoney was surprised his rangers had taken those steps to preserve evidence.

"After Dewar visited the ambush sight and took some pictures then left, we called the medevac. Sara and I decided we didn't trust Dewar. So to preserve the evidence we thought we'd give it to the Air Force for safe-keeping. The colonel signed for everything, including the bodies and I stressed the need for Chain of Custody. Sara and I are the only ones who saw the money packets. There is no record of the money at all."

"Probably good thinking. Right after we take care of the idiot in your office, I'll call the judge for advice. I don't think he'll be able to give any, but he might suggest an attorney you can call."

"What should we do with the agent if he does try to arrest us?"

"If he does, and he's a real smartass, depending on his actions, arrest him and I'll see if the sheriff will keep him until I can get him to Seattle."

Ken led the way to his office after Randy and Sara made sure the horses were settled for the night. As they approached the ranger office building, a man in a suit came out of the office to meet them. "You Springer?" he asked Randy, who nodded. "Then you must be Bennett?" He nodded at Sara.

"Yeah, that's us. What do you want?" Randy asked.

"Both of you are under arrest. Put your weapons on the ground in front of you along with your badges and credentials. Do it now!" The agent pulled his gun and found himself on the ground with Randy's knee on his throat.

"Your warrant has been cancelled and if you had asked you wouldn't be on the ground now," Ken told the agent.

"You've attacked a Federal Officer. I'm filing a report and you will be charged."

"Shut up asshole!" Ken cut him off. "I've about had it with you and your agency. If you had used your somewhat limited brain we could have avoided all this unpleasantness. The warrant was vacated by a federal district judge." Ken looked at his watch. "Almost six hours ago. Plenty of time to get that information to you. Sara, take his gun and Randy, cuff him. We'll go into my office and get this immediate problem solved." Randy used the agents' own handcuffs to cuff his hands behind his back. Following procedures, Randy with Ken as witness read the agent his rights, turned all the agents' pockets inside out. Randy found the handcuff key on the agent's key ring. He removed the key and handed it to Ken Behoney as the senior officer present.

Once in Randy's office, Ken again read the agent his rights and the reason for the arrest;: false arrest and attempted kidnapping using a deadly weapon. Sara, acting as the clerk, typed up the arrest papers and transfer papers to the Federal District Court in Seattle and custody papers to the U. S. Marshal's office. Ken called the sheriff, who was in Winthrop five minutes away. The sheriff agreed to keep the agent in jail until he could be transported to Seattle. Ken made one last call to the judge and explained what had occurred outside the office. He also asked what to do with the terrorists' bodies and other items taken at the ambush site to maintain the chain of evidence requirements. The Judge said he would have to study the situation and asked if the Jacobsens would be willing to visit the federal courthouse in Seattle and make confidential statements about the ambush and killing of the suspected terrorists. The judge said he would be happy to refer the matter over to the U.S. Marshal's Service and sign the confinement papers for the Homeland Security Agent. Ken asked if the judge knew any good attorneys within the Federal system he would recommend to his two rangers.

"Let me do some checking. I'll get back to you at your office this afternoon before 1700 hours. I'm sorry Ken, but I don't think this thing is going to go away either. Later." The Judge hung up.

Two hours later, the judge returned Ken's call. "I talked to a judge friend by the name of Barker in the California Superior Court and he suggested attorneys in San Diego. Graham-Butler & Associates Law Firm. It is run by two exceptional lawyers and they handle almost exclusively federal cases and capital cases for the California system. The Senior Founding Partner is Kathryn Graham-Caldwell. She's married to a U.S. Marshal in the Appeals system and the Special Projects and Operations Agency. They can be a bit pricy but are very good. They have excellent contacts throughout the Marshal's Service and judicial system." The judge read the telephone number to Ken who wrote it down and handed it to Randy.

"Now I want you two out of sight and out of mind for three days. Go home, clean your guns, and do something but not here. The new guys can take care of the horses until you get back in three days. You both did a great job with limited information. You saved a family and caught five terrorists—good work. Now, get out of your office!"

"What about the Homeland Security agent?" Sara asked.

"The sheriff and I are going to send him to Seattle and hand him into the custody of the U.S. Marshals. By using Homeland Security's own procedures, the Marshals can isolate him for 96 hours then book him for assault on two commissioned federal officers as a courtesy to us. It should take Homeland Security a day or two to find their agent and get him out of jail. Call your friend Colonel Wilson and see if he can get the terrorist bodies into a the Seattle District Court system where Homeland Security can't touch them. And, call that San Diego attorney tomorrow morning at the latest."

Sara and Randy shook their boss's hand and left for home. Sara wanted to spend some time to clean her rifle; red is not a good color for rifles or any firearm.

Sara opened the door to her apartment and Randy with their bags stepped inside. Sara carried Randy's rifle and both of hers. He had the Mini14 strapped to his bag. They laid the rifles on the kitchen table after putting down newspaper. Sara set her cleaning kit on the table and set about cleaning and oiling her M1A Springfield. She checked the M70 and refreshed the light coat of oil. Randy cleaned his Winchester and started cooking dinner while Sara finished with the rifles. Two hours later after a dinner of chops, baked potatoes, green beans and corn, Sara and Randy were ready to turn their attention to cleaning themselves. Sara stood in front of the apartment-sized clothes washer and stripped out of her dirty clothes. She put them directly into the washer.

When Sara turned around, Randy was standing across the room watching her a mischievous smile on his unshaven face.

"Oh no you don't. I know that look." Sara squealed as Randy crossed the room reaching for her. She escaped to the bathroom and Randy followed.

He caught her around the waist and pulled her back against him and kissed her neck. His hands moved up her sides as she leaned back against him. "I love you Sara Bennett." Randy turned her to face him. He lifted her face and kissed her gently on the lips. "I have an idea, we'll take a shower to get the dirt off, then a long soak together. After the bath, I want to make soft passionate love to you and hold you safe and warm."

"God I love you Randy Springer. I never thought there was a man just for me. I'm going to love you so good we'll never be apart or alone ever again." Sara sat on the commode. "Now strip. I want to watch and see what I'm getting. Hurry up so we can shower. I'm getting wet just thinking about you."

Randy finished and picked up his clothes and carried them to the washer where he dumped them in a basket. When he returned to the bathroom, Sara had the shower adjusted and waited for him to join her.

After the shower, Sara wiped out the extra large tub and began to fill it with hot water. She made sure the water was hot, but not uncomfortable. Randy stepped in first. Sara pulled the cork from a bottle of Malbec wine and poured two glasses. She lit two candles on the edge of the tub and turned out the light in the bathroom. In the tub, Sara leaned back against him, relaxed as they sipped their wine, content to be together.

"We need to make a trip to Montana and let the family know about the Homeland Security charges." He kissed Sara behind her ear. Sara twisted her face around to be kissed. "How long have you been planning this vacation?" Sara sat up and turned to face him.

Randy let a grin wash over his face. "Since the day I first met you. You were my love at first sight. You were made for me and just didn't know it."

"What about the charges against us?"

"Don't worry about them. I'll call the attorney after we soak some more, or better tomorrow morning."

"What about money? We can't afford high priced lawyers." Sara sighed and leaned back against her man.

"I suppose now is the time I revealed some more about me." Randy smiled at Sara's expression.

"You aren't married or have a bunch of kids or something like that?" she asked.

"No, its we don't have to worry about money. I've got enough for attorneys."

"How much is enough?" Sara asked.

"I don't rightly know exactly how much. I think it's around three million dollars, maybe a bit more actually."

Sara spun around and faced him. "Three million dollars? You have three million dollars?"

"Yeah, I think so. It might be a bit more, maybe five or six million. I'd have to call Wilma to find out exactly."

"Who's Wilma, your other woman?"

"No, she just handles the finances with my sister Margie."

"I don't want to hear any more about money. Everyone will think I'm with you because you're rich and not because you're the sexist man alive."

"Sara, the sex part sounds good, but money doesn't mean a lot to me or any of the family. Dad discovered he was a millionaire only because he wanted to foster three orphans: Margie, Michael and Mary Ann. He wouldn't adopt them because they need to carry on their family name. He did adopt Gail, but that's a story only Gail can tell you. You can ask, but Gail keeps that bit of family history. Bess is our step-mom and Bev's mother and my sister Lori's mother too. Sabrina says Bess is just like my mother. I barely remember her. I was still a toddler when she died. Now that's Dad's story to tell." He gave her another mischievous grin. "How many kids would you want? Zero, two, four, a dozen?"

"Let's let nature decide shall we?" Sara couldn't imagine herself a parent.

The couple relaxed in the water. Sara added hot water twice more before saying. "I think it's time to get out. I'm beginning to look and feel like a prune."

Randy dried Sara while she dried him. He picked her up and carried her to the queen-sized bed. He kissed her and lay down beside her and both were instantly asleep.

Chapter Twenty-Nine

The Lawyer and to the Ranch

Randy held thc card with the attorney's telephone number. He punched in the number and listened to the ring signal.

"Graham and Butler Attorneys, how may I direct your call?"

"Yes, my name is Randy Springer. I was referred to you for some legal problems."

"Can you say who referred you?"

"Well, kind of, a Judge Fullworth in Seattle called a Judge in San Diego who recommended your firm."

"Who was the San Diego referring Judge? Do you have a name?"

"Yes ma'am, actually their were two Judges, one was United States District Judge Aldrich and the other was San Diego Judge Barker of the California Superior Court. I personally don't know the Seattle Judge. But he is a U.S. District Court Judge."

"You said your name is Springer?"

"Yes ma'am."

"I am going to refer you to Ms Graham. She is available at this time. Would that be satisfactory Mr. Springer?"

"Yes ma'am." Randy didn't quite know what to say. He had limited contact with lawyers even though his job was as a Federal Commissioned Law Enforcement Officer.

"This is Kathy Graham, how may we assist you Mr. Springer?"

"Well ma'am, I'm a Federal Fish and Wildlife Law Enforcement Ranger. I work in the central part of Washington State. My partner and I are in a bit of a pickle with the Homeland Security Agency among other agencies. We think they want to charge us with a number of crimes including murder."

"Okay, did you murder anyone?"

"Well, yes and no. We did kill five people who we identified as terrorists who had a local family as hostages. None of the terrorists survived. We did rescue the hostages without any injuries to them."

"Listen Mr. Springer. I assume you know we are quite expensive and going up against the Department of Homeland Security could be a problem. Give me your contact number and I'll get back to you this afternoon or tomorrow at the latest."

Randy gave Ms. Graham his information including his Social Security number and permanent home address, the Rolling JH Ranch in Montana.

Kathy called Sam Hobert; it was his last official week on the Chief U.S. Marshals job. He would become the law enforcement director for a special new agency under the direction of the Assistant Attorney General and U.S. Court Judge Aldrich. "Sam, Kathy here. You ever hear of trouble with the Department of Homeland Security?" She listened for a couple of minutes. "You ever hear of a Fish and Wildlife Ranger named Springer from Montana working out of Winthrop, Washington? You did, what was his father's name?" There was a pause while Kathy listened. "You said Hank Springer, he owns the Rolling JH Ranch northwest of Missoula, Montana. I guess his son is in trouble. Do you think Jon might know him?"

Kathy listened to Sam for a few more minutes as he told her of Hank Springer and if Jon didn't know him, he had heard of him. Hank was an intelligence officer in the Marines for twenty-plus years.

That evening at home, Kathy asked Jon if she knew a Marine Intelligence Officer named Springer, a Chief Warrant Officer.

Jon stopped working replacing the electrical cord on the toaster and gave his full attention to his wife. "I heard of a CWO4 Hank Springer who is a legend in the Corps Intelligence. His wife was killed and he had three kids. He ended his career early and moved to Montana, nobody seems to know what happened to him. I'd like to know, why are you interested?"

Kathy explained her call from Randy Springer that morning. Jon listened quietly. A hard look came over his face when she told him of the conflict between the Fish and Wildlife Enforcement Rangers and the Department of Homeland Security. "Honey, if it's the Gunner's son you need to take the case. I bet Sam Hobert knows more about Springer than almost anyone else. Did he tell you anything."

"Yeah, he said almost word for word what you just said, the Corps owes him."

"Are you going to visit him? If you do, I want to go with you." Jon sat at the table with his wife.

"Okay, I'll visit him, but I want him away from the influence of the Homeland Security people. Think we can get to Missoula and find this JH Ranch?"

"No problem Honey. Can we take the kids? I'd like them to see a real ranch. Wait a minute, I'll look it up on the computer." Two minutes later, Jon had the web page for the Rolling JH Ranch and Guest Ranch on the screen. The first clue it was the right Springer was the Marine Corps flag below the American flag on the pole in front of the Guest Ranch lodge. "Honey, look at this, they have lots of fun stuff for the kids, swimming during the summer, fishing, horses. Let's go even if you don't take the job. The judge asked me if I was going to take a vacation since it's been over two years.

Missoula is only a couple of hundred miles from Priest Lake if we want to visit Grandpa. He's in his mid-eighties and he got married to that woman of seventy.

And your mother married that Navy friend of hers. If he gets her pregnant I'm putting him in a home." Jon laughed joined by Kathy. Her mother had married her retired Navy friend and was living in Cardiff by the Sea, a half hour from the Caldwell home.

"Come on Kathy, Pat can run the office for a week or two while we play with the kids. Dennis would love to go to a guest ranch. He'll be sixteen, or was sixteen two months ago. Things are passing us by."

"Okay, I'll set it up if the judge will give you time off." Kathy called the number Springer had given her on the off chance he was home.

"Hello." A woman answered.

"Yes, this is Katherine Graham, an attorney from San Diego. Is this the Springer residence?"

"No ma'am, but he's here most of the time. Do you want to talk to him?"

"Yes, please."

"This is Randy Springer."

"Yes Mr. Springer, this is Kathy Graham, we spoke this morning."

"Oh yes ma'am." Kathy could hear him explain to a woman who she was. "If I can, I'd like to put you on the speaker phone."

"Sure, no problem."

"I am going to record all the calls we make to each other from now on. I have accepted your case and you have attorney-client privilege and confidentiality. Do you understand?"

"Yes ma'am. Will the recording be available for Sara and myself?"

"Yes, just give me two days to get them to you, okay?"

"Yep, does that mean I've hired you?"

"Yes it does. Now, I would like to get you away from Winthrop while we go over your case. I noticed your father has a ranch in Montana. Would it be available and convenient for you to meet us at the Guest Ranch?"

"I'll call Dad and Brent and make sure you have a place to sleep. Will you be coming alone?"

"No, my husband and three children will be coming with me for a vacation if possible while you and I work. We can be there the day after tomorrow—will that work for you?"

"Yes ma'am. My partner is Sara Bennett. You can find her on the web as a national rifle marksman."

"We would be delighted to meet you. I'll see you the day after tomorrow in Montana." Kathy smiled as she hung up the phone. "Well it looks like you get to play cowboy Jon. We have reservations at the Rolling JH Guest Ranch."

They were eating dinner when the phone rang. It was Randy Springer.

"Ms. Graham, my sister is on her R&R from Afghanistan and is coming home, leaving California the day after tomorrow with her friend. They would like to know if you would like to fly with them to Missoula and we will pick you up at the airport, or at least someone will pick you up. They will be leaving from the private plane terminal at the San Diego International airport. Knowing Jeff, he'll want to be airborne by 10:00 a.m.. He'll have a reserved parking place for you and a valet to get you loaded. Since the only passengers are you and your family and my sister, there is plenty of room. Jeff is the command pilot and he has another pilot who takes care of the aircraft. For a smaller plane it is a very smooth ride. Shall I let him know you'll be flying Jeff Airline?"

"Sure, if you're sure it's no problem. We've got a sixteen year boy and twins, boy and girl six years old. What's the limit on the baggage?

Kathy listened. "No limit, bring what we need. Okay, we'll see you in about forty-eight hours. Thanks Randy." She hung up.

* * *

Randy and Sara called Ken Behoney and told him they were taking off for parts unknown for a month's vacation. They would have the Sat Phone, still encrypted and Ken could call them on it. Randy hauled Sara's baggage to the truck including her M70 Winchester and the Springfield M1A rifles. Randy slipped his Winchester into a carrying case and put the rifles in their hard case behind the back seat. Randy hooked up the horse trailer and loaded his mustangs and Sara's Buster. He put travel wraps on all the horses' legs for protection and hay in each horse's feeder. Randy wore his uniform with his pistol on his hip as did Sara. They left to find Rusty Williams, a team roper friend, and traded trucks with him. Rusty would put their truck in his barn until they returned. Randy felt better driving a truck unknown to the Department of Homeland Security.

It was still dark when Randy pulled onto the highway and the road to intercept Highway 2 to Spokane. They would take I-90 from Spokane to Missoula.

Randy talked to Brent, and Sabrina would arrive in Missoula on Jeff Price's Gulf Stream IV. Randy remembered Jeff told him he got a good deal on the plane and only paid half of what the plane was worth. Of course Jeff would have to do four benefits for abused children, which he would have done for free. But Jeff couldn't pass up the deal. A ten million dollar airplane for five million dollars.

Chapter Thirty

A Brief Stop on the Way to the Ranch

On the road since 5:00 a.m. before breakfast, they elected to drive along the river to Ephrata and intercept I-90. Sara volunteered to drive the first leg of the trip to Montana. Randy wasn't completely sure of the truck and trailer brakes with its three horse passengers. They decided to forego the Loop Loop Pass hills for the flatter route along the river.

At Moses Lake they stopped for fuel and a late breakfast. Randy pulled the truck and the five-horse silver stock trailer onto I-90 at Moses Lake. By the time they reached the old Simplot plant five miles east on the interstate Sara was asleep. He glanced down at Sara's left hand where he imagined the diamond engagement ring he had in his pocket would be. A little thrill passed up his back and a grin covered his face. He knew beyond a doubt she was his soul mate. His mind slipped to his family. He hoped Sue would understand and accept Sara. Sue was five years younger than Randy and very outspoken. She didn't like to share what she considered her time with Randy when he was home.

Sue Withrow was the daughter of the Rolling JH Ranch horse manager, Ben Withrow and his wife Wilma. Sue and her brother Robby worked for the JH Ranch. The family always thought Sue would partner with Randy. At first Randy and Sue were attracted to each other but found the attraction was more a sibling relationship. Included in the family were Josh and Charlene Reynolds and their three offspring. When Hank Springer married Bess Clemons the extended family was complete: Springers, Andersons, Withrows and Reynolds. Added to the family was Gail, Hank's adopted daughter and two of their steady ranch hands, Leonard Honey and his cousin George Honey. George and Leonard were favored uncles, babysitters and teachers. The two old bachelors watched over the children and the ranch as if they owned it and the children were their own, which in a sense they were.

Randy was the youngest of the three children of Hank's marriage to Lori who died when Randy was still a toddler. Sabrina, the older sister to Brent and Randy, met Sara when Sara participated in a National Match shooting competition at Camp Pendleton. The two women became good friends and talked on the telephone often. Their main subject was Randy and the relationship between Randy and Sara.

Sabrina thought Randy would propose to Sara while they were at the ranch so the whole family could be a part of the romance.

Sabrina was due for a two week R&R from Afghanistan within the month and wanted to be at the ranch while Randy and Sara vacationed. She arranged her leave and would meet them at the ranch before returning to Camp Pendleton and transportation back to IMEF. Sabrina was the senior medical doctor deployed to Camp Leatherneck, Afghanistan. Frocked to full commander in the Navy Medical Corps, she commanded the surgical team at the Navy Medical Facility.

Sara woke as they passed through Spokane. She looked over at Randy and he was looking at her with a wide grin on his face.

"What Randy, what's with the grin?"

"Sara, I'd like to make a stop before we get to Montana."

"Where and what for?" Sara knew there wasn't a lot between Spokane and Missoula.

"Well, other than Las Vegas or Reno, Couer d'Alene, Idaho is the marriage capital of the world. I thought we could stop and get hitched on the way through."

Sara stared at Randy and he reached into his coat pocket and pulled out a small jewelry box. Randy pulled off the road at the Liberty Lake exit and into a strip mall parking lot. He turned to face her, opened the box and removed an engagement ring and a white gold wedding ring. "Sara Bennett, will you marry me and become a Springer?"

Sara sat silent and stared first at the rings and then into Randy's eyes as tears flooded her own. "I've said it before, do you think I'm insane? Damn right I'll marry you."

Randy took the engagement ring and slipped it on her finger. "Now I think we've got about an hour before we use the other ring."

"Okay, where's your ring?"

"Right here." Randy removed a small envelop and placed it in Sara's hand. In it was a plain white gold man's wedding ring.

"What about your family?"

"They won't mind. Dad married Bess with only a couple of people in the Dutton Court House as witnesses. Brent and Bev eloped when he got back from Marine duties. The only wedding was Brent's and Bev's and they were already married and it was an excuse for a party."

Randy drove to a gas station in Couer d'Alene, looked up a marriage chapel and forty minutes later Mr. and Mrs. Randy Springer pulled their truck onto I-90 and drove to Missoula, where Randy checked and watered the horses. They had their marriage dinner at the X-roads Café before driving the last leg to the Rolling JH Ranch.

Randy drove through the gate and onto the infield—as Hank called it and parked next to the hitching rail in front of the split-log lodge. The lodge was home to the Springer family where each family member had his or her bedroom suite consisting of a small kitchen, bedroom and private bath. A second story had been added since Randy had been home last. The split-log house, started as a five bedroom home, was now almost a small hotel with twenty additional suites added to the original house in a horseshoe shape around the rear of the building.

Randy stepped down from the cab and ran around the truck to open the door for his bride. They stood together as the front door began to disgorge people. Bess led the herd as they swamped Randy. Bess kissed him on the cheek, gave him a brief hug and turned her attention to Sara.

"Welcome Sara, it's nice to finally meet you after listening to Randy brag about the great woman he found after she was wounded jumping out of airplanes. I'll let Gail introduce you to the rest of the family. Brent and Bev are on their way from the Guest Ranch." Bess noticed the wedding rings immediately but waited for Randy to take the floor and make the announcement.

"Wow!" Sara was tongue tied and embarrassed until Bess put her arm around her as people came over to meet her.

A beautiful strawberry blonde girl disengaged herself from Randy and before Bess could introduce her, introduced herself. "Hi, I'm Gail, Randy's sister. We heard from Bess you were on your way and we waited dinner until now. If Bess will excuse us, I'll introduce you to the herd." Gail took Sara by the arm. "Bess prepared a room for you where you can dump your stuff and wash up when we're done here. Bess will have Randy take your stuff to your room." Gail introduced Sara to the rest of the family. She started with Hank who put an arm around Bess and pulled Sara into a three-person welcome hug. Hank too had noticed the rings. Hank and Bess excused themselves and left to return to the house, leaving the rest of the family to get acquainted with what appeared to be a new member.

Sara noticed a beautiful blonde woman dismount a horse and ground tie him. When the blonde reached them, Randy picked her up and hugged and kissed her then introduced Sara to Sue. "Sara, I'd like you to meet Sue. Until you she was the love of my life, my trail buddy and my friend. Sue, this is Sara, my wife."

Sue stood still and studied Sara until the silence intruded, then a brilliant smile broke across Sue's face. "Sara, we need to talk. There are some things you need to know about this." Sue stopped and gave Randy a serious glare. "Oh whatever he is. When you're settled we'll go for a ride."

A pickup truck came around a large barn and slid to a stop behind the horse trailer ,and two older ranch hands stepped down. George and Leonard shouldered everyone aside, shook Randy's hand, stepped back and studied Sara for a minute before they both declared, "A right nice woman you brought home." They shook Sara's hand and went to the horse trailer and began to unload the horses. They led the horses around the infield to an empty paddock, checked the horses for travel injuries and turned them loose to run and roll. Sue left and took her horse to the stable. When she returned she brought three flakes of hay from the feed shed. She carried them to the paddock and tossed them to the horses.

Gail showed Sara to her and Randy's room. "I thought you would need a room to yourself. Now, it's just a place you can get away from Randy. He can be a pest and always underfoot. You are going to be very busy for the next few days and you don't need to be hassled by him." Gail paused. "You know Sue and Randy are so tight with each other you can't see any space between them."

"Do you think Sue is jealous?" Sara really feared the answer but the question needed to be asked.

"Heavens no. They are more brother and sister and protectors of each other. If Sue approves of you, you will know it right away. I saw the look she gave you, you're in."

Gail waited while Sara took a quick shower and changed clothes, putting on a well-worn soft pair of Wranglers and a faded Pendleton shirt. Sara followed Gail to the large dining room with a huge oak table. A woman she hadn't met was putting the finishing touches on the plates and eating utensils.

Finished setting the table, she came to stand in front of Sara. "I'm Charlene Reynolds. You need anything these Springers can't get for you come see me. Welcome to the Rolling JH Ranch and the Springer clan." Charlene gave her a quick hug when Bess came into the room. "Bess, I told you to relax. It's my turn to do the table setting. Wilma will be here in a minute and Lori needs supervising, so go." Charlene shooed Bess away. "Bess is always underfoot. She's worse than a toddler. She just can't relax when Hank isn't in the house. By the way, Hank and Randy are with the horses with George and Leonard. They'll be back pretty soon.

Sara watched Charlene before she asked, "Is there anything I can do to help?"

"No, you go visit. Oh by the way, do you mind if Mary Ann and Sue ride your horse? I promise they are good riders."

Sara was surprised by the question; this was a horse ranch and there were plenty of horses to ride. "No not at all."

"I suppose Randy told you Sue is our vet and Mary Ann is probably the best young rider in the State." Charlene grinned. "And two riders, Jess and Cassie are her competition and they are my overactive offspring. You'll meet my brood at dinner."

Sara looked at the table again and counted twenty place settings. Mary Ann came through the kitchen door into the dining room."Is that buckskin yours?"

"Yes, why?"

"I'd like to ride him tomorrow of you don't mind. Randy said he was a roper, that true?"

"Yes, I head off him. I'd like it if you exercised him. I don't know when I'll have time. Looks like I'm going to be pretty busy. You're Mary Ann, Randy's sister?"

"Yep!" she said with a grin.

A girl about the same age as Mary Ann came in. "Sara, this is my younger daughter Cassie." Charlene introduced them. "Jess will be here as soon as the food hits the table, never fails. The older boys, Robby Withrow and Michael, Randy's foster brother are in the Marines. Hank could pull strings and get the two time off, but he won't. I hope you understand."

A tall ash-blonde woman came in. "This is Wilma Withrow, Ben's wife. Ben is the horse business manager, while Josh, my husband runs the cattle side of the ranch. Wilma is our money person along with Margie, who will be here tomorrow. They take care of payroll, expenses, and savings accounts. Between them they do all the money matters. The ranch is a corporation."

* * *

Sara was lounging in her rooms; there was a soft knock on her door. She expected Randy to come and they could go to breakfast together. After sending an email to Ken Behoney and asking about the legal situation on the charges against her and Randy, she waited for his reply. The knock came again. Randy would have knocked, waited a few seconds and entered without waiting for her to answer the door.

Opening the door, she found Hank with a brown envelop in his hand. "Mind if I come in.? I know Randy will be here in a few minutes. He's helping the girls and Jess feed the horses."

"No, please Mister Springer, come in." Sara held the door open.

"Thanks, I've got a couple of things to talk about. Bess will corner you sometime today to talk. Sabrina will be here tomorrow for two week's leave before she needs to be back at Pendleton." Hank sat on the sofa. "I hope the room's okay. Anything you need?"

"No everything is wonderful and everyone is so friendly." She sat in the overstuffed leather easy chair. "Randy told me everyone was great, but not this great."

He took a deep breath. "I hope you don't feel we are prying, but Bess looked you up on the Internet and a couple of other places I don't know anything about. Bottom line, I think Randy is getting the better part of this deal. Not that he doesn't deserve the best, but you are a very impressive young woman. Worked your way through college as a waitress and fighting forest fires. A team leader as a smokejumper. A Fish and Wildlife Ranger, even the sniper on an ad hoc SWAT team. You've been a very busy girl. Oh yeah, on the national shooting team starting as a teenager." Hank leaned back against the sofa's back. "Is there more?"

"God, I hope not. You make me sound like a super hero; maybe I should be wearing a cape." Sara was clearly embarrassed by Hank's revelations.

"Now, I used to be pretty good with a rifle when I was still in the Corps. Brent and my two ranch hands, George and Leonard think they're hot too with a rifle. Randy said you brought your rifles with you. If that's the case, would you care for a little shoot—not really competition but I'd really like to shoot with you. It would be an honor."

"Sure Mr. Springer. It would be my pleasure."

"About the Mr. Springer thing, my name is Hank and I hope you'll call me Dad. I'd be honored."

"Sure Hank, Dad, thank you." Sara's eyes became glassy. She quickly wiped a tear away.

"Great Sara. On the sly, Ralph, who you will meet later, had George and Leonard build a 300 meter, 500 meter, 1,000 meter and 1,500 meter range. There are only six regular targets. Each of us will have our own. Brent used the backhoe and dug a place for the scorer at each distance. Each shooter will have three rounds to get dope for the sights at each range. Does that work for you?"

"Sounds fair to me. Could we use paper targets with ten inch blacks up through 500 meters and 20 inch blacks beyond 500 meters with X rings?"

"Now that makes a challenge. Everyone has the same rifle, Winchester M70 with a Redfield scope at 1,000 meters and beyond. At 300, we will all shoot Winchester Model 94 with iron sights, okay?"

"Darn Dad, you are making it interesting. What Caliber M94s?"

"Any Caliber you want: 30-30, 25-35, 32 or .45 Calibers."

They talked for a few more minutes when Randy knocked lightly on the door and entered. Hank clapped him on the shoulder and left the couple alone.

Chapter Thirty-One

The Gulf Stream IV

Kathy and Jon with Dennis and the twins arrived at the private terminal of the San Diego airport and were met by a uniformed valet who directed them to private parking. A blue and white Gulf Stream IV sat with its passenger door and baggage hatches open. The valet transported their baggage to the plane and loaded them. He led them to the open door behind the cockpit. A man with the three stripes of a copilot met them, introduced himself and ushered them to their seats. He told them Mr. Price was filing the flight plan and would return in a few minutes. As they were getting settled a beautiful blonde woman climbed aboard and introduced herself as Sabrina Springer, Randy's sister. A man with the four stripes of a captain climbed aboard, kissed Sabrina on the cheek and introduced himself as their pilot.

Kathy knew she had seen him before, while Jon began to grin. "What are you grinning for?" Kathy challenged.

"You don't recognize our pilot?" When she shook her head, "That's Jeff Price, the movie actor." Kathy's mouth dropped open. Dennis just stared at the actor.

Jeff left the door open to the cockpit and had Dennis move to the seat where he could see all the gauges and dials. The boy's eyes were about to pop out of his head if they got any wider or stared any harder. Jeff started the engines, went over the check list with his copilot. Dennis could hear Jeff ask the tower for clearance to taxi to the main runway. Jeff turned around and handed Dennis a set of earphones so he could hear the tower.

"Gulf Stream niner three niner, you are cleared to stage, you are number four for departure. We have a United heavy on approach." Dennis watched a Boeing 757 land and an Alaska Airlines 737 moved onto the main runway. "Alaska 514 you are cleared for departure, have a nice flight. Roger, Alaska 514 rolling." Two more planes took off, then, "Gulf Stream niner three niner you are cleared to main runway." Jeff moved the throttles forward and the plane moved to the main runway and lined up on the center line. "Gulf Stream niner three niner you are cleared for departure, have a nice flight."

"Roger tower, niner three niner rolling." Jeff, pushed the throttles to full takeoff power and the plane quickly rolled down the runway and lifted into the sky.

Dennis turned around and saw his father watch him all smiles. "Niner three niner, you are cleared to angels one five come to heading 060 magnetic. You are cleared VFR, Los Angeles Control. Niner three niner, Los Angeles Control, you are cleared on this heading to flight level 41, to 600 knots."

Dennis watched the sky change color through the windshield: it went from sky blue to a deep blue, almost black. He felt the plane level off. They transferred to the Denver control and changed the direction by a few numbers on the compass and increased speed to 590 knots. The copilot got out of his seat and motioned for Dennis to get out of his seat and move up into the cockpit with the pilot. When Dennis was in the copilot's seat and strapped in, Jeff switched his mic so only Dennis could hear him. Jeff explained what the dials and gauges showed. He let Dennis put his hands on the wheel or yoke. They could hear other airplanes talking to control and to each other about weather and bumpy air. Through his hands Dennis could feel the auto pilot adjust direction when high-altitude winds blew them off course.

Jeff pointed ahead and Dennis had to strain his neck to see but there was a Boeing 737 ahead and below them. They quickly passed the passenger jet four thousand feet below them. Jeff explained the plane was on its way to Spokane and would get there about the time Jeff and his passengers would be climbing into the vehicles for the trip to the ranch. Time flew past and the copilot needed his seat back. Dennis thanked Jeff and the copilot for the great time and returned to his seat. When he started to give the headphones to the copilot, Jeff motioned for Dennis to keep them until after them landed.

Dennis was surprised to see the twins asleep. How could anyone sleep when in a plane like the Gulf Stream.

Jeff landed the plane at Missoula and taxied to the private passenger terminal. A man met the plane and guided Jeff to his assigned parking place. When Jeff shut the motors down, the guide pulled a long-bed pickup close to the cargo space and began to unload the baggage. Jeff and the copilot locked up the plane and closed out their flight plan. Jeff ordered the plane to be refueled and made ready for the return flight two weeks away. Airport management would see the plane to the hanger space on permanent rental for Jeff Price.

Dennis noticed two Ford pickup trucks parked near the passenger terminal. Jeff waved and the door opened and Brent climbed down and walked around the fence to shake Jeff's hand and welcome Sabrina home. Kathy and Jon were impressed by the fondness each person had for one another. Sabrina introduced Kathy and Jon to Brent and then called Dennis over to introduce him to Brent. "Here's your new helper. And do not let Sue have him, she'll work him to death if you don't watch her. Also Mary Ann, I've heard she's become a bossy teen." Kathy laughed.

Brent spotted the gun and the U.S. Marshal's shield on Jon's belt. Only the breeze coming across the apron exposed the gun and shield. Brent squinted. "Hey, I know you. You're that Intel weenie who put Hawaii and San Diego together."

Jon squinted at Brent. "You a Major out of Fort Lewis?"

"Yeah. Put'er there buddy." Brent thrust his hand out for Jon.

Sabrina watched the action between Jon and her brother. "Oh God, another Marine. Can't I ever get away from these high testosterone he-men."

"Don't let Dad hear you say that," Brent said.

Jon introduced Kathy and the children to Brent.

"Who's driving the other rig?" Sabrina asked.

"That's Sue, she's busy texting Margie. Randy arrived last night just before dinner. He and his squeeze are probably still asleep."

"Is Sara here?" Sabrina was excited.

"Yeah, Randy said don't wake him from his afternoon nap unless you hear a blood-curdling scream from him. Not from Sara, he says she does that all the time anyway."

"Oh God, I'm going to tell her you said that and you'll be in trouble. Wait until you see the talent this young woman has. You know she jumped smoke." Sabrina informed Brent. "Not only was she a smokejumper, but she was or is on the National Large Bore Rifle Team. Sara has been in two shooting incidents: a hostage situation when she killed one man and aided the capture of another. She also saved the lives of two FBI agents and shot a domestic terrorist and recovered a deadly batch of Mexican heroin," Sabrina added. "Now she is being prosecuted for helping Randy take down some terrorists. They are trying to pin murder charges against them. Sara has been a very busy young lady and she possesses the heart of our baby brother."

"Sorry Sabrina, I didn't know. I was being a bit over protective. You know Dad isn't going to leave her and Randy alone." Brent said seriously. "Dad already had George and Leonard build a shooting range and Jon, you and I will be shooting against her and Dad. We'll be using the Winchesters, M70 and Model 94s. The 94s at 200 and 300 meters and the M70's at 500, 1000 and 1,500 meters. If she is a roper Dad will try to adopt her." The brother and sister laughed together; Sabrina and Brent walked toward Sue's truck.

"Oh oh, I almost forgot about Sue. Don't let them be alone together. Sue will run her through the third degree and back."

"Speaking of Sue, have either Sue or Margie found a boyfriend yet?" Sabrina and Sue were both attractive blonds while Margie was a Elizabeth Taylor beauty.

Sue was a graduate of the Veterinarian School at Washington Sate University and Margie a recent graduate CPA and Premed from the University of Montana. When they were alone Brent asked, "Sis, what do you know about the Caldwell's?"

"I just met them on the plane. Mrs. Caldwell, goes by Kathy, is a high-end lawyer who practices in the federal court system in Southern California. She was recommended by Judge Barker and by Marshall Sam Hobert, a friend of Dad's and of course a Marine. Jon Coldwell is a U.S. Marshal and a reserve Marine Major. I thought you would know him. He's a spook too. Jon was born and raised in Spokane, Kathy in Union south of Spokane. Their story is interesting and I bet Sam Hobert was involved." Sabrina paused. "What I find really interesting I don't think Randy and Sara have even met the Caldwell's."

Sabrina asked, "Is Dad at the ranch.? I'm surprised he didn't come to the airport."

"Dad, Ben and Leonard Honey are checking the north fence. Cattle have been getting out onto the BLM land. We'll probably have to do a roundup while you're here. They should be back this afternoon. I think Dad was dragging his heels waiting for Jeff to get here. Dad says if Jeff wasn't a movie star, he would make a great ranch foreman. Josh and Ben have so much to do Dad needs an overall manager to bring the two, and now three operations together. Speaking of Jeff, what are you going to do about him?"

"What do you mean do about him?"

"Damn Sabrina, you are probably the only person within a thousand miles who doesn't know Jeff loves you." Brent studied Sabrina's face for perhaps a minute. "Don't be stubborn Sabrina, the man loves you and I think you have been interested in him since he started to work part time for Dad."

Sabrina's face showed sadness. "I'm going to be returning to Afghanistan at the end of next week. Maybe after I get back to Pendleton I can think about me and Jeff. I'm assigned to Camp Leatherneck. Right now I have six more months in country. Jeff and I are just going to have to wait until I get back." Her sadness reflected in her eyes. "If he's still interested, well maybe then."

They turned off the highway at Lone Horse onto the State road toward the Rolling JH Cattle, Horse and Guest Ranch.

Chapter Thirty-Two

Home On the Ranch

Sara woke with thc sun shining in her eyes as it crested the low hills to the east of the ranch. She felt the body in the bed next to her, cracked open an eye and saw Randy awake as he watched her sleep. "Humm, how long have you been awake? Why didn't you wake me?"

"I was just enjoying watching you sleep. I love watching you." Randy brushed a strand of blonde hair from her face.

"What time is it? Shouldn't we be getting up?" Sara sat up and straightened the T-shirt Randy loaned her to sleep in. "I'm a little hungry. I could fix us some breakfast."

"What? And ruin Charlene's whole day. It's almost five and the morning feeding is just getting started. It's usually done by 5:30. If we hurry we can join them."

"Who's them?" Sara asked, somewhat intimidated.

"Mostly family, that's the Springers. the Withrows and Reynolds. Dad is still out checking fence with some of the hands and should be back by supper. I was going with them, but Bess nixed it. She wants to talk to us this morning. Sabrina and the lawyer are on the way here to talk to us so we should have quite a crowd for supper. The Caldwells will be staying at the guest ranch with their three children. Sabrina's room is just down the hall from our room. Brent mumbled something about eating at the Guest Ranch tonight. Leonard and George will be cooking, it'll probably be an outdoor thing. Of course the Caldwells are invited."

"What about your dad?"

"I don't suppose he'll want to miss anything. I bet he's on his way home right now. Bess would have called him this morning and told him Sabrina will arrive with Jeff this afternoon. That's where Brent is right now on the way to Missoula. He and Sue left about two hours ago."

Sara kissed Randy quickly on the lips then rolled out of bed shedding the T-shirt.

"Sara, you're not wearing any panties!" Randy grinned. "If I'd known that we'd miss breakfast."

Sara came back to the bed. "I was hoping we might use a little of our sleep time for other things. I came to bed last night and you were out like a light. But I was hoping and then I woke with you staring at me."

Randy leaned forward and kissed her flat belly. "If I kiss anything else we'll be late for breakfast and lunch. You go first, I'll be in a minute. Bess told me ladies like some free time in the morning and Bess knows everything."

Randy stood up. "You're naked!" Sara smiled and started to reach for him.

"Later Sweetheart, we don't want to start anything that will make us late. Bess, I am sure is expecting us for breakfast and it is being served now."

* * *

Hank and Leonard Honey rode onto the lawn of the main ranch house where Brent, Bev, Bess, Sara and Randy were having a late lunch on the porch. Hank dismounted Jake Junior, handed the reins to Leonard and climbed the steps to kiss Bess and then folded his youngest son in a bear hug. Hank turned toward Sara. "This beautiful strange blonde woman belong to you Randy?"

"Yes sir, all mine. You don't know what I had to do to get her to come visit you. That includes the whole family too." Sara had met the whole family and talked to Hank last night. For some reason, Randy wanted to go through introducing Sara again.

Sabrina choose that time to come onto the porch and kissed her father on the cheek. "Dad, don't you say a word about blondes. Sara is my friend and I'm sure Randy's future wife. Besides she can beat you on the rifle range and not even break a sweat."

"Now, you've got the word Hank my love," Bess added teasing. "You be nice or you'll spend the rest of the day in your room, alone. Sabrina, you're a bit late. Sara is Randy's wife."

There was silence on the porch until Hank shrugged. "Charlene, is there anything left in the larder after these freeloaders have picked over the groceries." Hank called through the door into the kitchen.

"Hank, you just sit there and be quiet. You'll eat when I get around to cooking it." Charlene came onto the porch with a large plate of hash browns, three eggs sunny side up set right on top of the spuds, a large pitcher of orange juice and a glass for Hank.

"You see what I have to put up with day after day?" Hank asked Sara. "Do you really want to join this herd, not that you wouldn't add some grace to it. Maybe they'll learn from you—they certainly need to learn some manners."

"It's not only Hank's manners that need a bit of tweaking," Bess said and leaned over and kissed her husband again. "Sara, it's like this every time he gets out into the back forty. He loses all his manners. I think he leaves them on the wire out there."

"Hey, where's Jeff? Sabrina, you scare him off again. Go find him and bring him back here. I've got a job for him."

Twenty minutes later, Sue drove onto the parking lot with Kathy and Jon Caldwell. She came onto the porch and kissed Hank on the cheek and introduced the Caldwells to Hank as the master of the spread. Hank stood and welcomed the Caldwell's to the Rolling JH Ranch.

"Dad, Jon's a U.S. Marshal, and a Marine spook," Brent said, giving Jon a free pass. Marines were Hank's favorite people. "Kathy is Randy and Sara's attorney and it's a working vacation for her. Their children are Dennis, sixteen and twins, boy and girl about six. I've already assigned Dennis to Gail's shovel work force. Sue promised to teach him to ride and has a horse picked out for him and another for Sara so her horses can rest after the trip. She likes mustangs."

A two-tone pink and brown pickup drove onto the parking lot. The strawberry blonde and Dennis climbed out and came to join the others on the porch. "You responsible for this kid?" she asked Jon.

"Yep, guilty." Jon smiled. He had talked earlier to Gail at the guest ranch and turned Dennis over to her for chores in exchange for riding lessons. Jon had given Dennis a set of riding lessons at the Camp Pendleton stables. Dennis knew quite a bit about riding and had a good seat. After Gail saw him ride that morning, she wanted to turn him over to either George or Leonard Honey for cowboy riding lessons. Leonard suggested Jeff would be better if he had the time. The two had already bonded after the plane ride from California.

"Now that everyone is here, we need to do a roundup of the late calves for branding and medications." Sue climbed up on the porch and sat down next to Hank.

* * *

Bess and the girls wanted to give Sara a bridal shower and Bess asked about her family.

"I was raised in Bellingham, yes, with a brother. He's actually a Marine F18 fighter pilot and deployed right now. I doubt if he will be able to make it from somewhere around a place called Diego Garcia. My folks are in a retirement home and need daily care. The doctors have advised they not travel and they aren't aware of much around them. They were injured in an auto accident some years ago. My father was driving and hit a bridge abutment. They both suffered head injuries."

"I hear you jumped out of airplanes to fight fires, Sara," Jon said.

"Yeah, it wasn't a big deal, just another job."

"No Sara, it is a big deal. I worked for almost three years as a smokejumper and it is a big deal. It was the hardest job I ever had," Jon Caldwell interjected. "Be proud of your contribution to our forests. I know you are." Jon looked embarrassed.

Kathy came into the kitchen followed by Hank. Hank volunteered his office for Kathy to use. He told her to feel free to use the phones, or anything else. "If you don't see what you need, ask Wilma, Charlene or Bess. Between them they run this outfit. I'm like George Washington on a quarter, just a figurehead." Everyone laughed when Kathy told them what Hank had said and his sudden modesty. They all knew his act; Bess ran the family, but Hank ran the ranch.

Chapter Thirty-Three

The Warrant and Command Influence

Ken Behoney was on the telephone in his office when the Homeland Security Agent came through the door.

"Mr. Behoney?" the agent asked as he pulled his suit coat aside to expose the heavy automatic pistol and Federal Law Enforcement badge.

"Yeah, who's asking and why?"

"I'm Special Agent Roland Asgard, Homeland Security. I have an arrest warrant for Randy Springer and Sara Bennett. You need to tell me where they are."

Behoney stood exposing his own heavy automatic pistol and the Federal Law Enforcement badge on his own belt. "I don't have to tell you anything. What are the charges and who signed the warrant?"

"They are charged with illegal seizure and illegal use of firearms, the murder of five foreign students, unlawful detention and kidnapping." He paused, looking at the warrant. Also threatening an law enforcement officer and attacking said officer resisting arrest. We also want to talk to them about the disappearance of Special Agent Dewar."

"You've got to be out of your minds. Who signed that warrant?"

"Judge Lawton of the Federal Court in Seattle."

"Well, that judge doesn't know his ass from a well. I don't know exactly where they are. You're just going to have to find them on your own." Behoney turned his back on the agent and poured himself a cup of coffee. He didn't offer Asgard a cup. He sat at his desk, sipped his coffee.

Asgard snorted. "Listen, we've already been to their apartments and they're not at either place." Asgard actually whined.

Behoney smiled, adjusted his pistol on his belt to a more comfortable position. "Agent, I can't tell you where they are. They left on vacation the day before yesterday and aren't scheduled to return for six weeks. They came in the other morning saying they were going to take six weeks of earned vacation. I knew of no reason to deny the time off and they left. If you want anything from me I need a copy of that warrant."

"You don't need one," Asgard replied gruffly in an attempt to regain the upper hand in his confrontation with Behoney.

"No warrant, then get out of my office."

Asgard spotted the copy machine, stomped over to it and made a copy of the warrant. "Here." He threw the copy on Behoney's desk.

"Why thank you Special Agent Asgard. That was very thoughtful of you." Behoney smiled at Asgard and didn't say another word. He sat silent until the Special Agent snarled, grunted and stomped out of the office. He slammed the door on his way out rattling the office windows. Behoney smiled and finished the patrol schedule he was working on.

Behoney left his office, after calling the ranger in Brewster telling him he would be going to Omak for a meeting with the chief ranger for the Colville Indian Reservation.

In Omak, Behoney used a public telephone and called the telephone number in Montana Randy had given him before he and Sara left.

"Hello, this is Ken Behoney, the Supervising Fish and Wildlife Law Enforcement Ranger for Central Washington. I'm trying to reach Randy Springer."

Bess listened to Ken introduce himself. "Randy isn't available right now. He's out on the range. Is there someone else you would like to speak to?"

"Sara Bennett would be my second choice," Behoney replied.

"Is this something about the charges against my son Randy and Sara?"

"Yes ma'am."

"Their lawyer is here right now, Katherine Graham. Would you like to speak to her?"

"Yes ma'am, that would be fine."

Bess put the phone down on the table and went to Hank's office where Kathy was working. "Mr. Behoney is on the telephone and would like to speak to you. Its something about the charges."

"Thanks Bess,. Can I pick up that line on this telephone?" Kathy indicated the phone on Hank's desk.

"Sure, just flash the switch hooks and you'll pick up the line. I'll go and hang up the other phone." Bess left closing the door.

"This is Katherine Graham, to whom am I speaking?"

"I'm Ken Behoney, Randy and Sara's boss. I just had a visit from a Special Agent of Homeland Security named Asgard. He had a warrant for Randy and Sara's arrest. There are multiple charges,—do you want me to read them to you?"

"Yes please, just skim them. Can you fax me a copy of the warrant? You did get a copy from the agent?"

"Yes ma'am. Give me the fax number and I'll have a copy to you in fifteen minutes. I'm in Omak right now. I need to talk to Randy and Sara so I'm taking a week's vacation and will come to the ranch. I can bring the copy he gave me. He used my machine, but his fingerprints are all over my copy."

"Yes, bring the warrant you have, but I would like the faxed copy too please." Kathy began to smile. "Can you tell me the judge who signed the warrant?"

"A Judge Lawton of the United States District Court in Seattle."

"Great, I'll call the judge's office and get a authenticated copy mailed to me. I know Judge Lawton and he would only issue the warrant if he thought there was a danger of unwarranted political influence. Thanks for your help here and I will be seeing you in a couple of days."

"Yes ma'am. Actually I'm leaving here tonight on my way to Montana. I have my luggage with me. I don't want to give Asgard and anyone helping him time to set up a tail on me. I know I'm clear to here. My sister lives in Omak and I'll use her car for the trip. No sense taking any chances of being followed."

"Okay, see you tomorrow. Thank you for the call. Goodbye." Kathy ended the call.

Bess knocked on the office door before she entered. "Everything okay?"

"Yes Bess, that was Randy and Sara's boss in Winthrop. He had some information I think I'll find very welcome. Say, I've got about a half hour of work here then I'm free till tomorrow. Would you mind terribly if you could show me around?"

* * *

Kathy and Jon Caldwell sat across the conference table from Randy and Sara. In addition to the table, Hank's desk, an old saddle on a saddle tree and a sofa completed the room's furniture. The walls were paneled with knotty pine and gave the office a bright, airy feeling. A small old potbelly stove was in one corner of the room, the walls and floor protected from the heat by used brick; a bucket of seasoned larch sat beside the stove. A large patio door opened to a small balcony where a patio table and two chairs sat under a protective roof.

Kathy's laptop computer was on the table in front of her. A small personal recorder was placed in the center of the table to insure the accuracy of what was said. When Kathy informed Homeland Security she was the attorney of record for Randy Springer and Sara Bennett, she was informed Homeland Security reduced the charges from murder to negligent homicide. Homeland Security also separated the charges so Randy and Sara could be tried separately. All the other charges were still in place and applied to each of her clients separately. The Director of Homeland Security and the Director of Fish and Wildlife Law Enforcement refused to reduce those charges further. The U.S. District Court in Seattle issued a temporary warrant good for 24 hours, but refused to reinstate the arrest warrants beyond one day. The Court did set a court date a month from the first attempted arrest. The Court Justice was to read the charges officially and accept a plea from the accused. Judge Fullworth invited the Jacobsen family to come to Seattle Federal Court for a deposition. Judge Lawton, the United States Attorney Ambrose and Kathy were invited to witness the Jacobsens statements.

The Homeland Security Special Agent who attempted to arrest Randy and Sara was still in jail. The charge of attempted kidnapping using a firearm required a Federal Grand Jury to hear the charges. The current Grand Jury term ended and the new Jury Panel would not be sworn until the following week. Meanwhile, the court had not set bail so the agent remained incarcerated until either Judge Lawton or Judge Fullworth granted bail.

Kathy connected her computer to Hank's server system and established a link to her office in San Diego. Jon was currently assigned to work as an investigator for the U.S. Marshal's Service and had taken a month's leave to assist Kathy in defending her clients. He felt he was qualified to put the pieces of evidence together. Hank offered to help Jon who was still in the Reserves as an Intelligence Officer. Brent was also an Intelligence Officer analyst with the Joint Intelligence Center Pacific (JICPAC) command and was considered one of JICPAC's best analysts. With Hank's assistance, Jon began to put the mystery together. Jon's U.S. Marshal's office provided a secure computer and he could interface with low-level classified material delivered by overnight courier to the ranch.

Kathy felt most of the evidence pointed at command influence over field agents prohibiting them from doing their jobs. She felt there was undue influence and a conspiracy on the part of the Director of Homeland Security and the Federal Fish and Wildlife Law Enforcement Service. She felt the key accusation of the use of deadly force by field agents was bogus and had already drawn up papers for dismissal sent to the Federal Court in Seattle. The take down of the terrorists was within current guidelines and the agents had followed procedures. Unfortunately, all the terrorists were killed by Sara Bennett and Randy Springer during the attempt to take them into custody and save the hostages.

Sue drove Kathy to Missoula to catch a flight to Seattle to attend the Jacobsen deposition. The Jacobsens visited the District Court and made a statement before Judge Fullworth. They indicated Randy had twice challenged the terrorists to surrender. At the first challenge, the terrorists did not surrender but threatened the hostages with lethal weapons.

Jon concluded in his reports to the Marshal's Service and Kathy, as defense attorney, the charges were unfounded and SAIC Dewar had done everything he could to hinder the operation against the terrorists and the rescue of the hostages. Jon's leave was cancelled and he was assigned to the Marshal's office in Missoula and was to investigate the bringing of charges against SAIC Dewar and the Directors of Homeland Security and the Director Fish and Wildlife Law Enforcement Service for interfering in an active operation and command influence of Federal Officers in the performance of their duties as defined by law.

Since leaving the Winthrop area, Dewar had flown to Seattle taking a box labeled material found in the possession of the deceased terrorists. Fortunately, the box he took was mislabeled and contained powered brown sugar taken in a drug raid the month before and the few items in the possession of the terrorists. The Marshals were in possession of the box containing the toxic mixture of Mexican brown heroin and a lethal biological agent. The box also contained the numerous passports in the possession of the terrorists, including the United States Passports, one of a block of passport blanks in the possession of the Department of Homeland Security months prior to the incident in Washington. Using his Marshal's badge and credentials, Jon was able to track Dewar's movements from Seattle to the Philippines and on to Iran where the trail ended. Airline tickets were purchased for flights to: Honolulu,, Hawaii; Manila, Philippines and Bangkok, Thailand. The ticket to Manila was used and Jon was able to use HumInt sources to track Dewar from there to Tehran, Iran.

Kathy wanted to find and arrest SAIC Dewar before he could escape. She felt he was the key element to the resolution of the negligent homicide charge and was a player in the terrorist actions. She wanted to effect an arrest of the agent. Dewar had done everything he could to inhibit Randy and Sara's attempt to rescue the hostages and allow the terrorists to escape to Canada.

In the course of the investigation, Jon went over the vetting process of the Homeland Security agents and found discrepancies where influence had been brought to bear to clear the subject prior to the completion of the required special background investigation. Chief Marshal Sam Hobert was brought back to active duty with the U.S. Marshal's Service and assigned to take over the case. He arranged for Jon to assist him. Sam insisted on another Special Background Investigation and found Dewar didn't exist seven years prior to his employment at Homeland Security. Some records were sealed, authorized by the Director and others missing. The Director of Homeland Security was suspended from work until the resolution of the Marshal's investigations. Other Homeland Security agents were background checked and found to be missing critical information. In more than one case, warrants were issued and served resulting in numerous arrests of both administrative and field agents. The Director of Homeland Security was found innocent of criminal wrong doing, but was quietly asked to resign, as was the Director of the Federal Fish and Wildlife Law Enforcement Service.

Kathy made a second trip to Seattle and presented evidence showing Sara Bennett and Randy Springer were acting within the parameters of their agency instructions and recommended all charges to be dismissed. With the assistance of Judges Lawton and Fullworth, all charges were dismissed and a warrant issued for the arrest of Dewar.

Sara and Randy decided to stay at the Rolling JH Ranch for a thirty day vacation granted by Ken Behoney as the acting director of the Federal Fish and Wildlife Law Enforcement Service. Sara thought it would be a nice place for their honeymoon with a short week to visit Hawaii and Maya Sutterland, Hank's foster mother.

When U.S. Marshals went to arrest the Director of the Fish and Wildlife Law Enforcement Service for obstruction of justice, he committed suicide in his office leaving a detailed confession to his involvement with Middle Eastern terrorists for money.

Chapter Thirty-Four

Sara and Sue ~ Kidnap and Rescue

Sue and Sara left on a horseback ride to the far corner of the ranch. Sue wanted to show Sara the ranch but mainly she wanted to spend time with the woman who captured the heart of her first crush. Sara rode Buster while Sue rode Bess's horse Buttermilk. In Sue's saddlebags were sandwiches and Sara's contained water and her favorite tuna salad sandwiches.

Sue brought her Winchester 30-30 rifle and Sara wore her service pistol. The 10mm weapon was intended to scare off any of the many predators living on the ranch. Hank thought the critters had the same rights to live there as did the human occupants of the ranch. Jason and Curt, two of the ranch cowboys rode along and would join the fence-mending crew working on the north fence line. The fence crew replaced rotted posts and restrung barbed wire. Some of the cattle found a hole in the fence and were out on BLM land and needed to be rounded up and returned to their home range.

The day was warm and the women wore only light jackets and wide brimmed straw Stetsons against the hot afternoon sun. The higher range could be windy and there existed snow in the less exposed places bringing a chill to the air. They reached the fence about six miles from the ranch house when Sara spotted the flash of the sun's reflection off a windshield.

"What's a helicopter doing up here?" Sara asked Curt who stood in the saddle stirrups shading his eyes to see better.

"Could be a BLM chopper. They come up this way to check on fence lines too and look for evidence of poachers. There are a few large elk herds." Curt was thrown out of the saddle and the report of a shot followed before he hit the ground. Sara looked down at Curt on the ground; a large pool of blood was forming beneath him and the blood stain on the back of his shirt spread where the large Caliber bullet had exited his body. Sara started to reach for her pistol when a cold voice with a heavy accent stopped her.

"Don't move a muscle unless I tell you to move. With your fingers, first you ranger, take the pistol from your holster and drop it on the ground behind the horse. Next you cowboy, remove your weapon and drop it behind the horse. Now you Blondie." The rifle pointed at them didn't waver but remained steady on Jason.

"One at a time, step down from the horses, slowly." The commands came from a second man with a rifle pointed at them from behind a fallen log. "I want to see your hands or I'll shoot you where you are."

The three climbed down from the saddles and watched a man come toward them. "You are Sara Bennett?" he addressed Sara.

"Yeah I am and you're under arrest."

The man backhanded Sara, knocking her back against her horse. "You're so brave little girl. You belong to me now. You only talk when I tell you." The second man came from behind the log and stood off to the side ten feet away from his closest victim.

"I think I like the gold haired girl. You are my slave." He smiled at Sue.

"Up yours asshole."

The man hit Sue with his fist. "You no talk unless I tell you."

Sue stood quietly and glared at the dark-skinned man but she remained silent.

When the man hit Sue, Buttermilk shied and started to run back down the trail. The man raised his rifle but the horse was in the trees before he could shoot. Sue liked to tie the reins onto the saddle horn and guide the horse with her legs and shift of her body weight. The other three horses were ground tied and would remain standing in place. Only Buttermilk escaped.

"Now you, down on your knees," the man who appeared to be the leader commanded. The two women and Jason dropped to their knees, while the second man led the horses to the log and tied them to it by their reins. When the two men were together again, the leader moved behind them. "Put hands behind back, now." He then handcuffed first Sara then Sue but added thumb cuffs so the thumbs were locked together in addition to the handcuffs. When Sara and Sue were firmly incapacitated, he moved to stand behind Jason, took a small pistol from his coat pocket and shot Jason on the back of the head. "Now it's just you and me and my friend. If you make trouble, I will shoot the gold haired one. Do you understand?"

"Yeah asshole," Sara snarled. The leader slapped her in the back of her head. "One more bad thing you do and I kill the other girl. I would like to kill you. You killed my brother but Leader wants to keep you for himself; so if you are bad, I kill your friend."

Sara remained silent. She watched Sue out of the corner of her eyes. Sue appeared to have accepted their condition.

The leader pulled them to their feet and pushed them in the direction of the helicopter. Once aboard, the pilot lifted the helicopter above the treetops but still very low and turned toward the west. Out of the window, Sara could see the fence crew stop what they were doing and watch the helicopter fly over them and start to climb. Sara pressed her face against the window and hoped one of the men recognized her. Before they disappeared, Sara thought she saw one of the men lift a cell phone to his ear.

Ben Withrow was working with a two-year old colt on cues when his cell phone rang. "This had better be good. I'm busy right now," Ben answered.

"Hey Ben, this is Will Harris. I just saw a helicopter lift off and fly over us from BLM land. I think I saw Sue and Randy's wife in the back seats. At least I saw her friend, one of the other men saw Sue. Her face, both their faces were pushed against the windows like they wanted to be seen. Is there something wrong?"

"I don't know, I'll call Hank. Thanks for the heads up." Ben ended the call and called Hank's cell. After telling him what Will saw, Hank called Will making it a three way conversation. It only took seconds for Hank and Ben to put it together, the two women had been kidnapped.

Ben's daughter and Randy's wife were on the helicopter but he needed confirmation. He asked Will to take a couple of the men and find the horses. If the women had been taken, the horses would still be there. Twenty minutes later, Will called and told Hank they had found the horses and two bodies., Jason and Curt, both shot, one with a rifle from ambush the other in the back of the head, executed. Hank told Will to stay there and called the FBI office in Missoula and reported the crime and said BLM land was involved and a Federal Law Enforcement officer was kidnapped.

Hank next called Randy who was with Jon and Jeff in Missoula. Randy was filing some papers at the Federal Court House while Jeff was having the Gulf Stream refueled and made ready for the return to California. Randy invited Jon to ride into Missoula with him and Jeff. Jon wanted to check into the Marshal's office personally and took advantage of Randy's offer of a ride.

The fugitive helicopter with the two women was clawing for altitude to pass over the Cabinet Mountains and Rockies as Hank was talking to Randy. Jon looked at Randy asking a question, what's going on? Quickly Randy explained what Hank had told him then he called Jeff and explained about the kidnapping. When he ended the call his phone rang almost immediately.

"I've got Will on the phone with us and he's going to give you a description of the helicopter also a partial registration or aircraft number. Can you get with Jeff and see if he can get airborne and locate the helicopter. it was heading west toward Spokane or Coeur d'Alene. That should be almost an hour flight time to the nearest airport of any size from where the girls were taken about thirty minutes ago."

Randy drove as he and Jon raced toward the airport. Jon talked to the Marshal's Service and explained about the kidnapping. Three minutes later the two Federal agents went through the gate and parked in the terminal parking lots. They left the truck and ran toward the Gulf Stream with one engine already turning. The Marshal's office called the airport tower and quickly explained what was happening. While taxing toward the main runway, Jeff lit off the second engine, let it warm up for a minute and a half, asked for and received clearance to take off under VFR. At 500 feet, Jeff pushed the throttles to the safe maximum and turned toward the west.

Jeff flew toward the closest airport without spotting the helicopter, then turned toward Spokane's Felts Field near the river in Spokane Valley. As the Gulf Stream sped along the river, Randy spotted a helicopter approaching the airport and saw it land. Jeff turned the jet and stood it on its port wing to look down. They saw three men drag two people from the helicopter and run toward a Gulf Stream V. As soon as the five were aboard, the plane moved toward the runway prepared for takeoff. Jeff came around behind the other jet and landed in front of it, preventing takeoff. The Gulf Stream V with a Saudi Arabian identification-registration number stopped on the runway with Jeff's jet fifty feet in front of it.

Jon used his cell phone and called the U.S. Marshal's office in Missoula and Spokane and put them on a conference call. The Gulf Stream V was registered to the diplomatic mission of Saudi Arabia. Jon had the duty officer with the U.S. Department of State and Federal Judge brought into the conference call. Before he was done, the White House was brought into the conference. The incident was reported on a local Spokane TV station and coverage of the standoff was live on each of the local channels.

The Saudi ambassador reported the aircraft had been taken without permission and lifted the diplomatic immunity from the aircraft and Saudi citizens.

"Jeff, do you have any firearms on the plane?"

"No, don't you have you guys have guns?"

"Yeah, but two pistols against at least three armed men, I don't know."

"You'll be okay."

Randy, followed by Jon, left Jeff's jet and walked up to the front of the Saudi jet. Jon shot the front tire, then the other tires. Jeff taxied his jet around and parked on the terminal aircraft apron. Jon walked to a sheriff's car and explained to the deputy what was happening aboard the Saudi jet and it contained two U.S. citizens, one a Federal Law Enforcement officer, held against their will. Within the next seven minutes four Deputy U.S. Marshals, two State Patrol cruisers, two more sheriff's cruisers and three Spokane Valley Police cruisers surrounded the Saudi jet.

Randy walked up to the front of the plane and stood quietly until the copilot's window opened and a man with a week's growth of beard stuck his head out, waved a gun and yelled for them to get out of the way or they would kill the passengers,

Sue and Sara. Randy smiled at the man and shot him in the face. Randy pointed the pistol at the other man in the cockpit. He already had his hands up in sight as Jon pointed his pistol at him. Randy motioned for him to remain quiet, no talking.

Another man came into the cockpit with an AK47 assault rifle and looked at Randy who stood in front of the plane. He pulled the co-pilot's body out of the way and started yelling at Randy who shot him in the face. Ten seconds later the door opened and the steps appeared. At the top of the steps a man with a pistol in his hand and an AK47 over his shoulder stood behind Sue and Sara. Jon and Randy moved up to the bottom of the steps. Sue grinned at Randy.

"Remember when?" she said. Then shoved Sara down the steps with her shoulder and fell sideways. The terrorist was uncovered and before he could move, Randy and Jon both shot him. The two heavy Caliber bullets threw the man back into the plane. Jon was up the steps into the plane in seconds. Randy motioned the Marshal's forward and had them go through the terrorists clothing until they found keys for the handcuffs and thumb cuffs. Two minutes later, a bruised but alive pair of women were in his arms while the twenty police officers watched and TV cameras whirred recording the events.

Jon stood in the doorway of the plane, stepped aside and two young blond girls, fourteen or fifteen, stepped down out of the plane. Jon followed as he pushed the pilot out in front of him. The man was handcuffed and turned over to the Marshals who hustled him quickly into one of the unmarked cars.

Jon and another Marshal interviewed the girls and answered their questions and were told they were from Seattle and had been taken outside a Lynnwood movie theatre, blindfolded and handcuffed. The kidnappers used some sort of medicine and the girls didn't remember anything until they were on the plane. They hadn't eaten, but were given water only and one power bar for the both of them. Jon released custody of the girls to the local Marshal's office and joined Randy holding Sara and Sue.

Jeff approached. "We've got plenty of fuel to return to Missoula if we can."

"Yeah, I'll clear it with the office and we should be out of here in a few minutes. We will have to make statements at the office. Do we have room for another Marshal?"

"Sure, no problem. What's going on with the girls?" Randy asked.

"They'll be returned to their folks. There was a missing person report with the local Lynnwood Police. The Seattle office will interview the girls at their home with their parents since they are both minors. We can go back to the ranch. I'll have one of the Missoula Marshals interview Sara and Sue at the ranch if that's okay with them."

Both women nodded and smiled up at Jon. "Sara and I would appreciate that." Sue said.

Thirty minutes later Jeff lifted the jet off the Felts Field runway on the way to Missoula. The stress of the kidnapping had finally hit Sue who was asleep when the wheels left the runway. Sara was in Randy's arms as they sat together. Jon sat in the co-pilot's seat and talked to Jeff about life in Hollywood as opposed to life on the ranch.

Jeff responded to Jon's questions. "Life on the ranch with Sabrina would be the greatest." He explained, Hollywood was just there until Sabrina made up her mind if she loved him enough for a ranch life. Or maybe a small medical practice in a small town like Lone Horse. Jeff would be happy working for Hank on the ranch; he had enough of the Hollywood life.

On the Spokane TV station evening news, Randy was front and center. When asked if he gave the terrorists a chance to surrender, he responded with, "Yeah sure. They didn't want to. They already killed two men in Montana and the captive's lives precluded giving them a chance to kill the hostages."

Chapter Thirty-Five

Home Again

After the flight to Missoula and the ride to the ranch, they were physically and mentally exhausted. When they arrived at the ranch, Sara, Sue, Randy, Jon and Jeff were fawned over, food was shoved at them, people asked questions until Bess put her foot down. "Okay, that's enough. Sue, where's my horse?"

Sue smiled and pointed; "Right out there, she just came wandering up to the porch a minute ago." Sue's grin became wider. "It looks like Jake Jr. has found a new love." Jake Jr. was standing beside Buttermilk and everyone would swear he was smiling.

Sabrina called the hospital at Camp Pendleton and said she would be another few days but would be there to catch the plane back to Afghanistan. The bachelor party was scheduled for the next night as was the bride's shower. Even though the wedding had already taken place the Springer family and friends wanted to celebrate.

Brent found the multi-colored halter he wore on his prewedding night and presented it to Randy at dinner.

Maya, Hank's foster mother, came in and saw the halter, took one look and fell into a chair laughing. She would fly back to Hawaii after spending a month with her foster son and granddaughter Lori. Randy and Sara could use her house during their honeymoon on Maui. Bev came in followed by her brood who went straight to Maya begging for stories. Maya was one of the best story tellers and could keep the children spellbound for hours.

Randy and Sara decided to spend two weeks in Hawaii instead of five days. Kathy Caldwell filed a petition in the Seattle Federal Courts to dismiss all charges against Randy and Sara. Judge Lawton approved the dismissal, and issued an arrest warrant for Dewar as a Terrorist.

Ken Behoney was appointed temporary Director of the Federal Fish and Wildlife Law Enforcement Service. The new Temporary Director appointed Randy Springer as the new District Supervisor for the Brewster/Winthrop District. The name of the Service was changed to National Fish and Wildlife Law Enforcement Agency. Randy would take Ken's place as the Probationary District Supervisor.

Chapter Thirty Six

Maui and Justice

Sara and Randy flew to Maui to honeymoon. While they visited the tourist market place, Sara spotted Dewar in an outdoor bar where he talked to three men. Randy observed the men and identified them as Muslim by the way they wore their shoes. The heels were crushed down to make it easy to slip them off for prayers.

Randy called the Marshal's office in Honolulu and four marshals were sent to assist Randy in the takedown of the four foreign agents. When the marshals arrived they were dressed in what military men assigned to the islands might wear while on liberty.

The four marshals talking loudly and behaved like loud semi-drunk men being nuisances. One of the marshals bumped into one of the men at the table under the banyan tree and before the seated men could react they were covered by four armed marshals. They were made to lie on the ground while one of the marshals searched them and relieved them of handguns and applied handcuffs. The marshals also put plastic ankle restraints on the men.

Pistols and sets of FBI credentials were found on each man. They protested loudly they were U.S. Government Agents on official business until Randy walked up with Sara and smiled down at the restrained Dewar. The last Randy saw of the men they were being ushered in full restraints onto a twin prop airplane with U.S. Marshals Service on the sides.

Sara and Randy stood at the air terminal and could plainly see Dewar in the window of the plane. They merrily waved while the plane taxied out onto the runway.

"Think we'll have to testify?" Sara asked.

"I don't think so, Dewar is a coward and he'll cop a plea to escape being sent to Gitmo or the death sentence if convicted of murder using the deadly drugs. A nice cell in a nice Federal Pen will suit him fine. I don't think he'll be on the streets for a long-while. It's too bad the Director offed himself. They could have been cell-mates.

About the Author

Bob Manion is a native of Spokane, Washington, and a graduate of Eastern Washington University.

He is retired from US West Communications as a Special Services Manager. Bob served in the Marine Corps in the Fleet Marine Force and was stationed with the U.S. State Department overseas. As a reservist he served as an artillery officer and intelligence officer and is now retired after completing thirty-six years of service.